Jack Clemo was born on 11  the heart of the china clay co The son of a clay-kiln work education. He has been ston blind since 1955.

With the encouragement of his devoted and courageous mother he began publishing stories and verse in his early teens and in 1948 his first novel, *Wilding Graft*, won an Atlantic Award in Literature from Birmingham University. It was followed by two remarkable volumes of autobiography, *Confession of a Rebel* and *The Invading Gospel* and three collections of poetry which were reissued in one volume, *The Map of Clay*, in 1961. A further volume of poetry, *Cactus on Carmel*, followed in 1967 and in 1968 he married Ruth Peaty. This was the culmination of an emotional quest, much explored in Jack Clemo's writings, and it has proved a most fruitful and inspiring partnership.

In 1971 and 1975 came two more poetry collections, *The Echoing Tip* and *Broad Autumn*, and in 1980 Jack Clemo published a companion volume of autobiography to *Confession of a Rebel*, *The Marriage of a Rebel*.

Jack Clemo was awarded a Civil List pension in 1961 and an Honorary Doctor of Literature degree from Exeter University in 1981.

He is now preparing a new book of poems, *A Different Drummer*, and planning a collected edition of all his published poetry to date. Jack and Ruth Clemo live, in the house where he was born, below the clay tips at Goonamarris.

THE CORNISH LIBRARY
NUMBER FIFTEEN

Wilding Graft

JACK CLEMO

The great Gardener grafts excellence
On wildings where He will.

That is our secret: go to sleep!
You will wake, and remember, and understand.
ROBERT BROWNING

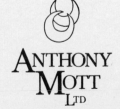

ANTHONY
MOTT
LTD

L O N D O N

Published by Anthony Mott Limited 1983
50 Stile Hall Gardens, London W4 3BU

First published by Chatto and Windus 1948

ISBN 0 907746 17 9

Printed in Great Britain by
Richard Clay (The Chaucer Press) Ltd

Chapter One

ON the evening of January the twenty-fourth, 1940, Garth Joslin was heading, on foot, across the bleak western fringe of the Cornish clay area, south of Fraddon and towards Meledor. His hands were in the pockets of his thick black overcoat, one of which held a purse containing nothing now but a cancelled bus ticket. He was young, about twenty-five, and his powerful build disclosed him as a labourer. His face was well tanned under a dark tweed cap, with a slant that gave prominence of bone to the lower part. A defensive habit of mind was expressed in the deep-set grey eyes, in the hard grip of the lips, but the chief impression given by the solitary figure was one of weariness.

Garth had had much to weary him of late years, before receiving the last inevitable blow that had taken him this afternoon to Bodmin, to attend his mother's funeral. The house at Meledor to which he was returning would be no more blank for him to-night than for four years past, but the knowledge that a phase had ended would strike him most poignantly there, and his pace slackened perceptibly as the huddled, shapeless white mass of Meledor clay-dumps jarred his vision above the frost-thinned scrub of downs.

Daylight was waning, and before Garth reached the village a thin drizzle had begun driving across the plateau. The path he was following headed just south of Meledor clay-pit, straight towards the dune. It passed through a gap in the lower edge of the dump itself, so that the waggon-track formed a bridge over Garth's head for a moment as he moved along the short defile. The refuse-heap bulged out as far as the hamlet, but Garth was soon free of it, passing the school standing on a branch road south-west—the school to which he could not honestly say he owed anything—and abreast of the first bare stone cottage of his birthplace.

Meledor was not arranged compactly, but scattered in groups of two or three houses each down the whole length of a long lane. The bends of the road and the thickness of the tree-growths were so pronounced that from none of the cottages was it possible to see many of the others. At several corners one came unexpectedly upon drying-sheds, their low roofs and stacks almost hidden among the trees, and trolley-lines crossed the road, connecting kilns with clay-tanks, the industrial features giving a false impression that the end of the village had been reached.

Garth had to pass most of the houses and a few of the drying-sheds before coming in sight of his home, a solitary dwelling half-way down the hill. It stood back from the road at the end of a path winding through a shrub-bordered garden, and the screen of elms and hawthorns around it was so dense that only the roof and chimneys could be clearly seen until one was level with the gateway.

As Garth approached it his eyes probed beyond to another dwelling tiny amid fields at the base of the dale. Stribley's farm ! His hands clenched, but the thoughts that would have surged anew at sight of that place were stemmed by a swift distraction. A movement! Something was happening down there. Narrowing his eyes he saw that a cart was being drawn through the farmyard and into the field. Slightly ahead of the horse walked two men, one of whom was holding the bridle. Garth's breathing tightened as he recognized this man. Martin Stribley!

The group passed slowly across the field, which sloped up to the edge of a ravine, thirty feet deep at this point. Along this gulch the clay-clogged Fal oozed turbidly, little more than a stream here, twenty miles north-east of Falmouth. Drawing near to it Stribley led the horse in a

8

broad curve until it faced the farmstead, and then backed it towards the fence that guarded the brink of the gorge. The group were soon hidden from Garth's view by a blob of trees on the higher bank. He heard Stribley bawling at the horse, then sounds of confused movement, the creak of the cart and the rattle of the fence, as if some bulky object had bounced against it.

Garth frowned, but in any case he would not have troubled to wonder much what they were doing. And his curiosity was sapped at once by a more direct challenge.

Reaching the gateway of his home he became aware of a dark form gliding along by the window and down the path. At the next minute a young woman, tall and of full figure, halted behind the black-painted iron gate and greeted him with strained pleasantry.

"You didn't used to keep me waiting like this, Garth! I've been here twenty minutes or more."

Garth started back, jerked a hand to his face and stared with a swift hardening of his whole expression. Edith! The last person he had thought to see here again, after four years' estrangement . . . though she lived close enough, with her parents, the Chirgwins, at Trethosa, only a mile off. Seth Spragg's wife—and showing signs of being the worse for wear. A typical village wife now, with a hum-drum harassed look—dowdily clad too in a grey raincoat with smears of whitewash on it and a small, shabby velour hat. The face that had been so richly dark when he loved it was now sallow, the lips thinned and pinched as if by constant nagging. But the eyes were as large and black as ever, and as black the hair that had not been bobbed and was coiled into a bun at the nape of her long neck.

Wishing to gain time for any serious duel she might force upon him Garth seized upon an opening sufficiently personal, and pointed to the field below.

"That's Seth down there wi' the cart, isn't it?"

"Yes. He went over to help Martin bury a dead cow —dump it in the gorge there."

"I thought they were getting rid of something. That seems to be their strong point."

"Not always. They didn't get rid of you."

Garth was not sure of his smile, but Edith thought it bitter.

"I'm still here, I admit," he said.

Edith leaned over the gate, speaking in a rapid undertone.

"That's why I've come up. . . . No, don't misunderstand. Seth knows about it and won't be jealous."

"You've come to offer your sympathy, I s'pose?"

"No, it's nothing . . . you needn't drag up that old affair unless you want to." She shrugged. "It's just a business call. . . . Shall we go in? I don't want to make more scandal for you."

Garth followed her to the door and left her there while he fetched a key from the tool shed adjoining. In tense silence they entered the house, Garth motioning her into the kitchen—a miserable little room, now so dusky that details of furniture could hardly be seen beyond the direct range of the window. Garth's black-out curtain, a green cloth on a white rod, lay across the table; beside it stood a lamp with a cracked white china shade, and a box of matches.

Garth sat heavily back on the table at the end farthest from the door, close to the fireless stove. He took off his cap and Edith looked musingly upon his curly brown hair outlined against the window-panes, the grey blob of his face. After a pause she stepped from the doorway and began fingering the black-out material.

"Shall I put up this for you?"

"No. I don't light the lamp till it's really dark."

"And you won't even for me?" She laughed. "I can see you don't want me to stay, Garth!"

"You couldn't expect that. And whatever your business, I should think it could have waited a day or two. I'm in the dumps now, naturally, wi' the funeral fresh in mind: aren't fit company for anybody to-night—least of all, you.

. . . . Why've you come ?''

She answered evasively:

"Seth thought it might spoil our chance if he tackled you about it himself. I daresay you hate him still and wouldn't toss him a civil word if he came here."

Garth's slow deep voice sounded ominous in the quiet room:

"'Twas your fault and Stribleys' more than Seth's. A weakling like him—he isn't worth hating."

"Well, anyhow, I don't see you need refuse us a tip. . . ." Edith leaned against the dresser, flicked her arm. "It's about the house here. You'll be sick of it now, I expect. We thought it might be empty soon."

"What put that in your head ?" he asked, surprised.

"Oh, nothing, we hadn't heard any hints, only it seemed you might be glad to shift off now the last link's gone. And you're so close, nobody'd know till 'twas all fixed. I expected you to move long ago."

"Thought you and Stribleys had made it too hot for me ?"

"Something like that."

"I had my work," said Garth doggedly. "And besides, I'd made up my mind to stick it. Nothing would ha' pleased you better than for me to run off and leave everybody sniggering. That's just where I wasn't going to oblige you."

Edith pursed her lips crossly, fidgeting with the collar of her raincoat.

"Well, I'm sorry. Me and Seth was hoping we'd get this house. It's time we had a home of our own, after four years cooped up with my people. Seven of us there now, in a little four-roomed hole no bigger than this."

"Couldn't you go across wi' Seth's lot at Goonamarris ? No kids there."

"No, nor any welcome either. We hardly ever visit them—only when we're hard up for a real good row. They've never forgiven Seth for marrying me."

"H'm! Well, I can give you forgiveness—not my home. I'm staying here for another twelve months, at least—till I'm called up. You may have a chance then, though if I'm bumped off"—he smiled grimly—"I shouldn't be surprised if you found the place haunted."

Edith smiled too—a sour, malicious enlivening of feature.

"Ah, yes—the war! That ought to give all of us a fresh opening." She paused, then observed with an abrupt change of manner:

"What's bottled you up so since we split? I've heard some funny rumours. Seems you've got like the old village women who used to get a bit cracked if their sons was drowned or something—shut themselves up and be for ever waiting for the boy to walk in. . . . D'you keep your door unlocked every night in case Irma should come?"

Garth changed colour, muttering:

"I thought you wasn't going to hash up that business."

"All right; I won't." Again Edith hesitated; she moistened her lips.

"This last stroke, about your mother: how did it happen? We hadn't heard any details, only that she'd gone."

"She died sudden—heart trouble, I believe. I didn't know she was ill—just had the word Monday about the funeral. A bit of a shock, o' course, but I'm glad it come that way—shouldn't ha' liked to've seen her pass out."

Edith sighed, edging nearer the door.

"Well, it's a release."

"Yes; I don't feel any loss now. 'Twas four year ago I really lost her. There's been nothing left since, the few times I've visited the asylum. She didn't always recognize me. 'Twas a bad case."

The woman's face grew hard again suddenly; she turned with a sort of defiance, her hands clenched.

"If you'd put her away when I was urging you to, all that trouble would have been saved. I s'pose I'd have married you, and p'raps been happier than I am with Seth. You know how we used to squabble, and I'd say you had to choose between us. Because you was so pig-headed, sticking out that she might get better, when every-one who saw her knew she was going over headlong."

"A man don't like to have his mother put away like that unless he's forced to," murmured Garth. "She was all I had after father died. I was hoping right up to the last—till Irma came—hoping you'd overlook it and settle down—lift up that worry from her and see if 'twould check things."

"You couldn't expect me to run the risk. I was scared when I'd once seen her in one o' those moods—I was, honest. The way she'd look at me. . . . We'd have had to live here with her, and goodness knows what might have happened, we being left alone together all day while you was at work. She might have stabbed me or something."

"No," said Garth stubbornly. " 'Twas only the rumpus about Irma and you marrying Seth that gave a violent turn to the trouble—and even then 'twas only o' night-time she'd get they wild notions. You know when 'twas she meant to drown herself—the night you was married."

A hint of malice crept into Edith's face and tone as she answered:

"I shouldn't think she'd have needed that catastrophe to head things up if there was any truth in what we heard about her son. People said you was hanging round Stribley's farm acting like an idiot several nights just after Irma went back to London."

Garth looked shamefaced, sullen; he writhed on the table, fumbling with his cap.

"There's things that break a man," he said. "Plenty besides me'll be finding that during the next few years, while the war's on. They talk o' keeping their chins up, but that's a risky practice when you're standing up to the Almighty. It invites the knock-out."

"You're morbid, Garth."

"Is it any wonder ?"

His piercing glance made Edith feel uneasy.

13

"Well, anyhow," she said with a swift evasive look at the banisters partly screened by two of Garth's coats hanging from nails in the beam, "I don't think the war'll last years. It seems to be fizzling out already."

"You'll find your mistake there. Evil forces bide their time, getting up strength, and then pounce, as they did on me nearly five year ago. The wreckage that's left then takes a lifetime to clear up. All the questions this war'll bring to people I've had weighing on me since 1935 —while they've been doing their damnedest to forget there's any danger."

The passionate intensity of his speech—though his voice was quiet still—almost awed Edith there in that room now all but dark because of thickening rain-clouds, the room she had last entered in July, 1935, as his betrothed.

"It's true you deserved a better mother," she confessed. "Beastly bad luck she brought such trouble on us."

"I s'pose you didn't bring any trouble on anyone?" said Garth bitingly. "Even if you wanted to stop me hanging on you could ha' managed it without getting those Stribleys to do your dirty work for you. You knew pretty well that was the one thing that could knock me out for good. If you'd got me suspected o' being a thief, or made some brawl or other between me and Seth so that I bashed him and got in trouble that way—in any such case 'twould have blowed over and I'd have got a fresh chance. There'd be other girls. . . . But when a chap's once labelled wi' the sort o' carrying-on you put on me and Irma—well, he's about finished. He never lives it down. I feel it still in the way the girls look at me—girls now coming on in their teens what was only school-kids when it happened: they seem to think I aren't human. Their parents warn 'em against me, no doubt—and knowing what they do about mother only rubs it in worse."

Edith stepped forward and would have laid a hand on his arm, but he drew away, slid off the table and moved into the deepest gloom around the fireplace.

CHAPTER ONE

"I'm sorry, Garth. I didn't see all 'twould mean—thought you'd soon clear out when your mother was put away, and get work somewhere else. But you didn't try that." She bent a moody frown upon the floor, and said tremulously:

"I sometimes wish it never happened . . . because I *aren't* happy with Seth. . . ."

Garth's voice came curtly enough now:

"I don't want to hear any o' that cant. You made your choice and ought to be satisfied when you think how it got me cornered."

"That business was nasty, I know. I hadn't thought of throwing you off that way till Martin said the girl was making such good use of the time she spent waiting at the claywork with his dinner. After I'd heard that, of course I was jealous and didn't care!"

"Irma was only here a fortnight," Garth reminded her. "A kid just fifteen then, and a perfect stranger to me."

"Not when she left! Nobody knows how often she'd been alone with you in the workshop before that Thursday. But then 'twas plain enough. . . . Your luck turned when that kettle-boy came over the dump to tar the pulleys and almost walked into her as she was leaving the workshop—looking confused he said, and with her clothes rumpled as if she'd been in somebody's arms!"

A note which in less vital natures might have been called sneering toned Garth's retort:

"Just as you'd been in Seth's, I s'pose?"

"Well, perhaps! But you *were* struck on Irma: it wasn't all a put-up job between me and the Stribleys. We may have put some smoke, but there was flame there already. Only you and she know how much."

"I don't admit or deny anything," muttered Garth; she saw his eyes glowing, his arm jerk up to the mantel-shelf. "It's dead and done with except to me; and if there is any secret that keeps me going it isn't for *you* to know it."

Edith frowned sulkily.

"We could have made it worse for you if we brought it into court."

"No. That was bluff—I never took it serious. Irma denied it flat and must have known she was just a tool in some dirty scheme. Coming down on holiday, expecting a jolly time, and then caught up in a beastly village squabble and packed back to London in disgrace! 'Twas a low-down piece o' work to play on their own niece."

Edith edged, resolutely now, out into the passage.

"Don't let's wrangle again, especially about that kid. I'd better be off."

"Well, so long."

As the door closed Garth sat down afresh, this time upon a chair by the table. He did not remove his wet coat, nor feel that lamplight could comfort him. Until the room was quite dark he remained seated there, bent forward with his head in his hands, without motion.

Chapter Two

MARTIN STRIBLEY stood erect in the cart that remained motionless with its rear edge of flooring against the boundary fence of the larger of his two fields. He was coiling the rope which had been tied to the cow's legs, enabling him and Seth to haul the carcase from the shed floor on to the vehicle. Though burly in figure he seemed cowed in spirit, and his spasmodic winding of the rope was the mechanical index of a listless yet irritable mood.

His face, red and full-cheeked, was shadowed from without by a green trilby and from within by a nature which ten years of marriage had warped from its original geniality. It was as if his wife, who was six years his senior, had exerted some malign magnetism upon his features, drawing and twisting them to make sure that he did not look younger than she. His small blue eyes scowled

now down upon Seth, who was lounging against an elm
that grew near the fence, lighting a cigarette and peering
anxiously through his steel-rimmed spectacles up the slope
where Edith had not long since disappeared.

Seth was a weakly-looking young man with a prominent
Adam's apple and short-sighted eyes, grey and hollow
under a forehead whose height gave a false impression of
underlying intelligence. Though only twenty-three he had
already lost all his teeth, and was not at present wearing
his false set, so that he appeared peculiarly old and sunken
about the mouth. Having lit the cigarette he slouched
forward and picked up the tail-board of the cart, which
had been removed to let the carcase slide from the tipped
vehicle. In silence he carried this to the cart and fixed it
into position. He walked with a limp, never having recovered from an accident on Retew claywork two years
ago when his leg was crushed by a skip-waggon.

The two men were now ready to return to the farmstead, but both seemed reluctant to move, though the fine
rain was damping their clothes and dusk rapidly closing
in upon the base of the valley, which was very narrow and
itself little more than a gorge between the shadowing hills.
Several houses besides the Stribleys' showed vaguely in the
drizzle, dark blobs along the road that wound northward
into the wood-begirt hamlet of Virginia. Above these
woodlands, now a mere scabrous haze of bare branches,
the grey sand-dune of Kernick was thrown up on the swarth
moorland like a bastion; even nearer, behind Seth's home,
was the conical wedge of Trethosa clay-heap. Spilled
over the brow of the eastern scarp these pyramids seemed
to imply in their passive and gigantic domination some
threat to the dumps of Meledor on the opposite slope.
The two groups of dunes faced each other with a surly
antagonism, reduced to natural terms by the gloom that
was already isolating them as a distinct part of the landscape and blurring details of their structure which marked
them as industrial products.

Stribley had leapt from the cart and moved to the horse's head when the figure of an old man darkened the field gateway near the foot of Meledor hill. At once Martin led the horse briskly forward, ignoring the flurried shout that grated across to him. The rebuff was typical of the general custom of the district in relation to this man—Colly Snell by name, a queer, crafty old soul whose inquisitive habit of mind, baulked at home by a wife who could tell him nothing, made him a nuisance elsewhere.

Seth, however, lagged behind, and when he again limped out from under the tree it was to mutter a word of dissuasion.

"Shouldn't run away too soon, Mart. The company indoors isn't no improvement, wi' Bella worked up about that old affair. . . . And Colly may have some news for us."

Stribley stopped the horse, smiling unpleasantly.

"Yes; he may have seen Edith go past—may even have gone creeping around and heard something o' their talk if Garth ha'n't let her in. She've been up there a brave while. Something brewin' what'll whet up your jealousy, old boy!"

Seth with a shrug of his narrow shoulders received this taunt in silence.

Colly had entered the field by now and was plodding across the short wet turf. He was a man in the early sixties, but looked older, being white-haired, small and shrunken in frame, and like the two men who awaited him he wore the rude garments of a clay labourer, corduroy trousers and clay-smeared coat, with a ragged black cap drawn low over his wrinkled forehead and sharp, sour eyes.

Before addressing the pair he strode across to the fence and peered over it, pushing aside with his stick the matted bramble and fern that obscured his view of the river bed. The carcase could be vaguely seen, a dark bulk half covered by the sluggish, pale-glinting water and oozy slime.

18

CHAPTER TWO

Colly probed the mournful twilit scene with an expression of gloom that fitted it, licking his bare and pimpled lips before turning to join the couple who, now sheltering beside the cart, had watched him with a mixture of irritation and amusement.

"I thought you was burying your cow when I seed the cart come out," he announced as he drew level with them. "A bad job to have a case o' foot-and-mouth here—makes the place famous, though in a tame sort o' way, for it've been famous for more exciting things in its time."

He nodded towards Garth's home, and the pair expected at once some comment regarding Edith. But the old man reverted to the more prosaic matter.

"Risky, isn't it—dumping a cow down in the open like that? You'd be haled up if any dogs got down to it."

Stribley shook his head.

"They couldn't get down the bank—sheer drop from the fence both sides. She's dropped pretty square, too, right in the thick o' the mica stream. When they flush out Kernick tanks to-morrow the clay slime'll be coming down and bury up the carcase. 'Twill be sunk down and buried out o' sight in a day or two." His brows lifted with something of mockery, a faint ironic smile touched his lips.

"Seen anybody go up there to-night?"

"Where?"

"Up to Garth's place."

"No," said Colly in puzzled tones. "Who do 'ee think's going there now? We all know Garth's in Bodmin, and likely to stay there late from what we can judge of his past habits."

Martin sobered, and heeding a nudge from Seth he replied shortly:

"He told us at the claywork lodge yesterday that he'd be home by the first bus after the funeral, so we thought he might be expecting company o' some sort."

"No likelihood o' that. 'Tis years since Garth have had

19

visitors, and there's no reason why any should come now, as he won't have no money left him."

"I s'pose you'd have gone up too this afternoon if 'twasn't for your work over at Melbur?"

Colly fingered his lantern-jaw with slow deliberation; his response was dry, characteristic.

"I couldn't promise that, Mr. Stribley. I as good as went to Mrs. Joslin's funeral four year ago when me and Garth got her in from the tank wall. She was as near to a corpse then as any live woman can expect to be, if not nearer, for both of us was fair took aback when doctor said there was a spark left."

" 'Twas a spark in the wrong place, it seems," commented Seth.

"Yes, a cruel thing to bring her back to such a mentality, Mr. Spragg. Better he'd left her as she was and made a funeral of it what we could all pay our respects to—the sort o' funeral I've been hoping for in me own home this past nine years." As if regretting the tell-tale fervour of this remark Colly added quickly in a parenthetical tone:

" 'Tisn't nice to speak so o' your own wife, but there's predicaments, Mr. Spragg—predicaments what make the heart surprise itself in a man!"

"There is that!" mumbled Seth. "A fellow goes it blind when he ties the knot wi' any woman. The very next day something may happen to knock the whole thing flat. Edith never been the same to me since I had me accident—'shamed to be seen walking wi' me, lame like I are. But how could I know when we married that any such trouble was coming?"

Colly stepped forward, poking the muddy end of his stick several times against Seth's coat.

"Certainly, Mr. Spragg, certainly," he agreed. "Such things is hid from the wisest, and even in our most foolish moods we'm wise enough to wish they wasn't." He paused, and with a suggestive sweep of the arm around at the bleared landscape he confessed in a muffled tone:

CHAPTER TWO

"I'm in a bit of a fog at the moment about our Minnie."

Seth grunted, but his face showed keener interest.

"That's rather a different business, if she've started to make trouble again. You didn't go it blind there—you knowed what you might have to put up with."

"The woman's character wasn't exactly hid under a bushel, I admit," said Colly. "If proof can walk on two legs, there 'twas. That chiel of hers, that Shirley—poor come-be-chance we all know: Ted Blewett's brat."

Stribley nodded.

"Always a big risk taking in a girl after she've made a slip like that, 'specially as 'twasn't your own kith and kin. Perfect stranger to 'ee till she got in trouble."

"Yes, but me chief concern just then was how to find a housekeeper. Missus had crocked up and been pitched in her bed—as final a job as that cow is, dumped there in the clay. Never to move again, the doctor said. I had to do something, having no darter, and maids what was free to choose had heard too much o' my woman to come and chance it. And there was Minnie Lagor really in need of a place somewhere, not finding it too comfortable over to Egypt after the baby came." Colly nodded towards this curiously named village, lying beyond the woods of Virginia and Kernick dune, two miles northward.

Stribley appeared to muse, moving slowly and with head bowed back to the horse as the creature made a restless step forward.

"Seemed a decent maid up till then—quiet, sober young thing. Come as a shock to everybody when 'twas knowed she'd knuckled in to Ted Blewett."

"Yes; 'tis edifying, and mystifying too, to see how things worked just then: little pushes this side, little pushes that side, all helping to unsteady the maid. A lot of illness in the family—she got wore down wi' nursing, and then her grandfer died and old Mrs. Lagor came to live wi' Minnie's people. Proper nuisance—been stone deaf for years, and got on the girl's nerves, having to bawl and

21

shout all day long to no purpose, besides having extra work to do. Her mother couldn't manage without her, and there she was tied down. No wonder that Ted got to hear of her inclinings."

"No ; he was always on the lookout—had a talent for spotting the right girls in their wrong moods."

"A talent—nothing less, Mr. Spragg, though we may question which Power above had gived it to him. I can see the chap now as he used to sneak around the villages in the evenings—sometimes here to Meledor: not much to look at, but a dabster at one kind o' game, since practice is half the battle. Just a look at a maid in a certain mood, a few words dropped casual, and 'twas all up: the young woman could be wrote off as a loss to a respectable community such as we hope ours is." Colly cleared his throat importantly and raised his stick, pointing again towards Egypt as he continued his speech.

"So it happened wi' Minnie. There was a few sly meetings around Egypt, then people saw Minnie off on Ted's motor-bike in the summer evenings, and so the night come when he got her to go inside his house there to Carpalla—sometime when his wife was safe off on similar business, I suppose. A most mystifying thing when you consider Minnie's make-up. But as I say, Ted had a way with him—could put a spell on a girl so that she gived in without knowing what was happening, and couldn't mind afterwards whether 'twas moonlight or lamplight or no light at all that observed the deed."

"Yes; Blewetts' place was rowdy enough back then," remarked Seth with a reminiscent glance up the eastern slope past Trethosa dune, a mile or so beyond which lay the dwelling referred to. "Both Ted and his wife getting their own back for the mistake they made in marrying so hasty. Better for a lot o' girls if Ted had come to a dead end before he did."

Martin shook himself from reverie, and turning his head he asked in a brisk tone:

22

"Minnie wasn't upset about that, was she, back four year ago when she heard he'd kicked the bucket?"

"I wouldn't say upset: she isn't that sort. No hysterics about Minnie, and she hadn't demeaned herself by summonsing Ted or having anything more to do with'n after she had Shirley. Wanted to forget the man. But I could see her thoughts was hard for awhile—how she'd look at her little maid—eight year old come June she is—look at the maid wi' her lips shut tight as if she was tempted to blurt out what had happened: 'Your father's dead, Shirley—carried on wi' the maidens once too often and gone and hanged hisself.' But she soon got over it—seemed relieved when the news had time enough to cool. She could venture out around without the fear o' meeting the fellow again."

"His wife's married again and shifted to Goonamarris. A lot o' new moves around here lately."

"And we aren't come to the end of 'em yet, if I've any insight under my hair; and I aren't referring to what the war may do to any of us."

The young men shrugged impatiently.

"Why—what's Minnie up to?" asked Seth.

Colly blinked past the drying-sheds at his home, humanized by a faint gleam of lamplight that was quickly obscured by a black-out curtain drawn across the window.

"The first Thursday o' the New Year," he went on in a freshened manner, "just afore tea-time Minnie heard a knock at the door, and went back to find a gent there wi' some leaflets in his hand. Poetry or something it was, wi' his name printed at the bottom—Griffiths, I believe. O' course, Minnie told'n she didn't want to buy no sich rubbish; but the man hanged around the doorstep and went on to ask where he could get a cup o' tea: a cold, snowy afternoon, and he in such a remote spot without a car, feeling a bit lost. And what did Minnie do but ask him into our place!"

"Wanting a second dose!" Seth slyly interjected.

"And when I got home from work they was sitting at the table wi' Shirley between 'em. Minnie explained it casual enough, and the gent was respectful to me as I sat down in my clayey clothes. Told us more about hisself—how he'd come from Wales—called Griffiths as I said—where he'd been a miner as a young man and then mining engineer. Showed us his certificates from some mining college, all very genuine and straightforward. And now he'd lost his wife and come to Cornwall—been lodging to Truro for six months, trying to get his bearings. Something have got in the man's heart 'tis plain. A bitter Socialist I found, and bitter in his general talk. About his wife even, though he didn't say much—just a hint or two; and 'a got up sudden and thanked us and was gone out o' the house as if he couldn't trust hisself to say more."

"And now he's called again, has he?" Seth inquired.

Colly resumed leisurely, with a glance that rebuked Seth for his interruption:

"Now, there was nothing uncommon in all this. Such things have happened afore here in the village. We get these travellers coming around, and don't turn 'em from the door if they need a snack: though I s'pose Bella would, and p'raps Edith—different make-up from Minnie. But a few days later she got a letter from this gent, thanking her for her hospality and saying if she felt lonely as he did they could do worse than acquire one another's company. Minnie was took aback at this, but she's a woman that gets her impulses: twenty-six years of age, but her own Shirley couldn't be more unguarded at times—more wilful, Mr. Spragg. She'd took a liking to this gent—felt he'd been ill-used same as herself; so she wrote back that she'd be glad to provide further acquaintance with him. Last Saturday she went to Truro and met'n there; and all I can get out of her is that she'll be there to meet him again next Saturday."

"Went by herself?" asked Stribley, moving again nearer.

"Yes—could hardly put Shirley, though Griffiths must know the maid's a bastard. What'll come of it I don't know. He must be forty if he's a day—tough-looking man, but greying in the hair, and something queer under the man's surface. If he means to marry her 'twill be a surprising turn, yet in some ways a providence."

"Not he!" said Martin. "She've made a fool's move, old man—time you shook her out o' that dream-stuff instead of encouraging it."

"Well, she got to prepare for the future. Afore this war's over me and missus may both be took; and if we aren't we might be wishing she and Shirley was took. The kid may be nearly in her teens by that time, and then most likely we'll see the ancestry coming out in her."

Seth sniggered.

"Maids don't need ancestry these days," he commented. "You can trust 'em to run wild on their own juice now the schools and churches is so busy building character."

"True; they'm building up sad collapses, Mr. Spragg; the wild atmosphere in the air is too strong for 'em seemingly. . . . But 'twould be more trouble than 'twas worth to keep they Lagors there, p'raps to have another such slip o' Shirley's to cope with, another mouth to fill. Not that she's showing any bad leanings yet—a bright, openhearted little thing: none o' the sly ways wi' she as that Irma had in her."

"Ah! Irma!" said Stribley with a hard laugh. "You ha'n't forgot her yet?"

"None of us can while Garth's here."

The sternness of Colly's tone caused Martin to shrug uneasily as he admitted:

"Irma did seem to have something wrong wi' her, from the start. Got it from her mother, I s'pose—a pretty loose woman before Bert struck in with her. And then there was the London life. Anyhow, she was showing promise from the time she was Shirley's age or a bit older. Started to worry 'em before she come down here that last time

—too fast after the boys. 'Twasn't no shock to me when I heard she'd took advantage o' the ugly mood Garth was in. What happened was her fault as much as his. Nobody thinks he forced her."

Silence fell heavily, the drizzle thickened, pressed out from the flabby clouds like the cold sweat of fever. The trio, now scarcely distinguishable against the blur of the cart, peered intently up the slope towards the workshop under Meledor dune. Nothing could be seen but the faint whiteness of sand gleaming above the dark blob of the thicket, but in the weird melancholy of the scene was a sinister element that made the thought of vice appropriate and persuasive.

So completely did they come under its spell that they did not hear the dull thud of the field gate closing. Only when the horse made a further restless move and Seth was forced to lurch free of the jolted cart did he become aware that Edith was approaching, half-way across the field, a smudge of life gliding silently and showing something of conflicting impulse in her manner. The outer discomfort of clammy rain impelled her to haste, while the inner discomfort natural to the circumstances urged her to linger.

At once Seth stepped fully out into the open; he tossed aside his cigarette-end and crushed it with his boot, glowering resentfully at Colly.

Martin stooped sideways and whispered to the old man:

"She been up to see her old flame—she and Seth want to get his house if he's shifting."

"Ah!" Colly looked surprised and stared at the young woman, then sharply at Seth as his challenge broke upon the muggy air.

"Seen Garth?"

Edith nodded, but did not speak until she was close to them. She, too, cast a spiteful glance at Colly, bit her lip and murmured:

26

"Yes, though he's only just come. And it's no good."

"You asked about the house?"

"As you told me."

"And he isn't moving?"

"No—said he'd made up his mind to stick it." Edith halted beside Seth, and as if reminded thereby of a darker humiliation she added harshly with a flounce of her whole frame:

"It's sheer cussedness, that's all. He always was a pig-headed fool—no making him see reason when he's put his back up."

Stribley spat; again taking the bridle he eyed her with quiet mockery.

"Had another squabble by the look of it!"

"Hardly that, but I was glad to get away. He wouldn't light the lamp and kept me talking there almost in the dark. I wasn't sure he'd even let me in at first. We haven't stopped to speak to each other since the old flare-up: he did very well to waste so much of his tongue on me. He's still got the old gift o' the gab when he's once roused. There *is* something about him—I felt it again just now—not ordinary."

"Couldn't expect that, with his mother ending up where she have," said Martin in a tone of malice.

Colly, who had been listening open-mouthed, now turned his back to the married pair and dealt several smart blows with his stick upon the cart wheel. To this rather than to any human present he seemed to address his next remarks.

"I've never known what to make o' that man. I've knowed'n all his life: never a mischief-maker, even as a boy, and no dunce, though he wasn't clever in a scholarly way. A friendly chap, too, as he got older and picked in wi' Edith there. I met the lad a good many times o' Sundays strolling or sitting on the downs, or over around Virginia. Always ready for a chat—seemed happy and contented. He've changed into a new man since Irma come here—a man what's hugging his own mysteries, it strikes me."

"Yes; if he'd pulled hisself together and made a fresh start he might ha' been married by this time." Seth winked at Colly and vented something of his spleen. "Your Minnie might have had him if he asked her, seeing both of 'em had made the same kind o' slip."

Colly ignored this taunt, condescending to favour Stribley alone with the climax of his argument.

"Whenever I see Garth pass me garden wall, or go by his house of a evening and see the light shining in the window—before the war I mean—I d'feel the pitifulness o' something. 'In there,' I says to myself, 'is a man what've p'raps looked deeper into life than any other around here, yet whatever he've learned is bottled up inside his own waistcoat.'"

"He's got secrets enough—he told me that," said Edith. "Only I hadn't any right to known 'em—that was his words."

A stealthy glance through his blurred spectacles preceded Seth's strained query:

"Did he mention Irma?"

"Yes; and I believe he's still moony about her, after nearly five years' silence." She turned to Stribley and asked with cold carelessness:

"Has he ever dropped a hint when he sees you at the claywork?"

"No, though he's down around the pit often enough fixing things here and there. Keeps his mouth shut and hardly looks at me. I've felt the thought o' Irma is still working in him. Goodness knows what comfort he can get out of it at this time o' day."

"True; for all he knows," said Colly, "she may be dead."

"She isn't dead," replied Stribley, again with a short laugh. "But I reckon he'd wish she was if he knew all that we do, me and Bella."

CHAPTER TWO

Colly fell back a pace and eyed Martin with a suspicious rigidity of feature, observing at length in a tone of dry reserve:

"Seems you can be close too, Mr. Stribley. I've heard nothing of her since she left here, no more'n Garth have."

"Well, you see him sometimes and you might blab; and we don't want to rub it in too hard. The poor devil's to be pitied; Seth feels the same."

"I haven't let out any secrets to-night," remarked Edith.

Colly bent towards her, his bared gums giving an ape-like expression to his face.

"You mean—Irma've gone the same way as Minnie—got in trouble—hey?"

"P'raps—or she may have served him the same trick as Edith and married somebody else," Martin responded. "That would be bad enough."

"'Twould, considering his alleged memories. And she must be of a marriageable age by this time."

"Nineteen last August. I can't tell you more than that."

Stribley moved forward, leading the horse, the Spraggs walking beside him. The old man was left alone in the rain-swept field now almost drained of light, leaning upon his stick, watching them with baffled, resentful eyes and listening to the dull thumping of the horse's hoofs on the wet ground.

Chapter Three

THE pale winter sunlight spilling across Lemon Quay, Truro, had now left the short prong of the river that slanted back from the main waterway, but Minnie Lagor stayed by the railing, giving now and then a slight shiver, drawing the collar of her shabby grey raincoat closer about her neck, or moving a few paces towards the stone parapet overlooking the northern end of the canal.

Few passers-by troubled to observe her with more than
a casual glance. Her prettiness was stolid and countrified,
though none the less genuine. She had a good sturdy
figure, rather a big face, a little blanched with cold but
of healthy texture, framed by brown, slightly curling
hair. Her features, homely in themselves, were attractive
because they were unwarped by any extravagant demands
of the spirit. The lips, to which at intervals she raised a
gloved hand, were not twisted by cynicism, nor loosened
by laxity, nor hardened by bitterness, though they showed
that on occasions she could be obstinate. Her eyes under
the small green hat were grey and mild, narrowed expectantly whenever she peered across the huge car park that
stretched northward to Lemon Street. At any moment
Griffiths was due to come along that way to join her.
Several hundred cars there, gaily painted buses, some
Army lorries outside the gaunt barracks on the corner.
Little knots of soldiers hanging about—discussing the
latest war news, she supposed. Minnie was not much
troubled about that. She had nothing to lose by the war,
except through a chance air-raid—very unlikely in Cornwall, with France keeping the Jerries thumb-sucking
behind their old Siegfried Line. Minnie had no male
relatives who would be called up, and Griffiths—he'd told
her last week—was a pacifist. A man of queer views,
explosive speech—a firebrand, denouncing Capitalism
and the Church and the whole cosmic scheme in words
she didn't always understand and with a vehemence
which she couldn't feel to be justified.

To have his engineering career knocked at the outset
by the last world war, and then to marry the wrong
woman as a desperate insurance against moral collapse
—unfortunate, no doubt, but hundreds had fared similarly
without beginning to rant about the laws of the universe.
His defiant reaction seemed to be the signal for the piling
up of calamities. On his return to civilian life, during a
period of poverty and unemployment, his first child had

died of pneumonia, partly through his wife's neglect. The family had left Wales and lived for awhile in London —wretched, fretful years—hell on earth he had called them—until he obtained a post with a firm of mining engineers and contractors, travelling extensively in the Midlands as their representative. With his ghastly domestic background he was in no fit mood to see the widespread squalor brought about by industrial depression. His revolt had fiercened, become revolutionary, anarchic. Financially he had done pretty well, it seemed, but the inner drama had not changed for the turn of fortune in material affairs. Not until last year had the final blow released him, sent him to Cornwall to live for awhile on his means and his hawking of leaflets around the county. His wife had deserted him for another man, and then died —whether naturally or by accident, or in more dubious circumstances, he had not made clear to Minnie. That it was something dreadful was obvious from the agitation that overpowered him whenever he dropped a hint of it. Probably an indelicate thing which he thought unfit for the ears of a simple country woman, even though she was an unmarried mother. Perhaps his wife had died through some illegal operation, carrying on with so many men and that. Minnie treated the matter with stolid realism, neither shocked nor curious. These things happened, and there it was!

Minnie had suffered, but she remained anchored to ideas that were trite, safe and commonplace. She scarcely regretted her position. She'd made a slip, but so had lots of others, and if they put up with it, so could she. She bore no malice and was now, she hoped, no worse for her lapse. She didn't mean to cause Giffiths any fresh trouble unless he asked her to do something extravagant, like marrying him secretly or going away to live with him. She felt that he would make no rash proposals—there was Shirley to think of. Her sympathy, firm, shrewd, practical, would help him to recover whatever balance was possible to such a nature as his, and by that time they would know what best to do with themselves. For her the companionship had tinged monotony with a little green stab of freshness, like a grass blade amid the snow, a welcome sign of life underneath but with no tendency to embarrass her with the offer of forbidden fruit.

From these reflections on the background of her present venture Minnie was called abruptly by a voice close behind her, thin and high-pitched, but breezy:

"Well, Miss Lagor! So we've met at last!"

Minnie gave a start; she turned quickly.

Confronting her stood a middle-aged woman, tall and large-boned, wearing a brown coat, a blue straw hat, and a shabby fox fur around her long neck. Her face was small and ruddy, especially the nose, which supported horn-rimmed spectacles, and through these her blue eyes glinted with a sly, secretive pleasure.

Noting Minnie's bewilderment the stranger proceeded at once, grinning as she stepped up to the rail.

"I don't s'pose you recognize me—never seen me before, have 'ee?"

"Not that I know of," replied Minnie in a blank tone.

"Nor anybody like me?"

A keener glance into that pink, rather puffy face caused a flutter of apprehension to stir in Minnie, but she answered with even more firmness:

"No."

"Not even when you look at your little Shirley?"

With this hint Minnie's guess hardened into knowledge, forcing a recoil that was apparent in the stiffening of her frame, the swift flush of confusion and anger that darkened her cheeks.

"Oh!" she said, and her hand made a groping defensive movement. "So you—you're Ted's mother?"

"That's me, Miss Lagor—Sal Blewett. I s'pose 'tis me and you who got the closest memories o' Ted, as his wife didn't have any babies by him."

32

CHAPTER THREE

"Well, I dunno why you need to come here and speak
to me," said Minnie, assuming an attitude of aloof cold
scorn. "I finished with Ted eight year ago and have
almost forgot him. I daresay he told you plenty o' lies
about me. You're welcome to believe what you like, but
I'd rather be left alone if you don't mind."

"A bit late in the day for me to introduce meself to 'ee,
it is," confessed Sal, her eyes twinkling behind the thick
lenses. "I can't never be your mother-'law now, though
I may be Shirley's grannie long enough to make her
ashamed o' me if she hears too much."

Minnie shrugged.

"I don't want no help of any kind from Ted's family,
and if you mean to propose anything . . ."

"Well, I wasn't exactly meaning to adopt the chiel—
nothing extravagant like that, my dear. I'm a poor
woman—me husband bedridden these last two years, and
me youngest maid Jean have only just started work. Only
I've been a bit curious about 'ee off and on when your
name cropped up—natural 'nough."

"You was living in St. Austell when I—when I made
that slip, weren't you?"

"Yes, though I used to come out sometimes to see Ted
and his wife and heard about most of his scandals. But
after he ended hisself four years ago I didn't think much
more about 'ee till last August one evening when I was
out for a stroll with an old neighbour o' Ted's from Carpalla, Lily Lean. We was strolling through St. Stephen
and as we got a little past the pub we saw a couple turn
the corner, heading down Terras way towards Trethosa
Moor. A woman and a chiel, looking very steady and
respectable, 'specially the maid in her little pink frock.
Lily pointed to the kid and said all sly: 'Don't look much
like her father, do she?' 'What!' I says, 'is that the couple
I've heard of, that Minnie Lagor and her little increase?'
'Yes,' says Lily; 'that's the only maid around here who
got anything to show for Ted's spoonin'.'"

Minnie winced; her reply was almost bitter.

"Me and Shirley did pass that way through St. Stephen in August, but we didn't know such gentry was so close."

"No. I had half a mind to make meself known to 'ee, but Lily was there and I thought it might be awkward. I haven't seen 'ee since, but now, coming along the quay here, I couldn't mistake as I watched your little peepings across the car park. I know what's behind such signs, Minnie!"

Sal laughed, taking in with relish the increasing tokens of distress, humiliation and revolt on Minnie's face. The young woman was biting her lip, and presently, looking straight at Sal, she said tensely:

"I got used to being insulted long ago, else I should flare up, to be spoke to in this way. You can't have heard the truth about me since Ted hanged hisself if you think I'm still carrying on. . . ."

"I haven't heard much," admitted Sal. "But I knowed well enough that a maid who'd struck in thick wi' Ted must have something real promising in her, though it don't always show in the same way. . . ."

Minnie's eyes flashed dangerously, her hands clenched; and Sal added in a casual tone while watching a bus glide to a halt on the edge of the car park:

"I daresay you come into St. Austell sometimes?"

"Not often."

"Well, I was wondering. . . ." Sal checked herself, stepping back with a flick of her hand. "You'd be welcome in to our place any time, there to Grove Road. If you get fed up wi' that old couple—Snells isn't it?— and want to have some gay company to mind 'ee of old times, me and Jean would be glad to see 'ee drop in. I aren't so sure about me other maid, Doreen. She's eighteen and getting stuck up now she's courting steady —don't like to be minded o' Ted's little doxies. . . ."

Sal had gone too far. Minnie flounced out into the roadway, aroused, mutinous.

34

"I won't stop here and listen to any more o' this! If you think you can pester me just because you happen to be Ted's mother. . . ." Her eyes, that had been rather wild, grew fixed and startled as they lit upon the people now leaving the bus; she gasped out an abrupt: "Oh!"

"What's that?" inquired Sal, scowling. "Ted's ghost isn't likely to come back here in broad daylight. Who've 'ee seen?"

Minnie pointed and said in a muffled voice:

"You'd better shift off—that's my mother there, just coming away from the bus."

Sal glimpsed a frail little woman hurrying towards them, carrying a bunch of chrysanthemums that accentuated her drab, limp and colourless appearance. She had raised her hand in a jerky greeting to Minnie; and thus baffled, Sal too became less genial in mood. Her face twisted with a gust of rage, and as she moved off behind the parapet towards a number of alleys on the western side of the car park, she flung at Minnie a final blasting sneer.

"A pretty sort o' maid *you* are—no credit to me son. . . ."

Minnie's attention was now entirely occupied with the second apparition, and while she was relieved at being rid of Sal she felt irked by a keener embarrassment. A month since she last saw her mother at the Lagors' home at Egypt. Minnie still visited her parents, and between them old wounds had healed. But to find her mother here to-day! An awkward turn, if Griffiths——!

Mrs. Lagor was within a few yards before she spoke, nodding towards the alley into which Sal at that moment disappeared.

"Who's that woman, Minnie?"

"A Mrs. Blewett—I needn't say more than that. First time I've seen her, and I thought, after all these years, I'd got clear o' that set now. We nearly had a row. . . ."

"I felt 'twas something unpleasant. She was raking up about Ted, I s'pose—slapping that in your face again?"

"Yes. . . . But let's talk o' something else." Minnie pointed to the bouquet, her brows knit. "What you brought flowers here for ?"

"I've come to see Aunt Maud. She's up in hospital."

"Oh! Is she? I hadn't heard that," said Minnie stolidly.

"No; it's nothing very bad—appendicitis. She had her operation Tuesday and will go back home to Ladock again next week."

Minnie moistened her lips—must carry on the conversation somehow, make the usual inquiries, get it over so that mother would be gone before——!

"How's grannie ?" she asked.

"Pretty wished—had to stay up with her last night. She do get the asthma that bad, no heart could stand much more at her age. 'Twouldn't surprise me if she was to go this winter." Mrs. Lagor stepped close, almost whispering as she laid a hand on Minnie's arm. "And then—if you care to come home. . . ."

"I dunno," drawled Minnie. "We've talked that over several times as 'tis. We got over any ill-feeling we may have had, and the two girls is growed up now and wouldn't take no harm from the scandal now 'tis eight years gone."

"No." Mrs. Lagor stood back, her hands twitching nervously on the paper wrapped around the flower stems. "Muriel's courting—have 'ee heard about it ?"

"Colly've asked me if 'twas true. I don't know nothing beyond that. Who's she going with ?"

"Chap called Trebilcock from Retew—a decent young fellow, though a little studious at one time."

"I mind something," said Minnie. "Meant to go in for the ministry or something, didn't he, but backed out last summer ?"

"Yes; and now he'll be more than content to go on with his quarry work so long's Muriel do have him. 'Tis only been started a few weeks, but they seem genuinely attached. She brought'n in to see us Wednesday."

"Do they mean to marry soon?"

"This year, I believe. I shall really need someone to manage there: Doris is too delicate to help much—anæmia getting her down bad now she's in her teens. You'd have to come back: I don't see no other way, and you know father's willing."

Minnie toed the bottom rail, frowning in silence.

"You can't be very happy there wi' Snells, chiel," continued Mrs. Lagor persuasively.

" 'Tisn't no joke, o' course, to tend that woman, and Colly gets his crotchets, nagging away if everything isn't exactly what he wants. But I can shove along while I got Shirley—'tis a roof over our heads, and money enough to keep us decent. The only thing is, I don't think they'd want me there when Shirley gets a bit older. Colly've hinted as much, and I'm beginning to feel I don't want to stay where me child isn't wanted."

"I've thought o' that meself," said Mrs. Lagor. "'Tisn't the wisest thing for a young maid to be cooped up with a party like Snells, 'specially when they aren't no relations."

Minnie looked out across the car park to the crowds jostling through Lemon Street—darkened now, the sun gone; all somehow tense, threatening. If Griffiths should appear, or Sal come back! . . . She leaned against the rails, hands deep in her pockets, and replied in a subdued, halting tone:

"I'll think about it, mother, and when grannie's dead . . . well, we shall see. I may have other plans by that time."

An expression of perplexity, deepening to pain, over-spread Mrs. Lagor's pale and shrunken face under the blue straw hat.

"It's natural you should be tired o' living on as you are, a young woman, wi' no man or anything. But I hope you won't act rash, Minnie. There's a lot o' danger now wi' the war and soldiers and that around these towns."

The remark was so casual, and dropped with such

weariness, that it scarcely constituted a challenge; yet Minnie's heart fluttered. The rumour about herself and Griffiths had not spread far from Meledor, but it might have reached her old home.

"I know," she mumbled. "You needn't be 'fraid I shall fall for any more tricks. Sal Blewett can think what she likes, but I aren't to be caught twice."

"We've heard nothing against you since you went to live wi' the Snells. You've been a credit, everybody says, since that first slip you made."

"Yes, I hope so." Minnie studied her mother's face, her suspicion slackened. No; they hadn't heard! But it might be better to give a hint, forestall those rumours. And biting her lip she stretched out an arm defensively.

"Some of 'em have changed their minds now, it seems—about me being a credit. It's true I . . . I have had a friend here in Truro lately—a man—but it's nothing. . . . I love Shirley too much to risk her future."

Mrs. Lagor showed no trace of shock or disapproval, only her thin lips twitched, her eyes grew stark, her voice tremulous as she answered:

"You're a woman now, Minnie, and must choose for yourself."

"Would you be glad if . . . if I could get married?"

"Why—is there any chance o' that?"

"Not at present, but later on I may have to face such an offer."

"From this man?"

"I might. But I don't love him yet and should refuse. . . . Only I see plain that marriage is the one way to get clear o' such pestering as I've just had from Sal."

"Yes. People think a maid's easy prey while she's on her own, after making a slip like yours. And 'twill get worse as Shirley d'grow older. You'll still be only thirty or so when she's in her teens, and I'm afraid sometimes there's another Ted Blewett waiting for 'ee somewhere."

A queer, half-playful smile touched Minnie's lips as her mother began sidling away.

"He won't be in Truro, anyhow," she replied.

Chapter Four

Mrs. Lagor was gone, soon hidden by the rows of vehicles; and from the opposite direction, from the bridge above the main quay, a man was approaching, whose form and gait struck Minnie at once as also familiar to her. A burly figure in black coat, grey cap, alone as he moved past some garages and strode across the wide open space towards the canal. It was not Griffiths, and surely it couldn't be——! Yes! Garth! As he lifted his face to follow the flight of a seagull overhead, she recognized him. Thought of her mother was dispersed by a fresh link of interest. She'd mentioned Garth to Griffiths last week, casually referred to his experience, because Griffiths spoke as if he were the only man with whom Fate had dealt incomprehensibly. And as she watched the young fellow approach, walking with slow firm steps, hands in his pockets, head raised with a certain massive dignity, she found herself comparing him with Griffiths and voting him the more attractive character. Garth had become unsociable, hugged his suffering, but without bitterness. A faith burned amid his isolation; there was also a grandeur, a quiet strength about him which, even now as he crossed the square, was forcing several people to stare long and curiously at him. It was as if he were always busy about some secret work, finding in it both joy and anguish of spirit.

He came slowly on, halting now and then to peer over the railing, watching the activity on the lower wharf. Smoke from the warehouse chimneys was adding to the haze, the trees and cottages on the river slopes hardly visible now; gulls spectral, gliding past the bleared sun, under the snow-clouds.

Garth was near the end of the little channel before he observed Minnie with anything but an impersonal, passing glance. As recognition came, his surprise was momentary; he stopped and greeted her with a slow, whimsical smile.

"Well, Minnie! Be pretty cold here to-night."

Minnie, too, smiled, nodding.

"I didn't expect to see you here, gallivanting around so soon after your mother's funeral."

"That's more than a week ago now," he answered, sobering at once. "Nothing in it worth remembering—private burial, you know, in the asylum grounds: and I haven't come here exactly for amusement."

"Shadowing me, I s'pose? It looks so. You're the third person from our district I've met here this afternoon."

"Why—who's here besides?"

"My mother—and Ted Blewett's."

"Sal Blewett from St. Austell?"

"Yes. I've never met her before, and it ruffled me up a bit. I didn't expect to run into any more reminders at this time o' day. Must be a stroke o' this destiny you're always talking about?"

Garth's eyes twinkled under the thick brows.

"Am I?"

"They tell me so—and I should guess it from the queer way you live. I know you don't come to town to try and throw off your blues—never think o' picking up a girl here: though it might be better if you did."

Minnie's candour brought a quick flush to Garth's cheeks; his glance darted to some seagulls wheeling and fluttering just above the mud banks. He shrugged.

"There's other reasons why I might come here," he murmured. "Edith, for instance. Every street here has its memories if I cared to dwell on 'em. I wasn't exactly cut out for a hermit in those days, as you know. Back in my teens I used to come here with Edith nearly every week; and if I still come back. . . ."

"It isn't for love of *her*." Minnie swept an arm towards the hubbub of Lemon Street. "All this racket, crowds o' people, and the gaiety and that here in the evenings before the war, when you used to stay till nearly midnight. . . ."

"How d'you know that ?" He looked startled.

"We'd hear you come back: several times your motor-bike woke me up, rattling up the hill, nearly always between eleven and twelve o'clock."

"I hadn't been to Truro every time," muttered Garth. "Sometimes 'twas St. Austell, sometimes Plymouth."

"Yes; we heard neighbours had seen you around those places, walking to and fro with your head down, not seeing a soul, or standing at street corners all tensed up like a fellow in purgatory. And when your bike woke me up I'd lie awake and think: 'Poor old Garth's been off for another dose!' I knew you was forcing yourself to it. Because town life isn't in your line at all. Only it's more like London: that was all that mattered."

A wry humour mellowed Garth's face; he shivered, felt emotionally bare—had never guessed that this stolid young woman whom he casually met so often had so truly diagnosed his case.

"H'm!" he commented. "How long've you been probing into me at this rate ?"

Minnie stamped her foot—mainly because she was cold, but there was genuine earnestness of feeling in her retort.

"You don't think I could have a close-up of that . . . that scandal, without getting an insight into it, after what I'd been through ? I believe I felt more sympathy for you than anyone else around our way. I didn't say any-thing, because 'twas just sympathy and no more. But the way you've acted since tells tales to anybody who's got their eyes open. If you meant to marry anyone else you'd have got going long ago."

41

"Perhaps I don't mean to marry at all," said Garth.

"You won't if you're expecting someone to turn up at Stribley's farm again one night."

Garth seemed to deliberate for a few moments, peering down the river with eyes narrowed. Then he turned back to her and remarked with an odd mixture of playfulness and mockery:

"I s'pose you think my conscience is pricking me all these years—won't let me marry anyone else because 'twouldn't be honourable or something? But it isn't that. It's no morbid conscience, or anything else, that keeps me a bachelor."

"I know," said Minnie, fixing him with a frank stare. "You love Irma still. It's queer. I've never heard anything like it."

An impulse towards anger was checked in Garth; a boyish grin lighted up his broad rugged face.

"Well, since you've snooped that much isn't it fair to give me a bit of insight into this other scandal? I've heard a word or two at the claywork about a certain Mr. Griffiths—commercial traveller or something, but I didn't believe much of it—sure you had too much sense to be gulled as easy as they made out."

"Who?"

"Martin Stribley and his pals."

"Well, that's it," said Minnie heavily, passing a hand slowly down her cheek. "About Mr. Griffiths. I've only met him four times: he called at Snells' last month and . . . took a fancy to me, so they're saying. I expected such talk, but Mr. Griffiths is a real gent and we're just being friends. Funny how it happened—quite a surprise; but I don't feel none o' this sense o' destiny about it!" She laughed—a low honest sound.

"Griffiths lives here in Truro, does he?"

"In digs over by the Waterfall Gardens, near the viaduct."

"And you're meeting him again to-day?"

"I agreed to, though I'm feeling nervous now. Mother may see us together and put the wrong sense to it." A spasm almost of misgiving seemed to tug for a moment. "I wonder sometimes if it's worth while. I don't want to make myself a laughing-stock. I may soon slip out of it and go back Egypt to live."

"Well, you must please yourself, Minnie." Garth began sidling away, mumbling over his shoulder.

"I'll move on and leave you now—for safety!"

She watched him stride forward among the mass of cars, past the doorway of the barracks and into Lemon Street. He was heading towards the heart of the city and had only the narrow neck of Lemon Street to pass through. He moved dreamily along it, gazing up at the roof and spires of the cathedral which loomed above an intervening line of shops, vague in frosty haze but almost filling the width of sky visible between the walls of Lemon Street. From the shade of these he soon emerged into Boscawen Street, the main shopping centre of the city—a broad thoroughfare with fashionable hotels and stores, a War Memorial and a taxi stand at its southern end where a block of buildings split the wide road into two narrow alleys leading out to the bridge.

Garth stood on the corner for awhile, watching the traffic, jolted now and then by the polished figures that seemed to belong to another world than his. Girls glanced at him, faces impersonally close: he felt the stab of their contempt, and a keener pain when one or two smiled. London! So Minnie had guessed! Others, too, might be suspicious, but he often felt that he did not care who knew. No one could appreciate the absurdity of the position more than he did with his reasoning powers. Irma! Who could expect——? As if——! The protests broke as always against something in him deeper than reason. . . .

He peered along the street at a group waiting impatiently for the policeman to let them cross; and as his eyes lit upon the second-hand bookstall over there his own face showed a thrust of impatience. Though except when passionately aroused Garth's speech was as crude as that of other labourers, he had not stayed mentally on the level at which his Council school education left him. He read much alone in the evenings, and seldom returned from town without a book or two—usually tattered second-hand volumes—in his pocket.

Moving forward he took his place behind a knot of women at the Belisha beacon, and as the policeman lowered his arm Garth hurried across the road and was soon at the bookstall. Over a hundred volumes there on a long rack outside the shop window, unattended. Most of them were old—peeling binds, foxed edges, musty smell. Victorian novels—the very titles caused Garth to pass them by with derision, for his intellectual approach to sex was bluntly realistic. Biographies, history books, theological works. . . . H'm! His gaze slipped along the line of faded lettering. Occasionally he picked up a volume, idly turning the leaves, reading a sentence here and there, then pushed it back on to the shelf.

Five minutes had passed thus when, glancing over his shoulder, he became aware that a man was watching him with the keenest attention, standing a dozen yards away, on the edge of the pavement. A stocky, middle-aged figure, the face ruddy and ravaged, with a close-clipped grey moustache, vitality and restless power in every feature. As Garth observed him he stepped quickly forward; his smile, like his greeting, was rather forced.

"You're a student, I see!"

Garth dropped a book hurriedly and gave a nervous laugh—confused, for he had seldom been accosted by strangers in a town, except late at night, and then the advances had come from women. . . .

"Not much of a student," he muttered. "Never had much schooling. Live out in the country, up around the clayworks."

44

CHAPTER FOUR

"Ah!" He was conscious of a fiercer scrutiny as the stranger stepped close and touched his arm. "Then— excuse my asking, but—are you Garth Joslin?"

"Yes," replied Garth, staring back in astonishment.

"Well, my name is Griffiths—Mervyn Griffiths. I daresay that conveys something to you."

Garth recoiled, catching at his breath, and leaned heavily against the book-rack.

"Oh! yes. I've heard a little—gossip around Meledor village and . . . ."

"From Miss Lagor?"

"Only the bare outline of your . . . friendship," said Garth.

"Well, I happen to have heard of you also, rather more details. Miss Lagor told me here last week. . . ." Griffiths lowered his voice; a continual stream of people was passing within a few yards, an elderly man had paused at the stall and bent over the books, adjusting his spectacles. . . . Griffiths drew Garth back a few paces, into a shop doorway. His voice grated, suppressed, sudden:

"Pardon me, but . . . is there any understanding between you and Miss Lagor?"

"Between me and Minnie? Good gosh, no!" cried Garth, almost forgetting himself under the grotesque challenge. "She's several years older than me, and a chap don't want to be bothered with a kid like Shirley. How did you suppose . . . ?"

"I saw you talking with her on Lemon Quay just now. I'd turned into the car park, on my way to meet her, and when I saw you there I thought it might be less embarrassing for us all if I had a word with you privately. I suspected you were the fellow she had spoken to me about."

"You can ease your mind on that point," said Garth curtly. "There's nobody standing in your way if you're serious about the woman."

"I meant no offence, Mr. Joslin, but I've ventured too often already without recognizing the odds." Griffiths

moistened his twitching lips, seemed lost in thought for
a few moments, then roused with a violent gesture.

"I must be going now—Miss Lagor will be anxious.
But next time I'm up around your district with my leaflets
I should like to drop in and have a chat with you."

Garth checked a little sardonic grunt. The fellow's
leaflets! A queer fish certainly, to shadow him back here
from the car park and begin probing——! He followed
Griffiths out on to the pavement with a sort of irritation.

"All right—you can call if I'm at home," he mumbled,
and turned back to his exploration of the bookstall.

Chapter Five

THERE was a double reason for the hesitancy with
which, at noon on Wednesday, February the twenty-
eighth, Bella Stribley turned into the short lane leading to
Meledor claywork. She was carrying dinner to her husband, whose face she had slapped that morning; so the
meeting might be a little awkward. And sounds of brisk
hammering that came clearly from further in the lane told
her that Garth was busy outside the carpenter's workshop;
so she would have to pass him on her way to the pit head.
She had seen him so often at work—for Garth had been
a carpenter here since he was eighteen—that the proximity
would not have troubled her but for the news which two
hours ago had startled her into acid reminiscence.

Having left the road and passed from view of the houses
standing at the lane entrance, Bella hurried. The threat
of snow earlier in the month had gone, the weather was
almost warm, though dull, and she wore a light brown
coat over her dirty apron. Most of the farm work fell to
her, for like many other smallholders in the district Martin
had to rely upon clay labouring for a regular income,

and could only attend to his crops and livestock in the evenings and at week-ends. Bella was quite capable of the arduous manual toil thus imposed upon her—a brawny, large-boned figure, though rather short, a woman of the soil, with no interest in the refinements of social life, always slovenly in appearance, her thin greying hair blown now by the wind.

The lane was narrow, completely isolated, lying in the massive shade of the sand-dump. On the western side a concrete tank stretched back to the dune's base, its wall twenty feet high at the lower end, dwarfing Bella as she drew abreast of it. But the lane sloped so steeply that ahead of her the wall slanted away to nothing, and within a few minutes she was able to look over the top of the tank, across the shimmering green water to the long mica-channels laid at ground level close to the sand-heap. At this point, however, her eyes slid in the opposite direction— to a small clearing fringed on the one side by the northern bulge of the dump and on the other by a dense thicket of thorn and hazel spreading to the hedge of the nearest field. Buds were coming out on the blackthorn boughs, stamen catkins ripe on the hazels, and amid the brittle grass primroses were opening. Now and then a bird rustled the branches, darting about with laconic twitters of practice for the full mating chorus of spring.

On a bank near the thicket was a carpenter's workshop, a small building with a red-painted zinc roof and leaded windows. The ground in front of it, overlooking the lane on the south and joining it a dozen yards further on, was littered with scraps of timber, two broken waggons, part of a wheelbarrow, a number of discarded axles and wheels. A large cogged wheel was lying against the window-sill.

But all this was a mere background for the human figure upon which Bella's eyes became riveted. Just outside the doorway Garth was bent over a winch now almost complete. He had nailed a final cross-piece to

47

the frame and was fitting in the roller—bare armed, wearing a blue overall smeared with clay and a black cap. His back was towards Bella now. He had glanced up as he heard the approaching footsteps, and recognizing Bella he promptly turned again to his work, obviously meaning to ignore her presence as he had done a hundred times before when encountering her here or on neighbouring roadways. Not a word had passed between him and the Stribleys since Irma returned to London.

But to-day Bella had important news; she was feeling reckless: and something in Garth's stooping form, very still and tense, urged her to fling some challenge that might further help to strip her emotionally for the imminent meeting with her husband.

She paused in the lane, a few feet below the level at which Garth stood. For a minute she watched him, gripping tighter the handle of her basket; then, as he did not turn, her fat red face hardened, coldly hostile—an expression thrown out by a nature cheated in its emotional experience and therefore very prone to believe that the relation between him and Irma had been of the most revolting kind. She greeted him with cutting raillery.

"Well, Garth! I s'pose you're tired of seeing me pass here so often, when you're still wishing it was somebody else!"

Garth gave no sign of having heard her; he remained bent over the winch, giving the handle a few slow turns.

Bella moved forward, stung, resolute.

"Oh, you needn't be sulky, Garth! You owe a good bit of pleasure to me, you know. If I hadn't sent Irma up here with my man's dinner you'd never have known what marriage is like."

At this Garth straightened, looked back at her—lips set, a danger-light in his eyes. But Bella, a coarse-grained woman, was so physically robust that she never shrank from a scene, feeling always that she was more than a match for her opponent, even were he a male, even

48

should the quarrel end in violence. A smirk twisted unpleasantly her thick pulpy lips, while her little green eyes jeered at him.

"By the way, Garth, I thought you might as well know: You've got a new stepfather-in-law."

He let go of the winch, stood rigid. "Eh?"

"Irma's mother's married again—a soldier this time, called Slade: a Londoner, of course."

A sort of stupor settled on Garth's face; he stared open-mouthed, shaken to the soul by this the first news of Irma that had reached him for four years.

"Married again?" he repeated blankly. "But I didn't know. . . ."

"You hadn't heard Bert was dead—no, I s'pose not. Me and Martin don't know more than the bare fact. His wife's been pretty clip with us since you made that rumpus here—didn't write to us for six months afterwards, and since then we've only heard from 'em once in a blue moon. Last year Mrs. Stribley just dropped us a line to say Bert was gone, and now, to-day, I've had another letter saying she's changed her name and so good-bye and good riddance to us all. No more news of Irma for us, I'm afraid. Pity, isn't it?"

The taunt caused Garth to flush angrily, but his mind still groped; he made a vague gesture of protest, muttering:

"You must have heard enough already now . . . now she's nineteen. You can't keep me in the dark for ever. It's time I knew. I'm getting desperate sometimes. What . . . what *has* happened to her?"

Bella shook her head, glancing aside as a pair of bullfinches fluttered among the blackthorn clump behind the workshop.

"Ah! That's safer with me at present. Too much bad news isn't good for your family, judging by the effect it had on your mother."

Garth took a fresh grip on himself and met her eye steadily, an arm outstretched.

49

"People are always dragging in about my mother—a cheap sneer, and unfair too when you consider the facts. She'd had little moods now and then ever since I was born—sound as a bell before that, everybody says. There was no streak in the family. She had this child-birth fever—just as you might if you had guts enough to go that far."

Bella stared; her gasp told that Garth's pointed thrust had surprised her. She'd heard that he could be deadly in speech when touched on a raw spot, but she wasn't prepared for that sudden stab, and preserved a mortified silence, biting tightly her lip while Garth continued:

" 'Twas nothing serious, even then, till five years ago —no worse than some other village women."

"No worse than me I s'pose you mean?"

"I don't say there's anything wrong with your brains," said Garth with a hint of malice. "But if you went through as much as mother did. . . ." Irritably he kicked away the hammer he had dropped beside the winch. " 'Twas only when she had the strain o' nursing father through his last illness, when he was laid up wi' cancer for twelve months, that she sort o' broke down. A ghastly time— would have broke me down too, I felt, if I hadn't had Edith going smooth with me then. Stands to reason, if there'd been anything much wrong wi' mother before that time Edith'd never have started going with me at all."

"Well, it's no good hashing that up again," retorted Bella. "Edith's fixed—though I don't say she's gained much by it. Seth's getting a moody beggar, almost as bad as you—though only about the war. Afraid he'll be called up and get in the way of a Jerry whizz-bang somewhere."

Garth peered up the sand-dune as a waggon rumbled up from the pit, moving smoothly against the skyline until it was two hundred feet above him. The jutting bulk of the dump prevented him from seeing it reach the tip, but the slither of sand and crash of boulders down the southern face of the pyramid jarred on his hesitant inquiry:

"Is . . . is Irma still in London?"

"Yes; I can tell you that much. You're thinking of air raids, I s'pose? I'm afraid we shouldn't know if she was killed. Her mother says in her letter to-day that if London's bombed they'll go to sleep in the shelters or even in the Tube stations." As Garth winced, Bella drove the point in recklessly.

"You can guess what that'd mean. Mrs. Slade says those places'll be little better than bawdy-holes: all the people lying around together, forgetting which belongs to which, but never hard up for a good cuddle." She pointed towards the doorway of the workshop. "Irma won't forget the lesson she learnt in there—though she may have made too much use of it already."

Garth's face had grown uglier every moment as he listened to this ugly talk; his frame quivered, he drew his breath in long, hard gasps. Like most men who have loved and suffered deeply he was liable to gusts of unbalanced passion under provocations such as this, and felt one swirl through his brain now. Something blazed in his eyes suddenly, his fists clenched, and stepping forward to the edge of the bank, glaring down at her, he said between his teeth:

"You devil!"

Bella reined back; she dropped her basket on the tank wall and stood free, flaming, formidable, like a tigress. He did not flinch, even when she cried furiously:

"I slapped Martin's face this morning, and I'll slap yours if you dare——!"

"Treat me as you treated Irma. I ask nothing better."

"Yes, I slapped her face all right—just where you kissed it!"

"And she gave you a few stingers back, I'll warrant."

"She tried it—and found who was top dog," said Bella with a hard grunt. "Since then I expect she's done most of her cheek-slapping at street corners, or in Clissold Park. The chaps up there are pretty fast, you know—can't keep to decent friendship for more than a few minutes, any more than you could."

Garth writhed, his face twitching, white—she felt almost a twinge of pity amid the natural satisfaction at finding him still so vulnerable. To her view he was outlined against the cogged iron wheel outside the workshop window, and to an imaginative mind—which hers was not—his attitude, thus superimposed, might have suggested some Ixionian torture.

"I've never cared what you thought of it," he said thickly. "When you sent your man up that evening, while Irma was still here, I just told him he could think I'd raped her or any darn thing he liked—challenged him to do his worst. He slunk off like a beaten dog with his tail between his legs."

"I know he hadn't any heart for the job. Irma denied at first that she even went into the workshop—seemed indignant that Martin should have believed what the kettle-boy said, or mentioned it. But when we were alone she flared up at me and as good as admitted everything. Told you her age, didn't she ?"

"Yes."

"Only fifteen the week before she came down—though she looked big and plump enough, I admit. If she's grown at the same rate since, she's about my size by now. I don't expect you'd recognize her. Not that you'll get the chance. I wouldn't have her in my home again even if she was found dying here in the gutter."

"My house would be nearest, certainly," said Garth with a queer, enigmatic smile.

"She not only made that fuss with you—I shouldn't have minded that so much : it helped Edith no end. But she made trouble between me and Martin : he almost sided with her sometimes—said 'twas her parents' fault if she was wild and out of hand, not hers."

"And that may have been true." Garth's voice was unsteady; he looked back at the workshop—a glance which, apart from any words, would have told that something tremendous had happened to him there. "She dropped a few hints about her home life—pretty rotten. You couldn't expect much from Bert. He left here in rather fishy circumstances, didn't he? I was only a kid at the time, seven or eight years old, but I mind some traces of a scandal."

"There was; but not the sort to make Irma turn the way she did. Bert embezzled money at St. Stephen, where he was an accountant, and nearly got sent to gaol, only his father paid back what he'd took—sixty pounds or so —and 'twas all hushed up as far as it could be, and Bert flitted to London."

"Irma told me he'd got steady work—driving a van for a brewery."

Bella nodded.

"That's all he's done in London, so far as I know—except to get half-a-dozen kids besides the one who got you."

Garth would have answered with fresh heat had not the stopping of the waggon on the dune—this is in lieu of the peace-time blare of a siren in the engine-house— informed Bella that the morning shift was ended and Martin free to come and meet her for his dinner. With a flounce of her arm she picked up the basket and hurried on, past the clearing into a narrow defile that opened on to the clay-pit some fifty yards further around the dump.

Garth slowly followed her. His dinner, too—a pasty which he had cooked last night and brought to the clay-work this morning—was awaiting him, warmed in the pit-head lodge. Passing through the defile he heard the chatter of other pit-head workmen, of whom he saw practically nothing during the hours of labour—the blacksmith, the "kettle-boy" and the mica-worker who attended to the clay-tank sluices. He heard also the footsteps of a man ascending the pit path, and then the vast chasm came into view, its scarred white cliffs descending two hundred feet below the point visible to him in his first glimpse of them; and beyond, the level moor which he had crossed on his return from Bodmin a month ago, with the grey melancholy dunes rising in groups as far as the eye could reach. Bella's podgy bulk was superimposed upon the scene like a gliding blot, and presently as she reached the lodge—a stone hut almost on the pit's rim—Martin appeared at the top of the precipitous path.

He was obviously steeling himself for this contact with Bella. He approached her nervously, spat over his shoulder, then tried to whistle, keeping his eyes downcast.

Garth halted by a clump of scrubby gorse, not wishing to join those two. The other three labourers had already entered the lodge, and Garth supposed Martin would return at once with his dinner to the pit-bed, where his mates who had brought their own food had repaired to a similar lodge. But having handed him the basket Bella leaned close, whispering; then suddenly, screened by the hut corner, she drew Martin's face forward and drove her lips upon his with a violent craving ardour.

It was partly a natural reaction from the morning's tiff; she was always fiercely sensual after they had quarrelled. But it was also partly because she knew Garth was watching and took an added pleasure in thus stabbing him.

She had not miscalculated. The heat of passion in that swift kiss almost made Garth feel sick as he stumbled again out on to the path. He was pale, haggard and trembling when a few minutes later she passed him in the defile.

"I'm going up to tell Edith the good news now—about Mrs. Slade," she said mockingly.

Chapter Six

DINNER in the Chirgwins' home at Trethosa had passed tensely. The children were at school; only Edith and her parents were present, with Prince, the brown spaniel, rather cross too because of persistent fleas that prevented him from concentrating upon the bone he had carried to the mat at the foot of the stairway.

The kitchen in which they were taking the meal was cramped and not too tidy. Its window was very small— a quaint, antiquated affair with wooden shutters swung back on each side. The cottage was one of a group of dumpy thatched houses standing on a broad mound slightly north of the road. At various angles in the immediate vicinity stood a number of slate-roofed dwellings, with trees foaming greyly now overhead, bent and bitten by the fierce winds that swept up the valley in winter.

About a dozen houses composed the hamlet, clustered around one sharp corner of the hill that wound upward to Trethosa Downs and the main St. Stephen–St. Dennis road. The lane was extremely narrow and tortuous; no buses ever passed along it, and few cars. The place was one of those old-world beauty spots often missed by tourists keeping to main roads only a few hundred yards away.

From the front windows of the Chirgwins' home a fine view was obtainable over the dale. Most of Meledor was in sight, even Garth's abode, a mile off, though in summer several of these cottages were hidden by the dense leafage of surrounding trees.

Edith had kept glancing out during the meal, her eyes hard and resentful, frowning upon Garth's home, then probing back to her parents who sat side by side on the bench in the corner. She had no appetite, and merely pecked at the heaped pie on her plate, pausing frequently with fork half raised, tightening her thin grey lips before parting them slightly to receive a morsel.

Not until dinner was finished and the two women rose to clear away the dishes did Edith express the feeling of crisis that had kept Chirgwin's sharp bristly face dark and morose, and brought restless pouts and furrows to the round, mellower countenance of his wife.

As Edith stood at the table pouring hot water into an enamel bowl, watching the steam writhe up and cloud the window, she remarked abruptly:

"Seth's down in the waiting-room now, I s'pose, at Redruth, trembling in his shoes; or he may have gone in to the doctor johnnies by this time. Poor old boy! I almost wish I'd gone with him to make sure he gets home safe. If they pass him A1 he'll be so desperate he might even . . . even jump out o' the train on the way home!"

Mrs. Chirgwin, returning from the doorway with the table-cloth, gave it a reproachful flounce.

"Now, Edith, you needn't go jeering at the poor fellow behind his back. You know he wouldn't do such a thing. And if he've been worked up lately 'tis as much through you and your sulks as through this registerin' and that."

"I don't think so," retorted Edith. "This past week since he got his papers from the military people it'd take more than I could do to shake him out of his blues."

Chirgwin, reaching up to the mantelshelf for his pipe, growled out:

"He needn't worry about his medical. He knows he won't pass."

"Not for real fighting, p'raps—though he may squeeze through for some form of it. He couldn't join the Army —couldn't march with his lame leg; and he's a bit short-sighted. But apart from that he's tougher than he looks."

Chirgwin tapped her shoulder as she moved back to set the kettle on the stove.

" 'Twouldn't surprise me if he had consumption, maid."

CHAPTER SIX

"Get out!" said Edith testily. "Seth's no more consumptive than I am—never has a cough. He's been on the claywork for seven years now with hardly a day's illness, doing some of the hardest work he could be put to there, loading."

"You seem pretty eager to make out that man to be a fine specimen," observed Chirgwin sarcastically as he sat down—a tall, ill-proportioned man in clayey labourer's garb. " 'Tisn't that you'm so proud of him, I know. Want'n to be called up and git rid of him, 'a b'lieve."

"Well, I may; but I'm not taking all the blame—nor putting it all on Seth for that matter. It's partly through being cooped up here with you ever since we married. What chance have we *ever* had ?"

Mrs. Chirgwin paused in her transferring of dishes from the table to the bowl.

"Do 'ee think getting a home o' your own would mend things ?"

"It might be too late now, but if we'd settled like that a few years ago. . . ." Edith pushed a lock of black hair from her forehead, the hasty gesture leaving a smudge upon her cheek where her smutted hand brushed it. "Think what it means for us here with the three kids running and bawling around in the evenings. We're never alone and able to talk things over as we need."

"Done all the talk that was wanted in your courting days, I should think," said Chirgwin.

"I don't mean anything soppy. But about . . . about having a baby, for instance. We couldn't talk o' that with the kids here listening, or even with you here. And such things have got to be aired, all private between man and wife, from the start, if a girl's marriage isn't to be stifled."

Mrs. Chirgwin stared with bare arms akimbo. She was several inches shorter than Edith, though stouter; she jerked her big blonde head towards Edith challengingly.

"You don't tell me you'd have a kid now, no odds where you lived—even if you'd got Garth's place."

57

Edith winced. "No, I wouldn't. Things is gone too far."

"I should judge so," grated Chirgwin. "We d'keep our eyes open. Last week, for instance, when you was helping Seth to take out the works o' the clock—whenever his hand touched yours you'd whip your fingers away like if a bee had stinged 'ee. 'Tis little signs like that that show what state a marriage is in."

"Well, what d'you expect ?" returned Edith with a cold laugh; her sallow cheeks reddened as she stepped back to the table. "We're grown up now and can't sit around holding each other's hands like a couple o' spoony kids."

"You don't even kiss him good-bye when he goes to work now," protested the elder woman. "Only snub'n like you did yesterday. I heard 'ee when he went out to the fowl-house where you was throwin' in the maize. Went out o' purpose for a good-bye kiss, feeling the need o' some stimmilent wi' this medical to-day; and you up and told'n you didn't want none o' that silliness. I heard it plain; and he went back past the window here wi' his heart in his mouth, poor chap."

"These things is signs," announced Chirgwin, solemnly tapping his forehead. "When a wife starts to sneer at the way she acted in her courtin' days—well, I don't give much for the outlook."

"Nor I," his wife corroborated.

"And there's no natural reason it should come to this pass between you and Seth. Yours wasn't no wild affair where a couple kiss themselves cold. You never been more than lukewarm about'n. 'Twas all done in a muddle while the place here was in a uproar about Garth, his mother and that Stribley girl."

"And who helped to fire that scandal ?" demanded Edith hotly. "You made the most of it as a chance to make Garth let me go!"

Chirgwin leaned forward and said with dogged emphasis:

"Seth's beginning to feel you'm still in love wi' Garth, more'n with your husband."

"And so she is, 'a b'lieve," said Mrs. Chirgwin, peering suspiciously askance into Edith's sour face. "She was very set on going up to see him herself last month. Wanted to be alone with him. I dunno what you was telling about up there with'n so long."

"I wasn't long there with him, as I've told you before. I was down in the field talking with Martin and Colly longer than I spent with Garth."

"Was 'ee really so bent on getting the house, or was it the man pulling? He's twenty-five now, and a man that age, if he's bottled up, can be dangerous to a wife in your cricumstances."

Again Edith laughed, bitterly.

"He's finding all the help he needs, I expect. We know he goes to town still, though he sold his motor-bike two years ago—so we shouldn't know what time he got home, I s'pose. There may be women in Truro or Plymouth who could blab if they liked."

"For shame, Edith!" cried Mrs. Chirgwin, dropping a washed plate upon the bare table and scanning her daughter with arched brows. "You must feel something for'n or you wouldn't talk such spite."

"Anyhow, he'll soon be called up," observed Chirgwin in a conciliatory tone.

"Not yet. He's nearly three years older than Seth—wouldn't leave here till next year, and by that time the war'll be over."

There was a brief silence, broken only by the rattle of dishes, the splash of water, and Prince's gnawing of his bone on the mat. Then abruptly Chirgwin said, kicking moodily at the fender:

"Garth'll pass *his* medical all right—a tough bloke; and no conchie either—as tough in his views as in his muscles. I never disliked the chap. Biggest mistake o' your life when you chucked him over just because people

was sniggerin' a bit about Mrs. Joslin. That would ha'
passed, and now she's dead and gone you'd be fixed happy
up there—would have had four year o' this private talk
you speak of, and p'raps a few kids to show for it."

"Oh, shut up!" flashed Edith, and pushing her mother
aside she carried the bowl of water outdoors. Having
emptied it down the drain she stood for a few minutes,
wiping out the bowl with the sodden cloth, looking
mutinously across the dale at the straggling houses of
Meledor and the sand-dunes spilled along the skyline.
From the doorstep Prince watched her quizzically, his
fluffy tail making a few hesitant overtures before further
itching caused him to squat back and begin a savage
snapping at fresh fleas.

As Edith glanced towards him she caught the sound of
heavy footsteps approaching the corner, and at the next
moment Bella had appeared, swaying up the mound with
long lurching strides, her face fevered, grinning.

"Oh! You!" said Edith in no very genial tone.

"Yes. Cheer up. I've got some news for you. You'll
be tickled, I'm sure. . . ."

Shrugging, Edith led the way back into the house. She
crossed the kitchen to the "spence," a sort of cupboard
under the stairs, stooping beneath the low doorway and
keeping her back towards Bella as she came in. Mrs.
Chirgwin was wiping the table and her husband taking
his cap from a nail in the beams. He was about to leave
for Trethosa clay-pit, where he was employed this week
on an afternoon shift.

Bella gave a swift glance round, nodded brightly and
announced at once:

"I thought I'd slip across with the news—thought
Edith might be a bit in the dumps about Seth having to
go down there to-day. I've just been up with Martin's
dinner—saw Garth and . . . oh, we had a grand little
scene!" She laughed.

"Had a row?" repeated Mrs. Chirgwin, staring over

her shoulder. "I didn't know you was on speakin' terms with'n."

"I haven't been, but to-day—I just couldn't resist the temptation. Poor devil—he'll cry himself to sleep to-night, I expect. He wasn't ready for that shock—though it was nothing to what I could have said."

"Martin there too, was he?" asked Edith from inside the "spence."

"No; he doesn't know it yet. I just told him to hurry home from work, as there was something special waiting for him. I daresay he thinks the 'something special' is from me—to make up for the scrap we had at breakfast. But we've made up that already—had a good kiss outside the lodge."

Chirgwin strode past her and donned his overcoat, which had been hung above the banisters.

"I wish sometimes that Seth and Edith here would have such flare-ups now and again," he muttered. "Might put a bit o' fire into 'em. One sort o' heat usually leads to another: a blaze o' temper'll turn to a warm little piece o' spoonin' as often as not. But these two is always cold and stand-offish: sometimes from one end o' the day to the other Edith won't hardly speak to Seth or go near'n—snub'n if he tries to make any advances."

Edith slammed the "spence" door and turned curtly.

"What's your news, Bella?"

"I've had a letter this morning." Bella drew from her coat pocket a sheet of folded paper and waved it airily. "From Church Walk, Stoke Newington again."

"You mean—from the Stribleys?"

"No; you're wrong this time," replied Bella mysteriously. She sat down on a chair near the doorway, wriggling with malicious satisfaction as she opened the paper. "Listen!"

She read in slow, mocking tones:

"DEAR MR. AND MRS. STRIBLEY,

"This is just to let you know that I am again respect-
ably licenced to be loved—by a new man. He is in
the Army and we were married on his leave a fortnight
ago. He has gone back to his regiment again now—
I can't tell you where as this letter may get into Hitler's
hands so the Government says. If it does he'll get some
insight into English morals I expect, and decide to
attack us, seeing we're so brittle in the ham-bone. My
man says he'll be sent abroad if there's a big flare-up
like last time, but we don't think there will. It looks
like the war'll fizzle out this summer with nobody the
worse except the old politicians who hoped to make a
pile of money out of it. It hasn't touched London yet
except for the black-out, and that's rather a treat when
your man is in the Army and you don't want him to
know too much."

Bella sniggered, lowering her voice as she read the
next paragraph. It dealt with the possible use of public
air-raid shelters, and was unprintable.

Edith's face remained stony; she stepped forward and
laid a hand on the back of Bella's chair, peering over the
woman's hunched shoulder.

"Is that all? Hasn't she mentioned . . . Irma?"

"Only a few lines. This:

"I daresay you are wondering what has happened to
Irma by this time after what I wrote last year. But
I feel the less said about her the better. She didn't
come to the wedding.

"Wishing you all the best—though I don't suppose
I shall write again, having had all I need of your family.
                                    "MRS. P. J. SLADE."

Bella folded the letter and pushed it back into her
pocket. She rolled her eyes up at Edith, her lips pursed.

"Well? What d'you think of that?"

Edith shrugged without answering.

Chirgwin, now on the doorstep, shook his head.

"A pretty loose woman—her way o' writing shows that."

"She always was."

"This turn won't prove helpful to the girl, I should judge, whatever's become of her."

"Hardly."

"And what could 'ee expect o' the chiel," asked Mrs. Chirgwin, sitting down on the bench with a blank, rather shocked look still on her face—"hearing such language as that in her home every day?"

Chirgwin moved into the garden path, waving Prince back indoors with a jerk of his pipe.

"A thousand pities Irma ever come here," he muttered; "It brought wreckage to this house as well as Garth's, and there's no end to it that I can see."

Chapter Seven

WHEN Bella had passed him Garth approached the pit-head lodge reluctantly. He could have wished the shock had come during his leisure hours so that he might get away at once, shut himself indoors or in some secluded part of the heath, and brood alone until he reduced to measurable certainty the vast flux of confusion that now stormed through him. He was in no mood to face the possible banter of his workmates, and reaching the end of the defile he paused again with a dazed, startled air, listening to Martin's footsteps growing fainter down the pit-side, slithering now and then on the hard soil.

From here the path slanted down to a broad semi-circle of ridged sand, like a fantastic beach on the edge of the cliff. On this, besides the lodge, stood the smithy, a mass of scrap iron lying outside it amid bramble clumps that had pushed up through the gravel and almost hidden some of the old iron rods, wheels and pipes. To the north was a meadow fringed by dense bracken and with here and there a few stalky gorse bushes sticking up like mops from the flat turf. A fence divided it from the path and Garth laid a hand unsteadily upon the slack wire, throwing across the strip of waste land a glance as deep, hard and unfathomable as that which he had just now cast upon the workshop.

The place was a sort of Gethsemane to Garth, and Bella's double blow—her news, the kiss she had given Martin—seemed to have stripped him to the thrust of that old anguish. A lean grey rabbit stirred the undergrowth, a thrush swept up from a hollow beyond, and towards it, baulked and spiteful, the wind drove gusts of smoke from the lodge chimney. Garth followed the smoke with a vacant groping eye, as if it were a symbol of the murk assailing that living form, the prophetic image of Irma which had shaped itself in his mind during that tremendous period when night after night he had knelt there upon the turf while the moonlight broke mutely upon the white crags and broadened in level waves of fantasy upon the flowers and bushes, the sleeping birds and the rabbits that had watched him from their burrows.

Garth had reacted normally to those staggering events of 1935—that is, religiously. Having been reared in this remote area, having at that time never been to church, and having forgotten most of what he learnt at school, he was fortunately untouched by the emasculations of the twentieth century outlook. He was free to feel with full-blooded instinct that an experience which transfigured life must be essentially a religious experience. When a man was struck by lightning they called it an Act of God. And when a man was struck by the lightning of destiny, his old love stripped off like dead bark and a new stain of fire burnt along the whole length of his life by a momentary flash amid the density of circumstance—that too was an Act of God. And because it was a spiritual operation it must be creative as well as destructive. Some purpose was behind, discoverable if one kept in touch with spiritual realities. So Garth had felt, and his mystifying behaviour since had been merely the expression of his honesty to that belief. And now—this sudden stab ! No direct challenge, and still no answer possible except to wait as he had already waited four years. . . .

It was in Bella's own home that his true relation with Irma had begun, though he had seen her a time or two at the claywork, bringing Martin's dinner, before that fateful visit. Irma had only been down on holiday three days of that first week in September when he and Edith called in mid-evening at the Stribleys' farm. They often dropped in there, Bella and Edith being such close friends, though Garth had never been really welcomed by the Stribleys. His anticipations this time were more pleasurable, and he was not disappointed. Irma was present— a heavily-built girl with a full, fresh-coloured face that was not exactly pretty but had attracted him since he first saw it outside the workshop. She was wearing a red jumper that served both to reveal her well-developed figure and to throw into relief her fluffy golden hair; and as soon as he and Edith had seated themselves on the settee in the parlour Irma swung carelessly across the room and plumped down on the other side of him. He had no doubt that the hour he had spent thus, wedged between the two girls, had marked the beginning of his emotional cleavage. On his left sat Edith, cold and thin-lipped, talking in sour flat tones, with no sensuous colouring anywhere about her; on his right, the young warm Irma whose every movement seemed calculated to draw him away from the chilly sexlessness in Edith and pull him frankly to herself.

Bella guessed nothing of the turmoil of his senses, but

her behaviour could not have been more suitable had she deliberately wished to throw him and Irma together. She had gone out of her way to humiliate the girl, giving details of the poverty and general wretchedness of her London home.

"If they wasn't such a slummy lot you'd have seen her down oftener," Bella explained. "She was only five when she was here last—no brothers and sisters then. But when the big family started coming along so fast they just couldn't afford holidays. Irma had to wait till she got work and saved up her pocket-money. . . ."

As Garth listened and noted the flush of shame on Irma's face, the twitching of her small white hands, her swift mutinous glances, he was moved to a queer sympathy that made him fiercely sensitive, as if Irma's reaction were flowing into him. He felt himself fused with her, tense under the outrage. His face had looked as dark and stubborn as hers, and he had only mumbled unintelligibly in response to questions from Edith and Bella.

Before he left the house Irma had managed—while standing behind him in the doorway—to squeeze his hand as he slipped it back around his coat. He had responded, feeling a perverse pleasure as her hot slim fingers sent the soft wave of her understanding along his nerves.

On the following Saturday afternoon they had all gone out blackberrying together on Meledor Downs. Edith had kept close to Bella, seeming to resent Garth's presence, and Irma lagged behind, as near Garth as she could remain without arousing suspicion. All the afternoon the little group, tense with vague conflicts and jealousies, wandered from clump to clump of the heavily-berried brambles, sometimes clambering around the clay-dumps and the edges of the pits. When the couples were separated by bushes or rocks, Garth and Irma drew instinctively closer, exchanging shy smiles and jokes about prickles, stinging nettles, snakes and other nuisances that might spoil such a ramble. He had dropped some of his black-

berries into her jug, and again the touch of her hand, the
lure of her face as they stood almost breast to breast with
the jug between them, had set his pulses racing. Bare-
limbed and hatless, with scratches and fruit-stains on her
face and arms, she had been toned perfectly to the country
setting, more truly a child of Nature than Edith, who had
seemed to him in comparison a shrivelled, impersonal
thing as he glimpsed her bobbing among the dark thickets
and cutting irritably with a walking-stick at the fruit-
bearing stems. The idyllic quality of that afternoon, the
furtive snatches at awakening intimacy, remained unspoilt
in Garth's mind despite an outburst of temper from Bella
on the homeward journey.

Two days later he saw Irma again at the workshop, and
the showery weather of that day gave her an excuse for
entering the shed. He found the added privacy almost
guiltily attractive, and expressed clumsily and with some
bitterness his feeling about the Stribleys. They were
despising him because of his mother; they despised Irma
because of her shiftless family. The effect of this was a
peculiar strengthening of the bond between Irma and
himself. They had talked long and freely about their
respective predicaments, and he realised that her mood
was similar to his—the Ishmaelitish mood of a nature that
seemed unable to fit in or find understanding in the usual
quarters. She told him she had detested school, that she
had no liking for her shop work, that she was fed up with
her home life; yet this intransigence was not simply way-
wardness in her any more than his own revolt was merely
wayward. An odd streak in their temperaments was being
subjected to relentless pressure from circumstance, and
they were flung together at a time when a break of some
sort was inevitable. Garth's feeling for the girl, which
had at first been a kind of pity enlarging the field of his
fight against frustration, became subtly changed through
this fuller contact with her. His unhappy relation with
Edith made him careless, almost inclined to welcome any

breach of those standards of convention and good taste which had brought such misery to him. Yet he was restrained from any thought of a flirtation—restrained not only by his essentially serious and loyal nature but by the quality of his regard for Irma. He had indeed been clouded by the fascination she exerted over him: combined with the tragic threats of that period it blunted his normal perceptions and the ordinary commonsense arguments had not weighed with him at all. Irma's extreme youth, the probability that within a few days she would move finally out of his orbit, had been undertones that passed almost unregarded in that mood of fierce spiritual obsession. He knew instinctively that the fascination was mutual. His character was strangely attractive to her —solid and sympathetic, but with enough moodiness and mystery to keep her wondering, guessing and attempting fresh approaches. He was so totally unlike a town-dweller in the processes of his thought, and even in his appearance, while she stood in vivid contrast to the village girls by her swift frank ardours and gliding innuendoes that were somehow lifted above a mere seductive flashiness. There was a cheapness in her manner, but it was not the cheapness of pride. It seemed to be a veneer of vulgarity thrown on to her nature by the squalor of her upbringing and surroundings. He sensed an underlying depth, and when as they talked in the workshop he tried occasionally to reach it and draw it out he felt a warm, confused gratitude in her brief comments, her smiles and glances.

On the Tuesday evening they had spent an hour together in Virginia Wood, where Garth had found her looking for nuts. The meeting was not altogether accidental—she had told him she might stroll that way if she could manage to be alone; and their spiritual attachment took on a fulness of detail that was painful to both, trembling on the verge of an impulsive betrayal. Garth had not dared even to touch her hands there in the provocative half-tones and heavy, earthy scents of the coppice.

They had spoken fitfully while throwing sticks up into the horse-chestnut trees to try and bring down the pale, unripe nuts, and the poise of her body as she swung the missiles was achingly lovely to him. Several times she scrambled up into a cleft of an oak tree and sat amid the glancing shadows of leaves, swinging her bare legs and peering up along the valley slopes to make sure that no one was approaching.

The primitive atmosphere, the weird flicking tongues of sunset among the trees, had driven Garth at last to turn the conversation into a channel almost bitterly religious—for his early insights into the mystery of faith were not comforting. He had spoken to her rather gloomily about God. He did not suppose she understood him, but as she also had never been to church the subject was fresh to her, and it came from him with an irony and bafflement that made it fit in and deepen the sense that they were isolated and powerless under destiny.

There was no contempt in her reaction whether he talked of God or his mother: he was surprised to find her sensitive to this grimmer vein of his personality that was so repellent to everyone else. She seemed to have caught his mood there in that remote place—just as, in London, she would catch the mood of frivolity. A highly impressionable girl, she was soon moved from one emotional extreme to another and was not cultured enough to be disdainful about anything expect the cold, balanced middle courses of safety.

Garth had left her as twilight darkened, and felt ruffled and unhappy about the whole complication. Irma appealed to him as Edith had never done and—he knew —as Edith never could. This girl, mere child though she was, could set her nature flowing into his in a way that was a revelation of new, undreamed-of possibilities. Nothing that Edith gave would ever satisfy him, for this affinity was not a crude matter of sex appeal. Its roots lay in a spiritual kinship that seemed arbitrary and cruel, linking him with a girl whom until a few days ago he had never heard of. In Edith there were no such germs of sympathy to be developed, while in Irma they were ripe, bursting upon him through a beauty of flesh that was irresistible.

He spent the night in agony, hearing at intervals his mother's gabbling in the next room.

Day broke with heavy rain, and he felt relieved that probably Irma would not come to Meledor with Stribley's dinner in such a downpour. All morning he worked in the shed with his big rugged face clouded and twitching, looking out through the small leaded window at the rain splashing down in the clay-tanks and forming puddles out there where she had passed on other days.

As he had expected, she did not come: and the memory of their long communion in Virginia Wood, the soft-voiced talk, the burdened silences, and the sight of her figure gliding against the tree-trunks, took on an unreal, fantastic quality which he felt impelled to break before retiring again to bed.

He spent the evening with Edith in town, but blundered the whole time like one dazed and stupefied, listening dully while Edith spoke disparagingly of Irma: "Cheap little baggage—Bella won't have her down again. . . ."

This news had increased Garth's sense of desperation; and he was given no time to recover his balance and put Irma resolutely out of his mind. The very next day the fateful lightning struck down in Meledor workshop.

It had been a tense, thundery noon when Irma appeared, the sky black and ominous over the clay-dumps. The heat was oppressive and enervating, and the stuffy gloom of the shed had affected Garth queerly, preparing him for the girl's mood. He realised as soon as she came in that her manner was very different from the subdued, dreamy one she had shown at Virginia. She was wearing a red beret and cream frock, puffing and sweating from her brisk walk up the hill. She looked reckless and began

telling him at once that she had just had another row with
Bella. This had drawn a wry challenge from Garth as he
straightened from planing a board and dropped the tool
on the bench.

"You'll be glad when you go back to London, I expect?"
he said, peering hard at her.

She put down her basket among a pile of shavings and
approached him, her small blue eyes narrowed, her smile
tantalising.

"Glad to leave you to Edith, you mean?"

"That won't last long," he muttered grimly.

Irma paused as he turned fully to face her; she
moistened her thick slack lips.

"Edith isn't any good to you," she said in smouldering
tones. "It's a shame. . . ."

"Never mind that"—he spoke hurriedly, fighting for
composure.

She pushed back the hair from her forehead and glanced
stealthily out through the doorway.

"I wish I could stop and make it up to you. I'd soon
make you happy. . . ." She hesitated, then, studying his
face she must have found in it some encouragement. She
slipped one bare arm up around his neck and thrust the
other hand into his palm, worming her moist fingers
between his.

"It's all right, Garth," she coaxed. "I won't tell Edith
—or anybody." And she had pouted out her lips. . . .

The flash struck them both at the next instant. Garth
did not even try to resist the lure. Dizzily he felt the
spiritual passion flood up into his senses so that with a
blind, convulsive movement he had pressed her in against
him, taking the flame of her lips full on his mouth and
returning her kisses—kisses such as Edith had never given
him—frankly and shamelessly.

A sigh of mingled triumph and fear escaped Irma when
that long embrace had ended. She stood looking at him,
pale and as if startled by feelings that she could neither

understand nor discipline. Both were awed by the knowledge that this was no mere sportive prank that could
soon be forgotten, but the serious instinctive expression
of fundamental rhythms which had stirred and leapt to
meet each other in the Stribleys' parlour, among the black-
berry clumps of Meledor Downs, and under the chestnut
trees of Virginia.

"I'll try to come over to the woods again to-night—
shall I ?" she whispered.

Trembling and mentally paralyzed by the shock, he
nodded.

But when she passed out on to the cinder-track it was
the last glimpse he had ever had of her. A workman had
seen her emerge and had drawn an obvious inference
from her confused manner, so nakedly emotional. He
had told Stribley and the scandal broke upon the village
the same day, Irma being forbidden to leave the farm
except with her relatives until the week-end, when her
father came down and fetched her back to London.

Chapter Eight

WHILE Garth mused thus a lanky, muddy-faced youth
had stepped outside the lodge doorway and was
scowling up towards the defile—Roy Keast, the "kettle-
boy" (a sort of general attendant on clayworks), a native
of Virginia. Seeing Garth standing moodily by the fence
he shouted in a rather squeaky, impatient tone, and with
emphatic gestures:

"Hustle on, Garth! I've let the fire out in there, and
your pasty and tea'll be gone cold."

"All right," muttered Garth, and giving a shiver—for
he had become chilled on the exposed ridge—he braced
himself and moved briskly down the slope to join his
comrades.

The lodge was cramped and bare, with benches set along the walls and a rusty stove in the centre, above which Keast was bending as Garth came in, extracting from the oven a warm pasty. The fire was almost out, thin wisps of smoke flagging around the deadened embers, and Garth closed the door to keep some amount of warmth and comfort within the hut.

In the deep shade beyond the tiny window that overlooked the clay-pit, a man was sitting, his clothes so dark that he was scarcely distinguishable except when he made a movement, stretching out a brawny arm to set his cup upon the top of the stove or take it therefrom, and bringing within the focus of daylight a face blackened also, his small teeth and the prominent whites of his eyes gleaming like a negro's. This was Reub Pollard, the blacksmith—middle-aged, but only just married for the first time, and showing in his heavily-cast features the genial gusto of one whose virtue has at last been rewarded. He lived still where he had been born—in one of the slate-roofed cottages of Trethosa.

Opposite him sat a man rather white than black—in garb and also in complexion. This was Enoch Hocking, the mica-worker—elderly, very tall, and inclined to stoop through the habitual bending required in his management of sluices and stirring of clay in the refining-beds. He was a slow, meek man who nevertheless held strong views on occasions, and Meledor had no need to be ashamed of him.

Both men glanced up at Garth's belated entrance, but his expression did not invite verbal greeting of any kind, and they knew him too well to waste words. They merely nodded as he sat down near the doorway, on the same bench as Hocking but as far from him as possible, and mechanically took his pasty from Keast.

The meal continued, amid a strained silence at first. Garth was relieved that they made no reference to the Stribleys—had probably not observed Martin's confusion

73

as he moved back past the window with his basket; and ignoring them Garth began nibbling at the dinner he had prepared—in a very different mood—last night.

He could eat little of it, and several times arose, opened the door and tossed out a handful of scraps, watching the birds—sparrows and starlings—flutter down on to the gravel and hop about as they fed greedily; then re-bolted the door, returning to the bench to sip at the hot tea Keast had given him.

His thoughts were fitful, cloudy, without coherence; and fevered by them he presently sought distraction in the talk that had started among his mates.

Keast, seated opposite, his long neck and narrow shoulders jerking against the window-panes, was saying with a snigger:

"Ted Blewett's sister Doreen's still going steady wi' Webbers' chap over Rescrowsa farm, from all accounts."

"Yes," answered Reub, wiping his mouth with a red handkerchief and peering earnestly at the stove-pipe. "She and Paul have got pretty thick in the marrying way, if kissing can be called real progress. I don't say it can. We'm living in a loose age, Mr. Keast."

"Loose enough," muttered Hocking; he tore off the last strip of tissue paper from his pasty and leaned forward to push it through the bars of the stove. Watching intently to see if a spark would kindle it, he added as if soliloquising:

"And yet there's people goin' around whining that they don't know why this war's allowed! What *I'd* like to know is, why these loose-livers got off scot-free as long as they did."

Reub was not to be side-tracked by the charms of argument. He continued to address the stove-pipe.

"Well, Doreen's turning out very different from Ted —or that younger sister, Jean, there to St. Austell. That little beggar's running wild, they say."

"Yes—*she's* started to go Ted's way all right," observed

Hocking as he straightened. "And her mother encouraging it, if you can believe what's whispered—letting her bring in chaps when Doreen isn't around."

Reub looked more narrowly at the stove as the greasy paper blazed up for a moment. Squeezing his eyes half shut he said with restraint:

"Nasty cut for Webbers if that's true, now Doreen's trying to lift her family up a bit."

"Yes; how strangely things do work around when folks is growed up!" exclaimed Hocking, glancing sideways at Garth to include him in the generalisation. "To see 'em in their prams you'd never have believed it."

"Beyond belief it is!" admitted Reub, shaking his head vehemently. "Not that I mind seeing Jean Blewett in her pram—born and reared in St. Austell. But I mind Ted's young days well enough. He was one of our boys—born there at Trethosa in the house where the Chirgwins come in later."

In the act of pouring another cup of tea from the pot on the broad window-sill, Keast turned.

"Was he? I didn't know that."

"Yes: I mind it very often in the mornings when I look across the road and see the smoke rising above the thatch. Houses do change hands, and if you'm of a thoughtful turn o' mind you do get a queer feeling sometimes. 'Why,' I says to myself, 'that used to be old Blewett's chimney smoke there, and now 'tis Chirgwins' and Seth Spragg's!' A very queer feeling it do give me. 'Tis the same chimney-pot—almost the same smoke you might say with a little imagination; but quite different people underneath—a new world indeed; and the house itself knowing nothing about it. Things isn't so jolly there these days as 'twas when Nick Blewett and Sal lived there wi' little Teddy."

"But he couldn't have stayed there long?" suggested Keast, sitting back and squinting at Garth, who was moving restlessly, his eyes fixed upon the cup he held on his knees.

"Well, not exactly," replied Reub. "A matter o' two or three year. Afore the last war was over the Blewetts had gone in St. Austell. But I mind seeing the little toddler out wi' Nick and Sal—pale little chap then, nothing very winsome about'n."

"Nor about his father, 'a b'lieve."

"No beauty, I admit, a plain-featured lot, they Blewetts. Up till then Nick had lived all his life at Trethosa—used to run the old hoss-bus from St. Stephen to Truro back before the charabancs and buses came along. He didn't complain o' being scat out o' business, for the hoss-bus had served a good turn. First fell in love wi' Sal through her being a passenger, so 'twas said—would pick her up down to Ladock."

"Well, they married," observed Hocking, dropping his cup on the floor in his haste to strike a tone and attitude of finality. "And then Ted arrived."

"Yes; and if I'd gone up to that little toddler when he was out walking, holding Nick's hand, and said to him: 'My sonny, when you grow up you'll ruin the maids and hang yerself'—why, I suppose Nick would have scat me flat in the road. Not that he was that sort o' man—very mild fellow Nick always was—would stand any insults without drawing a extra breath. But my meaning is that not even Ted's own father could have foreseen such a mess as that."

"And yet it happened," said Hocking, as if regarding Reub's statement as somewhat lacking in emphasis.

"It happened," agreed Reub. "And now there's his sisters taking such contrary ways—Jean following Ted's footsteps and Doreen aiming to settle in as a good hearty farmer's wife. Ted little dreamed such turns was coming when he went in Carpalla 'dry' four year ago and hanged hisself over the kiln."

Hocking blinked for a minute out of the window at the western cliff of Meledor clay-pit, then closed one eye, as if trying to visualise the scene of the suicide. After a pause he commented wryly:

"Ted may have been thinking more o' Minnie Lagor than of his sisters that night he said good-bye to hisself, for a man's conscience must be very alive at such a time."

"Well, Minnie didn't mourn him; and 'tis my opinion she won't mourn Griffiths."

"Won't marry the bloke you mean? I hardly think it meself—a downright atheist, they say. My woman bought one of his leaflets—thought 'twas a hymn, and burnt it afterwards when she found the real sense of it. Bitter stuff; and Minnie've had enough bitterness of her own."

"Yes, bitter; and yet a deep-thinking man."

"How often you find it these days!" exclaimed Hocking, rubbing a clayey forefinger along the top of his Wellington boot, as though writing the words thereon. "We'm beginning to have doubts, 'a b'lieve, whether all this learning have been worth while."

"A pretty pass it've brought us to, certainly," Reub admitted. "Eddication puts knowledge in the head all right, but that's more than offset by the sneer it puts on your face. Did 'ee ever see or hear of a eddicated man what didn't sneer at something?"

"Not in this world, Reub. They'm all of a pattern, as far as I can judge. 'You can have your religion and your love,' they says: 'what we want is the sneers. The Sneering Man is the real civilised product, far above the Loving Man, and as for the Believing Man—why, he's nowhere at all. And so whatever helps us to sneer most is the highest form o' eddication.' "

In spite of himself Garth could not repress an appreciative grin.

"That's pretty true, Enoch," he said over his cup.

With this unexpected encouragement Hocking rose, his lean white figure almost reaching the roof. He waved his pasty—what remained of it—in a slow zigzagging course, and resumed more earnestly.

"'Tis this wave o' scholarship, not suffering, what've drained the heartiness out o' life. Eddication do weaken a man's power to keep his faith under the troubles and trials that come along. It offers him the easy way out—says he needn't keep up his struggles to believe in God or such-like; here's some philospher or scientist or something says 'tis more reasonable to give in and chuck it all over. He'd never ha' thought o' giving in if he was a simple-minded man what the schools hadn't meddled wi'—would ha' struggled on and won through as our fore-fathers did." Hocking bent to the floor for his cup, peering out under his woolly brows at Garth.

"You now, Garth, with all you've been through, I dare-say you'd ha' become a atheist too if you'd gone to one o' these colleges."

"I expect I should," said Garth, quietly, yet with an undercurrent of moody emphasis that made him at once the object of puzzled scrutiny. "Me and Griffiths seem to represent the opposite ways o' taking a big spot o' trouble: the unreasonable Christian way o' choosing to stay put and cut away all the worldly helps so that deliver-ance when it comes'll be the work o' destiny; and the natural, rational way o' kicking back and grabbing what you can to make up for it." His smile, this time, was rather tense as he added:

"It seems pretty much of a toss-up sometimes—which method's the winner."

Reub, who had eaten his pasty, lay back against the wall with arms folded.

"You ha'n't met Griffiths yet, have 'ee ? Wasn't at home that day he come around here ?"

"No, but I've seen him."

"Where ?"

"At Truro three weeks ago. It seems Minnie told him something about me and made him curious. I only stayed with him a minute then. He said he'd call in on me next time he's up this way."

Reub chuckled as Hocking sat down. "You aren't looking forward to that, I reckon ?"

"Not much."

"No, 'tisn't no *man* Garth wants there," observed Keast, hugging himself in the draughty corner. "But if 'twas a tasty bit o' skirt—even if not Irma. . . ."

Garth's face hardened afresh into the ugly lines that had marked it when he first came in. He dropped his empty cup on the bench and made to rise, but was checked by Reub saying with fresh interest:

"Well, if 'tis Irma he still wants I reckon he'll soon be free to go to London and pick up with her."

"Eh? How's that?" asked Garth sharply.

Reub turned and jerked a thumb over his shoulder.

"All the signs point to a breakdown here afore long. Output's falling steady, and it only needs another move o' Hitler's to put the works back on half-time. Several clayworks around here have had to close down altogether."

"Yes, I know." Garth spoke in a dull tone, as if pre-occupied, surprised by a new trend of possibilities. He sat very still on the edge of the bench, face grim, eyes downcast—so suddenly withdrawn into himself that Hocking leaned sideways and poked him in the ribs to secure his attention for the mild comment:

"War's bound to knock out a industry like ours where so much depends on the exports. Germany was one of our biggest customers on that there continent o' Europe, and now, o' course, none of our clay isn't goin' there—though you'd think they'd need more clay instead o' less, considerin' the amount o' crockery Hitler must ha' smashed up in these tempers he'd get."

"Anyhow, 'tis a black outlook," commented Reub, unmoved by this levity. "And 'twouldn't surprise me if we was looking for fresh jobs before the summer's gone. Depends how many of our markets Hitler can put quiet, and how many of our men is called up. I mind in the last war we got so short o' hands that they was thinking of havin' women in again to do some o' the soft jobs, same as they used to back in the olden days."

"And you think as soon as Garth's out o' work he'll make a bolt for London, like Bert Stribley did, and"—Keast winked slyly—"*because* Bert did?"

"I wouldn't say it too serious, but there's unlikelier things. Garth have just told us he means to stay put and wait for this destiny he've spoke to us of so often. But that don't mean lying around dreaming all your life. It means that when the proper time have come you'm forced to act, even against your own will; and it look as if that time is pretty near for Garth now."

Again that tense, almost desperate look on Garth's face. Clumsily he rose, stepped to the door and pulled it roughly open, scattering the birds that had been hovering outside, awaiting fresh titbits. This time he passed out, closing the door behind him without a word of farewell to his mates. He stood for a few minutes on the steps, breathing in gusts, gazing down into the chasm at the black-roofed lodge set beside a pool of blue water under a scarred crag two hundred feet below; then with the erratic, jerky movements of one tortured by irresolution he hurried away up the slope towards the workshop.

Chapter Nine

JEAN BLEWETT paused on the short path outside her home. Her features were not clearly visible, but she was dark, with black hair, heavy slanting eyebrows and a weak chin receding from plump lips that were thickly smeared with make-up. She buttoned her green coat, casting about her a glance more hesitant than usual. Keen pale starlight spilled down, here and there dimmed with cloud but throwing even where unchecked a mere grudging luminosity over the house-roofs of this low-lying north-western suburb of St. Austell. The solid block of

Grove Road stretched away as a blurred excrescence, every window blank, lifeless.

No one was visible now in the whole length of the street. Noiselessly Jean swung open the gate, stepped out and strolled northward to the corner, then uphill, leaving the viaduct and wooded slopes of Trenance behind her, heading for the heart of the town.

The road was exposed on the western side, and frequently she halted, glancing with distaste over the scene rendered inhuman and comfortless and void of challenge by the necessities of war. Nothing served to quicken, to enchant; all was one grey monotony, soulless in haze of frost and starshine.

Her step was less buoyant to-night than last winter, when nearly every evening she had come up along this road, rarely halting then to peer back into the dale sprinkled so lavishly with lights from cars, windows, garages: long rows of lights twinkling against the dark bulge of grassy hillsides rolling down towards the viaduct from the claywork-scarred moorland to the north, and the wider undulations sweeping in south-west from the Pentewan Valley. The scene had exhilarated her without any studied regard; in the background of consciousness she accepted it vividly as a fit, a congenial setting.

Her ambition then—always realised—was to spend delicious moments at street corners, talking and giggling with youths who knew her talent; to be petted a little in some park, or taken into a cinema and be allowed to forget her beastly home, her mother, and the repressions, interests and ideals of school-life from which she was only just released.

Jean was one of those girls of a very high type who are doomed by cheap intellectual standards to remain unappreciated; girls on whom mental education is wasted and who can be morally educated only through love. Of no marked intelligence, she was forced to live on her emotions and let them be prostituted by pagan standards because she had never heard of any others. She had much in common with Irma Stribley, but she had never been kissed by such an oddity—in a Christian land—as Garth Joslin, and so the recent example of her sister Doreen in her steady courtship at Rescrowsa farm was less effective than that set in the past by her brother Ted, though she had been only eleven when he committed suicide.

The clouds thickened as Jean gained the higher rise of the hill. The broad sweep of landscape westward, sprawling towards the coast—fertile, suburban, with the rows of stylish villas on the by-pass road, the little park below Truro Road, the avenues of trees—became stripped of detail and impressed itself upon Jean's senses only as a weird hollow traversed by the wind and scowled upon by the congealed and blotchy sky. She drew a torch from her pocket and flashed it occasionally along the gutter as she quickened her steps. She had soon reached the end of the steep lane and emerged into Bodmin Road, with the first line of shops just ahead, a high wall slanting down to them above the pavement, friendly with huge coloured posters. A few minutes' walking would bring her to the bottle-neck of Fore Street, from which alleys leading to pubs, cinemas and ballrooms were readily accessible.

Jean had crossed the road and stepped on to the pavement when she became aware of a dark bulk slumped against the wall a few yards above the turning. The natural light showed nothing but a vague male shape, but something in its stillness aroused in Jean an impulsive curiosity. She, too, remained motionless for a minute, watching with narrowed eyes, then boldly flashed the torchlight.

Its pale beam played upon a young man of slight build, wearing a grey raincoat and cap, spectacles, and a look at once dazed and fervid. Jean felt no particular interest, but they were alone and recklessness prompted her to a familiar, cheeky greeting.

"Hello, old sport! Who're you waiting for?"

The fellow's voice came—weak, thick, eager: "Eh?"

" 'Who you waiting for?' I said. Guess you're drunk."

She saw the figure make a painful effort to regain its dignity as he returned with a hiccup:

"Who you, ol' dear?"

"Nobody in particular. If you're drunk I'll pass on: my mother don't let me speak to soakers."

The fellow slouched forward a pace, waving his hand emphatically.

"Aren't drunk. Only took a pint or two—forget how much. But I . . . I'm bit lost. Don't drink as a rule—not that sort; but to-day—got to the end o' tether and jush broke."

"That's a pity. . . . Aren't in uniform yet, are you, buddy?"

"No—shan't be in uniform. They didn't pash me— only for m-munitions. Be sent away shomewhere—war factory—Brishtol most likely. All upshet."

"Sure, the war's upset most people; but that's nothing to cry about. Gives you more chances. . . . How did you get here?"

"Came up from Redruth hour or two ago. Had to go there to-day—lots of others—m-military doctors there to grade all twenty-threes."

"Oh! yes. Is that exam to-day?" Jean caught her breath, her eyes slid down the road as the dimmed head-lamps of a car flashed into Fore Street, several tiny black human forms being revealed for a moment in the pale weird glow. "Then—there'll be plenty o' fresh men around the town this evening?"

"Expect so. Some gone home on the bus, back to villages."

"But you stayed here—all on your own?"

"Ravver."

"Live here at St. Austell?"

"No—out in the country, St. Stephen way—shix miles or so."

"H'm. What's your name?"

"Seth Spragg."

The name conveyed nothing to Jean, but having revealed this much Seth leaned forward with an almost violent curiosity.

"What's yours, ol' girl?"

"Ah! I can't tell you that—in case of accidents!" Jean laughed, stepping closer. "And you want to throw off your blues somehow before you go back home—that it?"

"Yesh. They expected me around tea-time—must think I missed bus. Edith may be worried: serve her right *I* shay."

Jean frowned. "Who's Edith?"

"Wife," replied Seth, throwing a sort of ferocity into the monosyllable.

"So you're married?"

"Yes, worsh luck: four year of it, and going to pieces —fash." Seth stretched both arms in an eloquent gesture that rather overtaxed his power of balance. "Edith don' care much—want me be killed in thish war so she can go ahead with other affair. Been twitting me for days about thish—said if they pash me for fighting I'd be b-blowing me brains out and wouldn't turn up alive."

"Well—d'you mean to?"

"Not yet. Couldn't face it yet. Shomething happen first."

Jean pondered a moment, tapping the kerbstone with her foot, a strained smile on her lips.

"Perhaps it will—if you aren't too drunk. You're jealous, and that's a good sign, buddy."

"Dunno 'bout jealous. True, Edith may be gone up see Garth again by this time—may be there now, telling him I han't come home. That's first place she'd carry her trouble—not far—jush across valley, and Garth living alone there."

"Garth?" repeated Jean, pursing her lips. "That's her second fiddle, I s'pose?"

"No; I'm second fiddle—always was. She meant to marry Garth four year ago, only his mother went off her nut and she took me jush t-to—save her pride. She's driftin' back to him again: felt it lately—colder to me 'n ice." Seth's manner changed abruptly, as if he had become aware of indiscretion; he added stiffly, in a muffled tone:

"Needn't 'splain to you—stranger."

"Oh, you can trust me!" Jean teased. "I aren't married yet, and I want to learn. I can keep secrets, duckie: I wonder if you can too?"

"Secrets? What mean?"

"Well, you're just in the right mood . . . only I've got to be careful. . . . You wouldn't let me down, would you, if I tried to do you a good turn?"

"Wouldn't let down a girl—pretty girl that is. Wish was moonlight—shee your face better." Seth coughed, made a shuffling movement and said apologetically:

"Can't take you to pictures, I'm afraid."

"I wasn't going to suggest that. Something more sociable, old sport—but not from me."

Seth scratched his head for a few minutes, then shook it, staring hard at her. His breath was thick and smelled strongly of liquor; his eyes gleamed with increasing excitement behind the spectacles. Presently he broke out in a tone darkly confidential:

"Wonder now: you that kid, are 'ee?"

"Who?" asked Jean, arching her brows in surprise.

"Ah! I expect so. Talk, y'know: we hear it out where Ted and his wife used live. Doreen goin' steady on farm there, and her sishter running wild, we been hearing— down there to Grove Road. Yesh, tha's it." He nodded heavily. "Bringin' chaps in—and other girls—rips, o' course. . . . S'pose you come out to find company for 'em —eh?" Seth laughed, and reaching out a hand he flicked Jean's hair in a familiar manner.

Jean drew back and said almost curtly:

85

"Well—are you coming in? You can still catch the last bus home when you've got square with Edith."

Again Seth nodded: his face looked tense with resolution.

"Yesh, awri'—I go along. Cold here—can't shtand around this wind." He shivered, and interrupted his fastening of a coat button to brush away some stray figment of conscience.

"Don' care: Edith's with Garth most likely—may ask her stay the night. Man got his feelings and can't be played with—needs lesh'n, ol' dear."

Jean watched him anxiously, even with irritation.

"You're sure you won't crock up when you get indoors with the warm fire and the girls dropping in to pull your leg a bit?"

"No, I'm shteady enough—hol' on me arm—I. . . ." He staggered out from the wall, leaning so heavily upon her arm that she had grave misgivings. He was in no reliable state, and to bring him in like this—it might be too much even for her mother's indulgence. Only a momentary recklessness impelled her to move with him slowly towards the corner from which the houses of Grove Road were visible.

Having crossed the road Seth stopped abruptly, swaying on his feet, and pointed down into the valley vague in starlight. He muttered some incoherent words about "Edith down there." Clearly he was becoming more and more fuddled. Jean's resolve steeled and stabbed to humiliation. She'd been too hasty—must throw him off somehow. . . . She relaxed her grip of his arm; and immediately he slumped sideways, clutched at her shoulder, almost drawing her over with him as he fell with a thud into the gutter.

Jean stood for several minutes bending above him, her lips tense, twisted. When she had recovered a little she flashed the torch. Its diffused light circled over Seth's purplish face, showing the eyes closed behind his spectacles

—fortunately unbroken—one cheek hidden in his cap, which had been knocked off, his mouth gaping. . . . Dead drunk!

With a shrug of disgust Jean left him lying there insensible and hurried away towards Fore Street.

Chapter Ten

A STRANGER, approaching Meledor claywork in the early afternoon of Easter Saturday, the twenty-third of March, might have expected to find the place deserted, a playground of fantasy and storm. The grey spotted sky above it heaved like the vast body of a cow; the clawing fingers of the tree-tops seemed to be milking the clouds, the black clouds that were hanging down like udders in various parts of the heavens, squirting rain wastefully.

The labourers had been on holiday since Thursday, and the huts, pit-workings and mica beds had taken on an aggrieved air of neglect. The waggon stood motionless on the track, a dull sullen shape about which the wind whistled and the rain poured, dripping from its frame, mingling with the tar of an underlying roller, and oozing slowly like black treacle into the cracks between the rotting sleepers.

The waggon was not alone, however, in breaking the smooth outline of the dune. Along its southern slope, from the bridge formed by the track near the open downs to the lane leading in to the workshop, a young girl was scrambling about with the agility of a chamois. She showed in all her movements a fearlessness born of long familiarity with these surfaces, and also a perverse urge that countered the natural desire to return as soon as possible to the shelter of her home.

The girl was Shirley Lagor, and she was collecting

87

firewood, clad specially for the job in an old, dirty rain-coat that reached to the tops of her Wellington boots. Now and then, as she climbed down into the ruts that rain had worn into the almost perpendicular slope, she became invisible from below, her presence disclosed only by the clatter of stones set rolling by her movements and presently by the whisk of a scrap of wood tossed up from the gulch; but soon the green beret reappeared and she resumed her search in the open.

At intervals Shirley paused and stood erect on the bare side of the pyramid, looking steadily down the vale. The quick, vivid flash of her brown eyes showed that something of Sal Blewett's spirit, as well as marked physical resem-blance, had passed to this grandchild of hers. Shirley's glance was deliberate; it probed, flitting over the in-different details of flouncing trees, red-roofed drying-sheds, clay-tanks gleaming whitely like leprous scabs amid the healthily cleansed meadows. Each time it pounced on the one object that had led her to interrupt the urgent task of gathering the wood. This object was a small yellow vehicle, a butcher's van, that stopped wherever there was a dwelling. She watched it glide across Trethosa Moor, and when next she looked it was half-way up the opposite hill, at Trethosa village. On an impulse she waved the scrap of wood in her hand, her face under its white muddy streaks became grave, yearning, and her full lips formed, almost soundlessly, the words:

"Come home to-night, mummy. . . ."

And then, as her gaze returned to the dune's foot to see if she had now thrown down sufficient sticks, she gave a quick start and again stood rigid. Her eyes had taken in the range of the flat heath stretching southward to the main road above Scarcewater, and noted a movement, a man approaching, whom she recognized at her second glance. The man who had cast a perplexing shadow on her thoughts of late, a vaguely disturbing figure, of whom she had said as the shower began an hour ago:

"I don't expect he'll come now it's wet. I hope he don't, anyway. . . ."

Griffiths!

She followed with distaste the progress of that burly form, moving with a dynamic and defiant energy that fused him with the tempestuous mood of his surroundings. His head and shoulders were hidden by an umbrella which he held lowered before him against the wind. He was alone on the ridge, but not long exposed after Shirley glimpsed him. He had soon drawn level with the school and the row of houses stretching out to the corner above the claywork lane.

Shirley edged slowly down the slope, her tongue between her lips, the rain running down her face and causing her to squeeze her eyes almost shut. She kicked at a stone now and then, stooping whenever she reached a piece of wood and gathering these fragments until, by the time she arrived at the bumpy base of the dune, she was balancing precariously an armful of sand-caked timber. But she did not seem pleased now at her success in gathering so much. There was a shrinking in her step, almost a sulky touch in the pouted mouth, the firm set of the receding jaw.

She moved out on to the road just as Griffiths turned the corner, and hearing a plank fall he raised his umbrella and glanced curiously around. His red wet face under the grey trilby popped out from its cover and softened at once in a surprised, appreciative smile.

"You're determined to keep warm, Shirley !"

The child picked up the dropped stick, and after several unsuccessful attempts she managed to balance the pile again, her chin dug into the topmost scrap, her wet little fingers clutching desperately at the lower pieces.

"Yes," she said as she drew closer, speaking hesitantly and with her eyes on the faggots. "I'm bringing this in because we've run short o' firewood and Uncle Colly wants it to chop for lighting fire to-morrow and Monday. He's waiting in the kitchen now with the chopper, and was going to spend all the afternoon splitting these pieces up to burn. We didn't think you'd come this weather."

"It wasn't raining when I left Truro. . . . But you're drenched, child. Why didn't Mr. Snell fetch the wood ?"

"He's got rheumatics—and anyhow, he couldn't climb around like me." Shirley smiled shyly up at Griffiths: she was never sulky long, and she continued in a sort of headlong confession:

"I love bringing in wood, it's such fun. And I like being out in the rain too, because all the other kids stop in then and I can have all the rain to myself."

"Don't you like playing with other children ?"

Shirley made a face.

"Not so much now I know I'm—different," she said slowly, and her eyes showed a lonelier depth of thought than was usual at her age. "They're always slapping it up, 'specially the older girls. They laugh about my daddy and what mummy done, and say I didn't ought to be here at all."

Griffiths, who secretly shared this opinion, viewing Shirley as an impediment to his plans, remained silent, and the oddly-contrasted pair moved on down the hill, past the dreary houses and the dripping trees.

Shirley was the next to speak, from a point several yards behind Griffiths: carrying the sticks, she could not keep pace with him.

"It's a pity you've come now, Mr. Griffs. You won't see mummy."

Griffiths turned, his eyes pierced sharply from under the umbrella.

"How's that ?"

"She isn't home."

"Not at home ? But she knew . . . surely she would-n't. . . ." He halted, biting his lip vexedly.

Shirley stopped too and tussled for a minute with her load, which had sagged upon her aching arms.

"Mummy couldn't help it," she said then. "There's a van over there, just called at our place and going over to Egypt: I don't know if you can see it now. But mummy's in it—took a lift because 'twas coming to rain hard."

A wry smile twisted Griffiths' lips.

"I'm afraid I need a little more explanation," he observed.

Shirley answered while peering intently towards Egypt:

"We was having our dinner just now—chips and fried egg—and I'd ate all my chips when Doris come in."

"Doris?"

"My auntie—mummy's sister, though she's only fourteen yet. She was looking awful scared, and said our old grannie been took bad with her heart and won't live till to-morrow, they think."

"What! ... Ah! I understand now."

"Yes. Mummy wouldn't ha' gone if she wasn't sent for."

Griffiths strode on, his head down, his face a mask amid the ribs of the umbrella.

"How long will your mother be away?" he inquired after a pause.

"I dunno," said Shirley gravely. "She may be back this evening, but she said she might have to stay up all night if grannie don't die 'fore then. I hope she do, 'cause I don't want to sleep in the room all by myself."

To evade his stormy revolt at thus being fooled afresh, Griffiths asked quickly:

"Is Uncle Colly kind to you?"

"Well, he tries to be sometimes, but he's old and keeps squabbling with his wife. She's a horrid old thing, near as bad as grannie. And then he works off his spite on mummy and me. He's vexed sometimes because I'm getting older and says girls is a nuisance as they grow up, running wild and that. It's silly, because I'll be only eight in June. If grannie dies I 'spect mummy'll take me over Egypt to live."

"Would you like that better?"

"Yes, lots, if grannie was gone—that is the *old* grannie —Tab she's called. My real grannie is always nice, and Doris and Muriel too, and grandfather. I haven't been to their place for ages because grannie Tab tried to hit me with a broom and called me a bitch last time I went. Mummy said she wouldn't take me there any more to be sweared at."

"Quite right," remarked Griffiths absently, peering between the white pillars of the drying-shed they were passing. Its front was open and rain beating in upon the clay cubes stacked around the kiln. Not far beyond this the smooth high wall of a clay-tank loomed up on a corner, and when they reached it the Snells' cottage was disclosed below.

They hurried towards it, and as Griffiths opened the gate Colly's voice was heard shouting from within:

"Drop 'em down outside, chiel. I'll bring out your shoes."

A minute later the old man appeared, and was obviously taken aback when he found Griffiths standing beside the girl among the scraps of wood, closing his umbrella. Colly's little peaked face shrunk under a peevish scowl; he handed Shirley her shoes almost mechanically.

"You, Mr. Griffiths! Didn't think you'd be here wi' sich a lig driving."

"I certainly wish I hadn't come," said Griffiths, stepping into the shelter of the doorway. "Shirley tells me Miss Lagor is gone to Egypt."

"Yes; bad luck, just as you'd agreed to visit us. But there 'tis—things always contrary in this world."

The two men went in, Colly leading the way, carrying some of the larger planks, while Shirley remained on the doorstep, changing her shoes and brushing the mud from her raincoat when she had removed it. She brought in at length the smaller chunks of wood, stealing into the kitchen quietly, her yellow frock, now exposed, giving her a daintier appearance. She moved past Griffiths, who had halted by the dresser, and bore the dripping faggots across to the hearth, then glided back to the "spence" under the stairs and stood with her back to the men, washing her face and hands in a bowl of water standing on a shelf within.

The kitchen was small, weirdly shadowed. A big fire burned in the stove; from this rather than from the sky came the light that mainly lit the room. The window was tiny and blurred with rain; only the vague tossing stems of pollard thorns could be seen through it. The floor was bare, the carpet having been rolled under the table, and on the board, also bare, lay a saw and a hatchet.

Colly had dropped his planks and eyed the strewn wood grumpily during the strained silence that followed, until Shirley had finished washing and turned, rubbing her face vigorously with a towel. The old man then took up one of the logs and seizing the axe he cast at Griffiths an apologetic, yet resentful glance.

"I hope you won't think me uncivil if I chop up these few sticks while you'm here," he mumbled. "They ought to be in the oven soon to dry, or they won't light fire well to-morrow, left damp."

Griffiths shrugged, remarking shortly:

"It's quite all right."

The chopping began, Colly's lean arm in its ragged coat sleeve rising and falling rhythmically past the glare of the fire, while his white head bobbed in the gloom like a snowball. Through the thud and clang, and the sound of splintering wood, his voice grated:

"Minnie's very put out to leave 'ee in the lurch like this, as it might seem. I told her you might take it as a real snub."

"I can hardly do that. Blood's thicker than water, they say."

"And sourer too, between Tab Lagor and Minnie. She wouldn't be sorry if she found the blinds drawed when she got there. And that's just why she needn't ha' gone: folks never die as long as they can be a nuisance. I've had experience enough on that point. Nine year ago my woman upstairs there—very deaf now, like old Tab, and can't hear what I'm saying to 'ee—she was said to be at death's door: had a stroke, and doctor kept me in high hopes. 'The least little excitement, Mr. Snell,' he says, 'and you'll be free to take the next number and make a better choice of it,' 'a says—or words to that meaning. But nothing come of it: winter followed winter and she'd never survive any of 'em I was told: yet here she is, and I verily believe she'll survive anything short of a direct bomb."

Colly tossed aside some fragments of the sliced wood as Shirley slipped past him to the chair at the table's head, where she sat down, leaning forward to warm herself at the fire.

Griffiths appeared to be deliberating, head bowed, lips pursed moodily, eyes intent upon the wet hat he held in his hand. Presently he said in a low tone:

"This'll mean new arrangements, I daresay, if the woman dies?"

"It may. Minnie've spoke o' leaving here—a little unsettled lately, and I can give a pretty fair guess who got something to do wi' it. 'Tis strange you should ever ha' come here, Mr. Griffiths, and got a trifle . . . well, I'd better say no more in front o' the chiel. A sharp little mite, and getting to make us feel uncomfortable, the questions she's asking lately. Wanting to know why Minnie han't took her over to see that shack at Carpalla. It seem she've heard she was born there."

Shirley sat erect, meeting Colly's leer with a cool defiance.

"I 'spect I'll get mummy to take me over if we go to Egypt to live," she said perversely. "And if she won't, then I'll go by myself. I'm sure I could find it."

"No reason why you should see that place," grumbled Colly, scraping the clotted sand from another stick. "Nobody living there now—all gone to wreck and ruin, most likely, and rotting away in this weather. 'Tisn't a proper house, only a old wood hut—nothing for a young maid to be pleased with. Swarming wi' rats, I daresay, by this time."

"But they say 'twas very important to me, uncle."

"Your father lived there for awhile, that's all."

"Didn't mummy too—before I was born?"

" 'Course she didn't: Minnie'd bided to Egypt all her life till she come here. . . . And now you must shut up: I can't be pestered wi' your tongue in front o' Mr. Griffiths."

An awkward pause ensued, until abruptly a fresh turn of thought caused Griffiths' face to relax; he stepped towards Colly and remarked with impulsive resolve:

"As Miss Lagor isn't at home I wonder if you'd mind my spending an hour with a neighbour of yours—Mr. Joslin?"

"Garth?" Colly's surprise scarcely equalled his relief; his face brightened into a perky and cautious enthusiasm. "Well, if you care to. 'Tis only a minute's walk up the hill, and he's more in your line than a common ignorant man like me—spends a lot of his time reading and perusing, I believe."

"So I thought. I'm very interested in that young man —saw him once at Truro, and he said I could call in when next I was at Meledor."

"Minnie been blabbing, I s'pose?"

"She told me a little about his life—something very much out of the ordinary, I should gather."

"Well, 'tisn't what his mother dreamed of, poor soul, nor what his school teachers hoped for—nor what many in this world would praise him for, I reckon, if he really did handle that London girl. . . . But I can only drop a hint wi' Shirley listening."

"I've a fair idea of the kind of scandal he blundered into," said Griffiths. "But his conduct since . . . ."

"That's the puzzle, and you'll be a lucky man if you can find the key to it. Garth's the mystery of the village, and folks've been kept guessing so long that they've sort o' got tired of him and let'n bide."

Griffiths glanced at the grandfather clock opposite Shirley as it began booming the hour of two.

"I suppose I shall find him at home?" he asked in the tone of one prepared for still further vexations.

"Sure to, weather like this," replied Colly, a grin baring his gums as he added: "Though what sort of welcome you'll find is another matter. Everything depends on the mood he's in at the moment: he may slam the door in your face, or may let 'ee in and talk by the hour together, pouring out his ideas in a style that would amaze the ear-holes of any citizen." Colly rose, clearing his throat importantly, leaving the axe embedded in the log on the floor.

"I'd better go up and show 'ee which house 'tis; there's so many along the hill, you mightn't find it else. . . . Jist wait a tick and I'll slip on me oilskins—keep me rheumatics warm for that little journey." He turned to Shirley, who was now hunched forward, examining a cut on her knee that had begun to bleed.

"You needn't be 'fraid, chiel—I'll only be gone a minute or two."

It was obvious from Shirley's quick nod and the broad smile on her face that she too was glad that Griffiths was not staying here. There was a repellant force in the man's personality, a force of mature revolt that jarred on the child's spirit and was too subtly intellectual for Colly's dull mind to welcome it.

A few minutes later Shirley was left alone in the room and the two men emerged into rain that had eased somewhat, though the wind was rising swiftly to the strength of a gale.

Chapter Eleven

Few houses in the district were drearier than Garth's when storms swept across the plateau, howling up the narrow gorge from the northern flat wastes of Goss Moor or driving in southward from the Channel. Always an abode of solitude, it seemed then a place hunted, scourged, the magnet of the storm, involving the whole village in an outburst of elemental spite that was directed mainly against itself and the young man whose prison at such times it became. The maledictions of the wind as it roared through the screen of elms and hawthorns about the cottage appeared to have a more sinister intent than its blusterings around other dwellings on the hillside; the lashings of the rain expressed a more mystic intensity of assault; and the frequent whirling of clouds of sand from the dune, blown furiously against the windows of the house and sometimes leaving the garden and path white as from a hail shower—a feature of storm landscape peculiar to the clay area—this seemed like a symbol of the mood of society in relation to this man, the stinging of petty malice.

Within the cottage all was still as the grave; only the frantic flapping of chimney smoke revealed the presence of the one who heard and took note, in his laconic, sphinxish way, of these challenges. There were no musical instruments in the house, no radio, and Garth was never heard to whistle or sing. He was regarded by his neighbours as a strange, silent young man; some of them thought him morbid, and all shunned the dwelling as a place of peculiar atmosphere, with something of the hermitage about it, something of the madhouse—a haunted abode and one upon which the destined doom was not yet played to its close.

97

The events that had marked the last days of Mrs.
Joslin's life here were still discussed around neighbouring
firesides in the winter evenings; and of recent weeks they
had become more vivid for Garth himself. His mother's
death had presented them afresh to his mind as a problem,
and the later shock of Bella's news, the sense that the time
for action in relation to Irma might be now at hand—
this had driven him to seize upon those old memories as
a relief from the sudden glare. However he might act, it
must be against that background. Reality, and no dream,
was there, and all fanciful extravagance in his thought of
Irma crumbled in contact with that stern truth, the bitter,
sombre thing that had unfolded here in this house when
Irma was freshest in his heart and life.

He was reviewing on this Saturday afternoon the details
of that final collapse. Sitting before the fire in the snug
front room, his eyes wandering from the swooping flames
to the arm-chair opposite in which Mrs. Joslin had sat so
often, he found the past scenes called to possessive intensity by a congenial atmosphere, the hushed twilit room,
the rain and the wind.

The last phase had begun with a visit from Mrs.
Hocking, Enoch's wife. Mrs. Joslin never called upon her
neighbours, and was never seen in the village. She knew
nothing of Garth's relation with Irma while the girl was
in Cornwall, and Garth resolved to give her no news of
it. But one day, a few weeks after Irma's return to
London, Mrs. Hocking dropped in—Garth being at work
—to borrow a cupful of flour: a common practice among
village housewives. Mrs. Hocking, however, had more
important motives than the urgency of baking. When
Garth returned he saw that his mother was much agitated,
and guessed that some hint of the scandal had reached
her. She asked no questions, but kept looking at him
strangely during tea-time, and at supper after he came in
from a gloomy ramble about Meledor Downs.

As they were going to bed she paused on the stairway,

her figure gaunt, shrivelled behind the banisters, her peaked face looking queer, the eyes glaring in the light of the guttering candle she carried.

"Garth," she said in a hoarse tone, "do 'ee know what be the best way to git rids o' woonself? I be tempted sometimes. . . . There's that old rope we hanged our pig with last year, and barrels is full o' rain-water what a body could slip quiet in. . . ."

"For God's sake, mother," cried Garth desperately, "don't get any notions o' that sort in your head."

He waited at the foot of the stairs until she entered her room, then stole back to the door, removed the key and took it to bed with him. The precaution was clearly needed. Every night thereafter he slept with the key under his pillow, until winter came.

In December Edith married Seth Spragg. Garth was not shocked; he had expected the development for some time. Throughout the autumn that pair had been walking out together, passing his home with deliberate regularity and always with arms ostentatiously around each other's waists. This victory parade foiled Garth's attempt to keep the ugly news from his mother. He would never forget the evening when his musings here by the parlour fire— sombre, stubborn, intense—were rudely shaken by the sound of his mother rushing across the bedroom, where she shut herself in her strange moods and where she had been all day—rushing across to the landing and calling him in a thick, gabbling tone:

"Garth! Thik Edith o' thine is nobbut trash. She be outside kissing Seth Spragg a minute ago. I zeed 'em up in field gateway, plain as day in the full moon. . . ."

He had replied quietly, soothingly, in a tired voice, saying he had known of their courtship and was not sorry: it was all for the best. . . .

The wedding day was cold, threatening snow early, but later the clouds broke at intervals to let in weird palpitations of sunlight. From the bedroom window Mrs. Joslin watched the hired car coming and going along the hill opposite above Trethosa, its white ribbons flapping fantastically like lashes whipping at her. Her brain groped resentfully and stumbled on the monstrous surmise that she, Sarah Joslin, had somehow set in motion that sleek car attending Edith's wedding at St. Stephen church. Because she was not always quite herself Edith had grown ashamed, humiliated; turned catty against Garth because he couldn't help it. . . .

Garth, too, was very grim that day, caring nothing for Edith but finding the workshop almost unbearable, moving about where Irma had stood and chatted on that fateful Thursday——. The unveiling! Strange irony, that had broken the spell that bound him foolishly to Edith, only to expose his life to a more tawdry and contemptible stroke.

At the close of the day, oppressed beyond measure by this sense of deepening anarchy, he forgot to remove the key from the door lock when he retired. It was long ere he slept, and towards twelve o'clock he awoke with an immediate feeling of alarm, though he could not be sure that any particular sound had roused him. But realisation stabbed him alert at once. The key ! His mother ! Fearfully he hurred across to her room, and found the bedclothes trailing on the floor, the bed empty. Gone! Then she really had——.

With a groan of dismay he flung on his clothes, raced down and out into the open. A crisp clear night, with the sickle moon just above Venus, shining calm in the southern sky, the white clay swamp below gleaming evilly close to the Stribleys' fields where manure heaps dotted foully the wan, thistle-pricked turf.

Which way had his mother taken ? She could not have gone far yet, even if she'd left the house before he awoke: her rheumatism would cripple her, with this frost. He dashed around to the cottage corner. No, she hadn't chosen the water-butts or the rope in the tool-shed. She must have gone down towards Trethosa, where Edith was now sleeping in Seth's arms. . . . Oh, God! He raced down the hill. The river, the clay tanks—which ? The tanks were nearest—one in particular—a big tank close beside the road, a flight of steps leading up to it.

Turning a corner he saw his mother lying shapelessly at the foot of the steps, having slipped on the frozen surface near the top of the wall.

Half-an-hour later he had got her indoors, with the aid of Colly Snell, who had heard his shout for help. Mrs. Joslin was carried into the parlour of her home and laid on the sofa—a limp, insensible, hideous burden. Garth looked stupefied, was dully aware that he was hoping—almost hoping it might be too late. Colly summoned a doctor from St. Stephen, and it was found that Mrs. Joslin had broken her leg, besides receiving many minor cuts and bruises. She regained consciousness the next morning, but was now hopelessly insane.

The following week she was removed to Bodmin asylum.

It was from these memories that Garth was roused, by none other than Colly himself, the thin piping voice piercing into the room from beyond the garden wall.

"Hey there, Garth ! I brought along a visitor for 'ee —and don't 'ee go arguing too hot so that the police need be sent for!"

Garth rose, looking dazed for a moment, and saw through the window the thick-set, virile figure of Griffiths moving up the garden path between the low stalky shrubs; Colly turning away from the gate, waving his hand in farewell.

Garth stepped mechanically towards the door, frowning, though rather with weariness than active displeasure. He had thought little of Griffiths during recent weeks, and had certainly not expected him to-day. A cloudy mood of transition lay upon him for several minutes, and was not fully lifted until both men had entered the parlour—

Griffiths' hat and coat being hung in the passage—and the visitor was seated opposite Garth, drying his plum-coloured trouser legs before the fire.

It was then that Garth realised with a slight flush of chagrin that his attire could scarcely make a favourable impression on one who was dressed in the exact fashion of a town-dweller. Garth's appearance was, indeed, a trifle slovenly. He was wearing an old grey flannel suit, a white woollen cardigan, and slippers split at the heels. The trousers were patched, the coat torn at the elbows, and he had not troubled to fit his neck with a collar and tie, since he had thought to see no one for the rest of the day. His curly brown hair was tousled, and several little tufts of stubble on his cheeks, jaw and upper lip told that he had last shaved without much regard for thoroughness.

Griffiths' bold eyes were taking in the details of the room, and he seemed to find these, at least, agreeable The apartment was small, but warm, cosily furnished and not untidy. The blue-and-gold floral pattern of the wallpaper had almost faded into a neutral smudge, as Garth had not re-papered any room of the house since his mother left it; but apart from this the look of the parlour was one of pleasing freshness.

Griffiths broke silence as soon as the men were settled in their chairs, flicking his thick fingers as he explained:

"I came up to see Miss Lagor, but she's been called away to her grandmother's death-bed, so I thought I'd better drop in here till tea-time."

"Old Mrs. Lagor dying, is she?" asked Garth, surprised.

"Mr. Snell seems to have his doubts—something of a character, isn't he?"

"A curious old fellow—not much liked around here, I'm afraid. I reckon you'd have found his talk as interesting as mine: he's got views of his own, Colly has."

"Yes, but he seemed rather suspicious of me and glad to be left alone; and I've been eager to look you up, as I told you at Truro. Thought you were likely to be cold-shouldered by the majority, feeling much the same kind of loneliness as myself."

Garth leaned forward, his elbows on his knees; he appeared to hesitate, his natural reserve struggling with an urge to fling out his secret, test it in speech as he was soon to test it in action. His next words showed that, for the present, he chose to remain on the defensive.

"Made many friends at Truro?"

"Very few, though I take some part in political gatherings in the town, Socialist and pacifist; all 'gone scat' now—as you Cornish say—with this war. And I'm such a plain blunt man that many people take offence where none is intended. If you, too, think me a man to be shunned, well, so be it."

"I aren't the sort to take offence at bluntness, anyway," replied Garth. "If you think me a fool you can say so— the police wouldn't have to be sent for, I reckon, whatever Colly may be afraid of."

Garth's laugh was so boyishly good-humoured that Griffiths probed him with keener scrutiny, puzzled, his admiration guarded and restrained by the knowledge that spiritually they were in opposite camps. A rugged, heavily-cast face the young fellow had, with deep twinkling eyes and an honest grin around the lips now. Nothing morbid there! The brain controlling that face was certainly not stagnant or given to mawkish day-dreaming. A mystic with his feet firmly planted among healthy commonplaces. Griffiths knew the type—familiar enough in Wales and Cornwall, where the Celtic strain sometimes broke out in religious revivalism—and, jealous for his creed, he felt an odd twinge of relief that Garth was spending his life here in this remote backwater, with no influence on the public.

Garth went on genially, as if an obscure life had its peculiar rewards in the field of scandal:

"Folks around here seem to be getting pretty sure you and Minnie'll make a match of it."

"Country gossip, as usual," commented Griffiths, shrugging. "I've experienced too many set-backs to think this can go according to plan. Already, to-day, there seems to be a new movement afoot. Miss Lagor's told me her mother wants her to live back at Egypt if the old woman dies, and in that case I daresay her family'd persuade her to drop what must seem to them a dangerous association."

He smiled, but Garth remarked soberly:

"It's surprising you should see anything in a maid like Minnie—nothing very brilliant, I'm afraid, for a bookish man who've seen the world a bit."

Griffiths gazed for some minutes into the fire—burning fiercely, as Garth had put in several chunks of wood brought from the carpenter's workshop, iron fastenings of axles still attached to them and tar congealed in the sockets. A shadow of violence lay on Griffiths' face, and when he straightened it was to throw dynamic force into his confession:

"I resolved last year that if ever I married again it wouldn't be one of these competent modern women. My wife was that sort. . . . It's natural I should look towards someone who has suffered as I suffered and can give me a taste of the simple domestic virtues after all the blasting of passion that sickened me. . . . It's curious that Shirley's father was apparently the same pattern as my wife—and came to the same end."

"Why!" exclaimed Garth, starting upright with brows arched in shocked apprehension. "You don't mean your wife . . . ?"

"Committed suicide—yes." Griffiths laughed grimly, a kind of muffled snort through the nose. "She'd had a pretty good run for her money after leaving me, before the end came." His face twitched, changed colour, and he added with an evasive glance at the little round table in the centre of the room:

"I'm sure you wouldn't wish me to harrow up my feelings by giving any detailed account of the affair: it's best forgotten. But I can say this much, at least—in fairness to you, as I know the main outline of your own tragedy."

Garth turned sideways, breathing more heavily, lips apart; his hand groped along the ridge of the bookcase standing in the corner. Its three shelves were packed with volumes, mainly second-hand, their original bindings covered with brown paper. Their titles would suggest that they were the property of a theological student, but it was significant that modern religious thought was not represented at all. . . . Glancing across at Griffiths, Garth found the man's eyes still intent upon him, expectant, eager, and with a nervous moistening of the lips he began haltingly:

"I don't know how much Minnie's told you. She could only guess, anyway, about the main point that's stumped people."

"About you and that London girl?"

"Yes. I aren't in the habit o' putting into words—anything o' what happened, then or since," said Garth. "There's never been anybody I could talk it over with; and I've felt that a handicap sometimes—makes it seem like dream stuff. But lately I've had one or two jolts what've made me pretty wide awake towards it. I've got a hunch this summer'll be as eventful for me as that of 1935."

Griffiths sat very still, then brushed up the little quiff of dark hair above his forehead. His voice was more gentle as he observed:

"Miss Lagor's said she's always regarded the worst side of the story as a fabrication of the girl's family, in collusion with the—er—the girl you were courting at that time."

"Well, perhaps; but the villagers and my workmates know that something sprung alive then what friendship couldn't account for. I won't shuffle and jib or try to hide facts, even from a stranger. I *did* love the girl—mostly just after she'd gone back, when our names was joined on everybody's tongue in the sort o' filth village people are so partial to. And when the little vendetta was over and I'd lost every round—lost my mother and Edith, and lost my character so that no local girls'd look at me, there was nothing I could cherish but the memories that kid'd left me, and nothing for me to do but try and find out the meaning of why she'd come. And that, of course, brought religion into it."

Garth nodded at the bookcase, and again paused defensively, scanning Griffiths' face as one enjoying a sense of release and taking the measure of an opposing element.

"At bottom," he stated frankly, " 'tis just an experiment in prayer—not much in your line if you're an atheist as people say."

"I'm rather an agnostic than an atheist. I simply don't know what to make of life. I can see no purpose or design in the continual misfits and deformities which are presented to us as the acceptable and perfect will of a higher Intelligence. The whole thing seems to me stupid, a ghastly joke."

"I felt that too, for awhile; but as months passed and I found that girl's coming had worked a revolution in me —my nature changing and opening out as I'd never dreamed possible while Edith was in the picture—well, I began wondering. I thought p'raps Irma'd got a similar shock from it, and that God had got close to us and done a bit o' grafting without our knowing it. I came to feel like that fellow Browning says, that God has a right to graft excellence on wildings how He likes, whether through a church service or a vulgar scandal, at the altar or in a workshop. The result's the only thing that matters; and I've staked my whole life on the belief that that result will come."

This burning avowal carried such conviction that Griffiths side-stepped.

"You've done nothing to try and get in touch with the girl since—never made any inquiries?"

"No: she was so young, I was pretty well handcuffed, and should have been even if she lived in Cornwall. I couldn't act without muddling things worse. But now— she's nineteen and 'twon't be long before I know what's been happening to her while I've waited."

"Four years," said Griffiths musingly. "And those who caused your suffering have been flaunting their triumph in your face all that time, without let or hindrance, it seems?"

"I wouldn't say that. Things work around, and when I look at those who pitched me into that trouble I don't envy 'em much. The girl's family—her uncle and aunt down on the farm here—live like cat and dog; and as for Edith—well, I could almost pity her when I think what *her* future's likely to be."

"A hasty marriage—couldn't expect it to turn out well," remarked Griffiths.

"She seemed pleased enough with it at first. But then Seth had a accident and got lamed, and had to take to wearing glasses too, and have false teeth. She felt 'twas hardly the same man, and turned spiteful against him. It've gone downhill pretty steep this year, I gather. There've been ugly rumours lately, and though I haven't seen Edith herself I shouldn't be surprised to find truth in 'em."

"Her man got struck on another, I suppose—the old story?"

"Hardly the usual line. Seth been very changed these last few weeks—going around like a beaten dog, they say, ashamed to be seen and hardly speaking to anybody. Been like it ever since he went to Redruth for his medical exam that last Wednesday o' February. He didn't get home till the Thursday morning—had a sort o' breakdown, it appears: got drunk in town, and there's hints o' something worse than that." A wry humour twisted Garth's mouth. "There's loose women in these towns, as you know, and it seems the pull of his wife wasn't strong enough at the right moment."

Griffiths' smile showed an agreeable surprise.

"You know the world, Mr. Joslin!"

"Yes. I haven't lived here in a dream. I knew Irma'd have to face the sordid stuff in London, so I decided to face the same risks. It's no good a fellow pitting himself against evil or vulgarity if he knows nothing about it."

"I agree—though even then he's likely to be an ineffectual martyr."

"I hardly expect you to think I've backed a winner in this business," remarked Garth. "You think I'll die a bachelor I daresay—self-deluded fanatic or something?"

Griffiths' mood seemed to harden, as if he felt the threat of compromise. He drew a handkerchief from his pocket, his manner becoming almost brusque as he spoke, jerking the square of linen as though it were a red flag.

"I fear I can say nothing to encourage you in your hope of—that girl. I think the time of disillusion will come—the sooner the better, probably. And the most I can do is to try and help you to gain that fortitude which Maeterlinck so finely expresses: 'Ask nothing, hope nothing; expect only the worst, and accept it in silence.' And of our To-morrow, with all our past faith and work regarding it—'let us be assured that it will be nearer the end and sadder than to-day.'"

The words were spoken with the persuasive power of a man whose whole nature expressed itself in them. Garth felt a clammy pressure upon his heart; though the room was hot he shivered, raised a hand to his throat to ease a sense of suffocation.

A cloud of the spirit darkened upon him. He looked out of the window with a tense, haggard appeal. Heavy rolling sky and fleering rain and the wind battering at the trees, the shrubs, the delicate little fuchsia stems over there in the garden corner. The whole scene was suddenly stripped of meaning, vacant, squalid, miserable. He saw the universe through Griffiths' eyes, a vast chasm unutterably dreary; laws jarring and jangling in confused strife

of Nature and pitiless oppréssion of the human material
they had produced.

The impact of this nightmare vision so chilled and
dazed Garth for a few minutes that when reaction came
it gave tremendous force to the redeeming certitude.

He stretched out an arm and said in a tone still quiet,
but passionately intense:

"That sort o' talk's just a sample o' the modern mood,
Mr. Griffiths. And it'll pass because here and there there's
people who won't knuckle in to it—ordinary people like
me who're forced by God to stake everything on His Mood
that doesn't pass."

Chapter Twelve

ON the following Tuesday evening Martin Stribley and
Seth Spragg were following the main highway from
Treviscoe to St. Dennis—the only road that passed
through Egypt. Their movements were slow, abject and
furtive, and while not being exactly in flight they were
obviously much scared.

The evening had brought them to a crisis. Seth, calling
at the farm just after tea-time, had been promptly ordered
off the premises by Bella, and Martin, not wishing to face
her tirade alone, had acompanied this unhappy young
man. They still wore their clay-labourer's garb, Martin
a green trilby, Seth a black cap, with clay-smeared rain-
coats, and at first they had shrunk from venturing far
afield in this sort of evening dress. But after hanging
around Virginia for awhile Seth suggested taking a stroll
to the site of a camp under Carne Hill, where a lot of
soldiers were soon to be quartered. Martin had agreed;
he could think of no better way of spending the next hour
or two.

Carne Hill was over two miles from Meledor, and they took a devious route, though the normal means of access to it was wild and tortuous, even for this area where villagers, in paying casual calls or even on shopping errands, are wont to climb over sand-dunes, along clay-tank walls and paths that zig-zag above the dizzying precipices of the pits. The pair had scrambled up the ragged slope past Kernick dump on to the railway-line, following this as far as Treviscoe. They could have followed it the whole way to Carne Hill, which was visible from it, remote and lonely on the northern skyline; but Seth having dropped a word about the Lagors, they had yielded to an impulse to make a detour through Egypt, and at Treviscoe bridge they descended to the roadway.

Once free of the two neat and solid rows of this village they were amid a scene that in its bleak, harsh beauty would have struck something of awe into a mind receptive of atmosphere in nature. The Cornish clay district possesses not only features all its own in the colossal sand-heaps and blasted bowels of clay strata, but also—particularly at this western end—a peculiar spiritual tone, unheeded and scarcely felt by local residents, though it moulds their characters. To Seth and Martin the landscape meant nothing at all, yet as they impressed themselves upon it, passing between the high hedges overhung here and there by stunted, misshapen trees, their figures blended with a mood, a pervasive power that dwarfed their humanity to a symbol. In winter, and at this hour of approaching dusk, the countryside around Egypt, dominated by the volcano-like swelling of Carne Hill, possessed a strange brooding quality that seems to combine the unearthly gloom of a Doré print with the weird, starved horror of the landscape in Browning's *Childe Roland*. The scrubby vegetation, the white muffled clay streams, the dunes and clay-beds glimpsed unexpectedly through snaky boughs, and the dimly-seen expanse of Goss Moor below, carrying the desolation to wilder and

more savage extremes of tarn, bog and featureless waste-
land until jarred six miles north-west by the low grim tors
around St. Columb—these details seem united in a
common withdrawal from the general tone of English
scenery.

The two men were on the outskirts of Egypt, with Carne
Hill again facing them, towering massively amid rain-
cloud, when as they approached a field gateway they
became aware that it was occupied by a young man and
a girl. Apparently the couple had paused there while out
for a stroll—either to watch the sunset or, more probably,
to enjoy some furtive love-making, as they were clasped
together when Seth and Martin came round the bend.
They dropped their arms discreetly, but did not move
further apart. The girl, who wore a brown coat and hat,
was very young and slim in figure, and her face, turned to
the almost rayless disc of the sun, was keenly-cut, though
rather cheap and common in expression. She continued
to gaze across the ploughed field where some rooks were
flapping about, busily repairing their old nests in the elms
on the farther hedge. The young man—tall and fair-
haired, wearing a light mackintosh—also kept his back
towards the approaching pair, and looked somewhat
embarrassed.

The two men hurried by without speaking, Seth limping along the gutter under the flowering blackthorns, the
sour twist of his face hidden by the deep shadow.

When they were out of earshot he cast a hard, stealthy
glance back to the gateway, from which the couple had
not moved out. His voice grated as he nudged Martin.

"Minnie Lagor's sister Muriel and that chap Trebilcock.
Don't look very comfortable, do 'em?"

"Couldn't expect that. They must know what talk's
gone round the villages this past week-end."

"Yes: only been courting four months, and the maid
in trouble already. But there's no doubt he'll marry her:
'twon't be Minnie and Ted Blewett all over again."

"Made a brave rumpus at Lagors', I believe. Muriel was needed there to help look after the old woman, and now this mess have cropped up and the maid got to be married, they've had to make other arrangements."

"Old Tab's going to be put in St. Austell workhouse to-night, so I heard at claywork—in to the Union hospital. 'Tis the only way out, though it seems Minnie's aunt, Maud Criddle, been up here ramping mad about having her mother sent to the workhouse because Muriel's played this little prank. Wanted the maid to be turned out instead and Minnie come back from Snells' to nurse Tab."

"P'raps Maud have come up to see the old woman off," said Martin, "and that's why Muriel and Trebilcock aren't back at Lagors'—'fraid there'd be bloodshed."

"Likely enough. Minnie's keeping clear too, it seems, and for the same reason. Maud ha'n't been on speaking terms with her since she had Shirley."

Martin shrugged.

"Well, 'tis good to feel we aren't the only ones who've tumbled in a mess this evening, though ours is a bit different from that couple back there in the gateway."

"You didn't look exactly bashful just now, I admit, when Bella showed us the door. But Muriel may be showing that chap the door in a few years' time."

Seth's face had cracked in a grin, but Martin was moved rather to irritation. His full red cheeks were creased unpleasantly.

"I've said you was asking for it, coming around the farm so often. Bella've complained about it and said people'd think you was running after her."

A grunt of derision broke from Seth.

"And she nearly forty—just a barrel on legs for figure. They must have a pretty idea o' me taste!"

"Still, it d'look a bit fishy now 'tis known how you and Edith have broke down—and Edith herself never visiting us now."

"A little crotchet, that's all—vexed to think how Bella

112

helped to split her from Garth in that scandal: a sore spot these last few weeks, naturally."

"Well, you'll have to find somewhere else to spend your evenings from now on. Things is bad enough between me and Bella without you making a fresh split."

Seth's eyes became jeering behind their screen of glass. "Been falling out over Irma again lately?"

"A few words—about the way Garth's likely to work off his latest fit o' worry about her."

"Bella afraid *he'll* be coming down after her next, now I'm sent packing—eh?"

Martin met this levity with a shrug and a sidelong scowl at the hobbling figure beside him.

"It's serious," he said. "Garth's on the verge o' something. Reub Pollard told me last week that if Meledor works closes down Garth'll be flitting to London to look for Irma—hinted as much at the lodge, Reub said."

"Wild talk, you may depend."

"I aren't so sure. He's getting keyed up bad. I've noticed it, 'specially this last month since Bella dropped the news about Mrs. Slade. Several times at the works I've seen him look as if he was tempted to come across and try to wring more truth out o' me."

Seth had sobered; he kicked at a lump of clay in the ditch, dropped from some passing lorry.

"Why not tell him all you know and see how 'twould work?"

"He wouldn't believe me or Bella on a matter that touched Irma's own character; and besides, Bella won't hear of any such blabbing. She's enjoying the fun, watching him drift, sure he'll crash on the rocks somehow; and it's as likely to be through dashing off to London as not if he gets the freedom."

"Bound to end tragic whether he stays here or quits, in my view," muttered Seth.

"Yes. If he did go to London he wouldn't come back, that's certain."

Seth laughed cynically.

"No: he might forget all about Irma once he was clear o' we lot and away from the only place he and Irma ever met. Having to go to the workshop every day have helped to keep his mind tied down to her. He might copy her father and slip in quiet wi' the first cockney slut who made eyes at him."

"You don't know your man if you think that," objected Martin. "It's got in him stubborn, like a mania. He wouldn't give up till he'd found the truth, even if it meant knocking at every door in Stoke Newington; and when he *did* come face to face with Irma, or learn from her family or friends how faithful she's been to his memory. . . ."

"He'd scuttle hisself, you think?"

"Well, it seem to be a family trait, though the freezing o' the tank steps spoilt Mrs. Joslin's effort. Bella says when she told him Irma's mother'd married again he took it pretty violent—swore at her and called her a devil, it seems: looked queer and half off his nut."

A grin deepened the mockery on Seth's face.

"I'd like to have seen they two going at it—more lively than the little one-sided affair at the farm just now, I bet!"

Martin flushed, returning taunt for taunt.

"You saw something better, by all accounts. That was the day you went to Redruth, remember!" He drew a cigarette from his case, and having lighted it he went on:

"But about Garth: If a little pin-prick like that can unbalance him it's pretty plain he'd never stand the shock o' knowing the worst. They'd be finding his body in the Thames one morning, that's what 'twould amount to."

"Good riddance, anyhow," mumbled Seth. "Nobody'd be sorry there was one crank less in the world. If he chose to take it so potty. . . . After all, 'tisn't nothing unusual: chaps nowadays expect a girl to be a bit shop-soiled before she marries. Irma's no worse than that little bit o' fluff what put me wise at St. Austell."

"Jean Blewett you mean? H'm!" Martin held his

cigarette at arm's length, frowning moodily down at it. "Say if any bloke that was real struck on her had seen her encouraged in that game—he'd smash in somewhere as bad as Garth, I expect."

"Maybe; but decent chaps shouldn't pick on a girl who got that streak in her. There's different sorts. Ted set the same example to his other sister, Doreen, but she didn't catch on to it."

Martin's face and tone grew sly, malicious:

"Told Edith the truth yet—about you and Jean?"

"No: I let her think what she likes. The home's broke up all right, and things must drift till they crash now. Old Chirgwin've turned sour and put his prickles up a time or two—thought he'd order me to clear out; and his missus have shed some crocodile tears. But hang it, I can't help what they suffer. 'Tisn't my fault. She ought to ha' married Garth."

Seth halted in the ditch under a gaunt yew tree, and seizing a bough he brushed from several of its matured flowers a thin pettish flurry of pollen, resuming in a tone as rash as the gesture:

"I aren't sure she won't before long—be living as his wife, anyhow. She may bring a unexpected twist into this business, and instead o' Garth being found in the Thames he may be found nearer home, settled wi' Mrs. Spragg. That's what I'm prepared for, and wouldn't complain: glad to be rid of her."

Martin spat as they again moved forward.

"She han't seen Garth since the day his mother was buried, have she?"

"Not that I know of. But she's planning something deep, I can tell that, 'specially as she thinks I've broke out and gived her a good reason for throwing over the traces. She wasn't naturally cut out for a flaming wedlock-buster —always tame, even to Garth during the two years they was courting—and she got to work herself up to it. But she'll come to breaking-point soon, and go bald-headed

at him: there's no other in the running. And the shock
of it may shake him out of his crack-brained notions about
Irma, and then . . . well, they'll be ending up where they
started or a bit further on, and 'tis me who'll have to do
a bunk—skit off to some war factory where I can flirt wi'
the munition girls."

Seth checked his ironic laugh, for they had now turned
into Egypt—a hamlet no bigger than Meledor, though
more compactly arranged. The cottages and farmsteads
flanked the flat road for a hundred yards or so, and were
mainly of the antiquated type usual in remote country
districts. There was nothing of quiet charm here, however; a drab melancholy seemed thrown upon the place
by the overshadowing scarp of Carne Hill, hardly a mile
off to the north-east and framed by the few stalky trees
growing beside the intervening lanes. The church tower
on its summit was scarcely visible now, so dark was the
sky, and blood-red veins of sunlight were dribbling and
creeping out over the higher part of St. Dennis village
that clustered around its bare slopes, producing an effect
almost ghastly.

Seth and Martin were not much impressed by this;
their attention was caught at once by evidence of grim
human drama.

Outside the Lagors' home near the centre of the row a
motor ambulance was drawn up. Behind it stood a small
blue saloon car—Maud Criddle's. Several neighbours,
with their children, had gathered in the road, watching
curiously the open doorway of the cottage. A hush of
morbid fascination gripped these tense figures; no one
spoke.

As Seth and Martin paused two men emerged from the
house, carrying between them a stretcher on which lay a
form covered with sheets. They were followed by Mrs.
Lagor and Maud, both dressed for the journey to St.
Austell, where they would see Tabitha comfortably
settled in her new quarters. Maud carried the big suitcases

while Mrs. Lagor, having closed and locked the door, put the key into her pocket, looking dazed, pitiful as she turned and moved shakily to the gate.

Maud flounced into the roadway, ignoring the neighbours, her face brazenly set between her expensive check-patterned coat and her feathered pink hat. She gazed with fierce humiliation upon the shrouded figure of Tabitha. Low mutters escaped the old woman, rising once into something like a choked wail of protest. Her arms lifted feebly under the sheets.

Gently the stretcher was raised and drawn into the body of the ambulance; its glass-panelled door clicked shut. The two women passed around to the small car, Maud with long defiant strides, Mrs. Lagor falteringly, her head lowered into the shadow. They entered the front seat and sat frowning through the windscreen at the back of the ambulance.

There was a stirring amid the grouped watchers, the red feelers of the sun wheeled down and split among them like the beams of a searchlight, and a minute later both vehicles had begun gliding, silent and sinister, away along the winding lane towards St. Dennis.

Chapter Thirteen

GARTH was sitting on a boulder at the top of Foxhole Beacon, at a higher altitude than any other human for miles around. His thoughts also possessed an elevation, and from the intensity of his gaze as he probed the massive and inspiring scene about him it seemed that his mind had struck an unfamiliar vein of interest.

Griffiths' visit had left him somewhat shaken. His first open confession of his spiritual adventure—for his remarks concerning it at the claywork lodge had always been ambiguous—had produced reactions of an unlooked-for kind. After Griffiths had gone a feeling of fierce shame and self-derision had seized Garth; the week-end threatened to be one of the gloomiest he had ever known. He had fought his way through the mood and stifled at last the Job-like cry that had been wrung from him almost continuously during the early part of Easter Day: "Why is light given to a man whose way is hid, and whom God hath hedged in?" Yesterday, Bank Holiday, he had regained confidence, but was in no mind to join the crowds who would throng the beaches around Newquay and on the south Cornish coast. The weather was dull and rainy, and he had spent the day indoors, reading and thinking.

On the whole, he was glad that Griffiths had come. To speak as he had done, venturing from the unchallenged shade of his own ego, was a step forward. He felt braced by a sense of achievement, of being equal now to any test. But to maintain this attitude, vivid, alert, competent—that was the problem. His ideas ran more or less in a groove, thinning to staleness, while the sand-dune above Meledor workshop, and Stribley's farm, fenced him in and forced him to approach the subject from that one vantage-point. To preserve a freshness of outlook he needed the stimulus of fresh scenery.

Usually at such times, when his craving was met rather by a long walk than by a bus ride into any town, he moved out across the moor north-west to Fraddon or Blue Anchor, or followed the path along the ridge southward to the hilly roadway leading down to the few cottages of Brighton on the turnpike road. He knew intimately every feature of that wide sweep of landscape, to traverse which from end to end was like passing from one world to another, out of the clay area into the rich agricultural lands of the western valleys.

But to-night impulse had led him to strike eastward towards a part of the countryside he habitually shunned because he could not conveniently reach it without passing through Trethosa and running the risk of meeting Edith, Seth, or one of the Chirgwins. The Chirgwin children were cheeky brats and always, if they saw him, called some taunting reference to his old love affair. He had not come through Trethosa now, but by-passed it by way of Treneague, skirting the northern fringe of St. Stephen and following a lonely cart-track into the heart of Tregargus Wood. From there, after scrambling over a gulch worn by the clay stream, he had crossed some fields to the roadway west of Carloggas. The journey of three miles had taken him almost as many hours, and by the time he reached the Beacon behind Carloggas he was tired and glad to sit down after the steep climb up its shaggy slope.

This Beacon was just an ordinary bulge of English soil, turfed, matted here and there with dense undergrowth, broad and bare at the summit, curving down on the east to the straggling village of Foxhole, while to the west and south it dipped to clayworks, the dumps of which were dwarfed by its massive bulk. It lacked the grandeur of Carne Hill, since it rose from a general ridge extending several miles, and its background was placidly rural. Even at nightfall it failed to intimidate, and was so entirely without an atmosphere that one could scarcely imagine Celts lighting bonfires here in pre-historic times.

It was of a very different kind of bonfire that Garth was reminded, suddenly, as he first glimpsed the great green dome humped against the rolling, rain-heavy cloud. His last visit here! May the sixth, 1935. Jubilee Day! Not since that riotous Monday had he set foot on the Beacon, and it was under the spell of reminiscence that he had climbed it, feeling something might be gained from fresh probing of the mood he had then felt.

The last public festival he and Edith had attended together: the weather brilliant, hot sunshine pouring down hour after hour upon the crowds thronging here, the breeze wafting the blare of brass bands down along the vales and out towards the sea that had gleamed, a wavering colourless slit, nine miles to the south. There in the centre of the grassy dome, only a few yards from where he now sat—the huge pile of faggots, a Union Jack fluttering and tugging on top of them. Spirit of carnival —dancing, parades, patriotic speeches with bland apologetic asides about "the—er—present troubled state of the world." He remembered what he had thought of it, even then, sobered by his father's death, his mother's strangeness; remembered what he had said to Edith as the evening drew on and they strolled across into Foxhole to get a better view of the illuminations. Something unsound, unhealthy in the mood. He was no killjoy, but he saw that this evasive jollity was not good training for a nation that might be called upon to resist a titanic onslaught of evil. A bit more grimness in the English temper at that time might have prevented a general deluge of gloom over Europe.

Edith had not agreed with him: she'd said he was becoming cranky, and that people with views like his were encouraging the warmongers. They had arrived back at Trethosa near midnight in strained silence, aware of disharmonies that grew steadily worse until, three months later, Irma cut them apart. . . .

Garth rose abruptly: the air was cold, the horizon blurred with rain eastward along the desolate ridge of Karslake. His feet were wet from a slip into the claystream while he was crossing Tregargus gorge; his trouser legs, too, were damp through brushing against sodden bushes. Specks of bracken clung to them, and he stooped to flick off most of these before moving a few steps out towards the brow of the scarp. He glanced down across the railway line to Foxhole, and at once stiffened.

An ambulance was passing slowly through the village a vague dark shape, but recognizable. He watched it glide from view beyond Carpalla claywork, and gave an odd creepy shiver. He did not connect it with Mrs.

Lagor—had heard nothing of the week-end disturbances at Egypt—but its appearance was for a few moments almost morbidly suggestive. It switched his thoughts to the present, the danger threatening Irma. If London were bombed——. He evaded the thrust, only to be met by the more obvious, more deadly thing. Bella's hint. The unknown events leading into the war shadow: Irma's father dead, her mother re-married. Young men of her own age. The black-out, shelter life—"never hard up for a good cuddle . . . ." His hands clenched as Bella's words stabbed back. He seemed to see again her hot loose lips pressed to Martin's above the white cliffs of Meledor pit, and the memory, with all it implied, was so tormenting that he turned fiercely, seeking relief in the drab, inhuman landscape westward.

His eyes slipped across the downs and fields, past the ruins of an engine-house to where, close beside Carpalla claywork, stood a building no longer used—a converted railway carriage, its roof and chimneys rusting, with a garden attached, now thickly grown with weed and menaced by the sprawling fringe of the sand-dump. Garth strode forward through the ferns, making on an impulse straight towards that deserted hut. Ted Blewett's old home! A fateful place. Minnie Lagor had been seduced there, and from that house Ted had gone out to hang himself just after being summonsed by the parents of a younger girl. There, as on the Beacon, Garth might find relics of past moods, traces of atmosphere that would deepen his knowledge of the ways of human passion under the Divine governance to which he, in his turn, must soon submit, either proving his faith a vain fancy, as Griffiths had forecast, or else——.

Garth came to a sudden halt, standing rigid. Hitherto he had been alone,—no one else in view along the whole ridge; but now he spotted an intrusive movement that filled him with the utmost curiosity.

Three men had appeared around a bend of the lane

further west towards St. Stephen. As they drew closer
he recognized them as Reub Pollard, Enoch Hocking and
Colly Snell. The presence of that trio here together at
this hour was singular enough, and Garth's feeling that
something unusual had occurred was strengthened as he
saw that Colly and Reub were carrying lanterns.

He remained motionless, watching and undetected.
He was half-way down the slope, knee-deep in fern, and
dusk was fast darkening as the rain-clouds lowered.

The men soon left the road, and skirting a water-logged
quarry they headed towards Carpalla. They had somehow the look of persons engaged on a grim errand, and
seemed to force themselves on. Colly pointed excitedly
across the downs as the old Blewett dwelling came in
view, and hobbled ahead of his companions in sudden
haste to reach it. The three moved in single file, in the
gutter, so that Garth glimpsed only their heads and
shoulders bobbing above the hedge-top. Drawing abreast
of the shack they passed through the gateway, which was
unbarred, the gate lying within, rotting on the garden.
A minute later they were invisible to Garth, hidden by
the building, but he heard the rattle of the zinc wall and
sounds as of confused scuffling close against it.

Garth frowned and debated for a few moments. His
first impulse was to hurry down and join them and find
the reason for this strange behaviour; and he was given
no time for second thoughts. Before he could have turned
away the back window of the shack was banged open and
Reub Pollard's head poked out—distinguishable because
he alone wore a trilby. His gaze lit almost at once upon
Garth's hesitant figure, a hundred yards off, facing him.
There was a short pause while the two men stared at
each other, then Reub's challenge rang through the
twilight:

"That you, Garth?"

Garth nodded, and with a long sigh, bracing himself,
he hastened down through the remaining strip of heath,

crossed into a field behind the engine-house, and had soon dropped over a hedge into the neglected garden. He approached the hut moodily, his lip bitten.

"What's doing here?" he asked.

"Looks like burglary, I admit," said Reub with a wry grin—"though the front window was ripped out already and we got in without doing any fresh damage."

He withdrew his head as Garth stepped to the window and leaned on the sill, peering into the dim interior. A bare musty room, quite empty, the walls hung with cobwebs; a close mouldy smell pervading the place. A door on the left stood open, and he made out the shrunken form of Colly Snell beside it, jerking nearer to him through the shadows, panting and greatly agitated.

"Didn't know you belonged coming up around this way," Colly greeted in a suspicious tone.

"I don't often; and I've seen nothing to throw light on your coming here either."

"We'm here looking for our little Shirley, Garth—that's the length of it," said the old man, staring blankly around him.

"What! Shirley disappeared?"

Colly flung out an arm and began chattering shrilly.

"I knowed it had to come to it. I've expected this for weeks. The maid been begging Minnie to take her over to see this old shack—got terrible interested in it lately, for some reason. Hearing the talk around, I s'pose, and getting old enough to understand it. We've tried to turn her off that subject, but 'twas no use: she would come here to see the place where she was born, as she called it."

"She must know she wasn't born here," objected Garth.

"O' course; and I reckon that's just her way o' putting what she've picked up. 'Tisn't easy for little maids to find words for describing all they know. She've been hearing too much, Garth, and I believe she d'know as well as we do what Ted done to her mother here in one o' these rooms."

123

Garth nodded, standing very tense at the window, frowning over his shoulder at the Beacon, now a blurred black crescent like a gigantic tortoise humping the sky-line.

"Fascinated her, I daresay," he mumbled. "Come here this evening, has she ?"

"I'd be a happier man if I could tell 'ee, Garth. She went out around two o'clock this afternoon to play wi' t'other children: I saw her meself climbing up our sand-burrow about half-past two. But when tea-time come there was no Shirley to be seen, and Mrs. Best's little maid told me and Minnie Shirley'd run off from 'em down Trethosa way, saying all secret that she had a special visit to make."

"And that's the last you've heard of her ?" inquired Garth.

"All to a few remarks from folks down St. Stephen. Minnie came that far with us and is waiting down to Mrs. Sampson's. They told us they'd seen Shirley going down around the church just after three o'clock—heading for this house, no doubt about that."

Colly passed a hand over his forehead, wiping away sweat; his face was drawn, fevered in the sickly light a yard beyond the window. Again he looked dazedly round.

"But now we'm here—and we've drawed blank. . . . Dunno what to do next—shall have to tell the police. . . ."

At that moment there came a shout from Hocking in an adjoining room, and as the trio turned expectantly he appeared, holding up a small square of linen, upon which was a gaudy picture, almost washed out.

"Found it between the rotten floor boards jist under the window," he said. His tall figure stooped more than usual, his face was grey, strained. "She been here all right."

Colly took the handkerchief and held it up for inspection, Garth stepping aside to free the room of his shadow.

Colly trembled, his voice was shaky as he acknowledged:

"Yes, that's Shirley's hanky true enough—the very rag she blowed her nose in not many hours ago, safe and snug home there in me kitchen." He blinked from face to face, and broke out with a sort of worried irritation:

"Where can the young mortal be got to? Did she see us coming and hide somewhere?"

"Took a short cut home and lost herself, more likely," suggested Reub.

"But even then she'd be sure to meet somebody and could ask the way."

"She may have seen some other children around here, playing on the Beacon p'raps. They may ha' come down and helped her to get through the window where she dropped her hanky. If 'twas Foxhole kids she may have gone over to the village to play with 'em—childlike."

"But she'd be wanting tea before this," Hocking put in. "Wouldn't stop with 'em now 'tis coming dark."

Reub lurched to the window again, addressing Garth, who was standing outside with head bent, hands on his hips.

"You seed any kids around here, Garth?"

"No, but I haven't been up there long—nearly seven o'clock when I got to the Beacon. I struck in through Tregargus: Shirley must have been here before I left home if she came straight up."

"Well, 'tis no good to stay here looking at her hanky," announced Colly. "We must go on searching. We brought lanterns in case we was off till dark. Moon'll be up soon, but looks like we'm in for more rain and 'twon't be enough light to search by." He shuffled back to the corner, then turned.

"You lend a hand now, Garth?"

"Yes, glad to," Garth responded. "We'd better go different ways. . . ."

Colly nodded.

"I'll inquire at a house or two back to Carloggas first, then go up around Foxhole if there's no other hint. Reub and Hocking can go around Goonabarn and the clay-tanks over that side the valley, and as for you, Garth. . . ."

"I'll go down around Barrakellis woods," volunteered Garth, "and then ask up at Goonamarris. Somebody there may have seen her if she went that way."

"All right. . . . Little imp that that maid is, to give us this trouble! And her grannie put to the workhouse this very evening, too. What's meant by it all is beyond me."

Colly shook his head and disappeared, mumbling some complaint about the back window being too small to climb through. Reub and Hocking followed him into the dark interior, their footsteps echoing hollowly, while Garth stepped around the corner of the shack and along the downs path to the lane.

Chapter Fourteen

THIS abrupt turn had broken the coherence of Garth's mood, but as soon as he was alone, stealing eastward between high field hedges, he found that the pounce of dramatic possibility had opened up a fresher phase in his thought of Irma. It seemed united with an outer mood of urgency: a large raindrop, cold and wind-driven, stung his ear as if bidding him listen, and as he raised his head the mournful call of a wood pigeon smote up the vale from the copse where he was now going to look for Shirley. Something prophetic in this sudden quest! Just as unexpectedly, ere long, he might pass from thought to action regarding Irma herself. In what way the challenge would come he could not guess—perhaps through some such chance bit of news as had now startled him, perhaps through a direct move of Irma's. For several months after she returned to London, and at intervals more recent, Garth had come in from the claywork hoping to find a letter from her on the doormat. His house had no name or number, and a message addressed to him at Meledor would be sure to arrive safely. The expectation had died out, unfulfilled. But that, too, was possible, when Irma's sense of the spiritual grafting begun at Meledor workshop took control of her tractile sap, made inevitable its immediate fusion with his. She could not be ignorant that something unusual had followed their brief intimacy. She must know somewhat of his reaction to her coming, and more of his subsequent life than he knew of hers. Bella's malice would not have let her keep such congenial news to herself. He would give much to learn what she had written of him to Irma's family during the past four years—contemptuous stuff, no doubt. "The chap who seduced Irma is getting queerer and queerer—won't look at the girls around here, and he'll end up where his mother did if Irma doesn't come back and marry him. . . ." No, hardly anything so direct; but she may have dropped broad hints. "If you could see the way he hangs around the farm some evenings, gaping at the bedroom window where Irma slept. . . ." Something in that strain, very likely; and if Irma read such letters—what could she have thought? The reminders would, at least, have served to refresh her memories and add the necessary touch of mystery and suspense thereto. And now that the link was snapped, her mother breaking all contact with the Stribleys, she could hear no more of him until——.

Again the stab of raindrops on his face, swift, continuous: the shower had begun. Garth crossed the road, buttoning up the collar of his mackintosh, and turned with relief into a sort of cleft between fields, a long steep track dipping southward to another road some distance below Carloggas. High close-pressing hedges made the darkness almost complete here; ruts and boulders caused him to stumble frequently, and once his boot touched a soft spongy substance that immediately slid away under the wet grass—a toad or frog, he supposed, though he couldn't see it. He quickened his pace and had soon glimpsed, not far ahead, a greyish bulk looming beyond the dense foliage—the whitewashed cottage at the end of the path where the road slanting across from Goonabarn curved down into the dale.

There was a light in the tiny window that faced the hedge, and as Garth drew near he saw that a woman was kneeling on a table just within, arranging a green curtain on a rod. He did not remember having seen her before, but he knew that a family called Morcom lived here. This specimen of it was thin, middle-aged, and rather ugly, with prominent eyes, jutting teeth and a goitre.

The defile opened out so close to the house that Garth came within two yards of the window, and as the woman saw his shadowy form emerge thus near to her, an impulse led him to pause and drop a word of explanation.

"Excuse me, Mrs. Morcom—I wonder if you've seen a young girl around here this evening, about eight years old—Minnie Lagor's little kid from Meledor?"

The woman's figure, outlined against the yellow flare of the hanging oil lamp—for electricity had not been extended to such isolated dwellings—stiffened; she dropped the curtain and stared open-mouthed.

"Why—isn't she home yet?"

"No—or wasn't up to mid-evening. Colly and some others of us is out trying to find her—though she may be back waiting for us by now if she went down this way. Been up to Blewetts' shack, as they expected—just found her hanky there."

"Well, I can throw a little light on it," replied Mrs. Morcom in a rough, masculine voice. "After tea when I went out to the drain to shake the table-cloth, a maid was then turning the corner. Looked a bit tired and nervous, and asked me if she could get back to Meledor that way. I told her 'twould bring her out to Trethosa if she took the right turnings, and she went on down the hill."

A sigh of relief escaped Garth, but before moving away he probed for more details.

"That all she asked?"

"Yes, except to inquire if there was any short cut through the woods. I said there was, but she'd better keep to the road or she might lose herself."

"You're sure she went straight down the hill?"

"From here, yes, but I don't know how far. She may have climbed the stile below Barrakellis and got in the woods there, out o' sight o' this house."

"It'd be childlike, certainly. . . . D'you remember what she was wearing?"

"A red pixie hat and blue coat—torn, I noticed, and with a lot o' rust marks on it—through climbing around the shack up there, I s'pose. That's all I can say."

The curtain was again raised, and with a muttered word of thanks Garth strode out from the defile into the broader road.

There was scant shelter from the rain here in the open, but, though he was already chilled, Garth did not feel troubled by the discomfort or by any fear of consequent illness. He headed briskly into the vale, which dropped to the coppice and rose opposite to the hamlet of Goona-marris and a white rash of clay-dunes, the western edge of which was formed by the dump of Trethosa. He felt a tenseness, even though relieved that he had now a definite clue in his search for Shirley. The spirit of the hour was oppressive; its springs were hidden and he was awed by the enfolding phenomena. Weird and sinister, the meeting of the black clouds and the dark earth, himself pressed between the two glooms, swallowed up and slighted in the confused embrace of natural elements. He glanced eastward along the clay-tanks and drying-sheds below Goonabarn. Reub and Hocking would be going around there soon, on a fool's errand, but he did not feel inclined to return and tell them of Mrs. Morcom's news.

No doubt they would hear from other cottagers which way Shirley had taken. He wished to be free to follow the clue alone.

Drawing level with a stile near the clay-stream at the hill's foot Garth climbed over the bar and proceeded along a rough path winding between the downs and the coppice. His eyes ran feverishly along the sable wedge of the wood. If Shirley had strayed into it there was certainly a risk of mishap.

He was impatient to get the thing settled, for the idea of Shirley being in peril had a personal poignancy. He knew Shirley well. She was the only child of Meledor with whom he was closely acquainted. Minnie had allowed her a freedom denied to the other village children. She seemed genuinely fond of him and often came into his garden, especially when his gooseberries and peas were ripe. He loved to play with her and had a keen sense of fun when there were no adults present to chill him into dignity. But he was always careful, for the child's sake, to keep in the open where anyone passing along the road might see them both. Even so, there had been a good deal of gossip. Neighbours had reproached Minnie for her failure to join in the general boycott. "I'd never let a maid o' mine go near Garth," some of them had stated. "Who knows what he may do to her when there's nobody looking?" This sort of filth had angered Garth at times, though he knew it was inevitable, a part of the price he had to pay for Irma.

When he had gone a few hundred yards Garth espied a faint branch path that led down to the coppice, skirting a water-wheel. He halted, gazing at the huge structure, nearly thirty feet high, turning in slow, jerky fashion while the milky liquid streamed and splashed from the trough over the top of it, mingling with the rain and streaking the dusk with flying white flakes as of spume. He became almost hypnotised by this mechanical motion set amid the lush and primitive natural growths. Its stuttering roar, broken now and then by a shrill squeal, was eerie, suggesting some obscure torture.

Rousing, he moved down towards it, ducking under the trough that was supported by planks nailed crosswise, and fingering curiously the thick iron rod that tugged and jolted below. His feet became soaked afresh by the wet foliage, and he could not entirely escape the splashings from the water-wheel, though he kept to the extreme edge of the track opposite it. The cavity in which it revolved was fenced about, and just beyond a short ladder gave access to the bank of the stream a dozen feet lower down.

Reaching the top of the ladder Garth again paused, a creepy sense of apprehension pricking icily along his nerves. The scene had somehow the quality of a nightmare, a wild unreality. The wheel might have been Ixion's, the background Hades, for all the relevance they had to the workaday world. The clanking and grinding noises, the whirling spokes, the rush of water, the gliding motion of spiky rods and wooden beams against the trees, only half-visible in the gloom—these things jarred on the nerves while lulling the reasoning faculties into a trance-like stupor.

In the enclosure below was the ballast mechanism of the water-wheel—a large L-shaped framework moving rhythmically up and down as the wheel turned. The end of the horizontal beam supported a wooden box about five feet square, full of boulders. Its edge came within an inch or two of the ground when it lurched forward, rising six feet above the soil when the vertical beam was drawn back. Some overhanging hazel boughs were knocked senselessly about with each tilt and dip of the beams, sprinkling a shower of drops occasionally as they were freed from the entanglement. There was something inexorable, indescribably malignant in this ceaseless rise and fall of the inanimate.

Just outside the fence the streamlet could be vaguely

seen, frothing garrulously, and beyond that the base of
the wood, the huddled tree-trunks, the vast roof of plum-
ing branches—oak, yew, sycamore, chestnut—among
which the birds flapped disconsolately in the lateral wafts
of rain.

It was several minutes ere Garth threw off the morbid
fascination of the scene and turned to pursue his practical
business. Even then he descended the ladder with his
breath hard-drawn, face grim and strained, and with his
eyes fixed and shrinking. And when he stepped towards
the fence across the narrow strip of marsh and mire, he
chanced upon the key of this oppressive mood.

The ballast box was drawn up, seeming to be suspended
in the black heavens. He peered into the vacant space
underneath, and at once the spell of horror closed upon him.

There on the muddy turf sprawled a blurred form,
revealed fully to his view only for the few moments that
the box was aloft; but before it descended he had glimpsed
the red tint of clothing, the white blob of a face.

In an instant he realised, and stood petrified.

Shirley Lagor was lying there before him, and as the
heavy box ground down upon her again he could have
no doubt that she was dead. Her figure did not move as
the massive bulk crushed into its vitals.

Minutes passed, and like a gigantic hammer the box
rose and fell upon the prostrate body. In the copse an owl
hooted, and then came the scream of a hawk pouncing
upon some hapless little animal.

When the first shock had subsided and curiosity relieved
the blank sick torpor of incredulity, Garth bent down,
kneeling in the mire, and observed closely the position
in which the child lay. Flat on her back, her feet hidden
amid a mass of fern, one arm at her side, the other thrown
against the inner wall of the enclosure. Her head and the
upper part of her body, though under the box, were never
in contact with it, as the narrow beam supporting it was
thicker than her person.

The sight of that piteous form, mauled afresh every minute, became unsufferable to Garth. Cold sweat broke out on his face, which looked ghastly in its desperation; his hands clenched, jerked out towards the girl, were struck by the beam and fell limply. He crawled closer, so as to be able to reach the child while remaining just out of danger from the descending box. His fingers gripped the coat collar, and as soon as the pressure was released he pulled with all his strength, with a sort of fury.

It was enough. The box swung aloft, at a standstill for a few seconds, as if meditating the return blow, but its savage swoop, this time, was upon the naked turf. Garth had drawn the victim free of it, back through a puddle on to higher ground, and was crouching above her, a hand on the fence for support, trembling in every muscle.

Slowly, fitfully, as reason strengthened, he hit upon the likely cause of the accident. She must have slipped, either when climbing the fence or upon the mossy boulders studding the marsh behind it. The box being raised at that moment, she had struck her head against its edge in falling and rolled unconscious under the horizontal beam. Since then, perhaps for several hours, her body had been subjected to a regular crushing that must have fractured the bones of the pelvis and caused fearful rupture of the abdominal organs. This, with internal hæmorrhage, had brought the end—how soon he couldn't tell, but she was stiff and cold.

It was not the first time Garth had seen human death. Six years ago he had beheld the corpse of his father, wasted almost to a skeleton, hideous, repulsive. The spectacle before him now was so different as to confuse, even reverse his attitude towards the mortal stroke. Here was still beauty, freshness. Apart from some blood congealed around the cut on her temple where she had been stunned as she fell, Shirley was unstained in her final sleep. The round cheeks and pouting lips, the whole shape of her was retained as in perfect health; her little hands were plump still, though very dirty; only the staring eyes, the pallor, the rigidity, told of the irretrievable ravage within.

Garth never knew how long he stayed there, slumped against the fence, with the dead girl at his feet. His mind passed through phases of stupor until at length, as the rain came on more violently, chilling him and splashing the lifeless clay, he became conscious of the need for action.

He must go and get help somewhere, get her shifted. Colly and the other two might be here soon, but he couldn't go and look for them. It was just possible that they were still continuing their search around Foxhole and along the eastern side of the vale. He couldn't bear to leave her here long, exposed, defenceless, with the rain soaking her body, toads and birds likely to find and defile her. The nearest house was Rescrowsa farm; he could reach it in a few minutes, and he and Webber would be able to carry her indoors while Mrs. Webber went to Foxhole for the police constable and gave notice that the local doctor at St. Dennis was required.

Garth rose, shakily and with almost a guilty look at the little corpse. There flashed through him the thought that, had she only just died, he might have found himself charged with murdering her. His neighbours believed he had some criminal tendency in his nature regarding young girls. Having seduced one he might end by killing another, throwing up the suppressed violence of four years. . . . But she must have been dead before he left home, or not long after; several people had seen him pass through Meledor and across to Treneague. There was no need to fear any sinister complications.

He scrambled up to the path and stared about rather vacantly, trying to connect, to emerge. The moon was in view, as he had expected, but very bleared, jammed between the horizon and the black clouds—a spiteful, pettish thing, shining feebly as if it, too, were being crushed. No one coming along past Barrakellis yet. Garth shuddered, stumbling away across the downs face. Terrible news for them when they arrived! And Minnie at St. Stephen, waiting, hoping, praying perhaps. A ghastly business. What would she do when she learnt the worst? Griffiths! Had he been right? "Misfits and deformities"—was that the rule of existence? And this quenching of Shirley's clay: bitter jest of Fate or compassionate Intention—which?

Rescrowsa farm stood a few hundred yards up the slope southward, on the edge of a broad field dipping to the clay stream where it nosed back into Tregargus Wood. A hump of craggy heath hid the farmhouse from Garth's view and barred off also the remote region he had crossed two hours ago, seeking quietude and heading unwittingly towards this shocking revelation. He strode up through a matted patch of bracken and bramble to the nearest field hedge, and passing through a gap he traversed a couple of fields. The farmhouse was visible from these, and the pollard thorns fringing the long lane that wound out eastward to the road. He closed the last field gate feverishly and almost ran over the strip of pasture to the farmyard gate.

He was quite close to it when a young man appeared around the back corner of the house, wearing a grey cap and blue overcoat. He was slighter of build than Garth, but ruddy-faced, walking with a slow dreamy step unusual in a farmer's son. Garth stopped short as he recognized the fellow. Paul Webber, who had been courting Doreen Blewett during recent months.

The young man had observed the bedraggled figure of Garth, and was evidently astonished. He halted with a hand on the gate and stared for a full minute before issuing an awkward challenge:

"Hullo! Anything wrong?"

Garth braced himself and said thickly: "Is your . . . is Doreen here too?"

"Yes; we've been spending the evening wi'father and mother—now putting her home. Doreen's making the most o' the good-bye talk, as women will."

Paul's smile soon faded as he saw that Garth's agitation increased.

"I—I'm sorry. I wouldn't have come up if I'd known Doreen was here."

Paul frowned in bewilderment, and Garth went on:

"I daresay you've heard o' me—Garth Joslin from Meledor."

"Ah! Yes." Paul's grey eyes narrowed curiously. "I've heard. . . . But what've you come here about?"

Garth's arm jerked up; he replied hoarsely:

"A girl's been killed down there in the woods—just found her body under the water-wheel."

"Good gosh!" exclaimed Paul, starting rigidly back. "Killed, you say?"

"Yes. Must have falled under it as she was climbing out into the woods. Been missing all evening, and died several hours ago, I should judge."

"Anyone else there?"

"No: there's others searching. I left 'em up by the Beacon."

"A Foxhole girl, I s'pose—is it?"

Garth swallowed hard, but forced himself to tell all.

"No. That's why I—wish I hadn't come here," he muttered. "It's that . . . Minnie Lagor's kid, Shirley."

Paul's face paled, then showed a dull flush of humiliation.

"What—Doreen's little—niece or whatever 'tis?"

"I'm afraid so. It's a terrible shock. How her mother'll stand it I don't know, though in some ways. . . ."

Paul nodded, his expression softening as he moistened his lips.

"Bound to knock her up," he said. "Poor beggar— falling into Ted's clutches, and this the end of it."

Before Garth could reply fresh sounds came from beyond the house corner, and a minute later Doreen

Blewett emerged, wearing a brown coat and blue halo hat. She was as different from Jean in appearance as in character, a superb blonde, her face small and sensitive, the features clear-cut and vivid between the curly light brown hair.

She halted at sight of Garth, watching him lurch close up to the gate and lean beside it, very pale and dishevelled in the moonlight.

"What's happened?" she asked tensely.

Garth shot an appealing glance at Paul ; his head jerked; he could make no response.

Paul stepped back and tenderly put an arm about Doreen.

"There's some bad news, dearest," he said in a low soothing tone. "But it needn't shake you. It can't touch us. It's only about—Ted's kid—the one he had by that maid Lagor."

The girl turned to him, her brown eyes widening.

"Why—you mean . . . dead or something, is she?"

Paul nodded.

"An accident. Garth Joslin here just found her crushed under a water-wheel. Strayed off from Meledor this afternoon, it seems."

"She'd been up to Ted's old home," said Garth with a strange smile at Doreen.

"How d'you know that?"

"Found her hanky there. It was our first clue."

Paul stepped forward afresh, swinging open the gate.

"Want me to help in any way?"

"I don't think we need trouble you—no," Garth answered. "You two can get clear of it. The body may have to be brought in here when doctor comes. . . ."

Paul turned back again towards the farmhouse.

"I'll go in and tell dad—he'll go down with you if you wait a few minutes."

Garth noted the glance that passed between the lovers, the mutual strengthening: emotion was loosened in him as he contemplated that instinctive sufficiency. He lurched free of the gate-post, and without waiting for Webber to join him he hurried away back into the field.

Five minutes later he again passed the water-wheel and descended the ladder to the streamlet's bank. The rain had ceased; there was no sign of any living human but himself. All was as he had left it, only the stronger moonlight gave a more unearthly tone to the surroundings, a gentler symbolism to the young body lying there so unutterably still. It seemed no longer harsh, but mournful in its dignity and sublime in its triumph, eternally beyond the reach of harm. The swarmings of male lust, inevitable about such chance-sown beauty, were broken before that mute grandeur. Only that could turn them aside, at a stroke, once and for ever: all else seemed timid, brittle—all ideals, virtues, vows, pitting their boast against the flux of time.

It was the hideous potency of the ills she had escaped that now fleered in the soul of Garth and threw over him the pall of an abject melancholy. The terrible menace of the mood of nature, the loneliness, the inhuman gloom —all combined to enforce his surrender.

He sank on his knees beside the dead girl. He looked at her with a sort of agony, hands clasped; and now the tears came, falling one by one upon the remote white face.

Words came too, at last, relieving the awful strain.

"Blessed are the dead, Shirley," he murmured in a choked tone. "I wish to God that this was Irma and not you!"

Chapter Fifteen

GRIFFITHS was sitting at his desk in the snug back room of his lodgings in St. George's Road, Truro. He had been holding a pen in his hand at intervals for the past two hours, but the sheet of notepaper before him was still blank. His feelings were too tempestuous for doggerel, and as he stared through the high window he mentally cursed the stupidity of poets who could find inspiration in Nature.

The outer world was in a mood that must irritate any man consciously barren. The spring sunshine was almost hot, toning to every tint of fervid green the sub-tropical vegetation of the Waterfall Gardens across the causeway. Birds kept swooping through the sky that was pale blue with here and there small tufts of white cloud like wads of cotton-wool tossed from some heavenly surgery and floating down to the earth wounded by its long battle with winter.

Few people in Truro were more deeply wounded than Griffiths, but he stubbornly refused the healing of transient beauties. He was one of those men who stick to rationalism with a fierce fidelity that is unreasonable. After nine months spent in this quiet and cheerful suburb he found himself heading into a crazier balance of shade that threatened his agnostic muse—always inclined to stutter —with the same paralysis that had earlier befallen his faith.

He dropped the pen with a sigh of weariness and took up mechanically a little box-calendar standing on the ridge of his desk—a cheap thing of polished wood with glass-covered slots. He had not yet turned the cylinders to-day—sure proof of moodiness—and the record still stood at Tuesday, the ninth of April. His adjustment of the knobs showed chagrin and a certain grudge at the swift passing of time; and having put the gadget back in its place he sat hunched in the swivel chair, frowning across at the screened grate mellow with drifts of sunshine. A bee was droning about the room, and above its buzz a pleasant sound of running water came in through the partly opened window—the flurried motion of the River Kenwyn between the causeway and the garden wall. There was no exit from the premises at the rear, the stream, though invisible, flowing through a deep concrete moat that gave Griffiths at times a feeling of being marooned; the Gardens so near, yet inaccessible.

The clock on the mantelshelf struck eleven: he heard his landlady, Mrs. Rundle, bustling about in the kitchen, and then her heavy footsteps in the passage, coming towards his room. He was not curious or surprised; she sometimes dropped in to chat for a few minutes when they two were alone in the place. It was not a regular boarding-house, and Griffiths had taken up his abode here in an atmosphere of informality that was very agreeable to him, for he loathed the artificial stiffness of social etiquette. Mrs. Rundle, now nearly sixty, was a homely soul, not yet corrupted by city standards of mercenary, as opposed to human, values. She and her husband had settled in Truro only five years ago, moving in from the village of Tregavethan, four miles north-west of the city. Mr. Rundle, a man much mauled by his antiquarian interests, and now rather Cornish than human, since he had learnt the language too late to make love in it, was a curator of the museum here, and tiring of his job now that war had added to the pleasure of guardianship the real exertion of packing and storing away the more rare and precious exhibits each night in case of an air-raid.

The door opened and Griffiths' eyes lit at once upon the woman standing on the threshold—very short, not more than five feet high, and rather flabby in figure, though her face was pale, never really fat, and now appearing strained with suppressed excitement. A look of apology was in her hollow eyes, and she spoke hesitantly.

"I don't want to interrupt, Mr. Griffiths, if you'm busy writing of your poems. . . ."

"No, I can do nothing to it now," replied Griffiths, pushing the notepaper back in to its pigeon-hole. "I was thinking to go for a walk till dinner-time."

"Yes, the weather's too good for a body to bide indoors

CHAPTER FIFTEEN

—contrary weather you'd call it, wi' the news what it is.
You didn't hear the eight o'clock bulletin on the wireless,
Mr. Griffiths ?"

He shook his head. "I thought I might be writing all
morning and didn't want to be disturbed. I felt the mood
but it 'went scat' as soon as I took up my pen."

"Well, the news is bad to-day, sure enough," said Mrs.
Rundle in tragic tones. "Oslo was occupied by the
Germans last night, they say, and Denmark overrun, and
our Air Force rushing to try and stop the Nazis getting
further into Norway. And a great naval battle is raging
in the Scraggyrat, whatever that is. A real flare-up all
of a sudden."

Griffiths swung round on the chair seat, fully facing her.

"Ah, yes—the war," he said absently. "It'll be grimmer
from now on, no doubt. But they asked for it."

"Yes, I did think something was pretty close over the
week-end, wi' the crisis about our laying mines in Norwegian waters. My husband spoke of it there Monday
evening while you was out. He isn't a prophetic man as
a rule—looks backward rather than forward, as museum
people is apt to—but he says: ' 'Tilda,' he says—he do
always call me 'Tilda, as if we was still courting—I expect
you've overheard'n sometimes— 'Tilda,' he says, 'afore
next Monday there'll be sich a kick-up as the world never
knowed up to now.' He has a rather exaggerated way o'
putting things when he thinks he's telling the truth, but
his meaning was accurate."

"Quite," commented Griffiths ; a faint malicious
smile touched his lips.

"And we was hoping to be spared any real bloodshed
this time," Mrs. Rundle resumed, rubbing her cheek with
a hand still floury from pastry-making.

At this Griffiths put in cynically :

"And I suppose that if these pious hopes are disregarded
by any deity who happens to be hanging about, they'll be
staging more Days of Prayer as they did in the last war."

"Well, there's worse things than prayer, if I may make so bold. . . ."

"Perhaps; but it's disgusting to think of a building in a civilised city like this being used for an orgy of superstition more suited to savage tribes."

Mrs. Rundle sniffed and wiped her small red nose with her pinafore.

"You han't been in the cathedral yet, have you, Mr. Griffiths?"

"No, and I don't intend to," answered Griffiths gruffly. "I'd thank the Germans for coming over and bombing it up any night. It's an eyesore to those of us who don't want to be reminded of this commercialised mythology."

Mrs. Rundle came further into the room, eyeing her lodger warily but with spirited reproach.

"You aren't no Christian, Mr. Griffiths, if I may say so without offence."

"I'm not," Griffiths agreed, giving his leg a flounce as the bee threatened to alight on his trousers. "I believe in Christian ethics, but that isn't Christianity, though the modern Church is pitiably trying to pretend that it is. I couldn't accept any dogma, knowing life as I do. . . . But it isn't always easy to maintain one's doubts. One hears of strange things. . . ."

"Yes, sir, the war. . . ."

"I wasn't referring to that." Griffiths pursed his lips, his massive grey head bowed, the sunlight slanting warm across the nape of his neck.

Mrs. Rundle waited, discreetly clearing her throat. She knew that he was disturbingly unconventional and impulsive, apt to pour out his feelings with little regard for their formal relationship as landlady and lodger. A man always burning to make a confession of his bankruptcy, who could not suffer in silence, and must be forever hunting out and parading any like experiences of his fellow men.

Recent events had seemed to bring fresh confirmation

of his sombre creed. He had not seen Minnie on the day he visited Garth and he had heard nothing more of her since. Nearly three weeks of growing impatience, bitterness, resentment. He supposed something had occurred at Egypt to make Minnie banish him from her plans, as he had feared. Frustrated again! But his stubborn soul had its pride even if loss of dignity had become natural to his crises. He would not visit Meledor or communicate with Minnie in any way until she made the first move. He would scarcely admit that he loved her, though he knew that on that January day when she first opened the Snells' door to him, the thrill of promise had been unmistakable, a mysterious recognition of fitness. They'd seemed to have been prepared for that hour, yet now——! Meledor was another fated place: cursed be the urge that had led him there, into this torture. Minnie—Garth! Two more names that would be branded ironically upon his mind henceforth, mocking him—she with her shrewd practical triumph over ignominy and suffering, he with his calm tremendous grip on the Infinite. . . .

Griffiths roused and got up; obviously he had decided to unburden himself.

"The fact is," he said frankly, "a few weeks ago I met a young fellow who's—well, had a rather unsettling effect on me ever since."

"I thought you've been a bit down since Easter, Mr. Griffiths." The landlady's tone was sympathetic as she leaned an elbow against a big bookcase just inside the door. "We do all get our moods."

"Yes. In going about the county, calling at so many homes, I've come across a good many of these so-called Christians, and never found much trouble in dealing with them. They usually conform to type, huddled together in their sectarian ruts like a lot of fussy beetles. A good squirt of honest rationalism sends them choking and gasping into silence. . . . But this young fellow— called Joslin, a claywork carpenter—he stands apart, like

a giant among these pigmies. There's no church or club
that would have room for such a man, such a vision as he
has, lived out in a personal gamble where it hurts most.
He's staked everything on the supernatural."

"A very rare thing these days," remarked Mrs. Rundle.
"Too rare, or the world would never ha' got to this pass.
They tell us to pin our hopes on the young, but what've
the young got *their* hopes pinned to? They pinned their
hopes on froth, and now they'll get poison gas for their
pains."

"True; they treat a fellow like Joslin much as they'd
treat Christ or any other of these gloomy prophetic
characters that get in the way of their amusements. But
how the maggot's got into him—that's the mystery. One
expects to find old fogies stupidly hanging on to outworn
traditions, but when one sees the old faith springing up
spontaneously in such a young man, untouched by the
churches, one doesn't know how to account for it. And
if he should get results—*proof* as he would call it. . . ."

Griffiths' hands clenched, he almost glared through the
window, his expression so forbidding that Mrs. Rundle
edged uncomfortably nearer the door.

"Well, there's no knowing what may happen," she
brought out vaguely. "But I must be getting along wi'
me cooking or your dinner'll be late. I reckon we'll be
feeling the pinch in our stomachs now the war's come to
a real matter o' killing and occupying. A lot of our cheese
and bacon was imported from Denmark, I believe."

Griffiths nodded dully.

"Yes. . . . By the way," he added in a fresh tone as she
was closing the door: "haven't we new neighbours
across the street here? I thought there were some new
arrivals there last night, at Miss Jesty's."

Mrs. Rundle gave a quick gesture of assent.

"So there was. A party called Palmer—London
evacuees what've been here in Truro since last October,
in Moresk Road. They didn't settle in well there, it

seems—a pretty slummy place the house was—billeted with a Mrs. Fisher. Both she and this London woman is not very savoury—hanging around the pubs most nights —and a week or two ago they came to blows if reports can be credited. Mrs. Fisher's man was home on leave, and Mrs. Palmer tried to carry on with him; so 'tis no wonder they was shifted."

"No; such things will be a commonplace if the Government go on with this evacuation lunacy. They don't seem to know human nature. . . . How many of these Palmers have come ?"

"The woman and three children—girls, I believe. I hope they behave themselves here. These Londoners will turn the county into Bedlam as you say, if they swarm down like the billet committees is preparing for. A lot of 'em'll be scared now, I expect, wi' the war opened up rough—though Norway's a safe distance from we and if Hitler's head can be cracked open there, so much the better for us."

Griffiths followed Mrs. Rundle into the passage, and as she turned into the kitchen a little further on he took his hat from the hall-stand, opened the front door and went out.

Chapter Sixteen

THE street was quiet—only a luggage van coming along from the foot of the hill leading to the railway station on the bleak hilltop north-west. Near the corner a dowdily-clad woman was standing on the doorstep of the house outside which, as dusk fell last evening, Griffiths had noticed a taxi draw up and several people emerge with bundles, sacks and suitcases. The woman was a complete stranger to him, and he could see only her brawny figure, black hair and a red face without detail. This Mrs. Palmer, he supposed. His eyes hardened, he drew the trilby lower over them, swinging open the iron gate with a gesture of disgust. London! Scene of his own bitterest memories: life could never match *that* agony again. Odd that the puny thrusts from Meledor should trouble him after that scourging. . . .

Griffiths watched the van glide past, under the viaduct, as he stepped into the road, and a minute later he moved slowly in the same direction. Open country lay out there, as the bulk of the city sprawled southward, the mass of roofs, shopping centres and slum alleys hiding even the cathedral from his view, though seen from the top of the viaduct it dominated the whole expanse. He surveyed moodily the massive grey arches of that straddling erection, five of them rising from the northern end of the Waterfall Gardens, alternately obscured and framed by the thick foliage of trees as he approached. The entrance to the Gardens was about halfway between his abode and the viaduct, and reaching it he turned on an impulse in through the open gateway.

This little park was one of his favourite haunts here in the city; on its painted seats, in the shadow of its trees, he had brooded out much doggerel.

The path wound through a lawn flanked by shrubs, with benches set at intervals facing the road. The plashing of the artificial waterfall could be heard, and soon, passing through a gap in the shrubbery, he stood on the short concrete bridge spanning the river. No one was visible, only some seagulls strutting and flapping about, but he did not linger at the railing to view the tumbling cascade. He moved straight out on to the rough gravel causeway, and was again almost abreast of his lodgings before reaching the flight of steps that gave access to the upper and main section of the Gardens. From here paths climbed steeply up a broad slope, dividing flower beds and stretches of lawn and sheltered by exotic trees, ferns and bushes that often limited the view to a matter of yards.

Griffiths began following a path that slanted first towards the viaduct and then curved back under the fountain in the centre of the grounds. Not far from this a gap in the quickset border was rendered picturesque by a wooden bridge, on both sides of which benches had been placed against the bare turf. Griffiths was inclined to seat himself on one of these and try to grapple afresh with complexities that had scarcely needed Mrs. Rundle's news to edge them with desperation.

But as he turned a bend overhung by holly trees and came in sight of the bridge, he was brought to a sudden halt by the sound of girlish laughter on the other side of it. A man's voice murmured lightly in response: "You know, darling!" and then came a sound that sent an icy chill along Griffiths' nerves—the soft sucking of kisses. He smothered a fierce oath, annoyed. Some young fools there on the seat already, carrying on as moderns would! A newly married couple, most likely: lovers were not usually found in public gardens at eleven o'clock in the morning.

He stood close to the holly, covered by its shade, not daring to go on, yet reluctant to turn back for such a reason. Hs listened, scanning the open spaces of the Gardens furtively.

After a few minutes the girl spoke in more sober tones. Her voice was rough, and from its broad Cornish accent on certain words Griffiths judged that she was an uneducated country wench.

"In one way it's a good thing—clears up the whole muddle and salves our consciences. 'Twould have been rough on mother to have grannie on her hands with only Doris at home. But we couldn't stop to think o' that."

"No," the young man answered. "We'd have had to marry, whatever happened to your people. Minnie's bearing up like a brick, isn't she?"

"Yes, though I believe underneath it've shook her a lot more'n Ted hanging hisself. Shirley was all she had. But with grannie dumped in the workhouse she'll find it restful there at Egypt now. Mother and all are doing everything they can."

Griffiths stood rigid, breathing so heavily that he feared they would hear him. His eyes looked wild, and involuntarily he gripped the nearest bough, severely pricking his hand on the holly leaves.

The young man went on musingly;

"Must have jarred her a bit yesterday, seeing you married while she got all this to bear—rum contrast."

"Yes, it rather spoilt the wedding—we couldn't be as free as we'd like. Had to put a damper on any big splash —no guests or anything. Still, we couldn't expect much in any case, as people knew I was in trouble." Sounds of slurred feet and confused movement—another hug, Griffiths supposed; then from the girl, in hungry, sensuous undertones:

"Never mind, Stevie; we don't lose much. And now our honeymoon's come—a whole week here to enjoy ourselves; and when we're settled in at Foxhole next week there won't be anything to regret—or fear either. *We* needn't worry about the jolly old war—it can't touch us."

The strain was becoming unbearable to Griffiths. His mind was invaded by fevering half-truths. What were those fools discussing ? . . . He moved stealthily on to the turf, skirting some palms, until through the thinned edges of shrubbery he glimpsed the pair. Sitting as he had expected, very close together, fully in sunlight, just beyond a holly tree that made a dense, gleaming pillar by the bridge. Their arms were about each other's neck, their free hands interlocked on the knee of the youth's fawn trousers. Very young—neither of them looked twenty. The girl was slight, fair-haired, wearing a blue costume and a red felt hat. Her companion was slim, hatless, his

148

tawny hair ruffled, his cheeks rounder and pinker than the girl's. He had somehow the look of one undergoing a conversion from cynicism and still rather unbalanced by the process.

Griffiths stepped on to the bridge, within a dozen yards of them and fully in their view; and it was now their turn to exhibit all the outward signs of intense shock. They dropped their arms, facing him with cool defiance and antagonism.

He was much embarrassed, and making a clumsy gesture he addressed the girl.

"Excuse me, but I couldn't help overhearing something of your talk. It throws light on a matter that's been puzzling me a good deal. You'll have heard of me from your sister—Mr. Griffiths."

"Oh ! yes." Muriel's blue eyes widened, less hostile, though she spoke grudgingly. "You'll understand if Minnie hasn't wrote. She's been too upset over that blow, coming so sudden."

"I don't know precisely . . . ." Griffiths began.

"You haven't heard Shirley's dead ?"

"Dead ?" The word possessed a finality that Griffiths' brain had evaded hitherto. He had blanched, his stocky figure almost reeled for a moment. "How ? An illness ?"

"No—accidental. The Tuesday after you was up to Meledor last. Garth Joslin found her in the woods below Carloggas."

Griffiths' voice was faint, dull, unlike itself:

"How had she died there ?"

"Fell under a water-wheel—squashed her guts in, though they say she wasn't disfigured at all. I didn't see her, but me and Stephen went to the funeral."

"A lot of people there, I daresay ?"

"Not as many as turned out to see her father buried. Ted was better known. . . ."

Griffiths pressed a hand to his forehead, wiped away sweat, struggling for composure.

"I'd never dreamed anything so tragic was behind her silence. I supposed it was her grandmother who had died."

"No such luck, though we've got rid of her," returned Muriel. "Both of 'em was took the same evening, in different ways. I should think you'd have seen on the papers about Shirley: not that there was much put in about it. Minnie not being married made it awkward, and they hushed it up as much as they could to spare her feelings."

"I don't read the local papers often," Griffiths explained. He lurched free of the screening shrubs and looked dazedly across at the viaduct, most of which was on a lower level than this part of the Gardens.

"Shirley dead! I can hardly believe it. Everything's changed now."

The couple watched him, Trebilcock sulkily, as if resolved not to prolong the encounter by any speech of his own. Muriel, however, believed in more vigorous strategy.

"Sure," she agreed. "But I don't reckon Minnie's likely to follow my example. Mother'll need her at home now, and she won't want to be pestered."

This blunt and cheeky warning caused Griffiths to take firmer grip on the flux of his emotions. His whole face and figure tautened, and turning back to them he said with a strained, rather ugly smile:

"And it was Mr. Joslin who found the girl?"

"Yes. It upset him too, near as bad as Minnie—or worse even." Muriel shifted slightly away from Stephen, toeing the gravel. "She called over to see him several times that first week, and he spoke so comforting it did her good to hear him, she said. Religious, I s'pose. But after a few days it took a different line with him—reaction or something. Bound to give him a turn, inheriting what he have from his mother."

"I know about that," confessed Griffiths in response to the girl's uncertain questioning look.

She went on crisply, peering past him down upon the spires of St. George's chapel:

"And then there was the exposure—that's really what began it. He got soaked in the rain and was in his wet clothes till nearly midnight, and what with that and the excitement—bringing Shirley into Webbers' place and facing the questions from the police, and the inquest, and then the funeral—he was there, at St. Stephen's church-yard the following Saturday—it proved too much for him."

"And now he's ill—seriously?"

"Well, 'twas only a cold at first, but he didn't take any notice o' that with no woman there to tend him—went to work as usual and got worse. Last week-end the neighbours say he was fair staggering on his legs coming home from the workshop. Colly Snell came in and offered to take him in Snells' place over Sunday—have Minnie's room—but he wouldn't budge. Monday he went to work again with the fever on him, but in the afternoon he gave out. Enoch Hocking came over from the micas and found him half fainting against the workshop bench. He helped him in and got him to bed, and there he's been ever since."

Griffiths moved restlessly forward, then back to the grass verge. Noting some blood on his fingers where the holly had pricked them he wiped it off with his handkerchief, and they saw that his hand trembled.

"Who is there with him?"

"Nobody regular: some o' the neighbours is dropping in to get meals and see that he's comfortable. Poor old Colly goes in every evening—he seems knocked up too about the affair and is wondering what he'll do now Minnie's gone. Neighbours is managing for him as well as Garth."

"H'm! I thought Garth was generally shunned in the village?"

"So he is, but however much they may dislike the chap they can't let him die in his bed. Mrs. Hocking do cook for him, I believe. But most o' the time he's there alone, tossing about like a fellow in torment so they say, and moaning out Irma's name when he gets delirious."

"Terrible!"

"Yes; 'tis hard to see how he can get better, as he's been worked up so bad lately about that London girl. Unless she comes back—and of course she won't. . . ."

"I should think not." Griffiths' eyes swept the heavens; a seagull was swooping overhead, a white shape of life among the tiny drifting corpses of cloud.

"My God!" said Griffiths. "What he must be suffering."

Muriel nodded; her face showed the unconscious heartlessness of one to whom agony was an unknown extravagance.

"It's funny," she observed in a tone of flippant contempt, "to see what tangles people get themselves in through these superior notions. Silly chumps—they ought to be content to go on like the rest of us. Garth's had as many chances as any other chap—might even have cut out Stephen if he'd barged over around Egypt twelve months ago and acted like a man!"

She laughed, squeezing Stephen's arm, and as he flushed with a hint of displeasure she atoned for this teasing by giving him a bold swift kiss on the lips.

It was a sufficient move. Griffiths was stung and could stay there no longer.

"I must go up and look into this—and soon," he muttered, and to the Trebilcocks' relief he turned away immediately, striding down the path and behind the trees.

Chapter Seventeen

FROM the time it became known in Meledor that Garth was confined to his bed the road leading thither from Trethosa was, in daylight, closely watched; and on the afternoon of the following Saturday a few lucky house-wives were rewarded by the sight of Edith Spragg passing up the hill with a defiant bearing that left no one in doubt of her destination. That she should make the journey at such an hour, instead of under cover of darkness, seemed to prove that the state of things at the Chirgwins' was ripe for open drama, and that Edith's design was not compatible with secrecy. The neighbourhood was tense in expectation of another first-class scandal, and pro-phecies of a violent end for Garth were now linked with a conviction that Edith would in some way share the closing phase, possibly by being murdered as his mistress.

The weather was dull, though dry, and Edith wore the same shabby velour hat and smeared raincoat she had worn here on the day Mrs. Joslin was buried. She looked, indeed, rather a village drab than a woman schooled in the arts of coquetry. Fashion had no place in the crude, deadly warfare to which she was reduced.

In the garden of his home just above the stone bridge over the Fal, Colly Snell was planting a row of potatoes as she drew abreast. He appeared frail and shaken, and obviously had no heart for the job. He stopped shovelling on hearing her footsteps; his voice came over the wall, dull and lifeless.

"Going up to see Garth?"

"No odds to you where I'm going," she returned. "You seen him to-day?"

Colly nodded. "Went up this morning. He's a bit better now—not so feverish, and not rambling at all; but I dunno if 'twill do him any good to see you come in."

Edith shrugged.

"You've finished working at Melbur, so I hear?"

The old man's head jerked, he leaned heavily on the shovel.

"I couldn't leave missus indoors be herself all day, and when Minnie went. . . ." He snuffled, passing a grimy hand over his small peaked face, now pale and blotchy.

"I shan't work again, I s'pose—sixty-five next month, and must turn me hand to housekeeping if I can't git nobody else. I don't feel I want any strangers around now lil Shirley's gone. ...."

His hollow eyes brimmed suddenly; and with a hard titter of contempt at the sign of sentiment in this sour old man Edith hurried on towards the house where sentiment of another kind might soon comfort her.

Reaching the gate she was relieved to find no one in view, and quickly slipped inside the plot of ground which had produced all the vegetables Garth had eaten during the past five years. Birds were noisy in the surrounding trees; now and then a swallow or martin flashed overhead. The warm weather had brought these birds to England early this year and injurious insect life was having little chance to multiply.

Edith moved lingeringly up the path, noting the changed aspect of the garden brought about by the advance of spring. The border, edged with stones taken from the sand-dump, was colourful with chrysanthemums, budding pinks, and daffodils fully in flower. The red stems of the fuchsia in the corner were less wiry, putting out delicate green shoots. A row of gooseberry bushes was thickening with leaves just inside the hedge, in some places actually overhung by white clusters of blackthorn blossom. The garden itself was bare, with white patches where lime had recently fallen from a sack during potato planting. Half the year's potato seed was already sown, the row now open being straight, clean-cut. Garth was no slipshod workman, however much he might be engrossed in his dreams. And as Edith brooded upon what might have happened had she been mistress here, she was stung into fiercer jealousy by a chance reminder. Here in this garden four and a half years ago Garth and Martin Stribley had almost come to blows when Bella sent her husband up to demand an explanation of what had occurred in the workshop. There had been no verbal fireworks, as Mrs. Joslin was in the bedroom, but according to Bella Garth had "framed up" at Martin and offered to settle the dispute there and then by a stand-up fight—his animal energies very much to the fore, no doubt, after the practice with Irma! Edith's eyes probed the closed bedroom window. Was Garth in there remembering that now? . . .

The door was unlocked, and noiselessly she opened it, stealing in with a furtive glance back towards the road. The passage was dark, and she held her breath, oppressed by the memory of her last visit here—the unlighted room, Garth's shadowy form hunched on the table, their forced and pointless talk fraying off into taunt and counter-taunt about that kid.

Entering the kitchen she paused, and on an impulse removed her hat and raincoat—heavy garments with which she didn't wish to be cumbered indoors. She had dropped them, fluffed out her black hair and was smoothing her red woollen jumper when Garth's voice broke from the bedroom—irritable, but not as weak as she had expected it to be:

"That you, Mrs. Hocking?"

"No—me," she answered, and began ascending the stair.

The bedroom door was open, and reaching the landing she saw herself reflected in the long mirror of the wardrobe. Not as beautiful as when she last viewed herself in it; thin and haggard the image confronted her now. But there was something new and dynamic at work behind the blanched, warped shell, and buoyed by her sense of this power she stepped into the apartment.

It was small and the ceiling sloped so that on the farther side there was not room enough for Garth to stand upright. A dressing-table was set near the bed, in the corner beyond the tiny latched window, and upon it stood a bottle of medicine and several books. On a cane-bottomed chair within Garth's reach a tea-tray had been placed, containing the dishes he had used at dinner time.

Garth was sitting up in bed, looking strained and fevered as she came in. His eyes seemed unnaturally bright in the pale, sweat-heavy face; his hands were clenched on the pink quilt. He had drawn up his knees, and across them lay a copy of the *Daily Mail* with big headlines announcing the progress of the Battle of Narvik Fjord. He had been reading it as Edith entered the house, gripped and overshadowed by this epic phase of a world struggle, but the sound of her voice and her footsteps on the stairs had brought him back to the level of a man who still had a private life and for whom a woman might still be more dangerous than anything that could come from Germany.

"You!" he said in a blank tone.

Edith sensed the startled, defensive motion of his will behind the faint monosyllable. She glided forward, her shoes creaking on the bare patches of canvas.

"It's all right, Garth," she greeted in a tone which, though meant to be soothing, showed something incalculable and reckless in her mood. "I'm no stranger here, you know." She pointed to the faded blue-and-gold pattern on the walls. "That wallpaper—I helped your mother to paste it up. D'you remember?"

Garth continued to gaze at her, pushing a hand through his hair, that was rather long and matted with sweat.

"You can do no good here now," he said thickly, and attempting a smile: "The spring cleaning'll have to wait this year, I'm afraid!"

"A pity: this illness'll hold you up in your gardening, too."

"Enoch and Colly've offered to help there if I don't get around on time. Enoch'll put in a few rows o' spuds Monday evening if 'tisn't rain."

"I'm glad people are more neighbourly. I was afraid you'd be left in the lurch now you're laid up, and decided to drop in and see if I could help."

He answered with increasing reserve:

156

"Thanks; but I'm managing right enough as it is. Enoch's missus comes in at meal-times—though I can't eat much; and I'm better left quiet after being used to it so long."

"You've had the doctor, I s'pose?"

Garth nodded.

"He called Tuesday and said I must stop in bed till the fever's gone and take that medicine there. He doesn't understand what's wrong."

The smile that flickered out on Edith's face warned Garth of deep purpose underlying her casual reply:

"I should think he might guess if he remembers the last time he was here. . . . It was the last time, wasn't it?"

"The night mother was brought in from the tank wall, you mean?"

"Yes. You haven't had a day's illness since, but anybody could tell you was bound to have a breakdown sooner or later." She leaned over the bed-rail, idly turning the loose brass knob on top of the post. "Odd that it should come like this, though—through a tragedy that doesn't concern you at all. You must be sorry you went out that evening, over Foxhole way."

"No good being sorry," muttered Garth. "There was some purpose behind it, that I should find Shirley and feel what I did."

Edith straightened, a warped enticement thrown into her glance and speech.

"Won't you tell me? Though I can guess. . . ."

"I feel it even more now," he said, without looking at her. "And who knows?—Irma may be where Shirley is by this time, since her mother married, and if that's so I'm afraid the doctor'll be wasting his good intentions on me."

A scornful laugh broke from Edith.

"Well, if that's the sort o' morbid notions you're dwelling on it's a jolly good thing I've come up."

"'Tisn't no shock to me," he struck back, expressing his awareness of the duel. "I'd been expecting some move before now. Since Seth broke down I've heard from several quarters what was likely to come of it; and I'd had my suspicions even earlier."

Since when ?"

"Since the day mother was buried, when I came home to find you waiting here. You said you meant to shift, but there's been no sign of it since."

Again her laugh grated, now with attempted levity.

"You wouldn't let us have the house!"

"You may be able to get it soon," said Garth gloomily, "when I'm gone out o' the way."

This she ignored, continuing in a rapid tone as she stepped across to the window :

"It isn't easy to get houses now in war-time, and with Seth likely to be called up for munitions work it wouldn't be worth while."

Garth was sitting very still, watching her hands nervously twitching at the pink net curtain, her teeth biting hard on the lower lip. Worked up, certainly! He'd never before had to handle her in this state. Instinct told him that any approach to tenderness would be fatal, and there was a rough candour in his next remark.

"You can't kid me about your real motive. You owned that night you was sick o' your marriage and wishing you'd kept to your first choice; and now I'm weak wi' fever you think you may have a chance."

Her eyes, very wide, black, tragic, stabbed round to him.

"Well, I've suffered lately, as much as you," she murmured; "and we've both come to breaking point."

He studied her face, looking pinched and bony in the dull daylight.

"You've failed—even I can see that," he admitted.

"Yes; worry's pulled me down, naturally. I've lost twenty pounds since I was here last, less than three months ago. Seth keeps jeering and says you'll have nothing but a skeleton to hold in your arms if I don't hustle."

"Does he know you've come here now?"

"Of course. He wants to get it settled."

"And your parents——"

"They're fair stunned and may kick me out if I make scandal. I was brought up so strict, they can't understand me turning like this. I've no pity for 'em—none. 'Twas partly their fault that I lost you: they'd made me such a tame little prude—you'll remember."

"Yes, we were never really suited."

"But that's all changed now," Edith went on, her breasts heaving with the fuller swell of emotion. "I don't care what people think. I've found how much it's worth to keep straight for *them*. They all turned round on me and started sniggering or lecturing me when they saw what a flop I'd got for my virtue."

Garth shivered, drawing the bedclothes tighter around him.

"Have you any proof yet about Seth's breakdown at St. Austell?"

"All I want. He kept babbling about that Blewett kid while he was getting sober, and knows he gave everything away. . . . We can't go on: all of us know that—my people and Seth himself, and—and you can't stand aside as if you'd had no hand in it."

Garth lay back with a hard grunting laugh.

"Just like a woman! You threw me over and now blame me because you married the wrong man!"

"But it wasn't like an ordinary case. Irma threw us all into an uproar."

"Then carry your complaint to her, not me."

This curt advice suggested to Edith a fresh approach. She moved the chair back against the wall, then stood with hands clasped on her bosom.

"If I could only make you see it was *her* fault—that she made both of us pay for her little game—'twould be easy for us to make it up to each other, now she's gone out o' your life and Seth's gone out o' mine."

"News to me," said Garth dryly. "You're still his wife, I believe."

"Only in name since February. I won't make it up. I told him I'd rather sleep down on the kitchen floor than have him mauling me again."

"Well, it doesn't interest me, whatever domestic shifts you're put to." Garth glanced quickly through the window as a sparrow darted by to its unfinished nest in the eaves above.

Edith resumed in a tone of moody persuasion:

"I, too, would be breaking free from a sort o' dream. It's all unreal as I look back. I don't seem to be the same woman who married Seth. Life and everything looks so different, I'd never have believed I could change so in a few years."

"That's a commonplace," observed Garth, frowning up at the cracked whitewashed ceiling. "I look at love very different now from what I did when I had it."

"When you had it? D'you mean from me or Irma?"

He replied almost brutally:

"I shouldn't think you need to ask that. I didn't have any love from you. You were never meant to be my wife. God just used you as a stop-gap till Irma was ready."

"Very obliging of Him, wasn't it?"

"If you think so."

She made an impatient gesture, edging back to the wardrobe.

"It's all ghastly, how I've come to view things," she continued. "Even if I'd married you it might have turned the same. You understand as you get older—it's an awful business. You see that it *can't* be otherwise. A man naturally gets sick of kissing the same lips day after day, and when he's got another girl's mouth he goes on till he's got the rest of her. That's how it happens—not through him meaning to change or wanting to, but *naturally*, just through getting older."

"Original sin," commented Garth with a glum smile.

160

"Yes. The churches and educationists may prattle about their dainty little ideals and make out human nature to be sound, reliable stuff that only needs to be given its chance; but when you come up against real raw experience you soon learn the need o' some extra power grafted on to you if you're to hold out. I'm glad you see that, because if you once come to share my faith you'll be able to find your way out o' the whole tangle."

"It's nothing as tame as that I want now," replied Edith bitterly. "It's time we closed in and had the happiness we might have known long ago. We owe it to each other. We've both been cheated."

Garth smiled, his eyes seemed to brood on some inner vision as he said quietly:

"I haven't."

"Oh! So I didn't guess wrong?"

"In what way?"

"I've told mother and dad several times I bet you've had all you want off in town so often till nearly midnight."

"Setting Seth an example?"

"Yes—and p'raps even at Blewetts' lately: who knows?"

Garth's composure almost gave way for a moment.

"D'you think I meant that? Good God!"

"I know what you meant," rejoined Edith coldly. "You meant Irma'd been with you in spirit and all that tosh. Kidding yourself all these years—it's the limit. While you've been here dreaming and waiting for some miracle, she's been . . . well, I could tell if I liked."

This hint left Garth obviously shaken; he raised himself on an elbow, his manner tense, subdued.

"D'you know as much as the Stribleys?"

"Yes, and it's only fair you should be told—fair to me, I mean."

"Bella wouldn't let me hear a word."

"No, and she'd never forgive me for blabbing, I s'pose. But I don't care. We've fallen out already, in any case— I haven't spoke to her for weeks. . . . I've borne enough and I know there's only one way out, and once you get these cobwebs cleared away and see things as they are, we'll soon be on top—here together."

Garth stared; again a shudder ran through him.

"You're pretty far gone if you really would. . . ."

"I'd leave Seth and come with you—any time," she confessed in hard, joyless tones. "And after that past scandal you can't pretend you'd care more than I what a rumpus it made. And as for morals. . . ." Her hands clenched, she scowled through the window up at the trees veiling Meledor workshop, and went on with a hungry passion unlike anything he had heard from her hitherto:

"What's Seth ever been to me compared with you— weak, limping little fool as he is? I've felt mad when I see you about the village—a big healthy chap as you've been—and better looking than when you courted me. And everybody feels you're somehow above them all— that you've suffered and learnt more than any schools could teach."

"That's true enough," said Garth; "but what's soul and depth to a woman like you? You couldn't understand, or 'twould have been bred in me through your kisses instead of hers. For years it's been too late for you to catch up with me."

The curt finality of his tone was maddening to Edith; she stamped her foot, turning to him a face stark, fevered.

"But what can I do, Garth? You know I'm desperate and it can't end with you saying you're sorry and then drivelling back to your dreams."

"I'm afraid it must—till the awakening comes."

"Then it shall come now!" she cried harshly, stepping quickly up to the bed. "If the news makes you worse, you've asked for it. And there's nothing in it you couldn't guess. I don't know what you expected of such a girl. If you found her more than willing when she was only fourteen or so what could you think she'd be when she grew up?"

CHAPTER EIGHTEEN

Garth answered tremulously, while fumbling with the newspaper:

"I've seen in these towns what she'd be unless God stepped in."

"Well, He didn't, that's all; there was other examples too close. Her mother and father was both carrying on so, it hardly needed you to set her going. Before she was sixteen she was running wild—out late at night and all that. They couldn't do anything with her, and in the end it got so bad that they took her into court up there."

He sat erect, dazed and rigid. "Eh?"

"She was brought to a juvenile court and put on probation—two years ago."

Edith's voice was cold and pitiless; she watched with satisfaction the turmoil set loose in him and flinging out at last the dull query:

"What for?"

"Sort of stealing—you'll remember! Kisses and such-like—just what Jean Blewett stole from my man the other night."

Garth writhed on the bed; his face was ashy and terrible.

"For God's sake don't torture me!" he cried, lurching forward and gripping her arm. "If this isn't true. . . ."

"It is—I'll swear it on the Bible. I read the letters. . . . And then Bert got in some mess and died—we were never told exactly what that affair was, or whether Irma was mixed up in it; and we don't know what effect the proba-tion had, though I shouldn't judge 'twould tame her much. If it *did* cure her she's sure to be courting decent by now—may even be married. I should guess something pretty final had happened by the way her mother's hushed up every detail about her this last twelve months —ashamed to confess the disgrace, I expect."

Garth lay back, flagging in exhaustion, stupor clouding his face again for a moment.

"Put on probation because. . . . And I all the while

believing. . . . No, damn it, I won't believe it! If God's
served me such a trick. . . ."

"You needn't blame God. He has nothing to do with
it. It's just your own silliness. You must have been crazy
ever to think of marrying her. It's hopeless now, anyway,
and you can see it. Just in time, too: we heard you was
meaning to go to London soon to try and find her."

Garth responded drunkenly:

"And so I shall, as soon as I'm well enough. I'll stay
long enough to get the facts, and then. . . ."

Edith's lips quivered; rage and bafflement swept her.
Failure—even now! She couldn't get past this mania!

"Garth! You can't be such a fool. Seth's said if you
go up there it'll be only to drown yourself in the Thames."

A dreadful little smile broke into the fever of Garth's
face; he answered slowly, in a voice scarcely audible:

"Perhaps Irma's gone that way before me, and so it
would be a better end than yours."

"When we might both get free! . . . It's madness,
Garth!" She leaned over the bed, caught his shoulder
and shook him. "Can't you look back and think what
you dreamed of here in this room after we'd been out
together? It was *me* you wanted then. . . . And if I hurt
you because I was cold sometimes and wouldn't let you
kiss and fondle me as you wished to, it's different now.
I understand and I'm driven back. . . . I've only you in
the world. . . ."

"That's not my fault. It's too late. I can never love
you again—never. Don't tempt me, Edith!"

"But it's only these cobwebs. . . . Once you let me
prove how I understand, 'twould all seem so ridiculous to
you ; you'd be able to laugh at it as others have." She
pushed her face towards his, whispering:

"I expect your fever'll be bad to-night. You'll want
somebody here. I'll come up. . . ."

The fierce revolt in Garth that would have thrown her
off even with violence was checked by the sudden and

surprising click of the garden gate, the sound of footsteps outside, hesitant on the path.

Edith at once drew back, blundering against the chair, white, frightened.

A long sigh of relief quivered from Garth, though he, too, was trembling from head to foot.

"Mrs. Hocking, I s'pose—or Reub Pollard, p'raps. He said he'd call sometime to-day."

Edith, peering out between the wall and the curtain, shook her head.

"No ; it's a woman in black hat and coat. I think I've seen her before, when she lived. . . ."

"Who is it ?" he demanded hoarsely.

Throughout the whole wretched scene Edith's face had shown nothing as ugly as the smile which accompanied her reply:

"Sal Blewett."

Chapter Eighteen

An hour earlier Sal Blewett had alighted from a bus outside St. Stephen cemetery. While not showing the sad and chastened spirit of one who had come to visit the grave of a newly-lost relative, she looked unusually harassed and dejected. This, however, was not so much through having heard of Shirley's death as through the ripening of ironies suggested by the distant landscape around Foxhole Beacon, enclosing Carpalla and Rescrowsa.

She scanned it irritably, and had stepped off the kerb when she was arrested by the sound of a shop door opening just opposite the churchyard. Quickly she turned. A woman had emerged, a big flabby creature, carrying a parcel, wearing a fawn coat, a green hat riding amid her mousey hair. A smirk broke into her face at sight of the thin, black-garbed figure in the road.

"Good afternoon, Mrs. Blewett !"

Sal frowned, yet her response was not ungenial; she recognized a sympathetic coarseness in this stranger.

"Now, I believe I've seed you before somewhere, but I can't call to mind exactly. . . ."

"Mrs. Stribley—Bella, from the farm below Meledor."

"Ah! I dunno that I remember the name either. 'Tis only poor old souls like me wi' their scandals and troubles what do git famous."

"You've come to see your little granddaughter's grave, I s'pose ?"

"Well, I thought I'd just drop in to have a look while I was passing. I'm really out to fish up about the details, as there seem to be other things mixed up wi' it rather in my line." Sal lowered her voice, jerking her hand towards the straight row of garden walls overhung by shrubs and rhododendrons. "I'm going over to Meledor when I've paid me respects," she confided.

"To Meledor ?" repeated Bella in surprise.

"Yes. Want to pay a little visit."

Bella moistened her lips and gave Sal a sharp glance. "Minnie isn't living there now, and even if she was. . . ."

Sal reacted fiercely, her hands clenched.

" 'Tisn't she I'm after—no fear o' that. I only met the beggar once, and 'twas once too often. How she's bearing up under her bereavement I don't know or care, and wouldn't think o' going to her to make inquiries."

"Then who . . . ?"

"I'll tell 'ee as we go along back, if you'm goin' the same way." Sal lurched across the road and ascended the step of the churchyard gateway. "Whereabouts is Shirley buried ?"

"Just on the other side of the War Memorial. You'll be able to find it : it's the only grave made there recently."

"All right. You wait here. I shan't be more'n a minute."

Sal opened the gate and hurried up the gravel path, a bold defiant figure stalking amid the tombstones and at length hidden from Bella by the base of the War Memorial. Bella peered past the shrubs and the yew trees to where, above the farther wall, the mellow slopes of the landscape behind Carloggas could be seen, a few clay-cones fretful on the grey horizon. All was in shadow over there, but a waft of sunlight wavered forlornly around the grave-yard, slipping across it to stab the roof of the school just below. The church stood a hundred yards to the south, a dark square tower clean-cut among the scabrous frothy outline of trees. From the corner of the cemetery nearest it came the rhythmic thud of a pick, the grating of fallen earth: the sexton digging another grave, Bella supposed:

Within five minutes Sal had returned. No tender emotion had touched her; she was grinning.

"Well, the little thing is safe enough there, I reckon," she remarked as the gate clanged behind her and the two women moved abreast up the road. "Plenty o' flowers for company, too. None from me and Ted: neither of us heard of it in time, and maybe he han't even heard of it yet, as they aren't likely to meet in the next world." Sal laughed with angry satire.

"And you're going to Meledor, you say?" asked Bella.

"Ah, yes: I'll explain that as I promised, though 'tis rather roundabout. Partly through our maid Jean. 'Twas the papers what first brought the bad news to our place —though I believe Doreen heard of it the night it happened. She seemed a bit upset that week, though she didn't say anything—always 'shamed to mention Ted or anything to do with'n. But it knocked me, as you may suppose, when I read the headline: 'Tragedy near Fox-hole: girl crushed under water-wheel', and saw the name there, plain as print. I was helping Doreen to clean out the kitchen cupboard when the paper arrived, and felt a bit queer for a moment. 'My good gar!' I says over the whitewash bowl, 'here's another stroke of it. If Ted

hadn't hanged hisself four year ago he'd have had another
chance now through his own little daughter.' 'Twould
certainly have gived him a turn, wi' the guilty feelings
that would have come back."

Bella nodded as they drew level with the wide entrance
to the recreation ground, on the corner. Colour and
movement in there on the playing fields, the swings all
occupied, children noisy around the shrubs and the
pavilion.

"Yes," she said. " 'Twas through Shirley finding out
about Ted that she went over that way at all. Hearing
talk about that place and what was done there put a
sort o' spell on her, and she couldn't rest till she'd gone
over and seen it—to her death as it proved."

"I'd wondered how she got that far from her home. . . .
And did she get inside Ted's old shanty, or no ?"

"Yes. Colly Snell found her hanky there."

"Fancy that now!" exclaimed Sal, watching a girl, just
about Shirley's age, shrieking joyously as she urged herself
higher on the nearest swing. "Touching, isn't it, to think
o' that little mite wandering around the room where
Ted and Minnie had spooned for her, thinking her little
childish thoughts of it, and then hustled away to have
her insides crushed out ?" Sal's eyes grew bitter, and she
continued in a changed tone, hard, grating:

"I'm being stripped pretty close, Mrs. Stribley. Me
son hanging hisself, me grandchiel getting killed—exciting enough, but more excitement than sense to my view
of it."

A garage was just ahead, a van taking in petrol outside
it, several men about, and Bella waited until they had
passed out of earshot before replying:

"No need to be downhearted, my dear. You can't have
another son, but as for losing your granddaughter—that's
easy remedied."

"It don't look very likely wi' neither one o' me maids,"
responded Sal. "Doreen's going along stodgy and tame

—nothing won't happen there till they'm married, if it do even then; and as for Jean—she's a sly one and can take good care of herself: no innocent little village maid who could get caught through not knowing enough for safety."

Bella tucked the parcel under her arm and observed with a twisted, sidelong smirk:

"We've been hearing a good bit about that girl."

"Well, she is running a trifle wild: Ted would be proud of her if he'd lived to see all she's up to. Making it too hot for Doreen—and even her dad isn't so pleased as he ought to be when he hears the doings down in parlour some evenings. I let her bring in a chap to amuse herself with when Doreen's safe off at Rescrowsa; and one or two other maids drop in sometimes, though we shan't be honoured with Miss Lagor's company."

There was a short silence while Sal probed the widening landscape. Her gaze lit at length upon the rambling mass of sand-dunes across the valley, a mile north-west, and the cottages scattered along the hillside. She pointed, as one glad of a distraction.

"Ah! there's Meledor. Haven't been there for years, though I know it as well as you do, having lived at Trethosa so long."

Bella's curiosity seized on the fresh opening.

"And it's through Jean you're going there now?"

"Yes, partly. 'Tis like this: When Jean come in that day I seed on the paper about Shirley, she was naturally interested in it—read the account all tea-time. Then all at once I saw that she was looking across at me wi' a funny little smile on her face, all sly and secret. 'What's up now?' I says. 'Nothing to do wi' you, is it, that Ted's kid's dead and buried?' And she held out the paper, pointing for me to read. 'Noticed that?' she says. ' "The child was found by Mr. Garth Joslin." ' 'Well,' I flinged back at her, 'what about that? There's Joslins at Meledor, but I never heard o' Garth that I know of.' 'I've heard of him, anyhow,' says Jean, all sneering, and she went on in that quiet, mysterious tone she'd put on when she wants to madden me: 'I'd like to go out there and fish him up. I'd be able to get the details for 'ee.' Doreen looked tensed up, as if she knowed the details already and was minded o' something uncomfortable. 'I s'pose you've met him sometime here in town?' I asked over me tea-cup. 'No,' says Jean, 'not him.' 'Then what do 'ee mean,' I says, 'to make such a mystery o' finding his name in the paper?' She didn't answer for a minute, then she looked up at me and over to Doreen. 'You mind one night back in February there was a man found drunk up here in Bodmin Road?' 'Well, I did hear of it,' I said——or p'raps 'twas Doreen answered that time: I can't remember exactly, but I'm giving 'ee the sense of it, Mrs. Stribley.''

"Well," rejoined Bella in a light tone of secret enjoyment. "How did she link up that poor wreck with Garth?"

"We asked her what connection there could be, as she said she'd never met this Mr. Joslin; and she went on to tell how this drunk chap had meant to come in our place —surprised me, as she hadn't breathed a word of it before. She said he'd told her he was worked up because his wife was carrying on with this Joslin fellow. She couldn't mind his name, but from the account in the paper she knew the man who found Shirley was the one he'd spoke of."

Bella nodded.

"That's stale news to us. It's made quite a stir around here. The fellow's Seth Spragg: he and my husband are very thick. He rambled about Jean when he got home and his wife figured he'd had good cause to know she was Ted's sister."

Sal laughed, glancing stealthily at the houses—mainly bungalows at this northern end of the village, and on both sides of the road. She responded in a low tone, but with gusto:

"Well, his wife can put her mind at rest on that point.

The chap never darkened our doors, and I'm pretty certain nothing happened between he and Jean. He was too drunk to tickle her fancy—a little weakling with glasses, she said. Scarecrow like that'd never get even a kiss from Jean. She's very partic'lar about her boy friends —and woe betide the bloke who took liberties!"

They had now reached the top of Trethosa Road at the turning above Treneague, and Bella glanced along the lane Garth had followed on that fateful evening a fortnight ago, into Tregargus Wood. It was densely shadowed by trees, and in the gloom a labourer could be seen moving homeward to his dwelling in the heart of the copse.

Bella's face showed relish and some surprise, and she said musingly:

"Well, if that's so—if Seth never laid hands on the girl —that is a good joke! Edith's mad to get her own back because she's sure he went the whole hog that night."

"But hadn't she been carrying on wi' this Garth Joslin ? Jean said so."

"Garth was her first love, but they parted and have hardly exchanged a word for years. His mother was put to Bodmin. . . ."

"Yes, Jean mentioned that."

"And then—my family took a hand." Bella paused, as if deliberating whether to tell more, then resumed with a flick of her podgy fingers:

"My little niece—very much Jean's type—was down on holiday from London: only just fifteen then, though she was a fine girl in figure. And Garth happened to find it out."

"What—and she only fifteen ?" cried Sal.

"Yes. Didn't Jean mention it ?"

Sal shook her head.

"Couldn't have heard that part—and I shan't tell her. If she found he was that sort she might make a bolt out here, and things is tangled enough as they are. She said he was living alone there."

"He is—and in bed now. Caught a chill while he was out searching for Shirley. 'Twas heavy showers that night, and the shock o' finding a corpse was enough in itself to bring on a fever. You may find one o' the neighbours in with him."

A scowl darkened Sal's face, her voice held a rasp of vexation.

"Ah! I didn't expect this—always some snag. . . . But anyhow, they could hardly turn me from the door, knowing what a grannie must feel at losin' all that was left in the world of her famous son. You've already gived me some idea o' what happened, so I needn't stop long."

The pair hurried onward between the high hedges of a strip of road lonely, tortuous. Sal's lean figure bustled jerkily beside the swaying bulk of the younger woman. Bella had given several more details of Garth's old scandal before, when Meledor was again in view, they left the highway.

Coming to a stile by the roadside they crossed it, taking a short cut through some fields, and a few minutes later emerged at Trethosa village.

Here they almost collided with Edith's father, slumped moodily against a corner of the hedge where the field path ended. His face had the sulky, baffled look of one recovering from a scene in which his authority had been flouted.

Bella nodded a greeting, but Chirgwin continued to puff sourly at his pipe, frowning across the square at the thatched cottage on the mound where children could be heard noisily quarrelling.

When the two women were out of earshot Bella leaned her head close to Sal's and whispered:

"That's Seth's father-' law—looks hopeful, don't he ?"

Sal cocked her brows, but her response was glum, spiritless:

"Wishin' he never had a daughter, I bet. . . . You ha'n't got no kids, I s'pose, Mrs. Stribley ?"

"Oh! no. Garth told me once, when he was in a temper, that I haven't got guts enough; and I expect he's right." Bella tittered. "Edith hasn't sprung anything, either—luckily for 'em all if she and Seth mean to part, as I hear they do."

Silence ensued until the pair reached the level road scoring the dale, from which the heights of Meledor looked particularly wild and savage, a grandeur of grey peaks and craggy moorland and bud-swollen trees. Features lower down the slope had a cramped, fragile appearance. Virginia Wood seemed like a little green nut that was about to be cracked by the closing pincers of the gorge. The railway line that followed the upper bank of the Fal was occupied by a row of trucks, huddled like would-be suicides on a ledge backed by drying-sheds and with the river panting and crawling just below.

At the foot of Meledor hill Bella directed Sal to Garth's abode and the two women parted.

Sal did not hurry up the lane; she wished to ruminate a little on Bella's news before hearing Garth's account, and it was fully fifteen minutes later that she entered his garden.

Confused sounds came from the bedroom as she approached the house, but after she had knocked the whole dwelling remained deathly quiet. She waited awhile, then rapped again, and was about to lift the latch when the bedroom window was banged open and a voice that seemed to be trembling with rage and fright addressed her.

"What've you come here for?"

Sal stepped back on to the garden between the low shrubs that bordered it near the door. She raised her eyes, guardedly and with astonishment. The bedroom window was not far above her, and she could see clearly the features of the woman leaning out, her black hair disordered, her face white, tense, feverish.

"Shouldn't think you need to ask why I'm here, if you know who I be," observed Sal with a bland, conciliatory smile.

"I know that," returned Edith; she grimaced.

"Well, seeing on the papers about me little grandchiel, and how 'twas Mr. Joslin found her, I thought he'd be able to give me some particulars of it."

Edith remained stony, inflexible.

"I'm sorry. Garth's ill and can see no one. He's got to be kept quiet."

Edith's voice, and, indeed, her whole aspect, showed that further pressure would be dangerous. Sal glared around the garden for a minute, biting her lip, then accepted the repulse with an air of sardonic detachment.

"Well, if you won't let me in you won't," she mumbled. "I shan't make no unpleasantness. A Mrs. Stribley—friend o' yours, I believe—have told me most o' what I wanted to find out: met her down churchyard. She said, too, that I'd probably find a neighbour here. Be you a neighbour?"

"Yes."

"And might I be mistook if I guessed you was—er—Mrs. Spragg?"

Edith drew back; Sal heard her gasp, and saw her bony hand seize on the window frame.

"No offence, old dear," Sal insisted. "If you'm Seth's wife I got good news for 'ee."

Between tight lips came Edith's rejoinder:

"If you've seen Bella she's sure to have blabbed everything."

"And a good job," continued Sal, lowering her voice and brushing the flat top of a shrub with her hand. "It seem you've been under a missment about your man gettin' drunk and that in St. Austell back in February. He never come near our place, and as for carrying on with Jean—the idea could never ha' entered your head if you knowed the maid as I do. You jumped to the wrong sense, missus, and I'm sorry to find 'ee here, trying to make Mr. Joslin pay for what never happened—if I've guessed aright!" Sal's eyes twinkled, but she resumed earnestly:

CHAPTER EIGHTEEN

"If I was you I'd make it up wi' your man instead o' driving him to something worse."

A smile, icy, sneering, broke the fevered set of Edith's countenance.

"Thanks for your advice: you can take it back to St. Austell."

Sal had exhausted her persuasive power, and feared that a lengthy argument would spoil such dignity as remained in the situation. She lurched across the garden with a gesture of dismissal.

"Well, so long, and the same to you, Mr. Joslin, if you can hear me in there!"

Whether Garth heard or not, there came no response from within.

Sal hurried back along the path and into the road.

A few minutes later Edith also emerged, hastily attired, and followed the elder woman. The two figures passed down the hill, out of each other's sight but viewing the landscape through a similar spiritual miasma of humiliation and bankruptcy.

Chapter Nineteen

THE woman who greeted Griffiths in the square, dwarfed under the north-west front of Truro Cathedral, on the afternoon of May-day, looked more than three months older than the woman Sal Blewett had baited on Lemon Quay in February. Minnie's black clothes of mourning shrouded a figure wrenched and warped, the vitality drained from it, though her eyes, scanning Griffiths' twitching face, were brave and trustful, the pale lips forcing a smile weary but with no more of bitterness than they had shown when she last parted from him.

She had received a letter from Griffiths a week ago,

expressing deep sympathy and a desire to continue their friendship. The letter had revealed an ardent affection that left Minnie in no doubt of his motive, but it was surprisingly free from extravagance. She had decided that there was no risk in resuming her meetings with him; she seized even gratefully on what might prove an insurance. Life at Egypt was restful, but she knew that in time it would pall. With Muriel married, her parents ageing and Doris perhaps seeking another home in a few years, she would find the loneliness intolerable. The nature of Minnie's first trouble had shown her to be a woman made for love; beneath her stolid manner were deep tides of impulse. Now that Ted's death was followed by Shirley's that past affair was dead also. She could start afresh, and perhaps Griffiths——! She was conscious of a more intimate regard for him, and scarcely resisted it now that only her own life was concerned in the flooding out of her springs towards such a hazard. She knew no eligible young men; years of suffering were needed to make any one a fit mate for her.

She realised that Griffiths was passionate, and now in his prime of life his appetites were no doubt strong. But she was not squeamish, and if she married him she would give him all he wanted. She believed him to be sincere and strictly moral in his habits at present, whatever slough he had been dragged through during his luckless marriage. His agnosticism was of the Victorian rather than the modern type—not an excuse for laxity, but a genuine doubt allied with dynamic will-power still on the side of virtue. His ethical code was passably Christian and he had a vague reverence for the human spirit in its nobler expressions. This had given him a sneaking regard for Garth, while intensifying his hatred of the Christian superstitions that, in Griffiths' view, had seized like parasites upon the finest qualities of Garth's nature—its loyalty, self-sacrifice, stoic endurance—wasting them in a fruitless and fantastic bargaining with the dust.

CHAPTER NINETEEN

Griffiths had almost lurched up to Minnie now on sighting her in front of the cathedral steps. He held her hand a long while before dropping it; obviously he was much moved.

"This is our saddest meeting, Miss Lagor."

His voice trembled, seemed ready to break from restraint. Minnie's, too, was unsteady, though not emotional, as she answered:

"Yes. I wasn't sure 'twould be worth while, and thought first, when I got your letter, that I couldn't say I'd come. But then I felt 'twas no good to sit around up at Egypt and mope and worry: I must try to get out, get braced somehow. I've never been the sort to give way to me feelings—always bore up and went on, whatever happened."

"I admire your spirit," said Griffiths; his eyes glowed, fixed upon her big, homely face so intently that she glanced quickly aside. "I wish I had been nearer at the time, or heard sooner. You must have wondered at my silence."

"No." Again she looked up. "To tell the truth, I hardly thought of you at all the first week or so. The shock was too close."

He replied in a subdued tone, as one who has received a check:

"Naturally . . . . I had no idea what had happened until I went into the Gardens and overheard the talk of your sister and her husband. Have they given you any account of that?"

"Yes. Muriel called and said she'd seen you, the day before I got your letter last week. Rather awkward, she said, for all of 'ee."

"It was. I had no right to intrude as I did and spoil the first morning of their honeymoon; only when I heard of Shirley being gone and of your having shifted to Egypt and so forth, I couldn't rest till I'd got the fog cleared." His gloved hands clenched, he peered furtively back across the square in the direction of the Gardens. "It was very poignant when I got away alone and considered. It was Shirley I had to remember you by at that time, as I hadn't seen you on my visit to Meledor. Shirley was the first person I saw there that Easter Saturday, gathering wood on the sand-dump. She came down the hill with me, telling me about her 'daddy' and how she wished 'Grannie Tab' to die so that she could go and live at Egypt. . . . To think that exactly a week later she was to be laid in the churchyard! Monstrous it still seems to me—part of the derangement of the world. Even the optimists are feeling that derangement now, with the war upsetting all their prophecies."

Minnie nodded, watching the flow of people on the narrow pavements—tense and grave-faced for the most part.

"Yes; we seem to be bungling everything in Norway. Chamberlain'll have to go, they think. . . . Not that it matters to me. I've lost already, and the war's just dream-stuff compared wi' what I know to be real. If Shirley'd been killed by a bomb I s'pose I ought to be patriotic and curse the Germans—yet here she is took away at a stroke, and the war's had no hand in it at all."

"True," said Griffiths. "Even if we could banish man's inhumanity to man we should scarcely be more secure; there'd still be the inhumanity of Chance."

For a few minutes they stood in uneasy silence, detached, feeling neither the mood of sanctuary suggested by the overshadowing fane nor the brisk defiant tempo of surrounding streets. The weather was warm, but there was plenty of cloud, splitting the sunlight into shafts that glided, shuddered or stabbed across the roads and roof-tops, shifting with the shifting of those clouds. The veering rays threw into brilliant relief now the grey Victoria spire of the cathedral, furthest up, now the twin Edward VII and Queen Alexandra spires or the green coping of the west turret, now the massive moulding of a strip of wall, a pinnacle, the arched stone and stained glass of a window; at the same time picking out in the street, here a soldier swinging along with knapsack and tin hat, heartily in and of the human scene, there a black-robed Sister of Mercy shuffling past, devoutly aloof from the unpurged crowd.

Griffiths roused at length, adjusting his grey trilby.

"Shall we go over to the quay for awhile?" he asked. "It isn't far, and we can sit and talk there now the weather's fine."

The Waterfall Gardens would give more privacy, but he wished to avoid them at present. The memory of that Trebilcock couple spooning on the seat would be too galling in contrast to the decorum he must observe with Minnie; and the shock he had received there had made the place repellant apart from the direct emotional tones.

"As you like," responded Minnie, and side by side the pair moved forward.

They strolled around the north-western end of the cathedral and along an alley that lay completely in the shadow of the fane, breathing the peculiar oppressive atmosphere which is usual where a vast ecclesiastical structure overawes, by mere size and closeness, the human elements of shop and dwelling-place. The jutting wings of the building encroached upon the pavement, reducing it to a few inches in width. The ground in the recesses was turfed, and outside the chancel, enclosed by high railings, a triangular lawn sloped south-east towards the river. Having passed beyond this they threaded their way through several mean, crooked streets, and were soon confronted by the open suburb of the city, the broad river gleaming out towards Malpas, free of smoke from the warehouse chimneys, which was being blown inland.

Buildings here were of a harsher kind, suggesting the activities of a dock area. Outside one of them were a number of granite headstones and crosses, at which Minnie glanced with a deep sad look that held both tenderness and aversion. Shirley's grave! She had no money to spare for adorning it, but perhaps, if and when she married——!

They reached the bridge in silence and paused at the parapet. Griffiths leaned over the curved wall, taking in the quiet charm of this the most westerly city of England. Some boats drawn up on the shingle just north of the bridge, screened by thick bushes; the river winding back, fast narrowing, through the maze of walls and streets, upon which seagulls and sunshafts pulsed intermittently. The cathedral rising grey and lonely above the green water, beyond a bend where the next little bridge linked the centre of the city with the blob of dwellings on the eastern hillside. All very clear, and yet dreamy under the mute host of clouds, while, as Griffiths watched, the stabbing notes of a cuckoo trailed down on the river-scented breeze. Spring! Voiceless and colourless for him, unless——! Dare he——?

With an abrupt, impatient movement he stepped off the kerb and said in muffled tones:

"We'll go along to the quay—more comfortable to sit down."

Minnie inclined her head and slowly followed him.

Beside the bridge a flight of steps dropped southward to the quay, the landward side of which was prettily laid out with lawns, flower-beds, seats, a path slanting through the toll-booth to the landing-stage where the pleasure steamers plying between here and Falmouth were moored in peace-time. No vessels were in sight now, and few people—an elderly man seated, reading, on one of the benches, two women strolling on the outer wharf, a young couple talking together by the toll-booth wall.

Griffiths and Minnie descended the steps and seated themselves on the nearest bench, facing the river. A line of shrubs blocked their view of it where it passed under the bridge, but did not conceal the fringe of Lemon Quay beyond. Minnie remembered as she looked. That encounter with Sal Blewett! Mrs. Lagor's hints—the uncertainty about Shirley! And then—Garth! All part of a past life: inexorably those actors had been swept on, their problems taken and solved by Shirley's death, even Garth's—for who knew what might come, or have come already, through his finding of her ?

Griffiths broke in upon her reverie, leaning close, speaking as on an impulse and with a strained smile.

"What do your good people at Egypt say to your meeting me again ? Do they approve ?"

She turned her eyes quickly, frankly to his.

"They don't interfere."

"I can understand their anxiety," he went on. "I know country people have a dread of their daughters getting thick with strange men—foreigners as you Cornish call them. But it isn't as if you were a young girl."

"No. That's what they say."

"I suppose they wonder whether . . . they think there may be something serious developing ?"

"I don't know all they think. They're waiting to see; and they won't see any rash move."

Griffiths' face clouded, he breathed heavily and drew away to the end of the seat. It was a full minute before he had mastered and turned back the impulse that had led him towards indiscretion. Again his voice was subdued, though eager and sincere.

"I quite understand, Miss Lagor. I aren't the man to take advantage of these tragic circumstances. I will only say that in me you have a friend as long as you need one, and if—if as time goes on ‑you come to feel—to want anything deeper—then my lips will be unsealed."

Minnie had flushed, and she spoke feelingly.

"I thank you, Mr. Griffiths. I aren't sure o‘ meself yet. I need time to think it over. I've guessed, o' course, for a good while, how you felt, and that sooner or later. . . . But I know I'd regret acting hasty, on the spur o' the moment, if you was to speak now as I almost expected."

"I wouldn't think of rushing you into anything, committing you, until you've seen all round the situation. It's completely changed now and puts your whole future in the balance. For me, just another false step wouldn't matter much . . . though I don't feel it would be a false step. . . . I'll give you time—weeks or months as you may require; and you won't forget, I know, that I, too, am suffering."

A spasm of violence wrenched him; he drew a handkerchief from his pocket, but thrust it back unused, crumpled in his fist.

"I assure you that your friendship means more than ever to me now. Both of us seem singled out for the spite of whatever Power presides over human destinies."

Minnie glanced up at the bridge as an Army lorry rumbled across it, full of troops.

"It seemed hard, yet I'm coming to feel that Garth looked at it right. 'Twas wonderful how he spoke of his feelings when he came upon Shirley lying dead—that the worst was past, and not so bad as it might have been."

Griffiths nodded, adapting himself, yet not losing sincerity.

"I fully appreciate that viewpoint, and . . . in fact, I did feel it might perhaps be what pious people call a blessing in disguise."

"Yes. I'd begun to fear what Shirley'd be in a few years' time. She'd took a step the wrong way: her going over to that shack at all showed what a power the bad influence was having on her—the past coming back to claim and ruin her. Folks ought to have held their tongues, but you know how unkind they are to such children. They'd been glad to see her forced down in the mud; and Garth said when the first step had been took God caught her to Himself so that she could never take another."

Griffiths cleared his throat and asked evasively:

"You haven't been back to Mr. Snell's since?"

"No; I'm glad things worked that I could leave there. I dunno how I'd have borne it if grannie'd stayed at Egypt and I'd been tied down to Meledor still. To see the rooms where Shirley'd played every day since she learnt to walk. . . ." Minnie's lip quivered; and gently Griffiths put in:

"Your grandmother is still in the—er—hospital?"

"Yes: not likely to last long, doctor says. She had another bad attack last week: mother was called in there."

"And Mr. Joslin—have you seen him since the funeral?"

"Only once, when his illness was coming on. 'Twould only make talk if I'd kept going there afterwards—though my keeping away han't saved him from that. There's another scandal out about him—every day we get somebody dropping in and mentioning it." Minnie's arm flounced in a gesture of contempt.

"It makes me sick, the way people will go on badgering that chap. Whatever he did, he's suffered enough for it. Why can't they let him alone?"

Griffiths' thick brows were raised, ironic.

"What's the trouble this time?"

"It seems Edith—his old flame—came up to see him while he was in bed, and—of course, you can guess what they'd make of that."

"H'm!" said Griffiths, and a dry smile lifted his short grey moustache. "Well, human nature is a tricky thing, Miss Lagor. I told him the time of disillusion would come, and if it came through his first girl—he might slip back, you know. He's a rebel at heart, I felt that—outside all your little parochial morals."

Minnie's face was shadowed; she was staring across Lemon Quay with a puzzled air.

"Yes; and it does seem Edith sprung a bombshell o' some sort on him."

"Why—is he still in bed?"

"Not now. He's downstairs again and goes out, but they say he looks ghastly. Mr. Snell told me so when I met him at Treviscoe last Sunday. Like a man stunned and broke—indeed, Colly said he's as bad as Seth Spragg, and some think it's for the same reason."

Griffiths crossed his legs, his lips pursed for a moment.

"Garth told me Spragg had fallen for some—woman of the town. His wife would naturally be out for revenge. . . . A nasty fall for Garth if he gave in to her."

Minnie remained stubborn, her mouth and jaw set obstinately.

"I don't believe he's given in, or that he ever will. . . . He helped me through the shock—steadied me and gave me faith. I don't think you could have said anything to comfort me like he did, Mr. Griffiths."

This personal thrust caused Griffiths some embarrassment; he had not expected it, and replied almost irritably:

"Well, of course, one doesn't become a rationalist exactly for comfort. It's rather that an honest mind must admit that there's no such thing as real comfort, only various dodges of escapism, sentimentality and illusion. Most people dare not face the truth that life is cruel by the necessity involved in the defects of natural law, and kind only by accident or by some unlikely and very shirt-lived fluke in the timing of events."

Minnie looked at him steadily, questioning, ill at ease. Such talk was too deep for her comprehension, but it revealed the gulf between them and made her shrink as from an icy wind that smote up from it, chilling her sympathies.

"Wasn't it the . . . the way your wife carried on that made you feel that?" she inquired in slow, hesitant tones.

"Yes, chiefly, though the war had begun it, for me as for millions of others. But it was the conduct of my wife in London that at last cut into my vitals and cauterized every shred and fibre of religious belief."

Minnie straightened, gazing out through the toll-booth passage. The young couple had strolled to the far end of

184

the quay, the women had left it, the elderly man retired to the lavatory. She and Griffiths had this side of the little garden to themselves, and emboldened by the privacy she became more brisk in manner.

"That's the main trouble between us, Mr. Griffiths. I know nowadays people get married without bothering about each other's beliefs, but it don't seem to work well, judging by all these divorces and that. I don't think I could be happy with a man who *would* keep on believing that everything's meaningless. 'Twould take all the heart out o' me. What's the good of anything I might do, any sacrifice I'd make, if you'd treat it as a accident or fluke, as you just said ?"

She paused, shot him a stealthy glance and felt a twinge of pity for him: he looked haggard, tense, staring at some white butterflies that fluttered about the shrubbery.

"And if," she went on, resolved now to speak her mind fully on this point—"if some woman came into your life so that looking back you'd see that all the misery was only preparing you for the happiness at last, then if you still say it's without any purpose the experience would die out again. It couldn't live if you wouldn't give it air, and a sensible woman wouldn't try it if you was determined to stifle it like that."

He lifted his face, twitching—a gleam of torture in the deep baffled eyes.

"Honesty can be a bitter thing, Miss Lagor"—he almost muttered the words. "We must await developments, that's all. No good can come of arguing these things now: everything's in flux."

He passed a hand over his face, closing his eyes behind it for a minute, and when next he looked round he noted with a start that they were no longer alone.

A woman had descended the steps from the bridge and halted within a few yards of their seat. She was peering about the quay, evidently in search of someone. Gaudily attired, stout, middle-aged, with a dark coarse face too

185

heavily made-up. Griffiths recognised her, and as her eyes met his he forced a greeting.

"How d'you do, Mrs. Palmer?"

The woman lurched forward, leering at Minnie, a grin on her thick lips.

"Ah! You're the gent who lodges across the street from us, aren't yer?"

"Yes," he answered shortly, regretting that he had encouraged such freedom.

"Called Griffiths, I believe? I've heard Miss Jesty speak of yer—how you came down from London last year, same as I've done."

"I did; but not because o' the war."

"Well, I guess you're glad yer came, now you got company." Noting the quick angry flush on Minnie's face the woman added at once, jerking a long arm around the enclosure:

"I don't s'pose you've seen a young lady hanging around here—tall and thin, wearing a fawn coat and blue hat?"

"No," replied Griffiths. "We haven't been here long."

"Young pal o' mine she is—or was rather," Mrs. Palmer continued. "Agreed to meet me here on the bridge at half-past two. We was going to Falmouth for a spree, but I didn't feel sure of her—thought she might give me the slip again." Mrs. Palmer half turned, mumbling:

"I don't find it easy to get going with these Cornish —they're a snobby lot." Abruptly her mood changed, she cast at Griffiths a deep, sly, mysterious look, and said almost with mockery:

"A pity me friend isn't here now, though. She'd have been glad to meet you, I expect, if she knew who yer are as well as I do."

Minnie, glancing in surprise at the man beside her, saw that he, too, was speechless with astonishment.

Chapter Twenty

GARTH laid down the book on the wooden platform upon which he was sitting, part of the tip framework at the top of a clay-dump behind Meledor. He dropped his head, slumped forward with elbows on his knees, and remained motionless, supported by the rail that guarded the edge of the platform—a grey huddled shape, the only human figure visible in the wide waste of the plateau, and a fit match for its desolation.

This sand-hill was slightly north of the spot where he had halted on his return from Bodmin on that fateful January evening when his mother had passed from his life and Edith entered it afresh, paving the way for the blow under which he staggered yet, though three weeks had gone since that dreadful scene in the bedroom.

The succeeding days had dragged over Garth like a nightmare. His mind was still clouded, viewing all outward things distortedly as through smoked glass. He refused every distraction, and seemed to have recovered from his illness through a perverse resolve to be again master of the house, unmolested. He no longer even read the newspapers—merely glanced at the headlines when the paper came each day, then tossed it wearily aside and returned to his brooding. His brain received no clear idea of what was happening in the world: the Norwegian fiasco was as a phantasmagoria to him, dimly and monstrously flickering: he saw defeats, confusions, swelling out fantastically from the one spring, this opened vein of disaster in his own heart, the news of Irma. His actions were mechanical, slovenly; he ate little and kept no regular meal-times. Even now, though it was Sunday, he had not thought of putting on his best clothes, but wore his ordinary clayey corduroy trousers and ragged black coat, without a collar or tie. He hadn't shaved for two days, and the dark stubby growth showed more clearly the fevered pallor of his flesh. His hair had grown long and was tangled, bare to the breeze that swept gustily across these heights.

Now and then he had sought instinctively to throw off the torpor, regain balance, and had snatched at the obvious supposition. Edith may have lied. The whole story might be a falsehood conceived by her as a last desperate resort to break his will. But the effort to persuade himself of this soon collapsed now that he had no faith to support him against conclusions which he had always known to be natural. That Irma should have forgotten him, passed to others long ago, and be now—dead, married, seduced—anything but his prepared mate—this was so probable that he could not resist the spoken testimony, and now that his fevered revolt had ebbed he felt even disinclined to investigate it.

Yet there was still a nerve in Garth that resisted the final paralysis, one fact in which he found encouragement. Sal Blewett! Why had she come at that crucial hour, when Edith, having weakened him by her news, was bent on conquest? She had leaned over the bed to kiss him just as Sal's knock sounded. Had there been no interruption—who knew what he might now have had on his conscience? He'd certainly felt very queer and unbalanced —might have strangled her, or even, if the touch of her lips whetted his starved senses——! And instead—that abrupt turn, breaking the temptation, sending Edith away from him mortified, ashamed, silent.

Garth was sure he had nothing further to fear from her. She'd come to Meledor that day resolved that it should be "now or never"; and being baffled so, reminded by Sal of the misconception that had led her to that reckless assault, she would invite no more such indignities. He hadn't seen her since, but he brooded frequently upon that strange conjunction. Sal's coming had saved him from taking some irrevocable step into the dark. But why, if Irma was not to be his?

He stirred at length and mechanically picked up the book—a small Bible, much worn and tattered, its binding whitened with clay-dust and scratched through contact with gravel, rock, nails, iron fastenings and other rough materials around the moors and clayworks. It had long been his habit to take the Bible with him when he went out to spend an evening in the solitude of the heath. Sometimes, when there was a bright moon, he had stayed out till midnight, hunched as now upon some deserted dune or squatting on a ridge of the bare downs, drawing from this book the sustenance of his passion for Irma. He had not discarded it now; it still gave his mood, even his stupor, a language.

Pushing the Bible back into his coat pocket he rose with slow and painful effort, holding on to the handrail above the platform. He was standing on the edge of the pyramid, and beyond this the waggon-track projected for a dozen feet, unsupported. The platform was nailed beside it, enabling the tip workers to reach and lubricate the grooved wheel at the end of the track, over which the wire rope passed, taut, one end 'linked to the waggon half-way down the dune, the other wound about the big drum in the engine-house across the clay-pit.

Garth moved stiffly up the narrow gangway, that shook under his tread, and stood at the top of it, a sheer drop of a hundred feet beneath him. But he did not look down: he looked into the heavens. Change there too, exhaustion, decay. When he left home an hour ago all the clouds up there had been white, crisp as snowballs, but sunset had now stained them, adding a touch of symbolism to their appearance.   Those in the west were red and shiny as tomatoes, those overhead were purple, with here and there a brassy tinge on the underside, while those riding eastward were of a dull grey deepening to black. The clear spaces between them, that had been blue, were turning steely, and the distant ridges of the clay range beyond Kernick and Trethosa already dwelt in a sombre shade which was not that of cloud. Garth brooded upon that advancing wave of twilight, and upon the tinted cloud-groups, as if he saw the successive phases of his own life mirrored therein. Flamboyant hope passing to purple shame and grey misery.

He was aroused by a faint scrattling sound behind him, followed by the eager yelp of a dog. He turned, just in time to see a rabbit dart into a hole near the edge of the pyramid, under a sort of gravel bank thrown up by the cuddy. Close behind it came a brown spaniel, its tongue lolling and its pace already slackened by the chase up the steep side of the dune. The creature had not observed Garth, and as he watched it began scratching frantically with its forepaws at the mouth of the hole, thrusting in its nose and giving short, excited barks. Garth caught his breath in a slight gasp, recognising the animal. Edith's dog, Prince! He stared, harrowed by the sudden pounce of memory. Those courtship days of his at Trethosa! Prince had been only a pup when he spent those evenings in the Chirgwins' home, lived those scenes—false now, nostalgic, bitter! The firelit room, Edith crouching on the floor, smiling up at him while she played with that dog. So restful, so—so sure it had seemed; and then—his mother! . . .

The presence of Prince here on the dump suggested to Garth a more personal challenge in the neighbourhood. He glanced uneasily down upon the heath, and was hardly surprised to note the hobbling figure of Seth Spragg approaching along the hedgeless track from Meledor. In his best clothes—grey raincoat, trilby, navy blue trousers; but even this did not make him look less pitiful and weakly, at that distance. Seth's face was lifted, he was gazing straight at Garth, and as Garth spotted him he beckoned—a violent gesture.

Garth gave no response; he stood like a stone, scarcely breathing, his hands clenched on the rail, eyes hard, glowing. The only sound or movement on the ridge were those of Prince pawing and whimpering in bafflement about the rabbit-hole.

All doubt of Seth's intention was removed when he drew abreast of the sand-hill. Leaving the path he struck in across the rutted waste-land and around to the waggon-track where it reached the level of the moor at the clay-pit's verge. He began climbing up between the sleepers —the easiest means of ascent—his progress unobserved by Garth, who did not turn as Seth passed around to his rear. Not until Prince left his fruitless assault and trotted back with tail wagging to greet his master did Garth move stiffly down the platform to the solid ridge of the pyramid. The dog heard him and paused, looking from Seth to the stranger with a puzzled air, then gave a ringing bark and approached Garth with nose raised, sniffing, as if vaguely reminded of those old intimacies.

The two men faced each other, dwarfed by the beams of the tip, rising twenty feet on either side of the waggon-track, a cross-bar at the summit completing the gallows-like structure. Viewed from below, there was something fantastic in the sight of that pair, tiny and trivial figures, subtly antagonistic, framed up there on the pyramid's point against the sunset sky.

Seth broke the silence, jerking his arm clumsily, speaking with constraint and with an effort to make himself agreeable.

"Just wanted to see you, old man. Found your door locked, so I thought you might be out around the work-shop, and when I got there I seen you here on the burrow."

"Well?" Garth's tone was curt, his hands on his hips, his whole attitude defensive.

Seth shuffled, toeing the iron rail of the waggon-track as he asked evasively:

"Going to start work to-morrow?"

"No, next week—though I wish I needn't."

"Yes—a pity you held on to that job. I told Martin the other day that's what's kept you tied down in this rut."

"What rut?"

"About Irma." Seth moved a step closer, looking strained, earnest, and said in his flat, sulky voice: "All this tangle might never have happened if you'd got a job away from that place and never set eyes on it again."

Garth leaned back against the cuddy wall of rough piled stones, fingering the zinc roof that was less than six feet from the ground.

"No good thinking o' that now," he muttered. "We're here and got to go through wi' things as they are. Whatever your trouble, you're in a better plight than I am."

"I aren't so sure," replied Seth. "Say you'd married the wrong woman—wouldn't that ha' been worse?"

Garth's teeth gritted:

"God knows! I've got as much as I can bear, and what turn it'll take next. . . . I feel sometimes it may be the war'll solve everything—the one final way."

"You'll soon be called up, won't 'ee?"

"In a few months. I shouldn't mind if 'twas sooner —that is, if . . . ." He paused, peered again up into the sky, and stretching out an arm he said with sombre intensity:

"If there's some bomb wi' my number on it I'd thank God if it fell here now."

"Well, I don't say I'd have much objection to being wiped out, meself," responded Seth. "We're both in a hell of a fix—all through these women. 'Twas a bad patch we struck in 1935—played beastly tricks on us that year did."

Garth remained silent for a few minutes, hunched against the wall, his head bowed, watching Prince, who had returned to the rabbit-hole and was trying to wriggle himself inside. Seth also watched the dog, his hollow face catching the pale tint of the afterglow, the glare of clouds reflected on his spectacles.

Presently Garth straightened and spoke with more vigour, his eyes fixed upon Seth with awakening malice.

"You didn't come up to tell me that, did you? Don't it cut deeper—something more recent?" He glanced around at the narrow neck of sand, uneven, strewn with boulders, and a grim smile touched his lips.

"Rather dangerous place for a fight."

Seth shrugged.

"I don't want to fight," he mumbled. "Nothing between us that need be settled in that way."

"Oh! I thought there was." Garth's voice taunted now openly, his face was dark, with ugly lines playing about it, breaking up the dazed surface. "Men usually get a bit wild when their wives start kicking loose after other fellows."

"I can't in this case. You had her first, and ought to have hung on. I was a fool to marry the bitch."

"Well, you needn't call her names like that," said Garth dryly. "She's still faithful to you—though I'm afraid that's my fault rather than hers."

Seth frowned, blinking down over the scarp towards Trethosa, his hand on the tip beam.

"I know it took a wrong turn—could tell that the moment I seen her after she came back. She come up against something she didn't bargain for."

"From Sal Blewett—you've heard of it, I expect?"

"A few words—not from her in the first place. They was saying around the village that Sal and Edith came down Meledor hill one behind the other, and I asked her if 'twas true. She admitted Sal had called and spoilt the fun, though she wouldn't give no details."

Garth spat, stepping free of the wall.

"Sal told her you hadn't gone as far as gossip made out —that night in St. Austell, with Jean."

"Well, as a matter of fact, I didn't," confessed Seth casually lighting a cigarette; "only I was d—— well fed up and didn't care what Edith thought. Glad to make her believe the worst."

"Sal advised her to try and make it up with you, and

keep straight. In a virtuous mood Sal was, doing her good deed for the day."

Seth flushed, nettled by Garth's biting tone.

"There's nothing come of it. We've had to take the one bit o' relief we could find, and I thought I'd let you know and get the air cleared before we quit."

"Quit?" repeated Garth blankly.

"Yes. We're shifting at last."

"Leaving Trethosa?"

Seth nodded. "High time, too, better we'd gone in January instead o' Edith coming to see about your place."

"Yes; it would have saved me something I'd rather have died than know. . . . Where you setting up?"

"Down to Brighton—not far, but 'twill get us clear o' Chirgwins' lot and these neighbours here—and Edith won't be seeing you, nor anything to remind her."

"But your work——?"

"That's gone already. Retew closed down a fortnight ago. I don't s'pose you'd heard?"

"I hadn't."

"And that's what made it so urgent. . . . Not much of a house, this Brighton one—still, anything's better than staying at Trethosa. Me and Edith'd both go off our nuts if we had to stick it much longer, now I'm home all day long. Edith's people keep us muddled, and then there's the kids hanging round wi' their silly questions: 'Why don't Seth and Edith ever kiss each other now?'——or if Edith's in her sulks and won't answer a civil question it's: 'Why won't Edie speak to Seth, mummy? She's a proper baby.' And then there's a row, wi' Edith slapping the kids or shouting at 'em and her mother lecturing her, and old Chirgwin looking tensed up and ready to kick the lot of us outdoors."

"It'll be good to get free o' that . . . though it's a pity if you're called up for munitions. Edith'd have to leave the new house again and go back wi' her parents—or go to Bristol in lodgings with you."

"I know. 'Tis a desperate move, and I haven't much hope of it, as me and Edith never had any real love for each other. She blames you and'll keep on blaming 'ee, and you"—he looked closely, slyly at Garth—"I s'pose you got cause enough to blame Irma?"

Garth evaded this; his smile was bitter, his speech touched with cynicism—a quality unknown to him hitherto.

"Well, you've got your chance, and good reason for using it. Now the war's took a bad turn we must be patriotic and pull together—don't they say?"

Seth blew out a cloud of smoke—nervous, hesitant.

"I'm sorry if Edith blabbed too much what she'd heard from Bella. . . ."

"I don't want to hear more o' that," Garth broke in; he looked fevered again, backing towards the dune's edge. "If you've no more news I don't know already we may as well go down."

"Please yourself. There's nothing else, only I thought 'twould lift one worry off your mind to know Edith'll soon be out of harm's way—week after next 'tis we're shifting."

They began descending the dump, Seth returning as he had come, by the waggon-track, Garth moving straight down over the front of the pyramid directly under the platform. The gravel surface was hard now and he slithered most of the way, arriving at the bottom amid a shower of dust and sand. He stooped to flick out the gravels from the tops of his shoes, then stood erect, waiting in the shadow of the dune until Seth, preceded by Prince, appeared around its side. He strolled slowly then across the downland towards the path and said with a farewell jerk of his arm:

"You can go on out to the village. I want to turn into Meledor claywork for a bit." Defiance prompted a last glum confession. "I'm a homeless dog these days and would sleep there in the workshop instead of in me bed if the place wasn't locked up."

A warped grin spread about Seth's face, scarcely visible to Garth in the twilight.

"You're a queer devil, Garth." He sobered. "Don't mean to follow Ted Blewett's example, do 'ee ? They clay-tanks might do as well as a rope. . . ."

"No: tell Edith she needn't have that fear on her conscience."

Without a further word they parted, Seth limping on towards the bridge of Meledor clay-dump out on the brow of the scarp. He halted several times to call Prince, who kept pausing and looking back at Garth, as if he had doubts about which of these two should be his real master, Edith's husband.

Garth followed the track for some distance in the wake of Seth, then turned in along a narrow winding trail between Meledor clay-pit and the dune. Gorse grew thickly on each side, in places so tall that Garth had to hold his arms before his face as he pushed through the clumps. When he came to bare patches where layers of sand had slipped away he passed within inches of the precipice and glanced down the scarred white cliff at the clay-beds, buildings, trolleys two hundred feet below. He'd often worked down there, mending a broken window in the lodge, fitting pipes in the pump-house ; had helped to make several of those trolleys. He remembered also, dully, as he glimpsed the tip waggon half way up the incline, that he had been busy making the frame of that waggon the day Irma first came here with Stribley's dinner—had glanced up from his planing, outside the workshop, to find her standing behind him, lifting a basket and saying in rather a bored tone :

"Where must I take this ?" . . .

Garth strode wearily on around the corner of the dump, out past the pit-head lodge and up the slope towards the defile. Birds were fluttering about in there on the strip of common where he had knelt and prayed in those apocalyptic nights after Irma had gone home. The defile

was gloomy, the bushes black and blurred amid the
massing shadow. Hawthorn scent was in the air, stab-
bingly sweet; some scattered bluebells swayed on the
bank. Nature went its way, around him and in Irma,
caring nothing for his faith.

Soon he had come in sight of the workshop, the red
roof and grey stone walls looming grimly against the background of green boughs and white thorn spray. Across
the little square the clay-tanks glinted—round green pools
and long troughs of filtering slime stretching in the lee
of the dune. Several barrels containing silicate of soda
stood beside the tank steps, and passing these Garth moved
almost fearfully towards the workshop door. He hoped
against hope that it had been left unlocked by the tem-
porary carpenter—a fellow called Trevenna from Scarcewater. As he had confessed to Seth, he would rather
sleep there than at home: less repellent to lie on the bare
floor where Irma had stood in his arms than in the bed
over which Edith had so recently bent and stung him
with her deadliest venom. But as he approached he saw
the padlock hanging from the bar, and when mechanically
he lifted the latch and gave a slight push the bar merely
rattled mockingly in the socket. Shut out!

He stepped back, almost falling over the grindstone by
the doorway, and crossing to the window he peered
through the dust-laden glass. Faintly he could see the
bench just inside, and upon it some tools glimmered;
beyond that all was so dark that details were invisible.
His eyes grew hard, strained, as if he could hardly believe.
. . . Yet it was true : in there where dusk now brooded
Irma had been with him half a dozen times. There they
had talked bitterly and tensely, reverting to the mood
that had first struck them together in the Stribleys'
parlour rather than to the more light-hearted one they
had enjoyed while blackberrying on Meledor Downs.
There was so little of the usual gay badinage of youth in
their conversation that Garth should have been warned

of danger. He should have drawn back, even at the last moment when she stepped up to him for that embrace. . . .

He'd never been able to understand why he hadn't thrown her off at once. If he had just said : "Don't be silly!" and turned back to his work, he wouldn't have been mooning about here now—would probably have been married long ago to some village girl. Without that convulsion of the senses the few touches they had known elsewhere, and the spiritual idyll in Virginia coppice, would have remained for him a vague nostalgic drift of beauty, no complication of his real life. Under what spell had he consented to those moments of passion which had engrafted the sap that henceforth produced on every leaf and bud of his thought and desire the mark of Irma ?

The deserted building seemed to enforce the conclusion that it was but a momentary freak, of impulse in her and weakness in him. And leaning against the window-frame he let the waves of despair sway in, one with the darkening tide of twilight that had washed all colour from the clouds and fronted him, even in the west, with sullen grey. Minutes passed, while from the surrounding trees and the heath beyond birds flung into song the ache of the spring night, soft for them with mating bliss.

Presently Garth appeared to heed and respond, murmuring slowly some words—not words of endearment addressed to Irma as in past months, but words that he had read just now on the dune before Seth came, the language of Job.

"He breaketh down, and it cannot be built again : He shutteth up a man, and there can be no opening. . . . Where is now my hope ? As for my hope, who shall see it ?"

A long sigh followed, then his lips murmured on as his haggard face lifted towards the heavens.

"I made a covenant with mine eyes; why then should I think upon a maid ? For what portion of God is there from above ? And what inheritance of the Almighty from

198

on high ? . . . The thing which I greatly feared is come upon me, and that which I was afraid of is come unto me."

He bowed his head, slumped more heavily against the dark window, looking dazed and lifeless. And now the birds were hushed; only the moths seemed to be abroad, and flew past him silently.

Chapter Twenty-one

REMOTE country roads are usually deserted, save for a few stray lovers, at nine o'clock on Sunday evenings, but on this day, and at that hour, the wild and tortuous road between Egypt and Meledor was being followed by a young woman. She moved briskly, and though her business was not as personally gratifying as that of one going to meet a lover, it had, for the present, banished the tired, sorrowful mood to which her black clothes still bore witness.

The woman was Minnie Lagor, and not even her parents knew what mission was taking her thus abroad. Since her return from Truro four days ago she had lived in a state of suppressed excitement, a far-away look in her eyes. The Lagors suspected some crisis between her and Griffiths, and their concern had been expressed just now by Mrs. Lagor as Minnie donned hat and coat.

"You aren't goin' meet that there Griffiths somewhere around here, are 'ee—not goin' run off with'n ?"

Minnie's reply: "No, mother, it's nothing to do with him," had deepened the mystery, and they were inclined to think that her affair with Griffiths had collapsed and that she had gone out to-night, somewhat recklessly, to seek a partner among the local men.

She saw few of these on her journey, and not until she

reached Trethosa Moor did she observe one to whom she could give more than a casual greeting. The exception was Colly Snell, and he was standing alone on a step outside the little shop near the foot of Meledor hill. The green door was locked behind him, and the stick tucked under his arm rapped against it whenever he leaned backward to get a better view of some detail along the fronting slope. He kept licking his bare lips, several times jerking his head, and seemed to be engaged in a colloquy with the twilit landscape.

Minnie was surprised at this behaviour, and when he noted her approach she had more proof that his mood, too, had changed for the better since they last met. His little ape-like face was lit with the old perky humour; he drew the stick from under his arm and pointed it at her, stepping down with alacrity into the road.

"Well, Minnie! How's it goin', my dear?"

"Not so bad as I expected," she replied, halting a few yards off outside the gateway of the cottage adjoining the shop and speaking in a low tone so as not to be overheard by its occupants.

"No; you'm lookin' peart 'nough—more colour in your chacks than when I seed 'ee last. Brightened up all over."

Minnie did not explain the cause of her fresh animation, and Colly went on more guardedly:

"Keeping your friends, I hope?"

"Yes; everybody's been very kind."

"I'm glad you aren't bottling yourself up—though I shouldn't advise 'ee to make free where you belonged. Wasn't going up to our place now, was 'ee?"

"Oh no; I don't feel I want to go inside there again. You'll understand, I'm sure. . . ."

"Yes: me own nerves quailed a trifle when the house was left empty so sudden, though I believe I've got me second wind as I see how 'tis affecting my woman there in her bed."

Minnie's brows lifted in concern.

"Why—there's no bad news about your wife, I hope?"

"Bad news? No, my dear Minnie. Bad news is a thing that can never be connected wi' that woman again. She's gone too far for that. After being bedridden for nine years 'twouldn't be no bad news for me or the parish if the very worst happened."

"Well, of course I meant. . . . Have she had another stroke?"

Colly again ascended the doorstep, as if to increase the importance of his news by delivering it several inches above his normal height.

"It seems to me the worst isn't far off," he said with impressive emphasis. "She've had more rough handling lately than even her contrariness can stomach—not from me, I need hardly say; but she've been hit, Minnie. Shirley's end was a cut to her—not that she grieved about it—never had no love for the chiel; but naturally it shaked her a bit. And now wi' you gone there's plain signs of a crack coming. She's sickening, Minnie—sickening for her coffin as sure as the childern do sicken for measles. Strength giving out fast. I believe I'll be a free man afore the cuckoos do stop singing."

Minnie was looking up at the roof and chimneys of the Snells' home visible above the hedge, beyond the clay swamp.

"Well, I can understand you not being altogether sorry. . . ."

"Ah!" said Colly, leaning forward to prod the ground with his stick. "I could pitch a experience, I could, if I told all I've borne at her hands—twenty year of it afore you come there. But the end is in sight, and 'tisn't beyond a possibility that I may find meself settled wi' a real wife yet—may even give parson a christening where he'd be looking for a funeral only to follow my wedding."

Minnie smiled. "Yes, I s'pose it's possible, if you keep on the lookout."

"I've nobody definite in mind yet," Colly hastened to

explain—"wasn't thinking o' you, I mean. But the war is a handy convenience for old widowers—so many o' the young men called out o' the way. 'Tisn't always easy to keep a maid interested in a chap what isn't there. A man what's to be seen, Minnie, sometimes get the preference, though in peace time he might be too old and scraggy to be looked at twice. . . . Yes, I have me hopes; for 'tis a melancholy thing for a man to die and leave nothing behind him to carry on his crotchets."

Colly came nimbly down from the step, and crossing the road to the corner he pointed past the shop and the wild growth of trees and bushes behind it, up toward Trethosa.

"Take Reub Pollard up there," he continued with increasing fervour. "A middle-aged man half-way through his life afore he struck out for a woman he could fancy. And when that fancy come it seemed a surprisin' thing to most folks. He'd looked a bit too high, they was saying when 'twas first knowed he'd got sweet on little Miss Sandercock, our school teacher up to Meledor. Dainty little soul, fresh and pink as a daisy, and black-smithin' had made a real nigger o' Reub. Who'd have believed that such a black-faced ruffian of a man (I mean no disrespec'—quiet, decent fellow as Reub is: I was only referring to his outward looks as you see him going home from work)—but who could expect such a man to get Miss Sandercock under his arm, she so precise and correctful in all appearances? If Reub have done such a trick—why, there's hope for me yet!"

"Yes; we can all take heart at things that do happen—shows life isn't exactly what Griffiths and his clique think it."

"How I mind that Miss Sandercock!" Colly resumed, closing his eyes tight for a moment. "Used to see her every morning buckling up the lane there, books under her arm, on her way up school. Used to teach Garth in the infants' class ten year ago. . . . I wonder what she do think of him now?"

The abrupt reminder brought agitation to the forefront in Minnie. She breathed quickly, biting her lip, and glanced aside up the hill—just in time to see the dim figure of a man appear around the lower bend, emerging from the shade of massive elms. A minute later a dog bounded from the ditch out into the middle of the road, and Minnie recognized the pair. Seth Spragg and Prince!

Colly also had seen them and drew back against the hedge, something of the old suspicion sharpening his features. He leaned upon his stick and his mouth dropped open, his eyes rigidly intent upon the young man who came limping towards him with a reluctant, irritable air.

Before Seth had drawn level Colly called out with no preliminary greeting:

"I hear you'm shifting from Chirgwins' soon."

"Yes, we are." Seth jerked his thumb towards Meledor, smiling sourly. "I've just been up and told Garth."

"A pity you didn't go afore," remarked Colly, advancing from the hedge in a somewhat menacing attitude. "I seed your wife go up the hill that day—you'll know what I mean—very brassy in the face. Could see what she had in mind, and if I hadn't been a bit slight that afternoon—a bit down in me spirits and inclined to let things drift—I'd have boxed out and took her by the shoulders and marched her back to Trethosa. 'Garth's a lost man,' I thought as I watched her fling away up the road; and so 'twould appear from what I've seen of him since."

Seth flushed.

"Nothing more'n words behind it," he mumbled. "Indeed, if they'd got together and was guilty I shouldn't bother to move. I'd ha' been glad enough to turn her over to him if she could ha' broke him in to it; but 'twas all a flop."

"Where've you seen Garth—at home?" asked Minnie.

"No: out on Melbur burrow. He came down wi' me and is gone in to Meledor now. Told me he meant to sleep there in the workshop. He's half cracked I could see, and if something don't happen soon he'll be in Bodmin like his mother."

Minnie's smile puzzled both men—slow, dreamy, secret.

"Well—perhaps something will happen," she remarked.

"You don't mean you'd try *your* hand. . . ." Colly checked himself, then added as he turned to Seth: "though I have thought sometimes she seemed to have a insight into the chap. . . ."

"No—get along!" rejoined Minnie with homely bluntness. "It's nothing of that sort—as people will know before long."

Colly raised his cap and began scratching at his white head.

"What's become o' that Griffiths? Seen'n lately?"

"Yes, last week."

"And I s'pose he've proposed to 'ee—that your meaning?"

"You'll have to wait and see. . . . But I must be moving on now if I'm to get home before dark."

Dusk was, indeed, swiftly falling in along the valley, grim black outlines taking the place of detail, the clouds blown like dead ashes overhead.

Minnie hurried forward up the hill, past the Snells' abode, at which she glanced with a fearful fascination, noting the dark bedroom window behind which Shirley had slept every night for so many years. Just beyond the curtain was the bed where she had lain nearly six weeks ago, the mere clay, pale and beautiful. . . .

Reaching the hilltop Minnie turned into the lane leading to the clay-pit, her heart fluttering with a sense of apprehension. Garth was clearly desperate, at breaking point; there would be a certain emotional strain in the meeting which she dreaded. How would he react? . . .

As she turned the bend around the tank wall she looked straight across to the workshop, expecting to see either the door open or the man barred from his sanctuary.

CHAPTER TWENTY-ONE

It was the latter sight that met her, the blurred figure slumped by the window frame. His face was hidden in his coat sleeve as he supported himself with an arm against the wall. He did not hear her approach, and she stopped, hesitant, feeling something of awe at that revelation of tragic depth. Such mute despair she had never before witnessed, though she had felt something of it when the news of Shirley's death was brought to her. Garth remained quite motionless; it was difficult to conceive of that grey shape as a conscious, breathing organism.

Minnie stepped from the path on to the broad ledge in front of the workshop, advanced a few paces and said in a choked tone:

"Garth!"

His head jerked round, his arms dropped limply; she saw him sway and then stand glaring at her in a blank stupor for a full minute. At last he found his voice—dull, unnatural:

"Ah! Only you!"

The poignant pathos cut at Minnie's heart, but she forced herself to a casual opening.

"I met Seth down the hill. He told me you was here, and—and a bit upset still."

Tense silence followed, Garth struggling with the fever, the increased sense of nightmare in this fresh apparition. Presently he made a vague helpless gesture, his white dry lips barely moving as he confessed:

"I'm broke, Minnie—worse than you've been. I don't know why you've come, but you can't do anything—like I tried to do for you in your trouble."

Minnie came nearer; he noted signs of a sharp struggle in her, a hardening of resolve. She proceeded awkwardly:

"Seth tells me nothing happened between you and Edith . . . not that I believed what people said. . . ."

"No: Sal come and Edith made a bolt for it. She was a fool to try that game; only she had that card up her sleeve. . . ."

Minnie's eyes lit on his—unfathomable.

"Well, if you've nothing on your conscience—surely you needn't break down, whatever Edith blabbed? It seems strange after the way you spoke to me so recent. You had such faith—the grandeur of it gripped me; a faith that wouldn't stagger even when death struck."

He nodded, staring fixedly in through the window. Not even the bench could be seen now; all was dark.

"I know," he murmured; "and if I'd heard Irma was dead—dying true to . . . to what happened here—I'd have took it quiet, and—perhaps been thankful, feeling that our case was . . . was like Browning says about: 'high that proved too high, heroic for earth too hard, a passion that left the ground to lose itself in the sky.' I could ha' borne that—could ha' looked forward. . . . The sap being grafted, what matter which world we get the fruit in? Earth or heaven, 'twould all be one to me as long as the grafting was real and God saved it from drivelling out to such a miserable end as this."

"You've heard that Irma's—got like—like that Blewett girl at St. Austell?"

He grimaced.

"God knows! It isn't her fault, whatever she's done. It's simply that Griffiths and his crew must be right and we've got past the time when faith in a Divine purpose is any use in practical affairs. We must fall back on the defence line of ethics, self-reliance. . . . But if that's so there'll soon be no ethics left!"

His harsh, jerky laugh contrasted sharply with Minnie's mild persuasive speech:

"D'you think after you helped me as you did that God's going to let you down when you need help most? And all these years of sacrifice—is it all for nothing?"

"It seems so," he answered glumly.

"But look back. Your way to Irma was through Edith —through a false start and everything upset—losing your father and seeing your mother go cracked: all needed to make you ready. Why should you give up because . . . because Irma may have had to drift further off and take some false steps before she could learn enough to be fit for you ?"

Garth shrugged, lurching away from the window, and for several minutes he strode up and down in tortured indecision, hands clenched. Then, pausing by the grindstone, he cast a stealthy glance at Minnie's dark still figure, and said impatiently:

"I wouldn't mind her being hard-pressed, as long as she held out. I'd even hoped for that—indeed, I knew it must be, with such a home life. If she'd revolted against that . . . but she's given in to it."

"Perhaps—for awhile. Think how young she was. You mustn't be hard, Garth. Can you mean you wouldn't take her now even if she came ?"

He replied moodily:

"Depends. If that grafted power had come through, even after being choked by other growths—as long as it hadn't been messed up beyond remedy—God knows I'd take her and feel, even then, that I'd got more than I deserve."

Amid a hush that seemed awesome came Minnie's words, almost whispered:

"I believe it *has* come through."

Garth's smile was strained, bitter.

"Don't say things just to try and help. I'm beyond help from words—even these," he added, tapping the bulge in his pocket where the Bible lay.

Minnie swallowed hard.

"I wouldn't have come unless I had some real news for you—something I just *had* to let you know. The fact is, I—I believe . . . I don't think Irma's in London any longer."

A feverish interest took possession of Garth; he stood rigid as on that day when, from the lane a few yards behind where Minnie was standing now, Bella had flung at him her taunts, breaking the four years' silence.

"What d'you mean?" he brought out thickly. "You haven't heard anything from the Stribleys?"

Minnie shook her head.

"I wouldn't repeat anything I heard from that quarter. I don't think they know."

"Irma won't be there at the farm again: you reminded me o' that down on Lemon Quay last February."

"I don't take back that," said Minnie. "But—I believe Irma's in Cornwall."

"Where?"

"At Truro."

Garth leaned panting against the wall, clammy sweat on his face.

"This is crazy!" he spluttered. "How could she . . . ?"

"Evacuated. I'm just sure of it."

"Oh! You've heard some tall yarn from that fellow Griffiths, I s'pose?"

"No; and I haven't told him—haven't breathed a word to my people at Egypt either. I was determined you should be the first to hear of it."

Garth took a fresh grip on himself and inquired more soberly:

"When did you get the—hint or whatever it is?"

"Last Wednesday. I met Griffiths at Truro, and while we was sitting on the quay a woman came down and asked if we'd seen a young lady hanging round there, wearing a fawn coat and blue hat."

"What woman was that—not Irma's mother?"

"No—a Mrs. Palmer—London evacuee billeted in the same street as Griffiths. We hadn't seen any such girl, and Mrs. Palmer said she must ha' given her the slip again, and then she made a queer remark about the girl wanting to meet Griffiths—just a flash o' spite, I reckon."

The old haggard despair had dulled Garth's face; a long sigh quivered from him and with a gesture of sheer exhaustion he sank down upon the grindstone.

"Irma don't fit in wi' none o' this—waste o' time telling it to me."

"We'll see in a minute! Mr. Griffiths said he thought there'd a fresh lot come where Mrs. Palmer was billeted —arrived a week or two ago, though he didn't know their names or anything. It's a Miss Jesty lives there permanent —a gay woman, boozing and that: they all seem to be a rum lot."

"Well—about Irma?"

"It's like this. A little later me and Mr. Griffiths left the quay and went back into the town to a café—around tea-time. As we was passing the cathedral, in the narrow street outside the west door, a girl came out, wearing a fawn coat and blue hat. Her look struck me at once— quite different from most town girls: such a yearning on her face, and a sort o' scorn for some life that she was tied down to. I guessed right away that 'twas the girl Mrs. Palmer had spoke of—she'd gone in the cathedral to get clear o' such company."

Garth's eyes were glowing again; he half rose, trembling from head to foot.

"How old a girl?"

"About nineteen. She was quite close to me for a minute as she came out; I nearly bumped into her. And as I stared full in her face I had a queer feeling that I'd seen her before somewhere. She had fair hair and blue eyes—a big mouth, but drawn tight, and she stared straight ahead, not noticing me. And then as she moved on in front of us my heart gave a scat and it came like a flash to me: 'Why! That's Irma Stribley!' The very same face, only a lot older and thinner, as if she'd suffered —just as you have, Garth—suffered and been hunted and misunderstood everywhere—all alone in the world."

Garth stood up, looking queer, dazed; he peered vacantly past her at the clay-tanks now taking on an unearthly glimmer as the shadow of the dune blackened around them. When he spoke the restraint of his voice showed the intensity of the turmoil through which his mind groped.

"Minnie, if this is true—if 'twas really Irma . . . but d'you think . . . . You know I dare not hope unless I'm sure—dare not *lean* on anything that might break—*now*. I should go mad after the strain I've been through."

Minnie smiled.

"I haven't come to the end yet. If I'd only had that glimpse of her I think I'd have held back—perhaps asked Griffiths to inquire a little. . . . But a bit further on when we'd turned into Boscawen Street and Mr. Griffiths was at the bookstall, I saw that the girl, who'd come out another way from us, had stopped over by the alley facing Lemon Street. The children were coming home from school, and three of 'em ran up to her, and one, a girl about eight, called out: 'Irma! Why, we thought you was going to Falmouth with Auntie'—that's Mrs. Palmer, I s'pose. I heard the words plain."

"You heard the name—'Irma'? And the kids. . . ."

"Her brothers and sisters, no doubt. I don't know if all the family's come. I didn't say any more about it to Griffiths; he didn't seem in the right mood when he joined me. He'd got a book from the stall—some atheist affair—and began talking moody about the trouble he'd have in getting his verses printed now wi' the paper shortage. I felt really fed up with him . . . though if 'twasn't for him I shouldn't ha' been there and p'raps you'd never have heard in time; so things still fit, you see."

Garth lurched forward and caught her arm, as if to assure himself that he was not dreaming. He probed her with a look almost frightening in its savage fervour.

"If this is true—if she's so near and . . . and changed like you say—then it *must* mean . . . ?"

"Of course. I really believe you're going to marry Irma. I've felt so very strong since Shirley died. I felt you've paid too big a price to miss your reward."

Garth's hand dropped to the Bible in his pocket; his face had lit up, become beautiful.

"Can it be that this—Edith's stab—was just the final test ? If it is. . . . My God! I can hardly believe. . . . I can only wish you an equal deliverance, Minnie."

She stepped back into the lane, smiling wanly up at the overhanging trees, among which birds were still fluttered.

"I think mine'll come," she said. "But I'm getting less and less sure that it'll be through Griffiths. He's such a wet blanket: we nearly squabbled Wednesday about religion, and he seemed to think you'd given in to Edith. That's what put my back up: 'twas as if he'd be glad to see you go under so that he'd have more proof that religion's just a fraud."

"I'd expect that of him; and I've been too near the same mood lately to blame him much. And now—that mood's weakened me so, I aren't fit to tackle a job that needs a man with all his wits about him."

"Well, I'm no meddler," remarked Minnie, moving away into the deeper shade of the lane. "I can't advise 'ee about your next step. Anyhow, I should wait a day or two—not go rushing off to Truro to-night, for instance."

"No. . . . Don't mention it to Griffiths if you see him."

"I shan't see him this week. But you needn't fear— I won't blab a word till I know you're . . . courting."

Garth forced a smile, and as she disappeared around the tank wall he began stumbling drunkenly across the square towards the sand-dump. . . .

Just after midnight Colly Snell got out of bed to fetch brandy for his wife, who was threatened with a heart attack. He drew aside the curtain and stepping close to the window he peered out, up towards the ridge of the downs. The sky was moonless but brilliant with stars scarcely filmed now by any cloud. Colly noted the familiar landmarks, and he saw too, with sudden astonishment, that on Meledor pyramid a human shape thickened the bar of the fence beside the tip platform. The figure stood

like a sentinel, facing west, alone with the night wind,
mysteriously remote in starshine. As Colly watched the
young man half turned, wafting kisses out along the sky,
then remained with both arms stretched in vehement
yearning towards Truro.

Chapter Twenty-two

O N the morning of the following Saturday Griffiths was
in Truro museum, standing before the inner coffin of
Tefnekht close against the north wall. He was looking up
at the sphinxish carved face with a gravity that bore no
resemblance to its serene resignation. It was not only
that he was disappointed in a hope that might have
endeared to him the name of that other Egypt which
Tefnekht had never heard of. The week had unleashed
upon a stunned world events so sensational that even
lovers found it hard to maintain a true sense of values,
and to a middle-aged widower repulsed in fresh designs
rationalism seemed a personal monopoly that was galling.
The collapse of the Chamberlain Government, the
appointment of Churchill, the Nazi invasion of the Low
Countries yesterday morning—all this contributed to the
gloom that shrouded Griffiths' soul as he stood in the quiet
hall among the relics of past civilisations, preserved here
under glass for Heaven knew what benefit to the living.

Griffiths had just entered the main body of the museum
from the Reading Room, and towards him, between the
rows of glass cases, came at once a man who looked as
if he, at least, was benefited by these exhibits. This was
Mr. Rundle—a tall lean fellow, inclined to stoop, with
a ruddy clean-shaven face and rather owlish eyes blinking
behind horn-rimmed spectacles. He was smiling blandly.

"Thought I saw you come in, Mr. Griffiths. News isn't

very cheerful yet, is it?" His voice was soft, almost womanish, and he spoke with a drawl, making slow gestures with long black-sleeved arms.

Griffiths shrugged, peering up at the south gallery where stuffed animals and birds were on view. Sunshafts fluttered about up there, gleaming on the white stone arches and accentuating the shade of the lower floor.

"Depressing work, penned up with all this mouldy stuff day after day," he observed.

"Well, I don't know that I find it depressing—just a little tiring sometimes. It's surprising how remote our modern troubles seem, in here. I can look at these antique collections and brood away back into the past, see Cornish life as it was before the Saxons came, the roots of our land and language—*tyr ha tavas* as we say: very similar to those of old Wales, where you have your roots."

Griffiths answered grudgingly:

"I never bothered myself with Welsh nationalism. It's a nice pastime for the gentry, but I was a common man, a miner at the age of fourteen, and the iron entered too deeply into me for me to be gulled by such mock refinement."

"Very natural, Mr. Griffiths: you've had a hard life we always say, me and the missus, from the little we know of it. But as for myself, I get hope for the future when I look deep into what's behind."

"Pretty sort of hope," retorted Griffiths, "when even while we're here talking the people of Belgium and Holland are being massacred."

Mr. Rundle rubbed his bald head, his eyes wandering along the wide arch of skylights in the roof.

"The Dutch may be able to do something with their dykes," he said with an air of vague practicality. "Unless someone puts up a strong dyke there's no telling where this tide'll stop. . . . But somehow I feel the danger won't come too close. To look around here and see how peaceful these things lie after all the upheavals the world has

213

known—it helps a man to see things in true perspective."
He pointed at the mummy case, moving close to its glass
screen. "When that Tefnekht was alive there was Pharaohs
—Hitlers as you might call 'em; but they went down,
and here's the man's coffin safe and sound to encourage
the most timid-hearted man among us!"

"Well, I'm afraid I don't find the survival of coffins
very encouraging," muttered Griffiths. "You brood here
over the relics of barbarism—flints of the Stone Age,
weapons of the old Celtic peoples, and these mummy
cases carrying your mind back to ancient Egypt, the
Hyksos dynasty, the subjugation of the Egyptians by the
Asiatics; and from all this you go out to find the streets
plastered with directions to the nearest air-raid shelter.
And there's the cathedral stuck above it all to com-
memorate the complete and final triumph of right over
wrong two thousand years ago. What humbug!"

Mr. Rundle shifted uneasily and coughed into his hand;
he always felt nervous when Griffiths was in this bellicose
mood.

"Well, Mr. Griffiths, we can't see eye to eye on every
point. As a churchman I must say I get help from the
services back at St. George's—a quiet and soothing atmosphere. It strengthens one's ideals, and that's no bad
thing."

"Ideals !" repeated Griffiths. "But what do they
amount to when you've stripped off the smug slogans and
mock heroics ? Take this war. We pretend we're so concerned about decent ideals that we'd die rather than let
Hitler take them from us, yet in the very process of
defending them we're sending the flower of the nation
headlong into a life in which every ideal of decency goes
down in a welter of blood and muck. I can't help laugh-
ing sardonically when I see a soldier drunk or making
free with some professional rip out here in the streets after
dark. 'So this is the way we're going to preserve Christian
ideals, is it ?' I say to myself. 'This is the way we clean up

the world and put away the Hitlerite filth—just to make room for worse filth of our own !' . . . No, Mr. Rundle, idealistic talk's the merest twaddle to gloss over the facts we daren't face. We're fighting just on the animal instinct of survival, and that instinct calls up and gives rein to other animal instincts. And the Church condones war because it knows it has no answer to these instincts. Only the hospitals have an answer."

Again Mr. Rundle coughed, stepping across to a case near-by and stooping to examine its contents while he remarked:

"We must make allowances, Mr. Griffiths. Temptation may trip up the best of us."

"Just my point. It's no use pretending we're a scrap better at resisting temptation than people were when this Tefnekht was strutting about Egypt, or even when the Celtic tribes of Britain were using the most ancient relics preserved here. We're bankrupt, that's the truth. Every ideal is worm-eaten and rotted by instinct before we can link it up with the machinery of progress. . . ."

Griffiths' tirade was checked by a sound behind him, at the front of the building. The door at the end of the passage had opened and a young man appeared. There was something furtive in his manner, as if he dreaded the revelation that might strip him at the next instant. He stood for a few moments in the semi-darkness, a vague bulky figure, peering around the room and across at the broad marble staircase leading to the galleries; then his eyes fastened more particularly on the two men standing by the coffin of Tefnekht. Abruptly he turned, fumbled for the handle of the door, and stumbled rather than walked towards the steps outside. The main entrance door soon closed behind him with a sharp thud.

Griffiths face had taken on a look of intense surprise; he moved a few paces towards the passage, then leaned against a case containing pottery dating from B.C. 300, excavated at the East Cornwall earthworks of Castle Dore.

"That's funny!" he said under his breath, and with his eyes still on the entrance.

Mr. Rundle drew himself erect, his brows puckered in perplexity.

"I don't know who that young man is. I've seen him here twice already this week—Tuesday and Thursday. Something mysterious in his movements, I should say. I tried to get into conversation with him, but he wouldn't open up—wouldn't speak an intelligible word: just mumbled when I spoke to him and shuffled off upstairs to the Art Gallery."

"On the run—there'll tragedy come of this!" muttered Griffiths, shaking his bent head.

Mr. Rundle, mildly wondering, resumed:

"He had no interest whatever in any of the exhibits— hardly glanced at them. He seemed to be on the look-out for someone. He came in several times, went from room to room, up the stairs and around the galleries, then down and straight out again with a baffled set to his face. Very remarkable."

Griffiths smiled—a malicious curl of the lips.

"I can't throw any light on his intentions, but I know the fellow and can guess why he didn't like to come in when he saw me here."

"Not a Truro man, I think?" said Mr. Rundle with concern, as if the dignity of the city were at stake.

"No. I've spoken of him to you once or twice. That young—eccentric, Garth Joslin, from the clay area."

"Ah! Yes, I remember. Fancy!"

"A carpenter, as I've said, but not at all typical of his class."

"I should say not, Mr. Griffiths: he has a deep look."

"Yes. The last I heard of him he was recovering from an illness, and—rather disturbed. His old girl who married the other man had made a mess of her marriage and pounced back on Garth—successfully, so I'm told."

Mr. Rundle sniffed, wringing his hands.

"Not at all uncommon, Mr. Griffiths. A desperate state of things. . . . But I get comfort here from these relics. Think of the morals of those who used these flints and things—naked savages, Mr. Griffiths, and lived only a few miles from where we now stand. And the mummy that was inside there"—he tapped the glass screen, while peering up at the inscrutable face within it—"who knows how many women he may have had."

Griffiths shrugged irritably.

"I'm not sure there's any truth in the rumour," he went on: "though Garth certainly seems worked up, to rush out from here as soon as he recognized me. Ashamed to face me, I suppose, after the confident way he spoke when I visited him back at Easter."

"A religious young man, if I remember rightly?"

"Well, yes, in his own curious fashion: loathes the churches as much as I do, and harks after the grandeur of the desert fathers—applied in a way that would make him a real father. It's very interesting, but he'll have to sing it small, I should think, if he has to figure as a co-respondent of some sort."

"There's very tangled people in the world," murmured Mr. Rundle; he pursed his thin, humourless lips. I wonder . . . could he perhaps have come in here looking for—that other girl you spoke of, the London one he'd got so thick with?"

"Irma?"

"Yes. It isn't impossible he may have heard some rumour; now in war-time with so much shifting about the country you never know where a person may turn up. We're getting arrivals from London still."

Griffiths was breathing quickly, much agitated.

"Who's that girl who's come to lodge with Mrs. Palmer, in our road?" he asked in an abrupt, tense tone.

"I don't know her name—possibly a relative, though she seems of a more refined type. An unusual girl—holds herself aloof. I never see her in grown-up company, always alone or with the children. She's dropped in here a few times—no more interested in the museum specimens than . . . Garth."

"When was she here last ?"

"One day last week, I think. I aren't quite sure. I don't always spot everyone who comes in. But on that occasion I came upon her sitting in the Art Gallery, on a chair in front of Ernest Normand's huge canvas, *Bondage*."

" 'Bondage' ?" repeated Griffiths mechanically.

"Yes. Picture of Egyptian slaves—some nudes in the foreground. I don't know if she thought it symbolic."

"She didn't speak to you ?"

"Only a few words. . . . In fact, her manner was very much like Garth Joslin's." Mr Rundle caught his breath; his eyes looked wide, startled. "I wonder now: could she possibly be the same . . . ?"

Griffiths' face twitched, his hands clenching.

"We needn't waste time in conjectures of that sort. It's as I said just now—he's on the run—desperate; very likely to set off on a wild goose chase if some crazy rumour has reached him. Perhaps I can guess where such a rumour came from, if that *is* the explanation—someone whom he seems to have drugged with his own pious dope; and but for that I might. . . ."

Griffiths checked himself, flushing and biting his lip. He had spoken with emphatic bitterness—so savagely, indeed, that Mr. Rundle was dissuaded from further questioning. Griffiths was, of course, referring to Minnie, but he had not yet mentioned her to the Rundles.

An uneasy silence between the two men, who seemed to be alone in the building, was broken for several minutes only by the crackle of traffic stabbing in from the street. Griffiths moved restlessly nearer the door, clearly impatient to leave, but he appeared to be held back by a fear that Garth might be still lingering outside. He had no wish to meet that young man again: the brief glimpse, with the news that Garth was now seeking his deliverance here in Truro, had whetted antagonism, given it almost the edge of a personal hatred. It was as if he felt the approach of an unveiling, a touch of irony that would reveal him and Garth, not as mere champions of opposing creeds, but as figures placed in deadly juxtaposition in the same act of destiny.

The first practical hint of that ambush came sooner than he could have expected, and from an unlooked-for quarter.

The stillness overhead was snapped suddenly by an uncertain, almost stealthy footstep that echoed on the stone floor. Someone who must have been loitering on the threshold of the Art Gallery had stolen out on to the north corridor that jutted above the coffin of Tefnekht and the whole line of exhibits on that side.

Griffiths was now almost in the centre of the hall, and it was he who, looking up in surprise, first saw the intruder —a girl of about nineteen. She was standing just behind the balustrade, the split sunbeams filtering down through the skylights in wavering fingers that caressed her little red hat, the wisps of corn-coloured hair, the green frock and the small white hands gripping the marble bar. She was outlined against the entrance to the Art Gallery, which was full of a mellow golden blaze, sunlight stream-ing through the room unchecked. This background of radiance gave a strange vividness to her slim tall figure; it surrounded her like a halo, almost etherealized the lonely mould of youth, mystery and passion that were combined in her. Her face was in shadow, but Griffiths noted the rigidity of her pose, an intent watchfulness as of one startled, holding shut with all her strength some spiritual door from which the main bolt had slipped.

He soon recognized her, and felt his cheeks burn with confusion. This Palmer girl, or whatever her name was! How much had she heard of their talk ? . . . He nodded, greeting her rather stiffly:

"Good morning!"

Mr. Rundle now advanced from the shadow almost directly under that part of the gallery on which the girl stood. He looked more owlish than ever, clearing his throat many times, and pausing by a screen near the central row he turned and blinked up at the person Griffiths had addressed, and whose reply had been so faint that he had scarcely heard it. His face became at once red with embarrassment, though the feeling was not complicated by any of the somewhat ugly emotions that were shown in Griffiths' reaction.

"Why!" he exclaimed, a weak smile shifting his lips half-an-inch to the left. "I didn't see you come in to-day, miss."

"I've been here nearly an hour," said the girl dully.

"Haven't heard you moving around. Been sitting in the picture gallery again?"

"Yes. There's nothing much else to do." Her voice sounded tired, yet there was a suppressed excitement racing beneath its forced reserve.

Mr. Rundle nodded sympathetically; he too was wondering whether the girl had overheard their discussion of her, and became talkative through sheer nervousness.

"Must have a lot of time hanging on your hands, down here in a strange place with no work or anything. Nasty thing, this war."

She answered with a sort of defiance:

"I wanted to come."

"Ah! Well, I hope you find it interesting in here."

The girl gave a non-committal shrug, and without replying she turned away from the balustrade, moved out along the corridor to the upper staircase. Descending this she passed into a deep gloom in which the two men could see nothing of her features. Only when she came round the bend on to the main stairway did they note the signs of reckless resolve, the clenched hands, the evasive mutinous eyes and set lips.

She stepped towards them, moving in and out among

the glass cases and wooden screens—a figure whose easy swaying grace was hardened now, rendered almost jerky by emotional tension. No one else had entered the hall; and she looked as if the presence of a multitude would not have deflected her.

The men waited with growing concern, aware that something unusual was coming.

She halted in front of the big case that separated them, glancing from Griffiths to Mr. Rundle with an odd frankness, half appeal, half scorn, in her large blue eyes. She addressed Mr. Rundle, her accent clipped, slightly faltering:

"Did you speak of . . . of Garth Joslin a minute ago? I haven't heard your talk, only I thought I caught the name as I came out of the picture room."

The men exchanged glances, Mr. Rundle's accompanied by a brisk nod as of superior knowledge. Griffiths' head had jerked back as from a blow; he continued to stare at the girl in stony, hostile silence, and with a dazed face of incredulity.

"Why, yes, miss," replied Mr. Rundle, stretching an apologetic arm towards her. "We did mention that chap. He's just come in here—or as far as the door rather. He went out again on seeing us here. Not a sociable man, I should say."

"I heard the door close. . . ." She made a passionate gesture of regret; her face, fresh-coloured and with broad and prominent cheek-bones, glowed more nakedly. "Oh, if I'd only known! . . . Which way did he go?"

"Can't say, miss." Mr. Rundle's eyes narrowed upon her curiously. "Agreed to meet him or something?"

"No—oh, no. I've never met him here before—quite a stranger—only. . . ."

She was interrupted by Griffiths, who strode abruptly around the end of the case like one whose restraint is overborne.

"And who may you be?" he asked with a fierce unnatural smile.

She gave him a cold glance of aversion, and without a further word she hurried away to the door, opened it and passed out.

Mr. Rundle turned to Griffiths, somewhat shaken but unable to conceal his triumph.

"Well, Mr. Griffiths, what d'you think now? Rumour not so crazy after all, perhaps?"

Griffiths' stunned look had given place to that of a creature at bay, defenceless, uncertain of the concealed forces threatening him. His face was dark with something more desperate than anger; he ground his teeth.

"Damn her! Why wouldn't she answer me? If she *is* Irma"—his laugh sounded harsh, not altogether wholesome; his excitement grew as he lurched back to Mr. Rundle—"I . . . I won't stay here in Truro to see that develop under my nose. It's beyond endurance." He banged the edge of the case and flung out the truth of which he was now convinced: "The woman who's refused me—wrecked my life afresh—has set him after her!"

Mr. Rundle stared, pale and alarmed, licking his lips helplessly.

Chapter Twenty-three

EARLY in the evening of that day Mrs. Palmer was hurrying up the long hill past the Royal Cornwall Infirmary on the north-western outskirts of Truro. It was rather a lane than a street, with no pavements or houses; the high wall of the hospital grounds towered on one side, and on the other was a hedge dark and shady now with trees. Below her the city lay in a warm haze, filling the narrow valley, the cathedral rising in a vivid surge of contrast to the whitewashed slum tenements nearest Mrs. Palmer's view as occasionally she glanced back.

Mrs. Palmer was dressed gaudily in a costume striped in clover and blue, the top of a yellow jumper flaring under her thick red neck. Much of her bobbed black hair, greying at the sides, was visible outside the green hat she wore. Her bloated cheeks were powdered, her mouth was smeared with lipstick and twisted irritably. She glared out from the shadow of the trees upon the broad sunlit square ahead, marking the cross-roads at the hilltop, from which Lemon Street slanted south-east into the brisk shopping centres and the Falmouth road struck westward into the open countryside.

The corner was rendered elegant by a tall stone pillar bearing the statue of a man—Richard Lander, the Truro-born missionary. Mrs. Palmer did not think it incongruous that such a figure should remain looking down upon the careless queues that assembled daily outside the Plaza cinema. Her mind was rather dull for a modern one, and she never associated things vividly enough to find incongruities in life. All she sought were its spices, and almost all that she remembered were its hangovers. In all Truro there was not a woman more sincerely devoted to an ideal, or more bad-tempered at her success in reaching it. She was at present on her way to the cinema, not choosing to bring the children lest she should lose thereby an offer of fresh spice. And as she came round the railing at the corner, in full view of the square, she forgot even that piquancy in the sudden recognition of a figure standing a little back from the statue, near the shade of trees at the opening of the Falmouth road. A girl, there alone, richly a part of the spring beauty that was unstained and aching amid the more vulgar fevers of the crowd. Mrs. Palmer gave a short derisive grunt. Her niece, Irma Stribley! The girl was wearing the same clothes she had worn in the museum that morning, and stood with a stark and vivid look on her face which showed emotions still agitated by that chance visit to the Art Gallery.

Irma had seen her aunt approaching before the woman

noticed her. A frown of distaste and aversion settled in her eyes, she moved a step forward to the railing that enclosed the small grass plot framing the statue; then she continued to glance about, again calm, indifferent, raising a hand to pat her hair that now gleamed very light and powdery in the sunshine.

Mrs. Palmer lurched straight across the street, and as no one else was passing at the moment she vented the malice that grew daily through contact with this enigmatic girl.

"Oh! So you're up here, are you? We was wondering where you'd gone." Her eyes and voice became ironic, taunting. "Coming down to the flicks with me, sporty?"

Irma shook her head, gazing down Lemon Street at the queue already gathered outside the cinema.

"Not now. I've more important business."

"Made a dyte with some guy, eh? You look like it! Frighten off any chap to see that mug." She swayed close, tapping Irma's arm, jeering. "In one o' your sulks to-day, aren't yer? Came in very starched from your stroll this morning—hardly touched your dinner and kept staring out o' the window, shrugging away when you was spoke to. 'Got the hump, bless her little heart!' Miss Jesty said when you'd gone out again. 'She isn't disappointing us, you see!'"

"That's all right then; I thought you both had been disappointed."

The girl's quiet, cutting tone brought up the latent venom in Mrs. Palmer; her dark coarse face grew ugly, her voice rasped, she set her flabby arms akimbo.

"What the devil's come over you, Irma? I heard your mum complaining this last twelve months, but I never guess it was as bad as this. You been here three weeks now—either sitting around indoors like a wet blanket, or mooning away on your own in the stuffiest holes you can find here. Never where the chaps would have a fair chance. Only been to the flicks once or twice with the kids, and haven't been to a dance at all. You'll never get going with any boy friends if you don't loosen up."

Irma shrugged, pouting her full, heavy lips, that had no artificial colouring.

"I didn't come here to get boy friends. If I'd wanted that I should have stayed in London."

"Then why did yer come ?"

Irma was silent for a minute, then made a writhing gesture, her face clouded with a sort of disgust.

"You know I wasn't happy at home."

"Sure, I know that: mum pulling in Jim Slade was the last straw—looked like she did it just to spite you, eh ? But it goes deeper'n that, as Slade's off in the Army now —have to go to Belgium soon, I expect, and may never come back."

"I hope he don't," said Irma with sudden spirit, "for the kids' sakes. It'd be just hell for 'em—worse even than when dad was alive. God knows what the girls'd be driven to in a few years."

"Well . . . but that can't be all the cause, as I was saying." Mrs. Palmer cleared her throat, watching brazenly as a bus passed, then resumed in a tone of suspicion:

"You had some idea in your head—didn't come here because you thought auntie'd be lonely. You don't like me more'n the rest of our bunch—can't find it comfortable here in this billet any better than at Church Walk. Only you're putting up with it for some reason best known to yourself. I scented it from the start, and we thought —me and Miss Jesty did—that there'd be pretty high jinks by this time—figured you'd myke a fresh break here wi mum too far off to slap yer fyce and me not likely to try it. I've nearly got nabbed here in Truro already for having a little fireworks with Mrs. Fisher, where I was billeted first. Carried on a bit with her man, y'know: she didn't like it for some reason, and if we hadn't been pulled apart the hospital'd have had a pretty smash-up o' fyces to tend to."

Irma looked scornful.

"The kids is here with me," she remarked after a pause. "That's something to keep straight for."

"It didn't seem to be two years ago. I stick to what I've said before—there's some plan or other at the bottom o' yer mind what yer won't tell us."

Irma seemed to hesitate, her hands twitching, then stepping out to the edge of the pavement she said cryptically:

"You mayn't have long to wait now before you find it out. There may be some development that won't look very straight to you."

"I know you're a deep one—sly and mysterious—yer always was," muttered Mrs. Palmer. "Miss Jesty says very often you ain't so quiet as you look. 'It's always the ones that look quiet what's painting the town red in secret,' she says."

A faint smile played about Irma's mouth—deadly for all its quiet humour.

"I don't see how I could paint the town red in secret," she observed. "Still, I don't promise there won't be scandal before I leave."

"Well, you've had yer warning. Your mum said if you come home in trouble this time you'll have to find another roof: she'd wash her hands of you."

"I'd expect her to; and maybe I've already washed my hands of her and the drunken blackguard she's picked up. As if one man o' that sort wasn't enough!"

Mrs. Palmer drew back, glancing down the hill as an ambulance came through the hospital gateway.

"How long was you meaning to stop here—as long as I do, I s'pose?"

Again Irma smiled, her eyes following, not the ambulance, but the flight of a cuckoo above the trees.

"I mayn't go back at all," she answered.

"H'm! Well, yer mum wouldn't be sorry if you'd cleared out for good—certainly Slade wouldn't, if he's

spared to settle down there. You only been a nuisance
since you growed up, apart from earning a little and
helping to mind the brats. Got on her nerves, the way
you've shaped this last year or so."

"I don't see why it should. If she didn't want me to
chuck up the gay life she wouldn't have got me put on
probation."

"She and Bert was mad to get you knuckled in for a
bit, that's all. You'd only just left school, and it would
have made a mess for them if the worst happened—lucky
it didn't. But you've gone from one extreme to another
—made a real fool o' yourself. Lost all your friends by
turning into such a smug little penitent."

"Friends!" cried Irma scornfully. "I found soon enough
how much they was worth when the big trouble came last
year. The dimwits never guessed what was wrong: the
only help they offered was what would have pushed me
back where I'd started. I'm through with looking for
friendship from that bunch."

"Well, you won't myke new friends here either while
yer keep so high-and-mighty and pretend you haven't had
a past as spicy as the best of 'em. . . . I wonder what your
uncle and aunt—those Stribleys up in the clay area—
would say if they knowed you was so close to 'em, and
such a good girl now?"

Irma had flushed; she watched her foot toeing restlessly
the kerbstone as she replied:

"I don't care for their opinion."

"Aren't you going up to pay 'em a call one day?"

Irma's eyes looked straight into the woman's face—
cool, defiant, challenging.

"If I go to Meledor it won't be to see *them*!"

"Ah!" said Mrs. Palmer, her thick brows lifting as she
stared in sudden apprehension. "So that's at the bottom
of it, is it? That's what's been pulling you back to
Cornwall?"

"What?"

"That first slip at Meledor began it, your mum always said. You got a taste then that no girl'd ever throw off, and if you hadn't been artful—or lucky: I ain't sure which it was—you might still have something to show for it—a baby I mean. If you aim to get thick wi' that bloke again your mum'd never forgive you."

Irma stood very still, one hand on her hip, the other hanging limply.

"I shan't ask her forgiveness for what's to come. And I'm not telling you whether there's anything in the wind yet, or what it's concerned with. Only now I'm nineteen you needn't think you could put a spoke in my next affair."

Mrs. Palmer laughed, beginning to move away.

"I know yer too well to try and meddle in that when it comes: it'll be the real thing, Irma! You had yer first run three or four years ago, and then it cooled off, what with the probation business and missing yer dad's influence so sudden. If it's to break out again there's nothing in hell or earth that could stop yer, any more'n it could stop yer dad in his last fling."

Irma bit her lip, making no reply, and stood, breathing tremulously, watching Mrs. Palmer's solid figure sway off down the pavement, cross the street and become lost in the shifting crowd around the cinema doors.

When she had calmed her mind, ruffled by its own avowals under the abrupt pressure, Irma too stole away from the square, down the hill which Mrs. Palmer had just now ascended. She didn't wish to go past that cinema mob. Her aunt might point her out to some young man she knew, might make a joke, set them staring, sniggering.

Irma had soon passed the hospital and proceeded straight into the squalid built-up area, along a narrow alley backed by half-demolished slum houses, which opened into the Market Place. Children were squatting on the doorsteps—ragged, dirty little urchins; a few blowsy women and rough-looking men eyed her stolidly as she hurried by. She scarcely heeded them, yet her face held a tenseness. A month ago she had moved amid just such scenes in London, scenes with which she had been familiar all her life. Here—the same threat, the old oppression! Only one thing could make her flight from London worth while—one thing that even yesterday had seemed so fantastic that she'd had to huddle out under the arch of the viaduct towards midnight, in the dark, trying vainly to keep back the tears, the beastly talk indoors fresh in her mind. Miss Jesty, the worse for liquor, had come in late and recounted with much instructive detail what had just happened between herself and a soldier, after a dance, urging Irma to play the same game: "Only way to—hup!—enjoy the war, dearie...." Irma had awoken tired and dispirited this morning, had gone out early, wandering aimlessly about the streets, turning into the museum at last for greater privacy. As she passed now from the Market Place she gave an intent, strained glance north-east along River Street, in which the museum stood. Her nerves thrilled with the memory, the sudden stab of that name, blade-like through the dense drawn curtain: her cheeks grew hot as she recalled her impulsive appeal. Those two men must have thought her crazy! No matter! She'd got the clue, made sure that it was he, Garth. . . . And for a few minutes he had been in the same building! If he'd only come up to the Gallery! Those men had headed him off, and now—too late, perhaps! Not a glimpse of him, though she'd kept in the streets almost ever since, on the lookout. He might be gone again by now, back to Meledor, back to—not Edith, nor, she felt, to any wife. She hadn't heard much of the talk between Griffiths and Mr. Rundle, but she'd caught enough to assure her that Garth was still different, apart in the eyes of the world as he had always been in her mind when she thought of him at all. The feeling that had brought her to Cornwall was not yet fully love for him, rather a sense of need, a blind gravitation towards him because she could think of no one else who might understand the change which had come to her, this breaking up of an old world with but one reality salvaged as the core of the new; that first stabbing flow of communion in Meledor workshop. If the incident had loomed disproportionately it was no doubt partly through coarse-grained people so often taunting her with it. At home it had been sometimes treated as a joke, sometimes blamed for all the later trouble; and she had not escaped the teasing by coming among strangers. Almost the first words of Miss Jesty's greeting showed her knowledge of the affair:

"Ah! So this is the little girl who's been married in Cornwall already! You had a rare treat, my dear, and I'm afraid you won't find such hospitality in this house. I've no son—not even a husband I could spare. . . ."

These assaults upon the one memory that had survived and expanded with the growth of faith in her had caused Irma to invest it more and more with a passionate purity, inviolate, able to bind circumstances to its will, bring her to Garth again.

She did not hurry through the street; frequently she paused, looking into shop windows and scanning furtively the thronged pavements on both sides. Plenty of young couples about, clasped together, defensive—the shadow of the war giving sinister distortion to familiar tones of human intercourse. She watched them enviously, the ache of loneliness prodding here as in London during the past twelve months, with a keener urgency. Garth might be called up soon, sent abroad somewhere! Not a moment to be lost!

Irma's thoughts were keyed almost to desperation as she came in sight of Boscawen Street, probed it in vain, and turned up a quieter thoroughfare to the left. Probably it was useless to seek further to-night; she'd have to go back, face the fresh sneers and gibes—unbearable for long unless she could make good her boast. And how——?

CHAPTER TWENTY-THREE

The question was left unfinished; a possible answer
had disclosed itself. With a startled gasp she stood rigid
by the Belisha beacon on the corner.

Less than fifty yards up the side street a man had just
stepped off the pavement—a heavily-built figure, youth-
ful, yet with a tired, wasted appearance about it. His
movements were so peculiar that several people besides
herself watched him closely. His hands were in the pockets
of his black overcoat, his head was bowed, he walked
with jerky, uneven steps. He seemed like one lost in a
dream, dodging the traffic by instinct rather than conscious effort. The profile of his face was turned towards
Irma, and her heart leapt in recognition. Garth—at last.
His recent illness had taken off some of the bulk he had
acquired during the past four years; his figure was much
the same as when she had been pressed close to it. And
his face—though she couldn't distinguish its features
clearly—unmistakable! The same brooding, sphinxish
aspect that had fascinated her in the workshop! Alone
too—no girl beside him, and in his thoughts—perhaps—
dared she hope——?

She moved up the sidewalk, watching him gain the
opposite pavement and stride on, often bumping into
people, until he passed around the corner and into the
square in front of the cathedral where Minnie and Griffiths
had met nearly a fortnight ago.

Irma hurried now—somewhat paler, but vivid, alert,
dynamic. Her eyes glowed, her lips were parted, her
whole figure seemed transformed, its grace and rhythm
intensified by the blood stirred towards love. Most of the
men who brushed by shot at her a gloating, furtive glance,
but this no longer threatened, or even annoyed her. She
seemed to be lifted above trivial emotions, drawn away
from the level of the street with its tawdry laughs, frivolous
chatter. The new vision smote forth in outlines grand if
confused. This was no "date" with a boy friend! Destiny!

She had soon reached the corner, but the traffic was

heavy now—impossible to cross at once. Her hands clenched as she waited, feverish impatience tensing her face again. She *must* not let him slip this time! Her eyes darted among the stream of cars and lorries, brought her swift reassurance. Yes, there he was, even nearer than before, crossing the square—almost the only person in the open, looking very small under the massive façade of the cathedral. His head was raised now, he was peering intently up at the sunlit towers and spires; and though she could not see his face she noted that his step was slower, hesitant.

He was nearly abreast of the building by the time a gap in the traffic allowed Irma to leave the pavement. She almost ran across into the square, wondering if he might glance back as he turned the north-western corner of the edifice. But Garth proceeded stolidly along the alley until he drew level with the side entrance under the green-coped turret. Here he paused, and after a few moments' deliberation he began ascending the steps and passed into the building.

Irma was surprised, but her hope quickened as she hastened forward. Could it be that he'd heard she often visited the cathedral—that he had gone in there now, as into the museum this morning, seeking her? . . .

A minute later she too had reached the west entrance, and with trembling hand she pushed open the heavy door and stepped inside.

Chapter Twenty-four

IRMA had entered the cathedral a dozen times already, so that its interior was no longer strange to her, though still awe-inspiring; and even had this been her first glimpse of it she would scarcely have heeded the details of structure and furnishing. All her senses were fused, questing within the pure human limit, alert for Garth only.

A hazy gloom brooded over the great nave, a few shafts of sunlight wavering up among the white arches. The stained glass windows broke up the spilth of beams, toned them to unearthly hues, remote, gentle, floating out like aureoles over the carved symbols of worship. No one visible up towards the north transept. That part of the building was still unknown to her: the place had seemed so big that she hadn't ventured far beyond the west entrance for fear of getting lost.

She moved noiselessly out across the nave, holding her breath, treading stealthily as though she had come on some sacrilegious mission. Her eyes glided about, darting into every niche and among the rows of chairs and the pillars, where a blacker bulk might break the smooth flow of twilight. Nobody there! Her gaze swept up to St. Mary's chapel, dark and remote to the south—the only part of the building that had existed before 1877; and as she advanced the chancel was disclosed alongside. Which way——? Ah! Passing free of a pillar that had obscured a full view of the chancel she saw it as the place where the great moment of recognition was fated to strike—fitly, since the life they sought to consummate had been nourished by the truths acknowledged there.

Garth was standing within a few yards of the altar, near the row of chairs on the east side of the aisle. He held his cap in his hand, and a sunshaft pierced down upon his bowed head, lighting the curly brown hair, cut short now but rather tousled. He seemed much agitated, his whole frame wrenched now and then by spasms of emotion.

Very quietly Irma approached, moving past the main chancel steps, which were roped off, and around to the eastern end, past rows of carved images and beautiful stained glass work in the walls bordering the nave. She still kept a sharp look-out for intruders. All remained calm, like a stage purposely set for her and Garth. No vergers in view, no casual sightseers! They two would be alone in the chancel. And as she drew nearer, stealing through the hushed edifice, surrounded by the rich architectural tones that breathed around her an atmosphere of religious mystery, with the fresh scent of Whitsun flowers adding the touch of nature thereto, her instinct was driven into passionate certainty of what was meant by that figure so absorbed, broken and careless who should see his last agonised appeal for guidance and succour. She knew, as surely as if he had already declared all, that it was for her he prayed; and yielding dreamily she seemed to pass into a fantastic mood, as though she were back with him again in the workshop, the years between with their fever blotted out, the delicious intimacy just ahead. . . . This feeling burnt from her every trace of reserve, misgiving, apprehension; it gave her strength, the knowledge of her power over him and of a higher Power claiming them both. She ascended the side steps of the chancel with her gaze lifted to the figure of Christ carved in the centre of the reredos, gleaming gold. His hands outstretched behind the altar—grafting hands. . . .

Tip-toeing in on to the paved floor she touched Garth's arm and said in a gulpy tone, very different from her gay challenge of that earlier day:

"Garth! I've come!"

She was not surprised to see, as his face jerked round, that tears lay upon it; and the look which at the next instant mingled with them was indescribable. Stupor, joy, amazement—these combined, almost overwhelmed him. A low cry broke from his white lips, he swayed momentarily and stretched an arm to the back of a nearby chair.

"There's no mistake," she whispered. "It's really me—Irma."

A minute of awed silence followed, in which, eye to eye, they read each other's souls, then Garth turned and also looked up at the reredos—a beautiful look, groping towards adoration. He said with tremulous fervour:

"Thank God!"

Then his gaze swept back to her, burning, avid to feast on every feature that would link this moment with the past, reveal her to him, no stranger, but a girl whose lips he had kissed when they last parted.

She'd changed a good deal, was quite slim now, her face sharper, a hint of tragic beauty stamped where he remembered only the fresh bloom of childhood. But her appeal was the same, whetting love such as he had never known, never could know, for another.

After a long pause he inquired thickly:

"Who . . . who sent you here?"

"Nobody. I saw you come in. I—I'd heard already, at the museum this morning. . . . "

"Ah! Then it . . . it really *was* you? I'd felt it must be." He attempted a smile, an apologetic note softening his voice as the first shock subsided. "I aren't so much took aback now as I should ha' been earlier in the day. I wasn't sure then you weren't still in London."

"You'd have known if you came straight into the museum. I was in the picture gallery and . . . heard two men talking about you, saying you'd come as far as the door and then. . . . "

Irma raised her left hand to brush a wisp of hair from her forehead, and noted that his gaze followed the gesture eagerly. She understood. The hand that had once wormed its way into his! No rings on it! But he could scarcely need that proof that no one else claimed her.

He replied more briskly, almost natural in manner now, though he still kept his hand on the chair-back.

"Yes, it was stupid of me, only . . . I can't go into details here, but one o' those men . . . I felt I couldn't go in and think calm what I'd better do next, with him there. He's unsettled me a bit—tried to, anyway. An atheist."

"The one with a moustache?"

"Yes."

"I didn't like the look of him myself," said Irma,

peering across St. Mary's chapel towards the south tran-sept—dim, cloister-like. "He seemed to be sneering, and after I asked about you he looked real violent for a minute, as if he could have struck me. He asked me who I was, but I wasn't staying there to go into family history with a stranger, and just walked out. But you'd gone by that time."

Garth stepped free of the chairs, pale and twisting his cap nervously in both hands.

"Never mind. It all helped." He went on to explain haltingly:

"I was feeling pretty rattled as I left, and just walked up and down the streets—over the river first, then back around the viaduct—trying to get a grip on myself. Couldn't eat no dinner. Just before tea-time I went back to the museum—thought that bloke wouldn't be there again—and the curator or whatever he is came up to me —seemed rather nervous and bashful—and said a girl'd been there just after I quitted, asking for me. From his description I knew it must be you—same details I'd had already, hints what'd brought me to Truro."

"How did you hear first?" inquired Irma, lifting her brows—brows so light that they were scarcely visible here in the shadow.

"Neighbour o' mine had spotted you leaving the cathe-dral—last Wednesday week."

"Ah, yes: that was the day Auntie wanted me to go to Falmouth with her." Irma's face clouded; she was reminded afresh of the background to which she must return. "Who was it had seen me—not Martin or Bella, I hope?"

"No. Minnie Lagor. You may remember seeing her: used to keep house for Colly Snell, just opposite your uncle's farm."

"Oh, yes, I think. . . . Had a baby or something, didn't she?"

Garth nodded: he swallowed hard before resuming:

"That kid was killed back in March. It all started then, this last phase—set things moving up to a crisis. 'Twas me what found the girl—fell under a water-wheel and got crushed to death—and . . . well, I done what I could to give Minnie the faith to bear up; and she repaid me by coming last Sunday with the news that she'd spied you here—looking lonely and upset, she said."

"I expect I did; I felt so, God knows. . . . But why should that woman think it would help—to tell you she'd spotted me in Truro?"

Irma was smiling: it was a sly question, not prompted by any ignorance. And Garth smiled too, wryly, as he confessed:

"They all knew what I was waiting for—guessed so, anyway, as I wouldn't take on with any Cornish girl. . . . And when the museum fellow said just now you'd been wanting to meet me, I knew the miracle must have happened. I made up my mind I wouldn't go back to Meledor before I'd found you, even if it meant staying here overnight. I'm due to start work again Monday— been home with a illness for weeks—shock through finding that little kid dead and . . . other things. Anyhow, I felt I couldn't go back to the workshop till I'd got settled."

"So you're still working there?"

"Yes; it helped," he said simply. "When I've told you all. . . . God knows what I've been through since we met last. It's like a dream—so much off the common lines. This last month or so I knew I was in sight o' the end— some sort o' end. The enemy came in like a flood and it seemed the foundations must give way. But God stood by me, gave me the hint in time. . . . I've been here three times this week, and felt last night that I must either find you to-day or else. . . ." He shrugged, staring at the red altar frontal, the flowers above it.

"I've been praying here if ever a man prayed. And God wouldn't have answered—wouldn't have sent you —unless you was still free."

Irma shot him a very clear glance—the sort he'd known so well in the workshop, making his heart flutter.

"How long I'm free'll depend on you," she said softly.

"Well, if you mean that. . . ." Garth laid his hand on her arm, and she felt it trembling. "We can never have an ordinary affair, beginning like we did."

"No. It rests with you, Garth—after we've got the situation thrashed out."

He frowned moodily at the brass candlestick beside the altar for a few moments, then roused, moving back to the upper steps and descending the first two.

"Better go for a stroll, hadn't we—somewhere quiet? We can't just part here with practically nothing told. . . . It's all so sudden and strange."

"It is," Irma agreed—"like a dream for me too. Only ten minutes ago I was mooning round the streets, cut up to see the girls and chaps hugged together, and now. . . . I'm glad I spoke as I did to Auntie: it'll forestall anything she may hear."

"You've told your people—about me being in Truro?" asked Garth as they stole side by side down the lower steps and into the nave. A door was heard closing at the northern end of the building; a verger appeared from the transept. Irma lowered her voice.

"Not exactly. Auntie came on me just now in Lemon Street, and started ragging me—caught me off guard, and I let out more than I meant to. But it's O.K. now."

They were almost at the door when Garth inquired:

"Will your family get the wind up about us?"

Irma pursed her lips, shrugging.

"Mum's as good as finished with me, anyhow, since she married again. You've heard?"

"Yes, Bella told me. I thought it would head things up."

"It did. Mum overreached herself that time."

"She hasn't come with you?"

"No—still in London, and likely to stop there. She won't come here with me, anyway—lucky for us !"

Garth looked serious as he opened the door, and halting outside on the step he observed:

"Minnie said she'd gathered you was only just arrived Who brought you down?"

"No one. I brought the kids. I'm there with my Aunt Ethel—Mrs. Palmer."

"Minnie told me that."

."Yes." Irma followed him out past the railings on to the pavement—almost deserted now, very cool in the lengthening shadows. "She came down last year, and when I knew she was settled in Cornwall I got a bit restless. You can guess why."

"Because it was near me?"

"Perhaps! Anyway, it made things unbearable at home —me and mum always squabbling. She could see I wanted to clear out. She complained about the kids too —they kept her from enjoying herself so free as she wanted. She said she wished she'd evacuated 'em with Aunt Ethel's. And then—I lost my job and the way opened up."

Garth's face had grown tense under the cap that he was still fitting on; he stood very still, close to her, studying her face half fearfully, now distinct in the daylight. Mention of her practical life in London had reminded him of Edith's ugly tales. How much truth——?

"That shop work?" he said; his voice was dull, mechanical.

"No. I soon chucked up that and got in a factory in Stoke Newington. But the factory's reorganizing now— Government want it for munitions or something. At any rate, I dropped out—and here we are!"

"And where do we go next?" queried Garth, peering across at the sunlit streets to the south. "Back over the quay and outside the town that end—Tresillian way?"

"Just it. We might run across Miss Jesty or some o' the kids if we stayed around the streets; and I want to have a good feed before I face them again."

"No cafés out that way, I'm afraid," said Garth; but he knew what she meant.

Chapter Twenty-five

SIDE by side, though a little hesitant, they moved out along the alley, clear of the cathedral, following the same route taken by Minnie and Griffiths ten days ago. Garth kept his hands in his pockets, watching the passers-by with a defensive air, feeling that he was shepherding his treasure through enemy lines and that any ostentatious sign of possession would draw their fire. By the time they sighted the quay, however, his reaction was more healthy. He laid his hand on her waist and then, responding to her smile and quick nod of encouragement, he slipped his arm rather shyly round her. She clasped him likewise, and soon they found themselves on the bridge, passing long queues of people waiting for buses—people who regarded them with indifference, seeing in them just one more couple snatching bliss at random and ready to shift with a chance current. No one guessed the tremendous emotional transition through which they groped, desperately adapting themselves to new standards, new demands.

The atmosphere of the cathedral, remote from common life, had been in harmony with the thrill of their reunion, made it seem obvious and inevitable. But here in the crude glare and splutter of the street, the cool evening breeze blowing about them with its mingled smells of petrol and stagnant water, the novelty and strangeness smote them afresh, worked in confused fluctuations, now as an intoxicant, now a narcotic. They spoke little until they had passed beyond view of the river and were heading eastward along the drab, quieter suburban area. Even

then their talk was strained, impersonal—inquiries from
Irma about her aunt and uncle at Meledor, general references to the war situation; and both knew what was
keeping them from intimate speech. That interval—her
past life in London! Neither seemed able to broach that;
and their faces grew darker, their eyes hard and furtive,
intent on every distraction—the passing of a bus, the
opening of a door, the scudding of a white butterfly among
the shrubs and rhododendrons overhanging garden walls.

At length they drew level with the gaunt squat Roman
Catholic church at the foot of a side-street, and the big
hostel in the grounds beside it. Irma's eyes narrowed
upon the building; Garth saw that she was tensing herself
for confession, finding some hint and help in that scene.

No one was visible on the short strip of road ahead,
screened partly by a foaming green blob of trees. Irma
leaned close to him and said in a tremulous tone, half
serious, half playful:

"I might have been in a place like that if it weren't for
you."

Garth stared.

"Why. . . . Oh! yes." He realised and was silent. A
Home for Fallen Girls! Then she really had——! Proba-
tion! Edith's words stabbed in again, giving him agony.
He dropped his arm and they halted, faced one another—

"Have you heard?" she asked, almost in a whisper.

"A good bit—only this last month or so. I won't rake
it up if . . . if it's painful for you. It can't matter now."

At this evasion her eyes softened, probing deep into
his; she touched his sleeve gently, timidly.

"Would you rather not know?"

"Well, there's one or two points . . . might be better
to get 'em cleared up. 'Twas Edith's doing—tried to win
me back and thought the best way was to . . . blab about
what your party on the farm had told her. Said you'd
—got—running wild—put on probation. . . ."

Irma nodded, walking on beside him under the trees,

glad of the shade, herself subdued and even more lovely, so that his senses ached as he watched her, the green frock matching the verdure of the leafage, her red hat bobbing like a little flame above the fluffed bright hair.

"Yes, they tried that," she admitted. "But it wasn't really so bad. . . . It was all against—my people, not anything that—that's against you—*now*. None o' those chaps went further than you did with me—not one. Honest, Garth, it's true." Her voice had a wrenched pathos in it, carried conviction. "I got fed up at home and tried to kick loose—spent my evenings with a pretty fast crowd—stayed out late at dances and told 'em no end o' fibs, just for devilment. They took it serious and thought something had to be done; and it does seem a wonder now that I could go so far without getting trapped."

Garth mopped his face with a handkerchief. The crisis —passed! Relief flooded his whole being.

"Thank God! . . . But I sort o' knew, the moment I saw you in the cathedral—felt you wouldn't ha' come if . . . if there'd been anything too bad. I knew you was bound to have your back to the wall, living in such a beastly home."

"Yes. Mum'd lived wild as long as I can remember. Seemed to agree with her, too: she was always jolly and gay except when Dad was around. Made me think it was a happy life for a girl to get a lot o' men mad after her."

"But you found there was a snag in it ?"

"I should say so. You see, it drove dad to get his own back, and he made a mess of it and . . . ."

She checked herself, clenching her hands. They were heading uphill now, along a wide road past rows of smart villas, gardens gorgeously coloured with spring flowers. Several people were lounging about, and she waited until they were in sight of the crossroads near the War Memorial before completing her avowal.

"He . . . he got struck on a woman, early last year—

went to live with her. They took lodgings in Dulwich. I didn't see dad for two months or more. And then—one day they . . . they was found gassed in their bedroom."

"Gassed ?"

"Yes. A suicide pact. They'd burnt themselves out, I s'pose, and couldn't face it."

Sweat had broken out again on Garth's brow; he caught her arm violently.

"You mean . . . they were both dead ?"

"Dead enough. Dad left a letter—ghastly. . . ."

It needed all Garth's will-power to keep him from embracing her at that moment.

"Oh, my darling! No wonder God plagued me with prayer for you. How you needed it!"

Irma was silent until they reached the hilltop, the privacy of the road winding down towards Tresillian. A pleasantly rural landscape here—steep slopes of pasture-ground, some cows grazing down there in the valley, and further to the east rich woodland thinning out along field hedges where trees lurched up and sprawled like the exhausted remnants of an army.

"That was what pulled me up," she resumed after a long pause, when they were again clasped together and aware that compensation for all shocks was within reach, possible at any moment as the impulse mastered them both. "I didn't miss dad much, as we'd never got on. He'd threatened to thrash me lots of times, and did knock me about a bit when I'd got—out of hand as they called it. It only made me worse, wanting love more than ever just to score him off. And the stuff those court johnnies tried on me—the probation meddling and 'guidance' of well-intentioned people—oh, it makes me laugh, the way they thought that could do any good. It'd got too deep in my blood for any little tame good influence to stop the rot."

"I understand," said Garth gently. "That sort o' treatment's a waste o' time when the problem's spiritual

—when it's just the old poison working like mad to throw out the new sap Christ has grafted."

"They never thought it might be that—I don't think they'd ever heard of it. I hadn't, anyway. But with the shock o' the suicide and the scandal it made, everything changed. Love—what they called love—became a perfect horror to me, all beastly and miserable. I couldn't go on."

"And—you looked back—did you?" Garth let go of her body and passionately clasped her hands as they halted. "Irma, did you remember—that evening in Virginia Wood—and the workshop—that—love we had together?"

"I did sometimes. We'd had letters from Auntie Bella now and then, saying you'd got stuck or something and wouldn't strike up with any other girl."

Garth nodded.

"I'd rather banked on that," he said.

"Yes. It made me feel you was different from ordinary chaps, who'd carry on like that with any girl and think nothing of it. I'd felt from the start you weren't like them. I rather pitied you, I think, you seemed so broke up about Edith and that, and too slow and clumsy to find a way out on your own."

Garth smiled: the Moment was very near now, everything relaxing. . . .

"True enough. That streak in me that keeps me hanging stupidly on to things even when I know they're no good to me, had got me tied up in knots just then. I s'pose it's the same streak what's kept me waiting for you."

"Oh! Aren't I any good to you?"

"Sorry! I didn't mean. . . ."

He seized the chance offered by this slip, inclined his face towards hers. She was ready. Their kiss was swift, lips locked to lips for only a few seconds, but it brought them fully through to realisation, the perfectly natural sense of mateship begun so long ago, maturing in darkness and silence, budding out now with delicious, frank audacity. Only the hoot of a car approaching the corner prevented them from giving this reunion the length and intensity of that parting embrace in the workshop.

They strolled on, outwardly as before, but deliriously changed in mood. The earth around them palpitated with fresh colour, fresh music. Blackcaps fluttering among the trees kept imitating the notes of various other birds, as if they were not sure which would best suit that couple passing below, now in the shade of gleaming hollies, now under the spread boughs of blossoming sycamore, flowering elm or sweet-scented hawthorn. Quite naturally now they could talk, dropping more details of the intervening years—Garth of his lonely life at Meledor, lightly touched in with references to his workmates, neighbours; Irma of the squalid slum background, her brothers and sisters, her childhood and school life.

For nearly an hour they sauntered on through the lush, tranquil beauty of the dale, while the sunlight panted down behind the flaming gorse-clad hillocks and shadows bit deeper and darker into each warm golden patch, whether of field, road, woodland or cottage wall. By that time they had almost reached Tresillian. The creek was visible, quite close, to the south, though only now and then could they get a full view of it between the dense growth of trees and bushes. A group of old-world cottages overlooked the road, and below this were several bungalows and workshops, with a crane now unattended, on the embankment. In the distance a bridge, a single arch of grey stone, carried the road across the river and on towards Probus.

Garth and Irma paused, not wishing to enter the hamlet, and after some minutes' loitering they began slowly retracing their steps. Irma at once took up the serious, personal issue from which they had strayed without fully exploring it. The evening would soon be gone, Garth travelling back along this road in the bus. Every moment precious now; every word must stab to draw him out and fill her! . . . She slipped her arm through his and locked her hand between his big hot fingers. Her voice was a trifle breathless.

"As I said, Bella'd let us know you was in a pretty pickle through the . . . the notion people'd got about what happened between us. But when dad dropped out I knew I shouldn't hear any more: Bella wouldn't write again. It was nearly a year since she'd mentioned you in a letter, anyway, and I . . . I kept fearing I might have to slip back. If nobody understood there was nothing else . . . Several times I felt an itch to write to you, only I . . . well, I wasn't sure enough then—thought you might reckon I was cheap or—crazy. But the memory grew on me—our little affair in the workshop; something seemed pointing to that as the point it all turned on. There was something about it that gripped, bigger than all I'd known since. It seemed silly, because I was only a kid then and wouldn't understand, they'd say. But I did."

"I know you did," said Garth. "I never had the slightest feeling that you weren't my equal—never felt ashamed in looking back at it. It always seemed beautiful—one o' the great moments when life takes a new shape. There was the mystery of it; and as it worked on me I got convinced that, whatever it may have been on our side, it was God's doing, a experience I could use to find what prayer could still do for a man who'd sell out every other prospect."

Irma's eyes grew wistful, following the flight of a wood-pigeon over the creek.

"I've a lot to learn, Garth. I couldn't understand what was happening to me, only I knew something had marked me out from our set—mum and Slade, and dad and the beastly rip he deserted us for."

"Who was she—did you hear?"

Irma's glance lit casually upon the river bend where the bird had vanished; broad, sun-flecked, the water lying tideless there between the woods.

CHAPTER TWENTY-FIVE

"Yes," she answered with some reluctance. "A Mrs. Griffiths."

"Griffiths?" Garth staggered a pace backward, leaning against the hedge. "Good God! Can it be. . . . D'you know anything more about her?"

"Only that she and her man came from Wales. They were separated, I think—he going around the country as an engineer or something. Why?"

Garth drove his clenched fist into his palm, much excited.

"I know that man! It was he who stopped me running across you in the museum this morning—the one who asked you your name—the man with the moustache!"

"Cripes!" said Irma; she, too, had become pale, startled. "He down here? Could he . . . does he know I'm . . . Bert's daughter?"

"I can't say how much he may have picked up. All I know is, he came to see me back at Easter and said I was a fool to expect to get this girl, whoever she was. I didn't drop your name, only told him I believed God had done a bit o' grafting in the workshop and wasn't likely to lose the fruit of it by letting us marry the wrong partners."

"What brought him up to Meledor? You'd met him somewhere before?"

"Yes—at Truro for a minute back in February. That began through Minnie Lagor, too. He goes around peddling verses, got so far as Meledor by accident one day, called at the Snells' and fell in love with Minnie. The affair's breaking down now, I believe—his atheist stuff getting in the way. Anyhow, Minnie blabbed a bit about me, as neighbours will, and he called to try and make me 'expect only the worst, and accept it in silence,' as his experience—that tragedy about his wife—had convinced him there wasn't any God."

A look of wonder held Irma's eyes very wide and steady.

"And that same experience—how strange! It was that very thing that led me to find my feet and . . . and reward *your* faith."

247

"Yes; God seems to have been thinking of us rather than him." Garth's voice became passionate, he peered up through the trees at the faint evening clouds, pearly, aloof up there above human mysteries. "I can't explain —it's too vast, too deep, the puzzle of things. But there *are* facts enough to show that the way of faith is the right way and doubt and cynicism and bitterness warn God off a man's life so that it crumbles to disaster."

Fresh light had broken into Irma's face; she stared musingly back along the road leading to Truro, and murmured half to herself:

"So that's the secret Auntie and Miss Jesty've twitted me about! They've said there was a man living in Truro who'd make my eyes pop if I recognized him, only I might bolt back to London again if they told me who he was. I thought they was kidding me, and once or twice wondered even—if they might mean—you."

Garth grinned.

"No such luck! Wish I *did* live nearer."

"But now—if he hears we're—courting. . . ."

Garth's grin faded; he bit his lip and a frown of genuine anxiety clouded his countenance.

"Sooner we're married the better," he observed with an abrupt tenseness.

Irma's hand slipped up to his neck, fondling; she sighed as though from her a burden, a haunting fear, had passed.

"I'm glad. . . . I wasn't sure you'd look at it like that," she whispered. "I'd felt you might be one o' these slow country boobs who think a girl needs weeks or months to think it over."

"I did think so once," he confessed ruefully. "But somebody taught me better—in the workshop!" He took her face between his hands, and again they kissed. "I'd marry you next week if I could," he went on in more tremulous tones, feeling her press close, hungry to be claimed. "All's ready for you there at Meledor, the empty house just waiting for you to take charge of it."

248

"Well, we'll see. It's crazy to wait in our circumstances —and dangerous too, with that Griffiths guy and Aunt Ethel and Miss Jesty snooping round. It makes me feel scared, there at Truro, all strange and unfriendly. I've really no home now, and with you a dozen miles off, except for an hour or two a week. . . ."

"We'll soon have that mended," Garth assured her. His eyes grew sly, teasing; he glanced along the road— deserted to the corners on both sides. They had rounded the bend, were beyond view of the bridge and the houses, close to a roadside clearing overhung by dense elms. No sound of vehicles approaching, no footsteps! Alone with the gulls and cuckoos and the teeming ardour of wild life in the woods along the creek.

Chapter Twenty-six

L ATE in the afternoon of Wednesday, the twenty-second of May, a horse and cart stood outside a cottage at Brighton, the tiny hamlet on the cross-roads two miles south-west of Meledor. It was the same horse and cart that, in January, had drawn Martin Stribley's dead cow to the gulch of the Fal for burial in the clay-slime; and the four persons who had then chatted around the cart had been engaged for the past half-hour in the bustling activity which belongs to fresh beginnings. Seth and Edith were about to settle in their new home, and the few pieces of furniture that could be spared from the Chirgwins' abode had been brought from Trethosa in Martin's cart. Now that the Spraggs were to set up at a safe distance from the farm Bella had allowed her husband to resume his friendship with Seth, though relations between her and Edith were still strained pending a definite issue of their malicious assaults on Garth.

The two young men, bare-armed and sweating, seemed moderately cheerful; they had even jested as they passed in and out through the glass-panelled porch outside the front door, carrying the iron bedstead, a chest of drawers, carpets, clocks and other oddments. They were occasionally assisted by Colly Snell, who had plodded down on his own account, uninvited by the young people, though tolerated out of a feeling of sympathy for a man just bereaved. Colly was now a widower; his prophecy to Minnie on Trethosa Moor had been fulfilled within a week, Mrs. Snell sinking rapidly after the heart attack which had come at midnight on that Sunday. Relieved as he was to be rid of such a wife, Colly found the house lonely and rather depressing as he remembered how recently Shirley and her mother had occupied it, and he spent most of his time with neighbours, meddling in any special business that could distract his thoughts from the personal blank.

He was seated now, sunning himself on the edge of the shaft, peering up at the open bedroom window—quite close, as there was no garden in front of the cottage. Edith and Seth could be heard moving about inside; now and then he caught a glimpse of their shadowy figures as they came near the window to rearrange some article of furniture or straighten the fringe of a carpet. There was little talk between them, but happily no sign of bickering. Several times Edith had leaned out of the window and addressed the men as they unloaded the effects—looking rather pinched, Colly thought, but it was clear that the emotional crisis had passed and that this step was being taken with the deliberate aim of improving their marital prospects.

The cart was now empty, and as Colly began lighting his pipe Martin appeared, hastily throwing on his coat in the doorway. His full cheeks were red, and caught the diffused glow of colour from the panels of the porch. He stood for a few moments on the edge of the road, glancing to the foot of the hill twenty yards distant where the lane joined the Bodmin-Truro highway and the road leading to Summercourt nosed away to the north-west under the lee of wooded slopes. Half-a-dozen other cottages down there on the corner completed the hamlet, and plashy meadows tapering out southward completed the view—softly pretty, with none of the rugged grandeur of the plateau to which it was appended, like a lace fringe to a curtain of sombre and violent tones. No neighbours were visible, though doutbless the arrival of the furniture had been observed and appropriate comments were being made by housewives scowling up through the mist from steaming bowls as they washed the tea-dishes.

"Well, Colly," Martin greeted as he stepped forward and took the reins; "time for us to leave the happy couple to their honeymoon now. Seth isn't going back yet, so you can save your legs on the homeward journey."

He motioned Colly to the footboard, and with some difficulty the old man clambered up and seated himself on the high front rim of the cart. Martin leapt up beside him, his head level with the bedroom window, to which both Seth and Edith stepped at once. Seth's face showed a watery grin; he even put his arm—very timidly—around Edith's shoulder. She remained cold and unresponsive, speaking in a flat, unemotional tone.

"Thanks for the help, Martin. Tell Bella she can call when she likes, though now we're on the main bus routes I don't expect we'll be at home so often."

"Right-o; but you know what she is, and you may do better to find new friends," commented Stribley.

Colly pointed his stick past Martin's head, almost touching the window sash.

"Not a very promising time for making a fresh start, Mr. Spragg, but you was drove to it—and you too, Edith—and when folks is drove there's no more to be said, except to wish 'em good luck."

The cart jolted forward up the hill, and once it was

beyond the house and the adjoining shed in which Prince was penned, howling miserably, Martin expressed a more grudging view of the situation.

"They'll shove along as well as most, I daresay. Marriages is apt to show a crack here and there in wartime."

Colly tossed his stick into the cart and winked slyly over his pipe as he observed:

"Rather more than a crack was seen by they Chirgwins, if I've heard aright, Mr. Stribley. But Brighton's a nice tame little place—ought to smooth down the breakages if anything can."

"They've made it up a bit lately," Martin continued. "Edith climbed down, so Seth tells me, and asked if 'twas true what Sal Blewett said outside Garth's—that he'd never carried on with Jean. Seth thought he might as well make the best o' things and told her straight 'twas just ballyhoo, that he hadn't been more unfaithful to she than she'd been to him, so they could go on with a clean sheet as far as that was concerned. Put 'em square, I believe."

"H'm!" grunted Colly, spitting tobacco juice over the ferns above the gutter. "Seems that even the Sal Blewetts have their uses."

"Yes; that business turned her dead agin Garth— brought an end to all her schemings there, and now she appear to have got back some balance."

"Glad to hear it, Mr. Stribley. If Seth d'go careful he may live to rejoice that he married that woman—so far as a man can rejoice at his mistakes. The uncertainty o' the times is a stimmilent: wi' Hitler's parachutes likely to drop down through the sky any minute and blow us all up, there's no argument agin making the most of our last hours upon this earth." Colly's face sharpened lugubriously as he tapped Martin's elbow.

"A solemn time, Mr. Stribley: makes me doubt if I'll make the headway I was hoping for. Freedom have come too late, I'm afraid—stubborn as that woman was and not giving up till Hitler'd put all other illegible women in such a stewer o' fright that they couldn't get a calm view o' me good qualities. But if we'm still surviving in a few months' time I shall dare to look around, I hope, and pop me question where it d'look favourable."

Martin's lips twisted with humorous mockery. The cart had reached the hilltop now and jogged on between high hedges, rows of broken elms, one or two farmsteads by the roadside.

"You'll survive all right if you look high enough," he said.

"Well, there's Reub and Miss Sandercock to encourage me in the matter of height," responded Colly, wriggling on his uncomfortable seat and making an expansive gesture with his skinny, ragged-sleeved arms. "Why should I be put off wi' a broke-down, illiterate old widow when Reub have netted in such a well-tailored piece o' cultivation?"

"True: why should 'ee?"

"Only the war is a sad impediment at its present pitch —except to they what's already spliced. You and Bella now—wi' Hitler squeezing us in so close I daresay you've found some improvement?"

Martin sobered, flicking the reins and frowning glumly down upon the horse's tail.

"Not exactly. Bella's turned a bit spiteful about Garth again since I told her how different he come to work last Monday week. She was expecting some violent move— —bolting off to London or drowning hisself; and instead o' that he strolls back to the workshop as cool as a cucumber, happier'n I've seen him look for years. Got us all stumped: queerest turn of all this is—if it lasts."

Colly sniffed.

"I've heard there's a change come over him; high time it did, anyway. Last time I seen him was the Sunday me wife had her last heart attack: he was standing up on

Meledor burrow—after midnight 'twas—blowing kisses around the sky like if he thought there was a maid there. 'Gone too far at last, my sonny,' I thought. 'There's the makings of Bodmin in that spectacle.' "

"He seems steady enough now: a crisis o' some sort have passed, that's certain."

Colly puffed at his pipe for a few minutes, then ventured as one making an oblique approach:

"Meledor back on half-time from this week, isn't it ?"

"Yes; only wanting us every other week now. 'Twon't be long afore we drop out altogether. But I don't feel that's done the trick, even if Garth did mean to go to London."

"Edith's shifting may have something to do wi' it: he'll be breathing freer now he knows he's past danger from she." Colly removed his black cap and tried to hit with it some flies crawling about the horse's rump. "In my view that man have had a schooling lately what've made a clean break for'n. Since he found Shirley and got that illness I shouldn't wonder if the bubble had bust. Seth give him a hint or two, I believe, there on Melbur burrow t'other Sunday. And then Minnie arrived." Colly's voice sank to a slow mumble, he scratched his white head perplexedly.

"I wonder what she said to him that evening ? 'Twouldn't surprise me if Minnie had more to do wi' the change in him than anybody else."

"She han't called on 'ee since, I s'pose ?"

"No: I seed her down to the funeral, but wasn't no wiser about what she's up to, except that she told me she'd wrote to Griffiths saying 'twas all off—had thought it over and decided 'twas best not to see him any more."

"I felt there hadn't been much movement there. She's lucky to get off so light. I'd feared another Ted Blewett in that bloke."

"Still, 'tis funny, as it seemed a providence Griffiths should call at our place like he did—and then Shirley being

CHAPTER TWENTY-SIX

killed to open the way. . . . But if Garth isn't behind it
somehow—well, my head have failed me for once. I aren't
saying she and Garth's going to run off together. . . ."

"More likely he've picked up wi' some maid in town,"
remarked Martin. "He don't look like a man who's still
waiting. He've got back in touch wi' things. Whistling
away as he works, and going headlong into the arguments
there in the lodge, so they say, though up to now he kept
quiet about the war, as if it didn't interest him."

Colly pulled his cap again low over his sunken eyes,
which glowed with fresh excitement as they fastened on
the brim of Martin's green trilby.

"Well, what do 'a think's going to happen now wi' the
Jerries barging through France—only seventy miles from
England the wireless said this morning, and likely to get
the Channel ports afore the week's out. We'm seeing
things these days, Mr. Stribley—nations going down like
skittles, and the whole country keyed up, expecting
invasion."

Martin gave an uneasy shrug, glowering upon the white
stump of a signpost, recently stripped of its guiding fingers,
at the cross-roads they were passing.

"Yes, 'tis a black outlook. Better we hadn't been so
hasty to help the blinkin' Poles—only pushing other
countries in the same stew."

"I never seed sich times: a man can't but ask why it
have come to this after all the hopes and that, eddication
and whatnot that was supposed to be making such headway." Colly knocked some ashes from his pipe upon the
corner of the cart, and abruptly rapped:

"What do that man say?"

"Well, I ha'n't heard much of it, only a few scraps
outside the lodge. Yesterday he was in full spate with
Hocking, Reub and Keast when I come up to meet Bella
dinner-time. He nodded to us and smiled pretty deep at
Bella, as if he'd got her licked somehow; and then went
on with his argument as if we wasn't there. No rose-water

talk, either—seemed to think France'll knuckle in soon.
All sham strength with the heart rotted through, he said
—drugged and paralysed for want of spiritual sap grafted
in. That's all I heard: daresay he worked it up to a
regular sermon. He's still religious, whatever change
have come."

"And maybe his religion have brought the change:
there's unlikelier things," admitted Colly, giving a smart
nod at Scarcewater chapel as it loomed into view near
the summit of the ridge on which stood Meledor.

They had soon passed this little sanctuary, standing
gaunt and lonely by the roadside; and just then a heavy
vehicle was heard approaching from behind. As Martin
guided the horse and cart into the ditch a bus slid by, so
near that its windows were within a yard of Colly. He
caught a fleeting glimpse of a girl's face close to the window, looking pale and tense, as if she had feared a collision.
Both men watched the vehicle glide onward, expecting
it to disappear smoothly over the brow of the scarp; but
within a minute it had come to a halt at the end of a lane
leading in between open fields and downland to Meledor.
The girl Colly had observed got out—a slim figure in a
brown coat and green hat; and from her uncertain
manner as she lingered by the ditch as the bus whined
away, raising a cloud of dust from the road, the men
guessed that she was a stranger hereabouts.

"Wonder who that is," grated Colly, leaning forward
and half closing his eyes as he studied the hesitant, forlorn-
looking creature. "Seem to me I've spotted she afore
somewhere."

Martin stared at her with lips pursed, frowning in
silence.

The girl stepped into the lane, her head and shoulders
visible above the low hedge, moving slowly, with frequent
pauses while she gazed across at the mass of clay-dunes
dwarfing the few cottages of Meledor that were in view
from here. Her presence whetted more and more a

pleasurable curiosity in Martin, and he urged the horse to a faster pace until the cart also passed from the road into the lane—a short cut, saving the journey down the winding hill to Terras and across Trethosa Moor.

Hearing the cart lumbering and creaking behind her the girl glanced around, then stood still on a bank close under the hedge, watching the men approach, a faint strained smile upon her lips. The lurching of the wheels in the deep ruts caused the riders to bob, jerk and collide violently with one another, sometimes wrenching Colly's feet from the footboard and swinging them out like a pendulum, while he held rigidly to the edge of the cart on which he was seated. But more than amusement at these erratic movements underlay the girl's smile, and as the parties converged the true heart of the comedy was disclosed. Martin's face had whitened before he drew level with her, and once abreast he brought the horse to a standstill and looked the stranger up and down with a deliberation in which rudeness was lost in incredulous amazement.

His doubt was soon removed; the girl's blue eyes met his, defensive, with an odd mixture of playfulness and reserve.

"Yes, it's me," she said.

"What! Irma?" Stribley could hardly speak, and looked dazed, open-mouthed.

She nodded.

"Rather a surprise, isn't it, Uncle Martin? You didn't expect to see me here again." She added with a flick of her hand: "I aren't going down to the farm."

"Don't think Bella'd let you in if you showed up there," mumbled Martin in thick, unnatural tones; he passed a hand shakily across his forehead—dripping with sweat. "But why . . .ah! yes, I understand now."

Colly took upon himself the explanation of this remark, though he, too, was much shaken, standing in a crouching posture, his jaw hanging stupidly, his hand trembling on the pipe just below it. His voice sounded weak, muffled.

"We . . . we was jist telling what a change have come over Garth Joslin lately. I reckon you must know something about it."

"Perhaps I do."

"You'm going in to see him now?" asked Martin after a tense pause.

"Yes."

Suspicion followed shock to Colly's hollow face; he jerked his pipe at arm's length towards Meledor.

"Funny he han't come out to meet 'ee: so long since you was here, you must ha' forgot the lie o' the land—except for the workshop over there, I s'pose?"

Irma flushed, staring down at the daisies on the bank as she replied falteringly:

"He don't know I've come."

Stribley had recovered somewhat; his reaction was clearly sympathetic. It was only under pressure from Bella that he had ever disliked the girl, and her ripe, lonely beauty now won him back. He spoke again, in a more hearty manner.

"You may as well take a lift in now I've come across 'ee. Cart's clean: we just been shifting furniture in it. . . . You can get back behind there, Colly, and let the maid sit up beside me till we get to Garth's."

Colly mumbled grumpily, but he climbed back into the body of the cart and squatted upon its side after covering it with a strip of sacking that had been rolled up in the corner. Martin leaned towards the girl and took her hand, helping her to reach the footboard, where she stood a little more stolid and aloof, tensing herself against memories.

The cart again jolted on along the lane, drawing its occupants into full view of the great sweep of landscape across the valley, from Kernick to Terras, and southward, following the bends of the Fal, embracing the richly wooded hills around Coombe and Trelyon. St. Stephen gleamed just oppoite—church tower, trees, rows of houses thinning out north-east towards the vast pyramidal wedges of clay-dunes driven upward from the bleaker folds of moorland. The breadth and spaciousness of the scene were exhilarating under a sky so blue that contrast had full play, the tops of sand-heaps clear-cut as marble on sapphire, not smudged upon cloud, the verdure of turf and trees no passive background, but vivid, darkly palpitating. Cuckoos wheeled up and down the dale, uttering that aching call-note which Irma had never before heard in this setting. Her pulse quickened as she picked out details of the scene forgotten since her last fateful visit here, noting also that most of the sand-dunes had changed their shape, some bulging much further, covering ground which she remembered as open field or heath, others pared back to mere shells by the removal of quantities of gravel for use in the making of cement.

The men's interest was confined to the girl herself as slowly their startled minds received her image as a harmless intrusion.

"If I'd seed a ghost I couldn't ha' felt more like a dish-cloth," said Colly solemnly, prodding Martin in the back with his stick as he edged along the sacking nearer to Irma. "How did 'ee get this far again, my dear?"

Irma explained briefly the circumstances of her evacuation, and replying to further questions told how she had met Garth in Truro cathedral nearly a fortnight ago.

"So 'tis going steady now, then?" persisted Colly, craning his scraggy neck in a vain effort to glimpse her face.

"I hope so," she answered, still looking straight ahead. "We . . . we mean to be married this summer and . . . and settle here at Meledor."

Stribley was studying her face as one hypnotised; he gaped afresh at this news and said with a smothered laugh:

"Bella'll have a fit if you put that through!"

Colly stood up and tapped Irma's shoulder with a familiar and ingratiating air.

"There'll be different views, o' course, as to how this have come about, but when I think o' what Garth have gone through for 'ee—well, I really don't know what to think."

At this surprising collapse of his logical and imaginative powers Colly sat back again upon the cart's side, crossed his legs and began puffing steadily at his pipe, as if the thought of commenting at all upon such a delicate situation had never occurred to him.

Silence fell between the trio and the cart drew at length into Meledor, past the school and on to the hill where the sand-dune abutted. No cottagers were abroad, only a dog came out to yelp at them, and some fowls fluttered, squawking in alarm, across the road. Both men watched Irma closely as they passed the end of the lane leading in to Meledor clay-pit, expecting some sign of the tremendous stir of memory which must be evoked by that scene. They were not disappointed. She stared fixedly in along the shadowed track to the tank wall hiding the workshop, her lips thinned, eyes hard, brooding. Nearly five years ago—there! How far had those two——? Her expression left the matter an enigma still. . . .

Having turned the next bend it was only a few minutes before Martin reined in the horse and pointed over the hedge to a cottage intermittently disclosed beyond it.

"That's Garth's place—daresay you remember."

The cart stopped and Irma alighted. She seemed even more agitated now than when she had first glimpsed them, her voice shaky, her glance evasive.

"Thanks, uncle." She forced a smile, slightly mocking in its triumph. "Bella won't need to send you up this time to inquire what's happened!"

CHAPTER TWENTY-SEVEN

Chapter Twenty-seven

THE cart rumbled on down the hill, passed from sight around the corner, and Irma was left alone at the gate, trembling, peering into the garden as if it were forbidden ground. She felt overcome for a few minutes by a sense of unreality, as though she were lost in some foreign world. That grey house under the foam of trees—her future home! It seemed crazy. . . . But she had stood here before and looked in, thinking: "So that's where he lives! Dear Garth!" She repeated the words now: "Dear Garth!" just as she had done that Thursday, coming back from the workshop, confused, knowing they had been discovered. . . . Ah, yes, it *was* real! She felt again that reckless mood, her humiliation at the farm, the delicious, half-guilty storming of emotion which had led her to linger at the bedroom window, wafting kisses up towards his home, before she got into bed to lie awake and murmur passionately: "I don't care! Don't be sorry, Garth. . . ." And then—suddenly the forward sweep, Garth's lips on hers by the roadside at Tresillian!

Softly she opened the gate and stepped inside, encouraged as she noted that the front door was ajar. Sparrows and other birds fluttered away from the gooseberry bushes as she entered; butterflies nosed about the thick dark rhubarb leaves down by the adjoining toolshed. . . . Irma stole furtively along the path, and halting at the door she pushed it wide open with a timid knock, her heart thumping in expectancy of her first glimpse of the man within.

It came at once, and surprise checked her emotional impulse. Garth appeared in the middle doorway, outlined against the small kitchen window. He was in his workaday, clay-smeared trousers, stripped to his shirt above the waist, and had obviously been shaving when she knocked:

half his face was white with lather and he still held a
safety razor in his hand, which jerked up at sight of her,
the clean side of his face becoming almost as pale as the
soapy one. His reaction showed uneasiness as well as
astonishment, though he greeted her lightly.

"You've caught me this time—and you'll have to wait
till I finish my shave before you get what you've come for!"

She stepped hesitantly in, glancing into the parlour as
she passed its open doorway. All was strange and the
stress of crisis was upon her, so that she could not reply
with spontaneity and naturalness. Moving fully into the
kitchen as Garth backed towards the table she remarked
with forced calm:

"You was just getting ready to catch the bus, I s'pose?"

"Yes—thought I'd be with you in Truro in an hour
or two. . . . Did you manage to find the house easily?"

Irma's eyes brooded upon the table—still laid for tea,
with Garth's shaving outfit set among the empty plates,
a small mirror leaning against a jam-pot in the centre of
the white cloth.

"I rode in from the hill out there with . . . Uncle
Martin," she murmured. "He'd been down somewhere
with somebody's furniture in the cart."

Garth halted the razor half-way down his cheek.

"Ah, yes—Seth's and Edith's. They're setting up at
Brighton on the turnpike road—got too hot for 'em here
close to me. . . . Rather a bombshell for Martin, coming
on you here so near the farm."

"It was," she said, her troubled eyes meeting his and
her breast heaving; "but . . . but not a bigger bombshell
than I've had since we parted last Sunday."

"So it's . . . you haven't come up just to give me a
surprise?"

"No. I wish it was only that. But I *had* to come. This
is the only safe place to tell you—what's happened."

Garth hastily completed his shave, wiping his face with
a towel hung behind the door. Then he drew her back

in front of the dresser, and for several minutes they stood there embraced, very still, her lips drawing at his mouth as if it were the one duct of nourishment God had opened to her soul just then. At length, still clasping her, and with his cheek close to hers, he said gently:

"Now! What is it? Those ladies haven't changed their minds, have they? You told me last week they just laughed and urged you to go ahead when they learnt we'd linked up again."

"I know." Irma stiffened, her mouth twitching. "It's —that fellow Griffiths. *He's* found out now, and—goodness knows what he may try to do if he gets the chance!"

A sharp gasp from Garth:

"Ah! That's more what I'd feared. . . . You've seen him?"

"Yes, last Monday. I was in the Gardens in the morning, over by the viaduct where the river comes out under the bridge. I was just strolling up and down there, thinking of our meeting and wondering how things would open for us to get married. Then as I glanced back towards the lawn I saw that man hurrying across it and along the causeway. 'Twas too late to get clear—he'd spotted me and was waving his arms—more violent even than that day in the museum. He barged straight up to me and said between his teeth: 'So you're still here?' I tried to answer casual and said I was. And then he opened up close: 'Are you Irma Stribley—are you?'— it almost scared me, he was that fierce. I didn't think it would pay to turn cheeky or jib away, so I said yes, that was my name; and then he—he asked if I'd met you— if we was courting. I didn't answer to that, and he laid hold of my arm. . . ."

"Wasn't there anybody around, that you could call out?"

"I didn't want to make a scene. There was no one in sight there with the trees. I was stumped for a few minutes, then I owned up that we—had got together in

Truro. I feel sure he knew beforehand—may have seen us pass the Rundles' place Sunday evening. And then he gave a queer sort o' smile, trying to control himself, and ground out: 'You aren't going to marry that man!' Then he gripped me tighter and almost shouted: 'D'you know who I am?' I said I'd heard he was the—the man whose wife had carried on with dad, and told him I couldn't help that, though I was sorry if he was still upset about it. And just then a party o' women turned in from the road and he slunk off—a mercy, as it'd got me pretty flustered. But the danger isn't past; I'm almost afraid to move out alone."

Garth slumped back to the table and seated himself upon its lower end. She came across to him, and he lifted her hand to his lips passionately.

"Don't let it get you down, sweet—don't doubt for a moment we're going to come together all right. That's bloke's just a symbol o' the unbelief we *have* triumphed over, though it may still wriggle and try to sting beneath our feet. . . . Have you told your auntie?"

"No; I don't want her and Miss Jesty to hear of it. They'd only laugh and p'raps tell me to switch over from you and see if I could rope in Griffiths."

"H'm! Well, it'd be safest to keep in their company now, even if it isn't very congenial—just for the few weeks. . . ."

But Irma had caught his arm, interrupted.

"It's about them, too—that I've come now," she said gulpily. "Aunt Ethel's had a word that her man's been knocked down in the black-out: he's hurt bad and in hospital."

An abrupt move of Garth's overturned the shaving brush, which rolled on to the floor.

"Getting a bit tense," he observed, stooping to recover it. "What'll this mean?"

"It means she'll go back to London—next week-end. Going up by the train Saturday morning."

"Not to stay?"

"No; only for a few days. She may come back Monday night even. Her man's a deserter from the Army and if he don't die he'll be dealt with by the military people—won't need her round him. But—you see how awkward it'll be for me, Garth?"

"Yes; you and Miss Jesty there alone. . . ."

Irma shook her head; her eyes grew wider as she disclosed the full extent of the dilemma.

"No. Miss Jesty's going too. They told me yesterday. They've talked it over, and Miss Jesty's jumped at the chance to spend a day or two in London. She's never been there—and she's got plenty of money. They'll have a gay time, I bet."

Garth dropped the brush on the table with a thud.

"My gosh! They're the limit. Leaving you to look after the kids there alone in a strange city."

"I wouldn't mind that so much, now I've found you. You could have come down every evening. But I'm afraid Griffiths will know they've gone—may see 'em go up to the station, or hear of it, and then . . . I feel there's nothing he'd stop at in such a mood as I saw him in."

For awhile there was silence, Garth's face growing dark and puckered as he stared through the window at the blank hedge beside the tool-shed. Irma watched him, toeing the carpet restlessly, blindly trusting him.

Presently he moistened his lips and remarked as one trying to visualise and grasp the whole of a situation before deciding on a practical move:

"Funny how this affair between me and Griffiths has taken such a personal turn. I never expected that when I met him first at Truro in February, or even when he came up to see me last Easter."

"You didn't squabble with him then?"

"No. We parted quite friendly. I thought him a bit of a crank—just as he thought me, I reckon; but there was no ill-feeling in it. I believe at bottom he rather took

a liking to me—felt I was independent too in my own
way, not just drifting with the religious, church-going
crowd."

"And you—you couldn't have thought him a rotter."

"I don't think that now," said Garth. "If he'd been a
conceited ass, just out to shock people with nasty ideas,
I'd never have had anything to do with him—nor Minnie
Lagor wouldn't either. It was his solid, old-fashioned
way that got her struck on him for a bit. We both felt he
was putting up a stiff fight for the best values he could
figure out, only he was determined to trust his own nature
to see him through." Garth paused, and as Irma made
no comment he resumed in a subdued tone of perplexity:

"But somehow life wouldn't let it stay on that level.
It set something working between us what's come as a
shock to us both: bits of news digging in and twisting us
apart. It's a queer feeling: we're still strangers, and we
parted casual, thinking some friendship might develop;
yet if we meet again—well, it won't be exactly friendly!"

Irma shrugged, mechanically unfastening her coat.

"You haven't met him since he was here at Easter?"

"No—except for that glimpse in the museum; and
by that time things had begun to look ugly. When Minnie
Lagor threw him over he seemed to feel I'd got at her
with my religious dope and turned her against him. And
on top o' that he learns I've got you after all—and that
you're Stribley's daughter. It's a personal feud now,
though it's ripened out from our beliefs."

Irma seized his hand, tilting her face again up towards
his.

"But what'll you do, Garth—about this week-end?"

He bit his lip, then announced deliberately:

"No half measures. We've gone through too much
to stop at anything that may look a bit shady."

"You mean—we'll have to be together somehow?"

"Yes. Either I'll go down to Truro and stay with you
till those ladies come back, or else you and the kids must

come here from Saturday to Monday. By that time we may be able to see whether the threat's worth taking serious."

Irma nodded, glancing dreamily around the room, trying to apprehend the future beyond this entanglement, herself a housewife preparing meals daily in this kitchen.

"We'd be safer here—and I'd feel more comfortable—in my own home," she murmured with a little strained laugh. "I shouldn't care about the village talk. . . . D'you think Griffiths might show himself here again ?"

"There's no telling wi' a bloke o' that sort. His morbid, unbalanced streak might lead him back to where this last mess started for him—that day he came here trying to spread his atheism and got caught in the noose when Minnie Lagor opened Snells' door to him. . . . But there'd be less risk here than at Truro. More convenient about the kids too. They'd scent something queer and unnatural in me hiding with you in a stranger's house, but here—you can just tell 'em you're giving 'em a treat, a week-end holiday where they can play hide-and-seek around their uncle's farm !"

A more spontaneous ripple of laughter broke from Irma.

"All right then. We'll come up Saturday morning by the first bus that leaves after I've seen Aunt Ethel and Miss Jesty off at the station."

"Do they know—about your visit here to-day ?"

"I didn't blab; but they'll guess where I've gone."

Garth slid off the table as the clock in the parlour began striking six.

"Well—now you've come—wait while I change a minute and then we'll see about spending the evening around here—get you used to the old place, even if I can't introduce you down at the farm !"

A little earlier Bella emerged from the cowshed in the Stribleys' farmyard, carrying a pail of milk. Her mousey hair was flying in disorder; a sack, dirtied from contact with the byre, coarsened her sprawling form. Her sweating, moon-like face expressed curiosity, and she glanced at once over the big farmyard gate a few yards from the shed doorway, into the road outside. Footsteps were drawing near, and halting a moment she saw the dark solid figure of Minnie Lagor become framed by the gate bars. Minnie's face wore a troubled frown, and she would have passed without observing Bella had not a creak of the pail handle drawn her eyes sharply to the small "town-place." She nodded, though with no warmth of familiarity: she had never been very friendly with Bella, who at heart despised her and had vented much malice on her affairs.

Now, however, Bella dropped her pail by the cowhouse wall, and lurching to the gate set a bare flabby arm along its top bar.

"You been over to Foxhole, I s'pose," she greeted in an insinuating tone.

"Yes," said Minnie, pausing. "I daresay you've heard about Muriel."

Bella gave her head a toss while pushing her thick fingers through her hair.

"A pity—though I expect most people'll say she got her deserts. Running headlong into that mess when she was only just seventeen. . . ."

"'Tis a bad job," returned Minnie, frowning across the farmyard where some fowls and pigs were wandering aimlessly. "She and Stephen was both looking forward so to having their baby and settling in comfortable; and doctor says with this miscarriage it's possible . . . they think she mightn't be able to have any more. It's upset her, naturally."

Bella grunted.

"Silly to be upset about that: she ought to be glad there's no more risk. How's she doing in herself?"

"Stronger now. She'll pull through all right, but 'twas touch and go. Came quite sudden: she was over visiting us last week, quite happy—everything going smooth."

A low titter broke from Bella; the gate rattled as she leaned more heavily against it.

"Stephen's wishing he'd walked off with somebody else, I expect, with this slip making him a laughing-stock."

"No: he's knocked up a bit—stays with her every spare minute. There's is a real marriage as far as any can be where there's no religion."

"Religion!" scoffed Bella, her little green eyes bright with scorn. "So you're turning that way now? Rather late in the day, my dear. . . . It's under Mr. Griffiths' influence, no doubt?"

Minnie answered stubbornly:

"You know very well I've finished with him. I couldn't risk it. *He* wouldn't be a safe husband without religion."

"Kept comparing him with Garth, didn't you, till you decided he was too old and tough for a young lady?"

"Well, I couldn't help seeing the difference, especially when Shirley died. If you'd heard Garth speak as he did to me you'd ha' found something there you couldn't sneer down."

"I'm still waiting to see results," said Bella with dry sarcasm. "Garth seems very happy all of a sudden, but I reckon some petticoat in Truro has more to do with it than his religion."

"It may have as much," replied Minnie quietly, a deep enigmatic smile touching her lips.

Bella glowered, her own lips drawn in, tigerish in bafflement. Something underlay that smile of Minnie's, a disturbing quality that made Bella feel uncertain, threatened. It gave an almost ominous significance to the sounds that became audible to both women at the next moment—the rhythmic clatter of horse's hoof-beats and the rumble of an approaching cart. Bella leaned over the gate, peering back towards the foot of Meledor hill. Her face grew more unpleasant, feverish. Martin at last!

When he drew close to the squat farmhouse the women saw that he looked pale and tense, standing stiffly on the

269

footboard, his eyes furtive, hardly daring to glance straight at Bella. With a short nod at Minnie he dismounted, moving with head bent sulkily to the gate. Bella stepped back, shifted the pail to safety under the yard wall, then returned as Martin swung open the gate.

"Well, are they settled in all right this time?"

Martin made an impatient gesture, leading the horse through the opening into the yard.

"Oh, that pair—yes," he mumbled; "I've seen 'em fixed snug in their bedroom. But that's nothing now. I don't reckon they Spraggs'll be getting any words wasted on 'em when others around here know as much as I do."

Bella stiffened, standing quite close to him, searching his face, which looked more than ever unnatural, ugly and defiant.

"Why—you've heard news—about Garth?"

"Not only him!"

Bella glanced at Minnie, who lingered by the gatepost behind the cart, and noted again that strange far-away smile. It stung awake a swift, daring apprehension in Bella now; she gasped and her cheeks whitened.

"It surely can't be . . . he hasn't found *her*?"

Martin pointed up the sunlit slope to the trees around Garth's home.

"Go up and peep through Joslin's window and you may see something similar to that workshop business!"

Bella laughed—a brittle, choked sound.

"You're crazy, Martin! How on earth could—could Irma . . . ?"

"She's was one o' the Truro bunch of evacuees, that's all—came down on purpose to find Garth, though. She told me just now—very frank."

Minnie was staring at Martin, breathing quickly, her features lit up with hope deepening to assurance.

"Irma up at Garth's now, is she?"

"I just brought her in from the bus in me cart—there on the footboard." He pointed to it, and the women's eyes converged on the spot as if seeking some material evidence of its late occupant, though as the ground was dry there was not even the faint mark of a footprint left behind. "Near floored me when I seen her turn in Meledor lane—couldn't believe me senses. But she knowed me well enough, and had her little joke about Auntie Bella sending me up to demand a explanation."

Minnie peered at the dark walls of the farmstead, her eyes mirroring a dreamy throw-back of fancy to the days Irma had spent in that house.

"I'm glad it's come at last," she said tremulously. "It's what I've been waiting to hear for weeks—and people've thought 'twas some affair o' me own, some switch-over from Griffiths, that's kept me a bit quiet and secret lately. . . . You see, I happened to spot Irma at Truro when I was there last with Griffiths—and told Garth. They've done the rest, as young folks will."

Restraint slipped in Bella; she strode angrily back towards Minnie, past the open gate, her fists clenched.

"A pretty fool you were to go blabbing to him like that!" she spluttered. "No business o' yours. Why couldn't you keep your mouth shut?"

Minnie answered with a calm dignity, looking steadily into the woman's eyes:

"I'd known suffering myself—too well to let a man go on in it when I knew I could help him as he'd helped me."

Martin slouched forward to close the gate, and said briskly:

"It's going ahead like a whirlwind, I should judge. Irma told me she and Garth's going to splice it soon and settle up here at Joslin's. So you'll have to mind your temper, Bella, or you'll be getting in trouble, passing her here on the roads so often."

Martin's gibe brought Bella to the point of violence; she slammed the gate shut before Martin reached it, and defiantly fronted him.

"What's she like to look at—fat and stodgy, I s'pose?"

Martin shook his head, his face and tone frankly jeering.

"Nobody'd take her for a relation o' yours, if that's any comfort to you. Slim now—as tall as me, and wi' that way wi' her that town girls have—all film star-ish, though she don't muck up her face like most of 'em. No maid around here could hold a candle to her for style and looks: Edith's a regular old hag in front o' she." He turned to favour Minnie with the more agreeable comment:

"People been making fun o' Garth for nearly five year, calling him killjoy and crank and what not; but it seems he got the last laugh all right. And I aren't the man to deny it got something to do with his beliefs."

"'Tis as near a miracle as anything I've seen," admitted Minnie.

"Miracle?" Bella sneered, her whole appearance becoming more primitive as deadly emotions were unleashed. "There's no miracle about it. It's as I've always said: Garth saw so much of her in the workshop that he couldn't rest till he'd got it in bed with him."

Martin spat.

"It's easy to talk like that, Bella, but you know as well as I that there's something mysterious behind it, how Irma should change so after what we heard of her— nothing brassy and reckless in her now—and turn up at Truro just as Garth was at breaking-point."

"Nothing mysterious. Garth isn't the only fool in the world. It isn't surprising Irma's another when you consider who her family is."

"Meaning me, I s'pose? All right, old dear—get it off your chest! You're licked and may as well get your own back by pretending everybody's coarse-grained like yourself."

Bella set her fat hands on her hips, throwing out a challenge that would have cowed Martin had he not been emboldened by the novelty of his recent encounter.

"Coarse-grained am I?"

"You better ask Minnie if you think you look nice and refined."

Bella lurched forward but controlled herself; her face twitched, however, and she almost shouted:

"D'you think Garth's marrying the girl out of charity ?"

"No. . . . But you wouldn't understand. If you'd heard him talk at the claywork sometimes. . . . 'Tisn't that he's tame and cold-blooded, but he's mastered the trick o' cutting out the smoke and sparks from his love so that the flame keeps burning clear right on through a lifetime."

"Huh!" grunted Bella, leaning back against the cow-shed wall. "It's early days to make any claim o' that sort about Garth. Irma's only nineteen yet, and he may find out things about her that'd damp his fire pretty quick. She may have had a baby already for all he knows."

Minnie turned away, not wishing to be drawn into the wrangle, and while passing along the road towards Virginia she heard Martin's ironic laugh and further sharp exchanges.

"That's the ticket—you'll hit the bull's eye yet, Bella, before you've used up all your spleen !"

"You dare to speak to me——!"

"All right! Garth and Irma won't have far to go if they need extra lessons. Here's a perfect marriage right on their doorstep!"

"I wish I'd never married into your bloody family!"

"Needn't blame me. I didn't use much persuasion on the job."

"Liar !"

Minnie shrugged with distaste, then hurried on, peering westward as the roof and chimneys of Garth's home were disclosed above the drying-sheds. The birds which Irma had scattered from Garth's garden came wheeling down the slope and passed over Minnie's head, chirping excitedly as if they had some secret for her. She continued to gaze steadfastly at the house ; and not even the rumble

of Stribley's cart disturbed the inflow of fortitude, her
share of the triumph now ready to beacon from that
cottage.

Chapter Twenty-eight

THE week closed tensely over mid-Cornwall. Places of
amusement in the more populous villages were packed
with crowds who had decided to spend the eve of the
national Day of Prayer in an outburst of defiant jollity.
No one guessed that a hamlet on one of the most remote
ridges of the district was now the scene of a spiritual drama
whose grandeur, stain of bled sap and scars of grafting,
would have shown them the proper use of crisis and the
conditions of success in any appeal for Divine intervention.

Irma had arrived at Meledor just before noon, carrying
two suitcases and accompanied by the children—her
sisters, Pat, Irene, and Sheila, and the Palmer trio, David,
Clarence and Elsie. The village and the downs around
it were quiet, sun-drenched under a sky that had been
blue for so many consecutive days that it seemed incapable
of changing colour, and gave the sensitive an eerie feeling
that something in the general mechanism of things had
snapped, leaving all non-human phenomena static,
paralysed. The war news Irma had heard at Truro and
on the bus was sufficient proof that appearances were
deceptive, and her face was shadowed as her thoughts
slipped from the sinister march of events in Europe to the
crisis that had brought her to this sanctuary.

The fresh meeting with Garth in that house was
awkward, the children's presence making it impossible
to discuss the real motive of the visit. Even when, after
the mid-day meal, the youngsters had gone out to acquire
some mountaineering experience on Meledor clay-dump
and Garth and Irma were left alone, she on his knee by
the fireless stove, they felt ill at ease, threats and fantasies

all round: the vague fear of Griffiths, the thought of those two women now being borne towards London, the oddity of this culmination, forcing them afresh off the lines of a normal courtship, and over all the tightening menace of the war that had brought them thus together.

The room itself was not cheerful now, being cluttered up with two folded camp beds that were set leaning against the dresser, the mattresses and bedding belonging to them having been pushed under the table.

Irma gave a brief account of her aunt's departure, the farewell scene at the railway station, speaking with an undertone of resentment.

"They promised to come down again Monday—and they'll bring back mum's verdict about our marriage. I've no doubt she'll agree to it—glad to be rid o' me. They'll be calling on her early to-morrow and telling her I've—gone back to you. Miss Jesty was joking about it as the train moved off. 'You'll be able to go ahead this week-end, dearie,' she said: 'won't be lonely to-night, eh? Your mum can't be heartless enough to refuse: she'll know it'll have gone too far to mend by the time we see her.'"

"You've told 'em—what we arranged?"

"Part of it—because o' the kids. I just said we'd be visiting Meledor while they're in London—didn't give any details."

Garth listened stolidly, gazing through the window at the blue sky above the flowering hawthorns. Irma's hand was curled in his, and he squeezed it hard, his free arm tightening about her supple form, clad now in a cotton frock of floral pattern that was damp here and there from recent dish-washing. After a pause he reached out a leg and tapped the edge of a camp bed with his shoes.

"I borrowed one o' these from Colly Snell," he said musingly. "Used to be little Shirley Lagor's."

"The girl you found killed?"

"Yes. Brings those memories close home to me. That maid was about all that brought real happiness into my life since you left here. She was in around the garden nearly every week—the only person who I felt really liked me. Neighbours used to say I was cracked, playing around wi' that kid instead o' going off wi' grown-up friends, old school chums and such like." He straightened, meeting Irma's eyes with a whimsical sincerity. "I reckon that childlike spirit's a part o' my faith. It's true of other things besides love that results can't be got while you're dignified."

Irma's smile was deep, intimate, and belied the apparently casual nature of her response:

"Who'll have these camp beds to-night?"

"The Palmer boys can have one here in the kitchen, and I'll shake down on the other out in the front room. Don't reckon I shall sleep much—and I can tackle Griffiths quicker from downstairs if he does come up after you and try to get in through the window."

They both laughed, Irma rubbing her cheek against Garth's for a few minutes.

"I haven't seen that fellow since Monday," she confessed, "and if—if he doesn't know Aunt Ethel's gone, or that me and the kids have flitted, there won't be any danger. But I'll be glad when it's past and—and we're settled here for good: though, of course, there'll be other threats then—from the war."

Garth nodded, peering at the dull bars of the empty fireplace.

"True," he said; "we can't tell how things'll pan out before the winter. I was meaning to get in war work when Meledor closes down, and should try for a job at St. Eval aerodrome, out near the north coast. They'll be needing hundreds o' men there during the next twelve months."

"We could still live here at Meledor then?"

"Yes; I'd get a motor-bike and ride to and fro. But

CHAPTER TWENTY-EIGHT

I might be sent to Devonport or Bristol instead—if I'm lucky enough to escape active service; and you'd want to come with me, in digs up there."

Irma rose, frowning moodily back at the stairway.

"It's real enough, Garth—this miracle of ours: there's still so many things we could worry about."

"I'm glad you see it like that, dearest," said Garth gently. "It's the only way. Faith isn't magic, and there's no happy-ever-after guarantee with the things that matter. . . ."

The afternoon and evening passed without incident, Garth and Irma remaining indoors except for brief spells in the garden, from which they watched the youngsters scrambling warily around the sand-dump, too timid to imitate the feats of local children, who left them wide-eyed by taking running jumps from the tip and tobog-ganing over the entire slope on old scraps of corrugated iron.

It was eight o'clock when the little London group came finally in for supper, not exactly shy but braced afresh for the contact with this strange man, Irma's "boy friend." They paused just inside the kitchen door, forming a dis-hevelled battalion of restless bodies and faces screwed up into neutral expressions that resembled blankness. The eldest was Mrs. Palmer's son, Clarence, twelve years old, and the youngest Irma's sister Pat, only just past her sixth birthday. All three Stribley girls bore close likeness to Irma, being decided blondes, plumply built, with big mouths and blue gliding eyes now half hidden by their tousled hair. Mrs. Palmer's seven-year-old girl, Elsie, was less attractive than her cousins, black-haired, thin, with red bony hands and a shapeless spongy mouth that was usually gaping.

Garth had already frolicked a little with his prospec-tive sisters-in-law, and continued to win their confidence, both Pat and Sheila being perched on his keee before supper was over. After the meal was finished—the general hubbub and clatter of crockery sounding very strange in this house where meals had been taken in solitary silence for so many years—he kissed the girls good-night, all except Elsie, who curled her lip and turned sulkily away when he approached her for the purpose. Irma led the four girls upstairs, and having shown them their beds she came down and enjoyed a few minutes of privacy with Garth in the parlour, clinging to him, throwing into every pressure, every kiss, the increased sense of intimacy and hunger produced by this unconventional situation.

"Good night, my own love," said Garth at last, chokily. "Only a few yards from the workshop . . . we'll think of that, not Griffiths."

She glanced at the drawn curtain barring out the dying daylight from the room, making a shadowy world all round.

"Yes. Good night, Garth—till then!"

He knew what she meant, and as soon as he was alone he knelt beside the camp bed for a long while, his head bowed, praying earnestly, one hand in his coat pocket grasping the Bible he had read on Melbur dune just before Seth and Minnie brought the double news of deliverance three weeks ago. When he arose he stood musing in the darkened room where the details of furniture were indistinguishable and there was scarcely space for him to move, the bed being fixed between a sofa too narrow for him to sleep on and the large sideboard. He listened to every sound from overhead, the padding of footsteps on the canvas covered floor, the subdued voices of the children and Irma's almost inaudible responses, the creak of the bed as one by one they climbed into it.

When all was quiet and he knew that Irma too must be lying up there in all her loveliness, awaiting sleep, Garth leaned over the sofa and noiselessly drew back the curtain from the window. Moonlight streamed into the room, for the moon, just past full, was riding up behind Trethosa, the tree-tops cutting upon its silvery shrunken

disc like black veins, unmoving, while shadows all over
the valley and the clay ridges were becoming magical,
the triangular shade of sand-dumps broken upon the
folds of the pits, the shade of drying-sheds and tanks
groping out over the Fal and the marshland, over the
first war-time instalment of flowers, insects, microscopic
eggs and amphibian life. Hardly a cloud up there among
the stars, and no marauding apparition below. Was
Griffiths too abed, at Truro, or prowling around the
ghostly streets, still undecided ? . . .

Garth turned back into the room, and within a few
minutes he was reclining between the cool sheets, head
on the pillow, eyes wide open, staring at the vague bulk
of the arm-chair in which Griffiths had sat last Easter.
He lay awake for some time, every nerve alert, disturbed
more by the proximity of Irma than by the memory of
Griffiths' visit or apprehension of the fellow's next move.
It was well past midnight before he got his first long snatch
of slumber, and when he awoke from this he saw that
sunlight was filtering in through chinks in the curtain.
His brain had barely thrown off the tangled associations
of the dream-world when the clock struck six. Realisation
came, and he sighed with relief, his eyes fixed on the dark
beams above him.

At eight o'clock Garth and Irma were breakfasting
alone in the kitchen. The girls were still abed, the boys
playing about the garden path. The atmosphere, though
a trifle strained, was not now oppressive. Garth was in
high spirits, even jocular, and both of them yawned a
good deal, feeling tired after the broken sleep of this queer
night.

They did not mention Griffiths but talked as if Mrs.
Palmer's visit to London was the sole cause of any incon-
venience they had suffered.

"I expect Auntie and Miss Jesty are up with mum by
this time," Irma remarked while spreading jam for herself.

"Auntie won't call at the hospital and see her man till this afternoon. She isn't bothered much about him— rather glad o' the chance to get a whiff of London air."

"In search of a new sensation, probably," observed Garth, and taking a slice of saffron cake he added with a sardonic smile: "I don't s'pose she and Miss Jesty'll go to church up there?"

"To church ? . . . Oh, yes—the national Day of Prayer. . . . No. It won't mean anything to people like them."

"Nor to a good many who go to church, I'm afraid," said Garth glumly. "Millions are being driven now as I was five years ago, stripped back to reality; and if they was willing to get their faith real too I believe we'd see the biggest spiritual revival the world's ever known. But it'll be just a flash in the pan from what I can judge o' the general mood. People'll pray as wildings and want to be delivered as wildings—don't want to be shown the rot in themselves, much less have the Christian antidote grafted on to 'em."

Irma nodded in silence, pondering deeply as she frowned across at the stove, in which Garth had lit a fire that now kindled ruddily. She had responded with quick insight to Garth's guidance in their frequent talks on spiritual issues, and understood somewhat the unseen forces that had warred to decide their destiny.

Garth remained seated on the fireside chair long after the breakfast dishes were cleared away. He had romped with the Stribley girls when they came downstairs, and when they went out with Elsie to pick flowers on the moor he helped Irma to peel the mass of potatoes that would be roasted for dinner. He lapsed gradually into a state of profound religious meditation as the hour of morning service in the churches drew near. Irma too became thoughtful, seldom speaking as she moved to and fro, busied with her cooking.

It was just before eleven o'clock that this contemplative mood in them was broken, not by the return of the

children but by a completely unexpected development.
Both of them were suddenly startled by the click of the
garden gate and the sound of footsteps coming around the
path. The steps were rough and unsteady, and the knock
which came upon the front door when they ceased was
somewhat violent.

Garth hesitated, then rose, smiling tensely at Irma, who
was adjusting a saucepan at the stove.

"Stay here—nothing to be afraid of," he whispered,
but he looked grim and pale as he stepped warily out
into the passage.

When he opened the door a gasp of astonishment
escaped him. He found himself confronted by a person
he had scarcely thought of during recent weeks—the tall,
ungainly figure of Chirgwin, clad in workaday garb—
black cap and jacket and brown corduroy trousers tied
below the knee with string, all the garments clay-smeared,
though his face and hands were clean. His sharp dark
face relaxed in an uneasy smile as he met Garth's questioning glance.

"Surprised to see me here, no doubt," he greeted.

"Bit of a shock, certainly," replied Garth. "Minds me
o' the day I foun d Edith waiting here when I came back
from my mother's funeral. . . . But that's all dead and
done with now."

"Yes. Now Edith and Seth's cleared out and you got
your London miss back again, there's no risk o' more
tangles between our families." Chirgwin turned, spitting
sideways on to the garden.

"I han't come up nosing into things," he resumed after
an awkward pause. "I've heard you got the maid staying
with 'ee over the week-end, but that's your own affair."

He checked himself, his gaze darting past Garth with
an abrupt, vivid interest.

Irma had appeared in the middle doorway, looking
rather agitated but relieved that no personal threat was
implied in this interruption. She was outlined against

the window, warm and passionate, her gold hair hanging loosely about her face and shoulders, gleaming in the sunlight.

Chirgwin touched his cap, grinning sheepishly.

"Good morning, miss !"

"How d'you do ?" said Irma with cool reserve, and flushing under Chirgwin's gaze. No doubt he thought the worst about her being here with Garth overnight. But her pride and exultant sense of future possession sustained her, so that there was nothing of furtive guilt to harden her into defiance. She leaned back against the passage wall, pressing her palms to it, eyeing the stranger with mere guarded curiosity.

Garth attempted a clumsy introduction.

"Mr. Chirgwin—Edith's father," he muttered.

Chirgwin watched the girl narrowly for a minute, though his stolid bony features concealed the nature of his reaction except for the frank male satisfaction in her beauty.

"I don't wonder at Garth preferring you to Edith, Miss —Stribley," he said, bringing out her name uncertainly, as if he felt it incongruous to associate her with the couple down on the farm. "I'd ha' been proud to have him for a son-in-ſaw, but things work as they will and 'tis no good complaining. I hope he'll be happy with 'ee."

"Thanks," said Garth dryly. "There don't seem to be much doubt about that. . . . But what's your business ?"

Chirgwin shrugged his gaunt shoulders.

"Needing some help on a tricky bit o' work," he said hesitantly, as if fearing a rebuff. "One of our kids is just come in saying there's a man lying in Kernick clay-pit, down in a knot o' fuzzy-bushes on a ledge. Hurt somehow and can't get up or down till somebody comes along to lift him."

A tremor of apprehension ran through Garth; he changed colour and his voice shook as he inquired:

"Who is it—did the kid know ?"

CHAPTER TWENTY-EIGHT

"Yes; he recognised him all right. An old friend o' yours, I believe." Chirgwin's shrewd black eyes twinkled. "At least, 'twas only you and Minnie Lagor that encouraged him to come around here. That bloke Griffiths."

Garth glanced back at Irma, noting that she had turned her face away, her lip bitten as she stared at the kitchen floor. He passed a hand over his forehead, dazed for a moment.

"Griffiths lying injured in Kernick pit!" he exclaimed incredulously.

"So the boy says. Dunno what's behind it, whether 'tis a accident or whether he tried to commit suicide—can't think why he should be there at all on a Sunday morning. Can 'ee throw any light on it?"

Garth braced himself, looking straight into Chirgwin's face, a wary defensive smile twitching at his lips.

"Your guess is as good as mine—about why he should be so near Meledor," he replied.

"Ah! Well, I thought this was the nearest place I'd be likely to find a able-bodied man free for the job. Trethosa men is gone to chapel, and most here to Meledor, I expect—this Day o' Prayer stunt. No good to me; and I was pretty sure o' finding you at home—felt 'twould take something bigger'n that to get you inside church doors!"

"Yes; I'm afraid it'll take a wedding," responded Garth wryly. His tone showed that he suspected a more personal curiosity to be part of Chirgwin's motive in calling—a curiosity whetted by the news of Irma's presence here.

"But about this accident or whatever it is," he went on, forcing a casual air that was belied by his strained, thick voice—"I've no objection to going along and lending a hand. You can go straight up to the pit—I'll be coming as soon as I throw on my other clothes. Just you and me ought to be enough."

"Right you are," growled Chirgwin, lurching a few steps down the path. He shot a last sly glance at Irma as

283

Garth turned back into the passage towards her, and revealed a hint of malice in his parting comment:

"Don't stop too long saying good-bye, though I daresay you two got different habits from what Edith allowed 'ee when you was courting she!"

Chapter Twenty-nine

GRIFFITHS had decided to leave Truro. The place had become for him spiritually a lethal chamber from which both air and heat were being sucked out; he was smothered and chilled by the pressure of events. Since he had learnt, through a conversation with Mrs. Palmer, that Irma was Bert Stribley's daughter, the situation had taken on a nightmare quality; and his brief encounter with Irma in the Waterfall Gardens had warned him that safety, for himself and for others, lay only in flight.

Yet he could not simply pack up and leave for some destination that suited a momentary whim. Before he cut himself away from this horror he must design a plan for the future. He would in any case be mere flotsam on the tide of war during the next few years, too old for active participation even if he were not a pacifist. But some definite ambition must steady him amid the swirl of the national conflict. Without that, he felt that the strain would break him completely, leave him paralysed.

The problem of where next to settle was acute, a thorny growth barring him from impulsive movement. There was hardly a county in England that could offer him sanctuary; all had their bitter associations with his past. Wales would remind him of his early struggles, the Midlands of those tragic years when he travelled as an engineering agent, homeless, separated from his wife, and London of the last nauseating stages of that marriage. He felt hemmed in, cornered.

The clamour of the city and the daily sight of the Waterfall Gardens and the museum jabbing at his memories of Minnie, Garth and Irma, were not conducive to calm reflection. He needed a day in the country, a day given up to one final effort to grope his way out of this smothering current and adapt himself to the set of a new tide. He shrank instinctively from the lush natural landscape lying towards Falmouth: now in the full riot of May its soft beauties would be maddeningly incongruous. His mood was one for the desert, a stripped barren expanse suggesting the ultimate conflicts. And he realised through an imaginative, poetic nerve still keen at times amid the general cloudy flux, the fitness of the clay area as a setting for his desperate spiritual battle. Not Meledor itself, but perhaps on the uplands adjoining, where the menace could be kept at a distance yet made concrete and actual by the view of those mournful clay-dumps and scattered cottages—perhaps there he could best grapple with this Cornish phase of his life, wring from it at least some lesson in fortitude. Vividly there he could feel, while the great open spaces, the curt aggressive outlines of the clay-bearing plateau, would give his judgment the cool breadth of sanity.

By the middle of the week he had resolved to make his journey on the Sunday following, when the clayworks would be deserted and he was unlikely to be disturbed by strolling villagers; and it was with an added touch of malicious satisfaction that he realised that it would be for the superstitious, conventional weaklings the national Day of Prayer. If millions went to church seeking strength and guidance, he would use the day as a sort of grim parody, girding himself for the last years of his own warfare.

There was no bus service between Truro and St. Stephen on Sundays. Griffiths came early by train to St. Austell and thence by bus through St. Stephen to Trethosa Downs, where he arrived at about ten o'clock.

During the final two miles of his journey Meledor was in view, away to the west—not now vague in snowy haze as when he first visited it or dismally shrouded in pouring rain as when he last came there at Easter, but clear cut, sweltering in fierce May sunshine, every detail sharp, blade-like.

Dismounting at the railway bridge on Trethosa Downs Griffiths stood for awhile by the parapet, his short thick-set figure tense in its neat brown suit, his deeply-furrowed face haggard though still ruddy under the black bowler hat. Quite close to the bridge, beside the railway line, Kernick clay-pit formed a broad white chasm, and it was across this that he contemplated the fateful scarp of Meledor a mile to the south-west. He thought of Garth only as being within the range of his vision. He believed Irma to be still at Truro, and knew nothing of Mrs. Palmer's trip to London. He had been so morose and irritable during the week that the Rundles had not passed on to him the local gossip they had heard. But Meledor considered merely as Garth's abode was brusquely challenging; even now it showed nothing of rural charm but seemed to exult in its proud, savage independence of mood. And the knowledge of the changes that had occurred there during recent weeks—the fruition for Garth, the departure of Minnie Lagor following Shirley's death—was sufficient to arouse Griffiths' mind from its slack fever and set it working with cold deliberation on the problems he had come here to solve.

The blows he had received this year, if considered in themselves and with no relation to the past, were not formidable. His passion for Minnie Lagor had been genuine enough, but he had known similar attractions and rebuffs and had outgrown the obsession with no permanent scars on his memory. He had met other religious cranks who had temporarily disturbed his agnosticism as Garth Joslin had done. If there were no more to it than that, he could go his way, dismissing both contacts with an irritable shrug. But Minnie was not shadowy and casual like those other women; she had been used to bring Garth back to the daughter of a man who had died in a Dulwich flat with his, Griffiths', wife. Garth was apart from those other cranks: his faith had snatched Irma from the reeking menace of that Dulwich tragedy. It seemed to Griffiths that his moves in Cornwall had brought him into an ambush of fate, the denouement of apparently random friendships baring maliciously, and ripping open afresh, the old wounds he had hidden.

His personal animosity towards Garth had ebbed and flowed with his moods; but it was diminishing. As he surveyed Garth's home now from the bridge his hatred of the man seemed trivial, misplaced. He saw that it was useless blaming Garth; the fellow had done him no conscious wrong. After all, Garth himself had chosen Edith and expected to settle down to a quiet domestic life that interfered with nobody. It was not Garth who had chosen that the girl who pressed her virginity to him in Meledor workshop should be Irma Stribley; nor had he willed the death of Shirley Lagor. Behind these decisive events there was a Mood—the Mood of which Garth had spoken during their talk in his cottage last Easter. To Griffiths it was still impersonal; he would not admit that it was a God in the Christian sense. But he was compelled to acknowledge that there was a mysterious force in the universe with which human faith could be allied. It was what he had always been up against. And he was oppressed by a feeling that this last wreckage it had brought upon him was too complete to be repaired. It was not a new, separate blasting from which he could recover to grapple with the next elsewhere. It had ripened from roots that clawed back into his youth, to his meeting with the dissolute creature he had married. He felt that his whole life was drained out by it, the long attrition complete.

He was now over fifty and no longer possessed the

physical power to make a sustained effort at renewal. His health had suffered during recent months; he had had one or two heart attacks and had been further debilitated by the May heat wave. He looked tired now, glancing about in an instinctive search for some shade in which he could escape the fierce drilling of the sun. Only the underside of the bridge and the eastern cliff of Kernick pit were deeply shadowed as yet, and with steps that showed the severe sapping of his vitality he moved down the bank to the railway line, mopping his brow for a few minutes in the gloom beneath the greystone arch, then ventured out between the hot metal rails towards the clay-pit.

The downs around Meledor soon became hidden by the tapering neck of Kernick sand-dump. Griffiths frowned as he looked at it with a sort of childish petulance, then paused, fascinated by the sinuous white ridge boring out over the green slope of the dale. There was some shade upon it, cast by the main pyramid: it looked cool, secluded—just the place he sought for his prolonged brooding. He could stroll out along that flat broad pile, which in itself seemed to be stiffened in defiance to the dunes of Meledor across the valley, and there decide upon his active defiance, some retaliation. . . .

He descended a step-ladder from the embankment and moved back past the workshops to the pit-edge, where the path broke away into a flight of rough steps leading down into the "bottoms" which he would have to cross to reach the sand-dune. But the surfaces were dry, not muddy, and the pit was little more than a hundred feet deep. Slowly and with a scowl on his red sweating face he began climbing down.

The steps were cut in the gravel soil of the cliff, but the shape of each was preserved by a board set vertically in front of it, secured by iron spikes. The whole length of the path was guarded by a series of handrails and there was no danger of his losing foothold at any of the bends. Several times he halted and leaned over the bar, peering gloomily down the cliff-side that was matted with coarse knots of fern, hazel and broom bushes, and along the blasted ridges and hollows spreading out below. All natural landscape had disappeared: nothing was visible above him but the sky, the rim of the pit notched with stacks of drying-kilns, and the huge towering bulk of Kernick dump sprawling from north-west to south-west, dazzlingly white, glittering with a sort of fervid menace.

Griffiths was near the bottom of the pit when the jerky exertion of the descent and the intense heat thrown back from the surrounding rocks began to affect him uncomfortably. He felt a slight dizziness and a sickening flutter of the heart, and stopped at a turning where the cliff face was broken into ledges close to the path. Most of them were covered with thickets of gorse and hazel, and the shade of the bushes drew him with a blind groping movement towards the nearest ledge. He swayed as he released his grip on the handrail, and stumbled out on to the broad matted slope with arms wavering, his head sunk forward. He removed his hat as he stooped under the screen of prickly gorse boughs, and his whitening hair gave him a particularly frail appearance amid the darkened green growths. With a look of exhaustion and a twist of the lips lifting his grey moustache, showing the humiliation and anger he felt at this weakness, he dropped back, sitting on the cool tufts of heather and fern. He was trembling and his heart thumped violently, sending up waves of faintness that loosened his nerves and muscles. And as the minutes passed that swooping of his heart, the increasing giddiness, began to alarm him. He crouched there, panting, dazed, aware of vague pains and of threatening darkness, fighting desperately to recover strength for the mental battle which this sudden collapse had interrupted.

When Garth arrived at Kernick pit head after forcing himself with growing tension up the moorland slope from

Virginia, he found Chirgwin awaiting him at the top of the path, leaning against a waggon outside the carpenter's workshop. Chirgwin was bare-armed, dripping with sweat, his coat hanging on the rim of the waggon; his lean face showed relief, though it was rather strained as he lurched towards Garth and lifted his arm in welcome.

"You aren't too late," he said with gruff, laconic satisfaction.

Garth was clearly much agitated, his manner being in marked contrast to Chirgwin's cool, stolid efficiency. He looked dishevelled, his clothes as rough and dirty as Chirgwin's, though the smears on them were mainly of tar, rust and paint instead of clay. He was hatless, his hair clotted with sweat and falling untidily over his narrowed, feverish eyes.

"Been down and seen who 'tis ?" he asked thickly, as if hoping even now that this incident was unrelated to the personal drama which had brought Irma to Meledor.

Chirgwin replied in a brusque tone, stripping him of such fancies:

"Yes, I been down there—and 'tis Griffiths all right."

"H'm!" said Garth; his hands clenched, then with a glance of appeal across the pit at Meledor, the memory of Irma's parting embrace rallying him, he added:

"D'you know now—whether it was a—an accident ?"

Chirgwin shrugged, leading the way forward and down the steps.

" 'Tisn't exactly what the kid thought," he muttered. "He han't falled or hurt hisself at all—just gone a bit fainty wi' the heat: a touch o' heart trouble, I should judge. Won't be much bother in getting him up the path now there's two of us."

Garth's mouth was dry, his eyes fixed apprehensively, shrinking, on the lower bends of the path.

"Have you told him—I'm coming to help?" he inquired.

"Yes—and 'twasn't pleasant news to him, judging by the way he took it."

CHAPTER TWENTY-NINE

"It could hardly be that," said Garth grimly. "But— you didn't mention about Irma being at Meledor, did you?"

"No—private matter between yourselves: no concern o' Griffiths', I reckon." Chirgwin spoke without conviction, turning and peering up at Garth with a puzzled, questioning frown on his face. Evidently he had begun to suspect that the presence of Griffiths here to-day was somehow related to Garth's love affair.

Garth offered no further enlightenment, and the silence remained unbroken until they rounded the bend that brought them in view of Griffiths. He was sitting on the step where Chirgwin had left him, gripping the rail with both hands, his face, now wan and puffy under the bowler, raised slightly as he heard their footsteps approaching. At Garth's appearance he stiffened, then flinched, his gaze wavering down to the pit bed while he mustered the reserves of his proud, stubborn soul for this encounter.

Garth avoided looking at him after the first glance of recognition, but when he and Chirgwin had come within a few yards of the stricken man and halted abreast on the step, he was impelled to make a full scrutiny and learn how deeply fate had ravaged this strange antagonist since they parted two months ago, mere friendly opponents in abstract discussion.

Griffiths' eyes met Garth's and a flash of understanding passed between the two men—piercing, wary, ironical.

A bitter grimace twisted Griffiths' lips.

"It would be you!" he muttered hoarsely.

"I wouldn't have come if I'd known 'twas this," said Garth, his voice tremulous but hardening with irritation. "We thought you'd fallen and was really injured—bones broke or something. We'll soon get you to some house where you can have a drop o' stimulant—brandy or sal volatile—and rest till you're strong enough to take the bus to—wherever you wanted to go." He hesitated. "Were you meaning to—to call at Meledor?"

A spasm of violence wrenched Griffiths. He rose unsteadily and shook off Chirgwin's arm as he felt it touch his in support.

"You won't get me there again," he said between clenched teeth. "I'd rather die where I am."

"Well, you needn't do either, by the look of it," responded Garth with a hint of malice. "You seem to have thrown off the attack pretty good already."

"I believe it is—passing," murmured Griffiths. "The shock. . . . " He turned to Chirgwin and made an impatient gesture towards the pit head.

Amid a strained silence the laborious climb to the summit was begun. The steps were wide enough for all three men to move abreast, but Garth kept one step in front of the others, holding Griffiths' arm and partly drawing him up at each fresh level. His head was bowed, his eyes fixed stonily on the dark edge of the steps as they slipped under him one by one in a slow jerky rhythm that was hypnotic. Although the group paused frequently Garth did not turn round at such times, but remained tense, hearing Griffiths' heavy breathing just behind him, sharpening now and then into a gasp of pain.

At length the trio stepped out on to the cinder-track just in front of the workshops. Chirgwin led Griffiths to the waggon on which his coat had been hung and seated him on the broad wooden frame. Garth stood back a few paces, hands on his hips, his eyes lingering not on Griffiths but on the scarp of Meledor now again in view. There under the bristling clay-peaks—the cottage where Irma was waiting, where she had slept last night—because of this man. . . .

He was roused by the voice of Griffiths, who had also been meditating deeply as the cool upland breeze revived him from the fatigue of the ascent. Griffiths seemed no longer aware of Chirgwin's presence, but fiercely concentrating on the personal issues between him and Garth as revealed in the sudden oblique light of this meeting.

CHAPTER TWENTY-NINE

His mood was one of shame, bafflement and revolt.

"I wish to God this was the last stroke!" he said with vehemence, his eyes probing bitterly out at Garth. "It would be a fitting end with you here looking on. But it seems you're to be denied that pleasure. The attack's passed like others I've had lately. I'll soon get along to the bridge by myself and wait for a bus there."

"Glad to hear it, Mr. Griffiths," drawled Chirgwin. He was standing awkwardly by the waggon, glancing at these two in bewilderment, aware of some conflict between them—aware, too (though with no appropriate subtlety of feeling) that this conflict could never have arisen had Garth been his son-in-law.

Griffiths stood up, his hand clawing at the iron body of the waggon. He was still weak and a further shadow of pain clouded his face for a moment, leaving an ugly mark of cynicism in the twist of the lips.

"Our creeds have worked themselves out now with a vengeance, haven't they, Joslin?" he taunted. "Just like my fate that—so near the end—I should see what faith can do—in the family that confirmed my scepticism —Stribley's daughter. And that your part of it should turn Miss Lagor. . . ."

"I didn't mean to turn her against you," muttered Garth.

"I admit it. You remember—at the Truro bookstall— I asked if you loved her. Foolish: I saw there could be no jealousy between us as soon as she told me of that London girl. . . . But when her child died she turned to the faith in you, and that worked again to thwart me. . . . And now—this farewell glimpse—as I meant it to be— of this cursed landscape—and you're brought before me again. You see me struck down, and can tell Irma she has nothing more to fear from such a poor wreck. . . ." He gave a harsh, smothered laugh. "She needn't have feared in any case. I shan't be in Truro much longer."

"Irma won't either, so you needn't leave on her

account," replied Garth, glancing stealthily at Chirgwin and shifting a little nearer to the workshops.

"I shall leave in a week or two," said Griffiths doggedly. "I came here to-day to try and decide where to go; but I feel now, with this heart attack, it doesn't much matter, as it won't be for long. My heart wouldn't stand an air-raid, so perhaps it may as well be London."

Garth shrugged.

"It's your own life," he commented. "No business o' mine, however much you may try to drag me into it."

"I'm not blaming you—I've outgrown that. It's what you stand for." Griffiths braced himself and stepped forward, his eyes brooding out over the countryside drowsed in its Sunday calm: no sound or activity on the clayworks but those of the birds and the running water in the conduits. . . . He turned back to Garth with sober, hostile deliberation.

"The churches are full this morning, Joslin—superstitious crowds pretending to faith. But you—you've got some damned secret they'll never touch—you and your God. And it's broken me. Perhaps before many months it'll have finished off the jest and left me—as my wife is, or Shirley Lagor. . . ."

His voice hardened, he stood erect, tense and stubborn, something of the old aggressive fire in his eyes, only now it seemed pathetic, no longer formidable but clearly a spent force.

"So be it. We've both paid the price . . . and you've won, Joslin."

He threw a last defiant glance across the dale at the ridged skyline of Meledor, then, waving Garth and Chirgwin aside, he moved slowly towards the embankment, a hand pressed over his heart.

THE END

THE CORNISH LIBRARY

'Well-chosen works from a literary heritage which is as rich as clotted cream.'   *The Times*

The aim of *The Cornish Library* is to present, in attractive paperback editions, some of the best and most lasting books on Cornwall and the Cornish, both fiction and non-fiction.

Titles in print, or shortly to be published:

Up From the Lizard	*J. C. Trewin*
A Cornish Childhood	*A. L. Rowse*
Freedom of the Parish	*Geoffrey Grigson*
School House in the Wind	*Anne Treneer*
Rambles Beyond Railways	*Wilkie Collins*
A Pair of Blue Eyes	*Thomas Hardy*
The Owls' House	*Crosbie Garstin*
Twenty Years at St. Hilary	*Bernard Walke*
Troy Town	*Arthur Quiller-Couch*
The Ship of Stars	*Arthur Quiller-Couch*
Hands to Dance and Skylark	*Charles Causley*
High Noon	*Crosbie Garstin*
A Cornishman at Oxford	*A. L. Rowse*
China Court	*Rumer Godden*
Wilding Graft	*Jack Clemo*
The West Wind	*Crosbie Garstin*
Love in the Sun	*Leo Walmsley*
Lugworm: Island Hopping	*Ken Duxbury*
The Splendid Spur	*Arthur Quiller-Couch*
Hawker of Morwenstow	*Piers Brendon*
The Cathedral	*Hugh Walpole*
The Stone Peninsula	*James Turner*
Cornish Years	*Anne Treneer*
The Devil and the Floral Dance	*D. M. Thomas*
Deep Down	*R. M. Ballantyne*
Corporal Sam and Other Stories	*Arthur Quiller-Couch*
The Cornish Miner	*A. K. Hamilton-Jenkin*
Happy Button	*Anne Treneer*
A Short History of Cornwall	*E. V. Thompson*

All the books in *The Cornish Library* are numbered to encourage collectors. If you would like more information, or you would care to suggest other books that you think should appear in the series, please write to me at the following address: Anthony Mott, The Cornish Library, 50 Stile Hall Gardens, London W4 3BU.

THE DEVON LIBRARY

Following the warm welcome which has greeted *The Cornish Library* we have felt emboldened to cross the Tamar and explore the literary heritage of its neighbour, Devon. Both counties have outstanding and varied scenic beauty. Both have a powerful maritime tradition and each has a strongly marked local character. There the similarities might seem to cease. But Devon has a literature every bit as robust and distinguished as the Cornish. *The Devon Library* will seek to do justice to this and to present the best of Devonian fiction and non-fiction in attractive paperback editions.

Titles in print or shortly to be published:

A Devon Anthology	*Jack Simmons*
Widecombe Fair	*Eden Phillpotts*
Devon	*S. Baring-Gould*
Mrs. Beer's House	*Patricia Beer*
The Initials in the Heart	*Laurence Whistler*
Diary of a Provincial Lady	*E. M. Delafield*
Father and Son	*Edmund Gosse*
The Thief of Virtue	*Eden Phillpotts*
Dewer Rides	*L. A. G. Strong*
Crossing's Dartmoor Worker	*W. A. J. Crossing*
Lorna Doone	*R. D. Blackmore*
The Old Stag	*Henry Williamson*
Westward Ho!	*Charles Kingsley*
On the Moor of a Night	*Jan Stewer*
Devon Short Stories	Ed. *Wendy Monk*
The Hound of the Baskervilles	*Arthur Conan Doyle*

All the books in *The Devon Library* are numbered to encourage collectors. If you would like more information, or you would care to suggest other books that you think should appear in the series, please write to me at the following address: Anthony Mott, The Devon Library, 50 Stile Hall Gardens, London W4 3BU.

Up From The Lizard

First published in 1948 this is a loving celebration of the land
J. C. Trewin knows so well: the County of Cornwall and that part of
it, the Lizard peninsula, where he grew up before the First World
War. Born in sight and sound of the sea, within a few steps of
England's southernmost landfall, he was the son of a sea captain who
had learned his trade under sail and whose voyages inspired the boy's
imagination as much as the shelves of books in Kynance Bay House
which fuelled his love of the dramatic, the literary, and the
fantastical.

Around the story of his childhood in Cornwall, and his days as a
young journalist on the *Western Independent* in Plymouth, Trewin
weaves a fascinating pattern of recollection, anecdote, and
character sketch. One instant he is recalling the Cornish cleric and
antiquarian, Polwhele, who inadvertently caused the odious
Captain Bligh to be locked in an outhouse, the next describing
haunted Pistol's Meadow with its 700 drowned soldiers, then
remembering his excitement as a ten-year-old schoolboy at
witnessing Lady Astor's famous Plymouth election triumph in 1919,
and on to the day when Cornwall's rugby team scored a memorable
victory over the might of Middlesex and narrowly missed the
County Championship.

But always, at the centre of his story, is the sea: in all its changing
beauty and, particularly on the treacherous Lizard coast, its brutal
might. There are extracts from his father's journal of fifty years at
sea which read like Conrad and there is the moving account, which
the young Trewin must have learnt like a litany, of the many
terrible shipwrecks, almost within sight of his home, which The
Lizard counts on its rocks and reefs.

A Cornish Childhood

A Cornish Childhood is one of the most moving and remarkable works of autobiography of our time. First published in 1942 it has sold more than 400,000 copies.

Its author, the distinguished historian, Elizabethan scholar and poet, A. L. Rowse, was born in 1903 in the village of Tregonissey, just outside St. Austell in Cornwall. His father was a china clay worker and his mother kept a small shop to help out. Like D. H. Lawrence the young Rowse was something of an outsider in the tight-knit, simple, and rather primitive community in which he grew up. Like Lawrence he never wholly belonged and lived an inner life of his own, devoted to school and Church, to reading and writing. Through the widening of educational opportunity early this century he found escape. In those days there was only one university scholarship for the whole county of Cornwall; but he won an open scholarship in English Literature at Christ Church, Oxford.

This story of solitary struggle and endurance forms the background to his matchless description of Tregonissey, the village whose customs and characteristics – which all the time the boy was observing – had remained traditional. A good education for the future historian and poet which was to produce this unforgettable portrait of vanished village life.

'There are passages of singular literary beauty. This is a live and courageous book.' *The Daily Telegraph*

Freedom of the Parish

Geoffrey Grigson was born and brought up in East Cornwall, the seventh son of the Vicar of Pelynt. It is this parish of Pelynt, deep in the Cornish countryside and to most visitors just a stopping-place on the road to the coastal resorts of Polperro and the Looes, which he describes in this classic of country life.

When *Freedom of the Parish* first appeared in 1954 the author wrote 'I mean the book to be about all parishes and would like it to appeal as much to the parishioner in Northumberland as to one in Cornwall, and as much to a reader in the city as to one in the country. Even then I must confess how personal a book it has turned out to be. I have wanted to write it for thirty years, so it is also a kind of extra-autobiography.'

In Grigson's recollections of his childhood and youth in Pelynt – fishing by night, bird watching, plant-hunting, archaeologizing – and in his exploration of his church and its family monuments, in his tracing of the old industries of milling, fulling, weaving, lime-burning, we are not only made free of one of the richest minds of our time but are endowed with the sense of ourselves belonging to that long English continuity that has for over a thousand years been implicit in the word 'parish'.

THE CORNISH LIBRARY
NUMBER FOUR

School House in the Wind

'The book is Cornwall. The flowers and the wind and sea of
Cornwall are always there, conjured up by exquisitely accurate
writing which never becomes self-conscious or earnestly literary.'
Compton Mackenzie

When it first appeared in 1944 *School House in the Wind* was
immediately recognized as an outstanding piece of autobiographical
writing. Time has shown it to be something more than that. It is,
quite simply, one of the most enchanting recollections of childhood
to have been written in our time.

Anne Treneer was born in Cornwall, towards the end of the
nineteenth century, and brought up in the neighbouring parishes of
Gorran and Caerhays on the south Cornish coastland. Her father
was Headmaster at Gorran, where the large Treneer brood
occupied the school house set on a hill in the full force of the
Channel gales, and later at the more protected school in nearby
Caerhays. Even by the standards of the time these were isolated
communities, subsisting on farming and fishing, each with its own
character and fierce loyalties. Anne Treneer grew up a bright,
energetic, and intensely observant girl, well able to hold her own in a
family dominated by sons. She recalls life in Cornwall at the turn of
the century in a way which is loving but never sentimental,
nostalgic but shot through with rich humour and an unforced
perception of people and places.

In its portrayal of the changing seasons, the countryside, and the
unique Cornish character this is a book which stands proudly beside
those classics of rural life, *Lark Rise to Candelford* and *Cider with Rosie*.